Heartwarming praise for Lisa Jackson's bestselling novels

"Her books are compelling, her characters intriguing, and her plots ingenious."

—Debbie Macomber

"What a natural talent! Jackson delve[s] deeply into her characters' motivations, lives, loves, and hidden secrets . . . and boy, does it work!"

—*Literary Times*

"Heart-stopping. . . . Don't miss it!"

—*Old Book Barn Gazette*

"Superb! Lisa Jackson has outdone herself. . . . Highly recommended."

—*Reader to Reader Reviews*

"When it comes to providing gritty and sexy stories, Ms. Jackson certainly knows how to deliver."

—*Romantic Times*

"[S]pine-tingling. . . . [An] incredible tale."

—*Times Record News* (Wichita Falls, TX)

Books by Lisa Jackson

Enchantress

Kiss of the Moon

Published by POCKET BOOKS

LISA JACKSON

Kiss of the Moon

POCKET STAR BOOKS
New York London Toronto Sydney

A Pocket Star Book published by
POCKET BOOKS, a division of Simon & Schuster, Inc.
1230 Avenue of the Americas, New York, NY 10020

ISBN: 0-7434-9293-5

This Pocket Books paperback printing December 2004

10 9 8 7 6 5 4 3

Front cover art by Alan Ayers

Manufactured in the United States of America

Special thanks to Nancy Bush,
Sally Peters, and Kathy Okano

Kiss of the Moon

Prologue

Castle Prydd
November 1280

This night the gods were angry. The wind howled and the sea raged with a fury that tore at the cliffs on which Castle Prydd had stood for over a hundred years.

Shivering, Isolde held her precious basket close. A midwife whom some believed to be a witch, she caught her bony fingers in the cowl of her cloak and hurried toward the great hall. Rain, as cold as the soul of the very devil himself, lashed from a sky where black clouds roiled and blocked the moon. Whistling eerily, the wind raced from the sea, dancing in death-light footsteps up the back of Isolde's wrinkled old neck. Strong gusts tore at the thatch on the roofs of the stables and sheds in the outer bailey. Lightning split the sky in sizzling forks, and the low rumble of thunder could be heard over the steady pounding of the surf.

Isolde cast a fearful look to the stormy heavens and whispered a quick prayer, for she knew God was furious with her for practicing the pagan ways of the old people.

"Think not of what I do, Lord. Just be with the lady," she

begged, clutching the damp handle of her basket more tightly. As if God would turn His deaf ear her way!

Through the portcullis and across the inner bailey she dashed, her leather shoes sinking deep in the muddy trail caused by the horses and men who had trampled the grass on their way to the great hall. A few knights lingering on the steps wore grim countenances, for Lady Cleva, beloved wife of the baron, was losing blood, perhaps losing her life, in the birthing of her long-awaited second child.

Unless Isolde could help and change the course of destiny.

Cleva's firstborn, a boy named Tadd, was barely seven, but was already spoiled and stubborn, with a cruel streak that Isolde had witnessed too often. He was quick with a whip to his pony's back and quicker yet to kick at the hounds and send them yelping in pain. Tadd had wounded some of his playmates as well, scratching, kicking, biting, and punching, and knowing always that he would be the victor in any match, for he was the baron's eldest child: the chosen heir to Prydd.

Aye, he was a bad seed, that one. Yet there were no other children to Baron Eaton and his wife. Three times since Tadd had been delivered screaming into the world, Cleva had been with child. Two had miscarried early, but the last infant had been in Cleva's womb the full time, only to be born blue-lipped and weak. The newborn had died within hours of his birth, and the Lady Cleva, who had lost much blood, had been so distraught with her grief, the baron had put her under guard for fear she might take her own life.

And now the lady was in a difficult labor yet again. Isolde crossed herself quickly. She was no fool. The baron would only have called for her in the most dire of circumstances, for Father William, the chaplain of Prydd, disdained her use of herbs and spells.

"'Tis the magic of the devil. Witchcraft," he'd said on more than one occasion. Lifting a lofty brow, he'd added, "And it will be in hell you'll be dwellin', Isolde, for all eternity."

William was quick to preach the wages of sin to those who lived in Prydd, but Isolde suspected that he, too, was guilty of a few vices himself. Too often William's eyes wandered to the wenches during meals, and several times Isolde had watched as he'd stumbled near the altar and slurred the mass, as if he'd tasted frequently of the baron's wine.

Yea, William would have put up a fight at the thought of having Isolde birth this new baby. But the baron loved his wife more than he loved his God, and he would do anything to save Cleva—even call upon Isolde's sorcery, if needs be.

"This way, woman," the guard said as he shoved open the thick oaken door of the great hall. Inside, the sounds of the castle were muted. Four soldiers rolled dice near the staircase, maids spread clean rushes near the hearth, the smith stacked firewood in the corner, and the steward with his nasal voice barked orders to the cook in the kitchen.

A fire crackled and hissed, giving off a red glow, but the castle felt cold with the presence of death. Two yellow-eyed hounds growled at Isolde's approach, as if they, too, knew she wasn't a true believer in all that was holy.

"Isolde! Come quickly!" Baron Eaton hurried down the stairs. He grabbed her arms and half dragged her up the slick stone steps. He was a tall man with broad shoulders and a cap of thick red hair that framed a fair, freckled face. His eyes were as blue as the skies over Wales, and his features were sharp, whittled to steep, aristocratic angles. Rumored to be the bastard son of the king, he was a handsome and strong man. Yet his worry was deep; his usually clear eyes clouded with concern.

"Thank the saints you've come." Rowena hurried toward

them, causing the light from the sconces to flicker in her wake. A rotund woman with fine white hair and a red complexion, she, too, was a midwife. But she was a Christian woman of uncommon faith. No one would doubt her devotion to God, not even Father William. Rowena grabbed Isolde's hands in her plump fingers. "Lady Cleva calls for you. The labor . . ." Her words were choked off, and she bit her lip. "Well, come, come . . . there's no time to waste. The baby's turned, I fear, and . . . Oh, please, just hurry."

Low, pain-racked moans echoed through the upper hallway. The lady was in agony, to be sure. Isolde's footsteps quickened until she spied Father William standing guard at the door to Cleva's room. Isolde crossed herself, but William's fleshy fingers curled around her bent elbow, and he stopped her short before she could enter.

"This is a Christian house, midwife," he cautioned, his voice booming through the castle.

"Aye, Father."

"I know of your ways. There will be no devil magic here. No chanting. No witch's charms."

Isolde stared long into his red-veined eyes. "I am here to help with the birthing, Father. That is all."

The priest's lips thinned and he reached quickly into her basket, his thick fingers digging under the towels to the knife, herbs, and candles within. "Witch's tools?" he whispered, clucking his sanctimonious tongue.

"Nay, Father, only the tools of a good midwife." She tore her arm from his.

"Is this true?" Father William asked Rowena.

Rowena swallowed back the truth and avoided the priest's heavy gaze. "Isolde is here but to help in God's work of bringing the baron a son. M'lady needs assistance that only Isolde with all her practice can bring."

"But—"

"Remember, Father," Rowena added, "Isolde was not at the birthing of the still babe. Aye, and she was not here when the lady lost those poor little souls who had no chance to grow in her womb. I think 'tis God's will that the baron and his wife have many more sons and daughters."

From the chamber, Lady Cleva cried out, "Help me, please. Oh, God, help me!"

The priest opened his mouth, caught a glance from Baron Eaton, and snapped his teeth together. His face was a mask of his own iron will. "There will be no witchcraft in the house of Prydd, Isolde. 'Tis the law of God and country."

Isolde straightened her old spine and stared directly into the priest's righteous eyes. "I have work to do, Father. Mayhaps you can help by going to the chapel and praying for the soul of this unborn babe." She glanced at the baron. "'Twould help you as well."

"Aye." Without another word, Eaton led Father William down the stairs, and Isolde, offering a prayer of thanks to whatever god was listening, hastened to Lady Cleva's bedside.

The room was large, with fresh rushes spread upon the floor, clean tapestries draped over the whitewashed walls, and a fire glowing warmly in the hearth. Yet wafting over the scents of smoke and lavender came the acrid odors of sweat, urine, and blood.

Lady Cleva lay on her bed, her face flushed and damp, her eyes bright with pain. "Help me," she whispered, twisting her fingers in the wrinkled linen sheets. "Please, Isolde . . . you must . . ." She clamped her lips together and tears filled her eyes.

"Shh . . ." Isolde said softly as she touched Cleva's sweat-soaked hair. She ran bony, experienced hands along Cleva's body and didn't stop until she'd felt the baby, twisted in the birthing channel.

From the corner of her eye, she saw Rowena hastily cross her heavy bosom.

" 'Twill be all right," Isolde assured the lady, though she doubted her own words. There was more here than a simple birth, and would the baby not turn, it would strangle itself.

"God is punishing me," Cleva murmured, her pretty face twisting in agony as her body convulsed.

"Hush, m'lady! God punishes no one with a child."

Again Cleva cried out. Her skin, so perfect and white, was now mottled, flushed where the veins in her face had burst. "But this child . . . 'tis not Eaton's . . ."

Isolde turned her stern eyes on Rowena, cutting off further confession. "You, midwife. Get clean sheets from the laundress, fresh, hot water from the kitchen, and see that no one disturbs us."

"But I could be of assistance—"

Isolde wouldn't budge. "The lady is rambling; she knows not what she says."

Rowena swallowed. "You think that the child is a bas—"

"I think we need to save this babe and heed not the words of a woman in pain. All that is said here will remain in this chamber."

"But—"

"Should I hear one word of what goes on tonight gossiped in the kitchen or stables, believe me, Rowena, by all that is holy and all that is not, I will work my magic against you, for I will know that it is you who have spoken. Now, get the towels."

Cleva screamed, and Rowena, biting her fat lip, hurried into the hallway. Isolde wasted no time. She reached into her basket. Withdrawing herbs, she poured a combination of ground mistletoe, fern, and rosemary onto the candle holders before placing long tapers therein. Only then did she light each candle, murmuring a quiet spell of protection for the mother and infant. She cared not if the babe be Eaton's or that of a stableboy; Isolde loved the lady and would do whatever necessary to protect her.

Cleva sucked in a breath, and Isolde took a red cord, knotted it nine times, then threaded the cord around Lady Cleva's sweaty neck. "Now, m'lady, we must work fast, the babe's almost here." With deft fingers she took off her silver ring, in the shape of a serpent, and pressed it into Cleva's palm. "Hold tight to this and feel its healing power," she said, folding Cleva's sweaty fingers over the ring. "Now, the child . . ."

Carefully spreading Cleva's legs further, Isolde reached into the birthing channel, feeling with skilled fingers, praying that the child would turn as she eased the baby's slick head forward.

Rain pounded the thick walls, and the wind gave up a shriek as loud as Cleva's cries. "Merciful God! Please. Ohhh—" Her fingers curled over the ring until the metal cut into her palm.

"Come, Cleva, 'tis only a short time yet . . ."

Lightning split the night, casting the room in an eerie flash of brilliance.

Cleva moaned loudly, and with one last push, the infant slithered into Isolde's waiting hands.

"Oh, God, oh, God," Cleva whimpered, blood flowing from her in a warm rush.

" 'Tis a girl, m'lady," Isolde said as the child gave out a first, lusty cry, "and a beauty, she is . . ."

Cleva tried to rise up, but Isolde, still holding the baby, shoved her gently back on the sheets.

"Wait . . . 'tis not finished," she said, as the baby was still attached to the afterbirth. She tied the cord with strong thread, then severed it with her knife.

Skillfully Isolde washed the infant, her bony fingers touching each joint as she watched eyes as blue as the sky blink up at her. Dark curls surrounded a perfect little face, and Isolde's heart nearly stopped.

Wind shrieked over the battlements, and the prophecy she'd heard since childhood, the prediction of the old ones, swam in a wild current in Isolde's mind.

She mouthed the words and could not help opening the towel.

Born during a tempest, with hair the color of a raven's wing, eyes the blue of midnight, and the kiss of the moon upon skin like alabaster . . .

She let her gaze wander over the pale folds of newborn flesh until she spied it, the birthing mark at the base of the babe's neck, a perfect crescent . . . the kiss of the moon. "By all the saints," Isolde whispered, rewrapping the girl-child.

Her throat constricted in awe, for she knew she was looking upon the chosen one, the savior who would sacrifice herself for peace between her countrymen. She held the baby close, felt the infant's warmth, and closed her eyes. Aye, she saw in her mind's eye the future, filled with bloodshed and deceit, and somehow she knew this little one's destiny was wrapped in the words of the old people.

Isolde had heard of the visions—aye, she'd had more than her share of the sight herself—but never had she expected to help bring into the lady's house the chosen one who would become the savior of Prydd.

"A girl?" Cleva asked faintly, her voice filled with disappointment.

"Aye, and a fine one she is, m'lady. As beautiful as her

mother." She handed the swaddled baby to Cleva and worked to catch the blood still flowing from the lady's womb.

"What I said," Cleva whispered, guilt shadowing her eyes, "about the child—"

"What a woman says in the pain of birthing is between her and her God. No one else's ears hear a thing."

"But—"

"Shh." She placed a hand on Cleva's shoulder. " 'Tis a glorious babe you've got, m'lady, a daughter who will someday make you proud." She took the ring from Cleva's hand and slid it back on her finger.

The door creaked open as Rowena, her eyes averted, her lips turned down in disapproval, returned. She said nothing as she helped the babe suckle at Cleva's breast and washed the blood from her body.

With a thunder of boots, Baron Eaton burst into the room. His face was flushed, his smile stretched wide. " 'Tis a son?" he asked, dropping on his knees at his wife's bedside, kissing her sweat-soaked curls and gazing in awe at the newborn.

Cleva licked her lips nervously. Tears again filled her eyes. "A daughter."

The baron tried to hide his disappointment, and his wife laid a thin hand over his. "We have Tadd," she reminded him, her chin wobbling slightly as she cradled the baby. "You have your firstborn son."

"Aye, and now I have a daughter."

Cleva swallowed hard, started to say something, but glanced over her shoulder to Isolde and held her tongue.

"And a beauty she is. Like her mother." Eaton placed a huge hand on the back of the baby's head, but his smile disappeared. The tiny girl nursed hungrily, and he shook his great head. "I had hoped for another son," he admitted, and thin lines appeared at the corners of Cleva's mouth.

"One may yet come," the priest interposed. He glanced at the chamber and frowned at the tapers burning slowly and giving off their herbed scent. He noticed the knotted cord around Cleva's neck, and his gaze sharpened on Isolde. "I warned you, midwife—"

"This child is a gift," Isolde said quickly.

The baron lifted a brow, encouraging her to speak. "A gift?"

"To you. To all of Prydd." She held her chin defiantly, aware of the priest's eyes burning in rage. "Born during a tempest, with hair as black as a raven's wing, eyes the blue of midnight, and the kiss of the moon—"

" 'Tis nonsense!" Father William interrupted quickly. "Heresy."

Isolde dared not move as the angry servant of God walked with measured tread in her direction. His thick finger wagged beneath her nose. "I'm warning ye, woman, there is never to be any word of that old prophecy or I will see to it that the bishop hears of your pagan ways! He will not be as tolerant as I. There are tests that will prove whether ye be sinner or saint."

Isolde quivered inside; she'd heard of the tests to prove one's piety. Either by burning or drowning, she would be proclaimed a witch. "But the prophecy, Father . . ."

"Aye, I've heard it myself. I hear much when dying men confess their sins of heresy on their deathbeds." He offered Isolde what he considered a patient smile for the unenlightened. "And of course, the prophecy is false," he said, reaching into his deep pockets for his prayer book, "for what fool would think that this babe would be the savior of the house of Prydd?" He glanced pointedly at everyone in the room.

"A man-child, mayhap, but a woman?" He chuckled and shook his head, as if he alone had the knowledge of the future.

Baron Eaton turned his back on his wife and the new little one. "We will have more sons," he said firmly, and Cleva paled on the bed.

But Father William wasn't finished. He stripped the cord from Cleva's neck, tossed it into the fire, and said, "Mark my words, no woman will ever change the course of destiny. 'Tis sacrilege to say so. Now, if we could all pray for this tiny new soul . . ."

One

Castle Prydd
December 1296

"Leah, *please*, take my place," Sorcha begged of her younger sister as they passed by the dovecote and scattered seeds for the birds. In a flutter of feathers, the doves picked through the frozen gravel of a path running through the bedraggled garden.

"I know not," Leah said, shaking her head as she threw another handful of seeds onto the ground.

Sorcha's cloak billowed in the icy wind blowing across the sea, and she felt more than a twinge of guilt, for it was her turn to sit through one of Father William's long masses and pass out alms to the poor. "I promise next week I'll do the same for you."

Leah rubbed her tiny chin thoughtfully. Her eyes, green as the forest, were unreadable. "And what will Tadd say?"

Sorcha's lips turned down at the thought of her brother. "I care not."

"If he catches us?"

"I shall take all the blame," Sorcha replied, anxious to be

off. Leah could be so stubborn sometimes. "Asides, we won't be caught. You'll wear my cloak and ride my mare. Only the soldier who guards you will know the truth, and Sir Henry is easily bribed."

"I like this not. Tadd—"

"Curse Tadd." Sorcha couldn't hide her disgust for her older brother. He'd tormented her for as long as she could remember, tricking her into making a fool of herself, laughing at her expense, treating her as if she were somehow no better than the manure in the stables. For years she'd endured his torture. He was seven years older and had convinced her at the age of five to try and suckle milk from the mother cat's teats, then, in the company of the other young boys, laughed at her. When she was seven he'd shorn her head under the guise of letting her become one of the boys, then made fun of her ugly scalp. Just after she'd turned twelve, he'd sold her to a sixteen-year-old stableboy whom she'd had to kick in the groin to escape.

But things had changed. Sorcha had realized that to protect herself from Tadd's cruelty, she had to become more devious than he. By befriending several of the knights in her father's service, she'd learned how to ride a war-horse, how to shoot arrows as straight and true as any archer in the castle, and how to use a knife to defend herself. Still she hadn't been convinced that these skills alone would keep her safe from her brother's treachery, so she'd taught herself how to use a whip and a mace and even the heavy military flail. However, it was her wits upon which she relied. Though Tadd was stronger and swifter, he wasn't as smart as she, thank the good Mother Mary.

Leah, as if reading her mind, bit down on her lip. "While Father's away, Tadd's the lord of the castle."

"Remind me not," Sorcha replied, unable to hide her disgust for her older brother. Ever since their father had ridden off to fight the bloody Scots, leaving his eldest in charge of the castle, life in Prydd had changed. Some of the knights neglected their duties, preferring to roll dice, drink wine, and seduce the kitchen wenches. Surly and often drunk, they seemed to have forgotten Baron Eaton and his strict moral code. Only a few of those who remained could be trusted. "If Mother were alive, Tadd would dare not to put the castle in such jeopardy."

"But she's not." Leah threw the rest of the seeds to the wind, brushed the dust from her gloved hands, and turned back to the great hall.

"I'd not ask if it were not important."

Leah smiled and tucked a strand of hair beneath the cowl of her cape. " 'Tis Sir Keane you're meeting."

Sorcha's heart nearly stopped. She'd been so careful, and yet Leah had guessed the truth.

"It is, isn't it?"

"Aye," Sorcha admitted with a shrug, as if her secret romance were of no great concern. Truth to tell she cared for Keane, but knew that she didn't love him. "Is there gossip?"

"Not yet. But I've seen him watching you. You needs be careful or Tadd will get wind that you fancy Sir Keane."

She didn't have to say more. Tadd was sure to make life miserable for anyone interested in his sister. Why Tadd despised her, she knew not, but only guessed his hatred was because of her cursed birthmark. His feelings for Leah were not as bitter. But then Leah had always been the kind one, the pious one, the saint in the family, and Sorcha had been a thorn in her father's side from the day of her birth.

"Will you help me with the accounts?" Leah asked.

So simple. "Aye."

Leah scowled darkly. "I know not why Father insists we

learn the duties of the steward. All those numbers . . . Ah, well, if you will do the work."

Sorcha couldn't help but smile. The accounts were easy for her, no task at all. " 'Tis done," she said.

Within the hour, Leah had explained that she, too, wanted to attend mass, and Tadd, interested in a new dark-haired kitchen maid, waved her aside. With Sir Henry for protection and Leah's maid, Gwendolyn, as companion, they rode through the forest on the main road. Once Castle Prydd was out of sight, the two sisters exchanged cloaks and horses.

"You'll not be doing this," Henry insisted as he began to understand that he'd been played for a fool in part of a girlish scheme.

"M'lady, please, 'tis not a good idea," Gwendolyn agreed. A tiny woman with light hair, she worried far too much.

" 'Tis all right." Sorcha slipped the hood of Leah's purple cloak over her head.

Henry reined in his horse. "No good will come of it. I forbid you—"

" 'Tis not for you to forbid," Sorcha cut in, and Leah stifled a giggle as she adjusted the folds of Sorcha's crimson mantle around her slender body. "Asides, I'll see that you get some of the baron's best wine on our return."

Henry's heavy face folded upon itself. " 'Tis not drink that I need. 'Tis assurance that you'll be safe. With Castle Erbyn left in Sir Darton's hands while Lord Hagan is off fighting the war, no one is safe."

"Erbyn is far away," Leah said, though she seemed a little anxious.

Both Hagan and Darton, the twin brothers, were harsh men who ruled with cruel hands, but Hagan, the baron, was the more levelheaded of the two, and he had once traveled to

Prydd to make peace with Sorcha's father. Sorcha had not been allowed to meet Hagan, as he was considered the enemy, but she'd hidden herself in the minstrel's loft and gazed down upon him as he'd walked arrogantly into the great hall. A big man with dark hair the color of a falcon's wing and eyes that were set well back in his head, he strode into the great hall and nodded curtly to her father. Hagan's nose was not straight, but his features were bold and chiseled, and he had an air about him that caused most of the guards to keep their distance. His shoulders were wider than her father's, and he towered above the older man. For the first time in her young life, Sorcha doubted her father's ability to command an army against so formidable an opponent.

Commanding. Assured. As if he were ruler of Prydd, he warmed himself by the fire and spoke in low tones that Sorcha, try as she might, could not overhear. He came in the company of soldiers, all wearing the green and gold of his colors, and there was another man with him, at his right hand, who looked much like the baron, though slightly smaller in stature and not quite as handsome. His twin, no doubt. Though she was but ten at the time, she knew, as she gazed at Hagan of Erbyn, she would never see a more powerful man.

Danger seemed to radiate from him, and when he glanced up, she gasped, giving herself away. His green-gold eyes focused on her, and the lips tightened a bit as his gaze caught hers for but an instant. At that moment Sorcha gleaned what it was to be a rabbit caught in the archer's sights.

Her little heart pounded, but rather than hide, she stood defiantly, tossing her hair off her shoulders, and met his arrogant glare with her own prideful stare.

"Who is the waif?" he asked her father, and Baron Eaton glanced upward, grunting as he recognized his daughter.

"Sorcha—get down from there!" Eaton ordered.

The twin brother eyed her with interest, but it was Hagan who said, "Sorcha? Ahh . . . so she does exist. I have heard of you, little one." His eyes glinted in a kind mockery. "Some of the peasants—the people who believe in the old ways—have told me that you are to be the savior of this castle."

Sorcha lifted a brow and shrugged, trying not to notice how handsome a man he was. " 'Tis true," she replied, not knowing where her courage came from, but squaring her shoulders a bit.

" 'Tis a lie, the mutterings of a crazy old midwife who thinks she be a witch," Tadd interjected as he hurried down the stairs, his face flushed in the seething rage that seemed to be constantly with him. Always spoiling for a fight, he eyed Hagan and the soldiers from Erbyn with obvious loathing.

Hagan ignored him and continued to stare up at Sorcha. "Will you strike me dead?" he asked. Again the gentle ridicule in his voice.

"If you ever try to capture Prydd. Yes, Lord Hagan, I will cut out your black heart myself."

He laughed then, and the harsh lines of his face disappeared. "Well, little waif, I quiver in my boots, as does the entire castle, just knowing that mayhaps your wrath will be cast in the direction of Erbyn."

"Hush this nonsense!" her father bellowed. "Go see to your lessons, Sorcha. Lord Hagan and I have a truce to discuss. Tadd come along with us. 'Tis time you learned how to bring peace to the land . . ."

Sorcha had never seen the baron again. Now, as her breath steamed in the cold winter air of the forest outside of Prydd and Sir Henry looked as if he were ready to strangle her for her impudence, she wondered if Lord Hagan or his brother or their men really did consort with outlaws and thieves as was rumored.

"Worry not about Sorcha, Sir Henry. She'll be in good company," Leah said, her nose wrinkling as she chuckled. "Safe in the arms of—"

"Rest assured, Sir Henry, that I'll be fine, and breathe not a word of this to a soul." Sorcha climbed into the saddle of Leah's bay jennet as Leah tried in vain to scramble onto Sorcha's feisty black mare.

"This horse will be the very end of me," Leah said as she finally settled into the saddle.

"She'll be your savior," Sorcha predicted as she dug her heels into the little bay's flanks and tugged on the reins. The mare whirled and broke into an easy gallop, heading north, away from the village and toward the meadow where Keane had promised to meet her.

"God be with you," Henry shouted over the cold wind that rushed at Sorcha's face and chilled her bones. It screamed past her ears and shoved the hood off her head to tangle in the long waves of her hair. Sorcha felt free, her spirit riding with her on the wind. She urged Leah's jennet ever faster, but the bay was not as swift as her own mare, and the little horse labored up the forested hill until the road broke free to a frost-covered meadow of dry weeds and bent, bleached grass.

Keane, as promised, was waiting, standing beside his gray destrier as the big horse tried to graze. Sorcha's heart still soared at the sight of the tall knight. No more than twenty, he was broad-shouldered and trim, his skill in tournaments already established. His blond hair ruffled in the breeze, and his eyes, deep brown, flickered in recognition as she pulled on the reins and hopped to the ground.

"So you did come," he said, his breath making clouds in the crisp winter air.

"Did you doubt me?"

"Doubt you? Nay, but trust you . . ." His teasing smile stretched wide. "That is a different matter."

" 'Tis I who shouldn't trust you," she quipped, wondering why she could not agree to marry him.

"Come here."

She threw herself into his waiting arms and felt the warmth of his mouth close over hers. Her heart, already racing, beat even a little more quickly, but she knew that she'd made the right choice to tell him that she could no longer meet him this way. Lying to Tadd, trading chores with Leah, deceiving everyone in the castle, and putting Sir Henry's pride on the line were worth a few stolen moments with Keane to tell him how she felt.

His arms clasped more firmly around her, and she pulled away. "Keane, there is something I must tell you."

"I've missed you, Sorcha," he said quickly, as if he knew her thoughts, gently shoving the hair off her neck and kissing her behind the ear. He traced her birthmark with his finger.

"No, Keane, please listen to me. I cannot—"

"Hush, little one. Each night I dream of you and—"

THWACK!

Keane's body flexed in her arms. "Holy Christ!" He sucked in his breath. "Sorcha, run!"

HISS! THUNK! Again his body jolted, and this time Sorcha saw the arrow buried deep in his shoulder. Another had hit his thigh, and blood stained his breeches.

"No!" she screamed, trying to hold him upright.

"*RUN!*" He fell to the ground, his fingers scrabbling for the hilt of his sword, but Sorcha stood as if rooted to the spot. Her head swung around and she stared into the trees, the dark undergrowth where their attacker lay hidden somewhere to the south, cutting off the road back to Prydd. As if he'd been following her.

"Come with me," she pleaded, pulling Keane to his feet and helping him to his destrier.

"I'll stand and fight."

"And die!" she half screamed. Her heart was thudding with fear that they would both be killed. " 'Twill serve no purpose. Come! Now!"

"But—"

Desperate, she clung to him. "There is no honor in giving up your life like this. Come! I need you!"

Keane, his face white, took her lead. With a scream of agony, he yanked the shaft of the arrow from his thigh and threw it onto the ground. "Take the other one."

Swallowing hard, she stared at the arrow buried in his shoulder. " 'Tis not safe to—"

"Do it!"

He leaned down, and Sorcha placed her fingers over the shaft. She tugged, but the arrowhead caught on flesh and wouldn't budge.

"Hurry!"

Fingers slick with blood, she pulled again, and the shaft of the arrow splintered in her hands. Blood smeared on the red folds of Leah's mantle.

Keane moaned, writhing away from her.

"Oh, God, I knew—"

Another arrow screamed through the air, passing near Sorcha's ear.

"It matters not," Keane said raggedly, stains of scarlet discoloring his tunic. With an effort he whistled to his destrier. The war-horse was nervous, prancing anxiously, nose to the wind, his great ears flicking toward the woods. Keane hauled himself into the saddle as Sorcha climbed on Leah's little mare, yanked hard on the bridle, causing the jennet to rear as they turned.

"Run, you bloody nag," she yelled at the jennet. Her horse jumped forward, and Sorcha leaned low in the saddle, digging her heels into the mare's flanks, urging the tired bay to keep up with the longer, steady strides of Keane's charger.

The frozen ground whirled past and wind tore at Sorcha's face, bringing tears to her eyes. She could barely breathe, and fear grasped her heart in its terrible, clawlike grip. They couldn't die; not like this! *Please, God, not like this!*

Another arrow whizzed past Sorcha's shoulder and she glanced backward for just a second, long enough to see a band of outlaws moving out of the shadows. Filthy and ragged, five men she'd never seen in her life rode rangy horses, without using their hands. Bowstrings held taut, arrows in place, they took aim. "Oh, God, save us," she murmured, her throat constricting in terror.

"This way!" Keane shouted, turning into the woods again. The road they took was little more than a deer trail that wound through the dense undergrowth, and at the base of an ancient oak, split in several directions.

"We'll never lose them if they live here in the woods," she said as the horses slowed to a trot and picked their way through the gloomy undergrowth.

"We'll lose them," Keane vowed, though he had to hold on to the pommel of the saddle to keep himself astride.

As often as Sorcha had ridden in the woods, she'd never ventured this far from the castle. The dark forest felt hostile. Tall firs kept the ground in shadow while bare, black-barked oaks reached skyward and thorny, leafless briars rattled in a wind that was as cold as death.

"They'll expect us to double-back," Keane told her as

they took a fork in the path leading farther north, away from Prydd.

She bit her lip anxiously. "Should you not rest?" she asked, eyeing the pained set of his mouth.

"Not yet."

She watched as even more blood stained his tunic, but she said nothing. Keane was a proud man, and this time, Sorcha feared, his pride would become his undoing. "Please, let us stop. We can hide—"

"Nay!" His skin was taut and white around his mouth. With determination, he clucked his horse forward. "We must return to Prydd by nightfall, but 'twill be a long ride as we needs make our circle wide so as not to run into the outlaws again."

She thought of the horrid creatures who had tried to kill them. "Who were those men?"

Keane shrugged.

"But why would they attack us?"

"For money," he said with effort.

"I have no coin—"

"Ransom, then. You're the baron's daughter, are you not?"

"The baron is away."

"Tadd is at Prydd."

"Tadd wouldn't pay a single gold piece for my release," she muttered as they finally turned southeast, beginning to double-back.

"It matters not. Now, hush, lest they hear us." His gaze held hers for just a second, and she saw death in his kind eyes. "Ride silently, and should I . . . be unable to stay astride, leave me and take my horse."

"Keane, no—"

"Do not thwart me on this, woman. 'Tis our only chance!"

He kicked his mount onward. She saw him wobble in the

saddle, and her heart leapt to her throat. He held on, but she knew he would not stay conscious much longer.

Hours later, they arrived at the gates of Prydd. Sorcha's body was numb from the cold, her fingers rigid in the frozen leather reins. Keane slumped forward, falling off his destrier as his wounded body finally gave out.

"Help! Guards! Please, help!" Sorcha screamed as she jumped from her own mount. The little horse sprinted into the outer bailey, and Sorcha fell to the ground, where she cradled Keane's head upon her lap. "Do not die," she whispered, tears hot against her eyelids. "Keane, please, you must not die!"

"He's dead," Isolde whispered, and Brother Ignatius murmured last rites over Keane's body.

"Noooo!" Sorcha wailed, her cries of grief resounding to the rafters of the solar. Her heart felt as if it had been ripped from her chest, and tears burned behind her eyes. "Use your magic, do whatever you must, but do not let him die!"

Keane lay upon the bed, his wounds bound, his face a gray mask.

Isolde touched his neck, feeling for signs of life, a pulse, then leaned down, her ear to his chest, as she listened for the smallest breath. "I'm sorry, m'lady—"

"Nay! He cannot be dead. He cannot!" Sorcha wailed. She approached Isolde and grabbed the servant woman by the cloak. "Some say you are a witch. Have you no potion to cure this—"

"I cannot save the dead."

"But you must!" Sorcha cried, refusing to accept that Keane's life was over. Had he not planned to meet her, he might still be alive. Guilt gnawed at her. She threw herself against his unmoving body, holding on to him, knowing she would never love another. "Keane, Keane . . . please . . . merciful God—"

"Had there been more life force within him, mayhaps, but—"

" 'Tis in God's hands now, my child," Brother Ignatius whispered, gently pulling Sorcha off Keane's lifeless form.

"No!"

Tadd's voice rumbled through the hallway. "Bloody Christ, is there no end to her schemes?" he growled, kicking open the door. It banged against the stone wall. Sorcha jumped, blinking back tears as her brother strode into the room. He loomed above her, his shoulders as broad as an axe handle, his face twisted with a powerful rage. "You disobeyed me."

"I—"

"Do not bother to lie to me again, for I will not believe you. Did you not bargain with Leah to go to mass in your stead?"

"Yea, but—"

"With only Sir Henry as her guard?"

"Aye . . . and Gwendolyn," she answered more carefully.

"Even though she is not as quick with a knife as you be."

"I understand not why you care. Sir Keane is dead!" she said, finally accepting the terrible truth, her bones seeming to turn to water.

"Aye, and he's not the only one."

Tadd's words cut to her very soul. Sorcha's throat tightened and her pulse pounded with dread. Beyond the anger in Tadd's eyes there were vile accusations. "News of Father in the war?" she whispered, dread pulsing through her.

"Nay."

Suddenly Sorcha understood her brother's ire. Their sister. Where was Leah? In her worry for Keane's life, Sorcha had forgotten Leah. Now her stomach wrenched painfully and her tongue was thick with fear. "Not Leah."

Tadd didn't reply, and a new, horrid fear gripped Sorcha's heart. "Tell me," she demanded.

"Tell you," Tadd repeated, his rage retreating a little. Satisfaction gleamed in his eyes. He liked nothing better than to keep a secret from Sorcha, who deemed herself a princess, who was born with the damned birthmark, who, he suspected, might be his equal in everything but strength.

"Where is she?"

"Ask Sir Robert," he said, enjoying this game immensely.

"Sir Robert?" Sorcha repeated, stunned. Robert was one of Tadd's most trusted knights.

"The traitor in the dungeon. He has news from Castle Erbyn."

Sorcha felt as if a ghost had walked across her soul. Years ago, Hagan's father, Richard, had unsuccessfully tried to wrest control of Prydd from her father's hands. A black-heart himself, Richard had been known to consort with thieves and outlaws. His ambitions were boundless and were passed on to his sons, though for the past few years there had been no war, the peace the result of Hagan's fragile truce. No one at Prydd trusted him, and she remembered him well—how powerful and determined and cruel he'd seemed. Handsome, too, but the kind of man who made others tremble in fear. She swallowed back her apprehension. "What news?" she asked, her voice barely a whisper.

"Henry and Gwendolyn were killed by a band of outlaw knights—all sworn to serve Hagan."

"No!" Sorcha's knees threatened to buckle. "They were fine when I left them." Guilt swallowed her soul.

" 'Twas after."

Surely there was some mistake. Numb, she whispered, "But Robert; you say he was part of this band."

Tadd's lips tightened angrily. "Aye."

"What of Leah?" she hardly dared ask.

"Our sister has been stolen away. To Erbyn. And why is that, Sorcha?" Tadd demanded, his face mottling scarlet in the firelight. Dark red-brown locks fell over his eyes, and his fists opened and closed in his rage.

Sorcha could hardly believe her ears. First she and Keane ambushed by outlaws, and now this horrid news of Leah. Sir Henry's flushed face swam before her eyes, and Gwendolyn's soft voice filled her ears. No more laughter . . . Oh, God, and Keane, noble Keane. Tears burned in her eyes. She bit her lip and prayed she was dreaming, that she would wake up and Keane would still be alive and strong, and Leah would be within the safe walls of Prydd, stitching her embroidery, or walking in the garden, or trying to make sense of the bloody castle accounts.

Tadd's nostrils quivered with fury and his lips were white and flat over his teeth.

"God preserve us," Isolde whispered.

Fear clutched at Sorcha's heart. Blind, numbing fear. Tadd was playing with her. For all his anger, he was toying with her, and he only did so when he was certain of winning, or humiliating her. Perhaps this was one of his tricks. "I believe not—"

Tadd grabbed her arm in a grip that bruised, yanking her off her feet before dropping her on the floor again. "*Believe,* sister. Your disloyalty has led to death this time. Henry was a brave and trustworthy knight. He gave up his life so that you could meet your lover." He shoved her away as if her very touch disgusted him, and she fell back against the bed where Keane lay unmoving.

She felt like whimpering, but held back her cries, refusing to back down. "How is it that Sir Robert, if he be a traitor, has confided in you?"

Tadd's smile turned cruel. "Sir Henry managed to wound Robert in the attack. Robert's band of thugs left him to die, but a farmer found him and brought him, barely alive, back to Prydd. He's in the dungeon, and with a little encouragement, he told us that he was hired by the lord of Erbyn."

Sorcha felt sick. She had brought this horror to Leah. "Then you must gather all of your best knights and ride to Erbyn to free Leah at once," she said aloud.

"Nay, Sorcha. I'll not undo the mess you caused. You with your damned birthmark," he sneered, the malice in his eyes gleaming bright as the yellow eyes of the hounds. "The savior of Prydd, isn't that what the old woman says?" He cast a disdainful look at Isolde. " 'Tis the mark of the devil, methinks, and I be not the only one. Father William, too, sees the sign as blasphemy against the only true God."

As if Tadd were a Christian! However, Sorcha had no time for arguments. If what Tadd said was true, then Leah was in grave danger. Her virtue and her very life were at stake. Sorcha marched up to Tadd. "I will go with you."

"Go with me? Where?"

"To Erbyn."

His laugh was harsh. "You did not hear me, sister."

"But we must free Leah!"

"By fighting Hagan or that brother of his, Darton?"

"Aye."

"Ah, Sorcha, so foolish," he said on a sigh that spoke of her naïveté. "I'll not risk the lives of any more good knights. No doubt Leah will be ransomed."

Keane's words haunted her. Had he not suspected that the outlaws planned to ransom her? A shiver slithered down her spine.

"Then you will do nothing?" she asked, inching her chin up defiantly. Then she saw it: the cowardice in her brother's features.

"I'll not battle Hagan of Erbyn for Leah, for that is what he wants."

"Hagan has upheld his truce in the past few years," Sorcha said, though she didn't trust that the black-heart would not break his word. The unsteady peace between the two castles had lasted seven years, but was always in jeopardy.

"Which is why, sister, 'tis best to wait. Hagan is rumored to be off fighting the Scots."

"Then his brother, Darton, is behind this treachery."

"Or Hagan has returned." Tadd rubbed his chin thoughtfully, obviously unhappy with this turn of his thoughts. "Hagan is a liar, but a powerful warrior. His people fear him. 'Twould be best not to anger him when so many of our knights are with our father."

"Even if he has taken Leah?" Sorcha asked, astounded at the depth of her brother's cowardice. Leah had to be freed!

Tadd's eyes swept up Sorcha's stained mantle. "I'll deal with Hagan my own way. As for you, sister, you will be punished for your lies and treachery. 'Tis your fault that two of my best knights needs be buried. Your fault that Gwendolyn was savagely murdered. You shall carry that burden on your soul, and your penance is that you, oh bearer of the 'kiss of the moon,' shall be locked in your chamber until the moon is next full."

Isolde lifted her old hands in supplication. "M'lord, 'twill be nearly a full cycle . . . twenty-eight days—"

"Hush, old woman, or I shall punish you as well." He drew his sword swiftly.

Isolde stood firm, and Tadd merely admired the blade, pointed it into the oak floor, and leaned insolently on the hilt. He had to bend a bit, so that his nose was within inches of Sorcha's face. "You'll pray in your room, sister, and pray alone. Even Father William will abandon you during your penance. The old woman will bring you meals, but that is all." Standing quickly, he motioned with his sword. Two guards came into the room and grabbed her by the arms.

"I'll not be held prisoner in my own castle!" Sorcha cried.

" 'Tis for your safety."

"In a pig's eye!"

He clucked his tongue as she was dragged out of the solar. Brother Ignatius prayed over Keane's still body, and Tadd grinned, as if he was glad for an excuse to lock her away.

Though Sorcha fought with all the strength of her young body, she was no match for the two burly knights, who flung her into her chamber and dropped the heavy oaken bar across her door.

Wretched and cold, she huddled on the floor. Henry lay dead. Dear Keane's soul, too, had departed. Gwendolyn had given up her life. Leah was a prisoner in the bowels of Castle Erbyn. Tadd held her as his prisoner.

Her life, so carefree this morn, had become wretched. Tadd, curse his soul to the devil, was correct, however. All the death and disaster that had been wreaked upon the castle was her fault and hers alone. Some savior of Prydd was she—more like the plague of Prydd. Her insides felt as if they'd been torn apart by wolves, and it took all of her courage not to fall down and weep. But she couldn't. For, by the gods, she would have to find a way to avenge the deaths and save her sister.

Gritting her teeth, she pushed herself upright. She'd kneel to no man. Especially not to someone as dull and wicked as Tadd. Guilt drummed in her brain as she walked to the open window and stared at the night. Clouds drifted across the face of the full moon.

What tortures was Leah enduring in the dungeons of Erbyn? Sorcha's throat clogged with hot, unshed tears. Oh, if she could only trade places with her sister.

"By all that we hold dear, Sister Leah," Sorcha whispered onto the breeze, "I vow to save you." She shivered as the breath of wind blew against her hair and she thought of Baron Hagan, Lord of Erbyn. Since childhood, she'd heard of him, knew him to be a rogue, a treacherous man who would stop at nothing to gain his ends. For years he had wanted Prydd and the surrounding lands, but he'd bided his time, agreed to the truce, and now, while their father was off fighting the Scots, he had decided to make war, not with an army, mayhaps, but to the same end. "Hold on, Leah," she whispered over the rising wind. The castle walls seemed to mock her, for she was prisoner in her own beloved Prydd, but Sorcha was a woman who believed that no enemy was invincible, no dungeon without a means of escape, no plot complicated enough that it couldn't be thwarted.

She kicked off her boots and started planning her escape. 'Twould be easy to sneak out of this room; she only needed Isolde's help. The difficult part would come later.

Nay, freeing Leah would not be an easy matter, but she had no choice. For all of her sixteen years she had been self-ish, only interested in her own needs, but as of this night, her destiny had changed.

She would avenge Henry's death.

She would see that Gwendolyn's murderer be held responsible.

She would seek vengeance, dark and brutal, for the killing of Keane.

She would free her sister.

No matter what the cost.

No force, not even the power of Baron Hagan of Erbyn, would stop her.

Two

orcha's heart was in her throat as she stepped over the dozing guard.

"He will not sleep long," Isolde warned her as the man snored and Sorcha barred the door.

"It does not matter. He will never know I've gone." They sped along the hallway quietly and outside the great hall to the gate of the dungeon, which was unguarded. Together they hurried down the damp stone steps.

"You must hear me. The potion is made of . . ." Isolde's voice whispered through the dark hallways, and Sorcha only half listened.

The dungeon smelled of rotting hay and urine. Rats scurried beneath thin layers of musty straw, and Sorcha's heart hammered so loudly, she was certain the prisoner could hear it. If Tadd discovered that Isolde had placed a potion in the guards' mead during the meal and that now they both slept at their posts while the old woman helped Sorcha escape, he would surely flail them both.

Tadd was an angry man, a strong man, a man who hated being beaten, but he was also easily tricked. Sorcha loved fooling him almost as much as she loved defying him. He hated her. That much was certain. Ever since he'd heard the old wives' tale about the "kiss of the moon" and had seen the birthmark on her neck, he'd been resentful and malicious, though sometimes Sorcha was certain she saw fear in his eyes . . . as if he sometimes believed in the witchcraft and visions of the old ones.

Sorcha enjoyed this little bit of power, though she believed not in Isolde's old fable. As Father William had pointed out time after time, should she be the true savior of Prydd, she would have been born a man, though why Father William even bothered to give her this information was a mystery. As a true man of the cloth, he didn't believe in folk tales.

No doubt Tadd would whip her within an inch of her life if he thought she would be so bold as to talk to the traitor, Sir Robert. She had no choice. Since her father was off fighting the no-good Scots with King Edward, and Tadd would do nothing to free Leah, Sorcha would. The first step was to talk to the prisoner and find out what he knew.

Sorcha held her torch high, allowing the flickering light to fall into the cell. With a clanking of rusted metal, she unlocked the gate and shoved the filthy barrier open. The flames cast orange shadows over the prisoner, a man whom Tadd had foolishly once trusted with his very life. Now Sir Robert was barely alive. His lips were cracked, and blood trailed from one nostril. Both eyes were swollen to mere slits, and his breath rattled deep in his lungs as he breathed. Naked to the waist, he shuddered at the light. Purple welts on his back still oozed blood, and the wound where Sir Henry's arrow had pierced his shoulder was deep and raw.

"Please . . . no more . . ." he whispered, tears running from his puffed and blackened eyes at the thought of another beating. "I've told you all I know."

"Aye, Sir Robert, but you spoke to Lord Tadd," Sorcha said as Isolde brought in a bucket of water, towels, broth from the kitchen, and her oils and herbs for healing. "Now you must tell me of my sister. Tadd told me little, but 'tis rumored that you know what happened to her."

Isolde offered the man a cup of water. He drank too quickly and retched the cool liquid back up. "Slowly," Isolde said, refilling the cup from her pail.

Robert sipped carefully, licking his lips and groaning. When at last he'd had his fill, he leaned back against the cold, damp stones. "Aye," he said, his voice filled with remorse, "I know of the Lady Leah."

"Tell me."

Isolde motioned him to bend forward, then touched his back with a clean, wet towel. He sucked in his breath in a horrid hiss. " 'Twill help," Isolde whispered as she cleaned his wounds and added her balms and herbs. She offered him the broth of salmon she'd begged from the cook. Sir Robert drank long, then wiped his mouth with the back of his hand. "Leah was on her way back from mass and giving alms in town—"

"This much I know," Sorcha said, guilt riddling her soul.

Robert closed his bruised eyes. "The lady was stopped on the road by a band of outlaws. Her guard, in trying to defend her, was slain. And her maid . . ." He hesitated, drawing in a shaking breath. Then, with a curse, he added, "Gwendolyn was beaten, raped, and left for dead as well. Christ, Jesus, I'm sorry . . . so sorry . . ."

Sorcha felt as if a dagger had been twisted in her heart all over again. Gwendolyn had been with the castle for all her fifteen years, and she'd hoped to marry the baker's son. Sir Henry had taught Sorcha to ride and aim an arrow with precision. Henry, like Keane, had been a good man, a kind-hearted man, and he deserved not to die. "Tadd told me of Sir Henry's loyalty," she said, her voice filled with a need for vengeance. "And that Leah was taken to Erbyn."

"Aye."

Again Sorcha's soul turned to ice. She had hoped that Tadd had lied to her. "Why would Hagan want Leah?"

Robert spat blood through a hole in his teeth. "I know not." Sorcha knew he was lying. She leaned closer to the man she had once respected.

"You know more, and if you want me to see that you are a free man again, you will tell me the truth, Robert of Ainsley. And I want to know all. More than you told my brother."

In the smoky light from the torch, Sir Robert grimaced in pain. He gazed through the bloody slits that were his eyes. " 'Twas not Hagan who did the kidnapping," he admitted. "The baron is off fighting the Scots with your father."

"Darton, then," Sorcha said, thinking of the younger scheming brother, even more vile than his twin.

"Aye, and 'twas not Leah he wanted."

Sorcha's heart stood still. "Then why?"

" 'Twas you, m'lady."

"Nay!" she cried, though she knew he wasn't lying.

Isolde turned tortured eyes upon her. "He speaks the truth. My dreams have forewarned me."

"What dreams?" Sorcha asked, though she did not wish to hear them.

"Of you and Castle Erbyn." Isolde crossed herself deftly and dropped to the straw.

"Your visions mean naught," Sorcha whispered, but a cold drip of truth settled into her heart. She forgot about the stench of the cell and the rats rustling beneath the straw. "But why? I've never met that cur from Erbyn."

"But he has seen you," Robert said, "and he paid the outlaws to bring you to him. He knew you would never come to him on your own. The feud between Erbyn and Prydd may not cause war just yet, but 'tis just as strong as it was before Hagan demanded a truce."

Sorcha felt her insides turned to jelly and she licked suddenly dry lips. "And what were Sir Darton's plans for me?"

Robert's eyes closed in shame and he hesitated before whispering, "He intended to force you to marry him."

"But how? I would never—"

"He planned to get you with child."

As if she'd been struck, Sorcha stepped quickly backward, nearly stumbling over the water pail in her efforts to get away from the horrid words. "I would never lie with that dog!"

"Not willingly . . . but Darton cared not."

"And you . . . you were a part of this . . . this treachery?" Sorcha's lips curled in disgust.

"Forgive me, Lady Sorcha. I thought he meant but to ransom you, and for that I was offered gold and a small castle of my own, but . . . when I found out his true intentions, I tried to return."

"Too late," Sorcha said.

"Aye."

"Know you why Sir Keane was killed?"

"Keane? But he was not with Leah—"

"He was with me. We, too, were attacked by outlaws."

"God in heaven," Robert said in a rattling whisper. "I swear I knew nothing of it. I believed you would be riding with Henry to the village . . ."

She believed him, and yet she could not forget that were it not for his treachery, Leah would be in the castle, and Gwendolyn, Henry, and Keane would still be alive. "I will never offer you my forgiveness, Sir Robert," she said, "for your disloyalty has caused too much grief, but I will ask my brother to spare your miserable life when I return safely with my sister."

"You cannot think of going to Erbyn!" Isolde shook her head side to side. "Oh, child, no . . ."

Sorcha ignored her. "Now, Sir Robert, you must tell me everything of Erbyn; how the keep is built, and how Darton spends his days. And . . . I needs know about Baron Hagan. When he is expected to return and what he will do when he discovers Leah within the castle walls."

Robert grunted. "I will tell you everything, my lady."

"If you lie to me, Robert, you will die."

The moon rode high in the night-black sky, casting a silver glow over the frozen ground of the inner bailey. The castle was asleep; even the sentries nodded at their posts as Sorcha led her favorite mount, her brother's war-horse, McBannon, from the stables.

Only Isolde knew of her hastily conceived plan. " 'Tis tempting the fates, ye are," Isolde said, her wrinkled features drawn into a frown of worry as the nervous horse sidestepped and snorted. "This . . . this plot of yours . . . 'tis a fool's journey! As the saints are my witness, if Baron Hagan finds out that you've entered his castle as an enemy—"

"The black-heart will discover me not. You heard Sir Robert last night; Hagan's off warring with the Scots," Sorcha assured the superstitious old woman. "Hagan, that beast, I won't have to fear." She took the cloak and old burnet tunic from Isolde's hands and stuffed both pieces of clothing into her pack.

"Then what of Hagan's brother?" Isolde persisted as she gave Sorcha the basket she would use as part of her deception. "Sir Darton . . . he's a mean one, he is. Ye'd best not be tryin' to outfox him."

"He won't be expecting me."

Isolde wrung her hands. "Holy Mother, you're a stubborn one. Yer own brother will skin ye alive when he finds ye missin' on the morrow."

"He'll not know I'm gone."

"But takin' his favorite horse—the one only a few can ride." Isolde clucked her tongue with worry. "Satan himself would not be so foolish."

" 'Twill be good for Tadd to be angry. He should have gone after Leah himself, and he knows not that I can tame McBannon," Sorcha replied rebelliously, her fury with her older brother burning bright as a smith's forge. Tired of the argument, she climbed astride Tadd's anxious destrier, but Isolde's fingers twined in the reins.

"If you must go," the midwife cautioned, her voice low and filled with premonition, " 'twill end up in pain and bloodshed." Her old eyes glazed as she stared up at Sorcha. In the light of the moon, Isolde's face with its hooked nose and hollow cheeks did seem to have the visage of a witch, as many had claimed. "I've seen it."

Sorcha's lungs constricted, but she would not let fear stop her. "You've had a vision of Leah."

"Nay, my child, 'tis your face that I see when I sleep. Always yours."

Sorcha's throat tightened in dread. "And what see you?"

"Ah, child. 'Tis ye who are imprisoned in the towers of Erbyn, 'tis ye who are held captive by Lord Hagan himself, 'tis ye who will not return."

"You're trying to frighten me."

"Aye, and I hope I have, m'lady, for the wrath of the devil Hagan is swift as the strike of an asp and twice as deadly. Like a dragon, he is, but more crafty. You'd best be staying."

"You know I can't."

With a sorrowful sigh, Isolde said, "Then take this . . ."

She pressed a tiny necklace into Sorcha's hand. " 'Tis for protection. Wear it over your heart always."

Sorcha looked into her palm and saw, in the faint light of the moon, a small cross of twigs tied with red string.

"And this as well." Isolde removed the ring she had worn as long as Sorcha could remember. Tooled of silver, the band wound around the old woman's finger in the shape of a snake. " 'Tis magic, you know. Never take it off."

"Isolde, I cannot—"

But Isolde caught her hand and forced the ring onto Sorcha's finger, and the silver seemed hot against her skin.

"You do not know the ways of the old people—this is your choice," Isolde said, "but in your heart you are with us and you know the chants and spells, though Eaton forbade that knowledge."

"I know not—"

"But you do, Sorcha. Listen to your heart; the magic will be with you. You will need your faith in the Christian God as well as your inner strength from the ways of the old ones."

Sorcha took up the reins, stripping them from Isolde's bony hands. "I have no use for this talk of nonsense. I must save Leah."

"And sacrifice yourself."

Icy fingers of fear clutched Sorcha's heart. "If needs be. Now, come. 'Tis time."

Isolde did as she was bid, walking briskly to the gate. While Sorcha held the nervous stallion from bolting, Isolde threw her back into the task of pulling on the rope that turned the gears and lifted the heavy portcullis.

"Halt! Who goes there?" The tower guard's voice was sharp.

" 'Tis only me," Isolde called upward toward the battlement where the sentry was posted. "Isolde."

"You again!" he said, then let out a sound of disgust. "I'll be lettin' the baron know that you've been out diggin' up yer witch's 'erbs again, old woman."

"But he'll not mind, now, will he, Sir Michael?" Isolde cranked the huge gate upward.

Staying close to the wall, Sorcha held her breath and quietly urged the horse forward through the opening.

Isolde kept the sentry distracted. "Go ahead and tell the baron what you know."

" 'E'll not be likin' your witchcraft. Nor will Father Will."

Isolde chuckled. "Wasn't it my magic that saved the baron's daughter at her birth?"

Sorcha winced. 'Twas true. Without Isolde's magic, she might not have been born, but the old midwife had managed to bring her into the world as well as save the life of her mother seventeen years before. Isolde hadn't been so lucky the next time, with Leah. Lady Cleva had died shortly after her second daughter's delivery, and none of Isolde's magic had been able to save her. The snake ring seemed to tighten around her finger.

"Your own son came into this world with the help of chants and—"

"So be it, witch!" the sentry said in disgust. "But ye'd best be diggin' your roots in the light of day."

"Nay. Only with the moon's blessing will they bear medicine," she said.

"Your black arts will be the end of ye, Isolde," he grumbled. "I'll close the gate behind ye, but don't be expectin' to come back through the gate tonight. You can bloody well stay out till morning!" The great horse walked quickly to the outer bailey. They only had a few minutes until the guard climbed down the steps from the tower to the gatehouse.

Isolde grabbed Sorcha's hand one last time. "Be careful,

'tis the Christmas revels, my girl, and many who visit Erbyn might know ye."

"You worry too much," Sorcha replied, though the old woman's words settled deep in her soul.

"And you worry not enough! Now, be off with ye, if ye insist on going."

"Ha!" With a swift kick to McBannon's sides, Sorcha leaned forward in the saddle. The feisty bay bolted, his strong legs digging into the soft loam of the outer bailey. As she passed through the gates of the castle, she wondered if she'd ever see the thick stone walls of Prydd again. From the corner of her eye she noticed Isolde pick up a handful of earth and toss it in Sorcha's wake—for protection; a custom of the old ways.

Yea, for her plan might not be perfect, but she had no time to improve it. She had to rescue Leah before the devil himself—Hagan of Erbyn—returned.

With breath as cold as a demon's soul, the wind blew through the trees, shaking the leafless black branches and bringing driving sleet that pounded on Hagan's neck and head and dripped down his nose.

He rode on, and with every step of his war-horse, he gritted his teeth against the pain, as hot as the day was cold, that seared his thigh.

The wound was two weeks old and healing well. He'd developed no fever and had wanted to return to battle, but King Edward had insisted Hagan return to Erbyn.

"Lord Hagan." Sir Royce, astride a restless gray steed, commanded Hagan's attention. Royce was a big man with good intentions and little brains. His courage and loyalty were never in doubt, though sometimes his judgment faltered. "Could I have a word?"

Hagan swung his head around, but didn't allow his horse to stop. They trudged through the icy rain, splashing water from puddles and heading ever west. "What troubles you?"

"Mayhaps we should rest." The heavy man's gaze drifted from Hagan's face to his thigh, the very thigh the arrow had pierced.

"We're close to Erbyn."

"Yea, but Sir Darton expects us not until the morrow."

"All the better."

Royce seemed perplexed, but Hagan didn't explain. For several years he had begun to worry about his twin brother's ambitions, but he'd kept his fears to himself, content to observe. Darton had every reason to feel slighted; he'd inherited from their father, Richard, only a small piece of land in the northwest corner of Erbyn. And Anne, his sister, had been left with naught. Consequently, Hagan was always at odds with his siblings. Leaving Erbyn in their care during his pilgrimage to help the king with the Scots had been difficult. 'Twould be interesting to see how Darton ran the castle without his brother's wary eye upon him.

"We ride on," Hagan said, setting his features in grim determination and allowing no evidence of the pain to show on his face. "We'll be at Erbyn by nightfall and can plan the Christmas revels."

Sorcha shivered in the sleet. The sky was an ominous gray, and she couldn't shake the feeling of dread that had ridden with her on her journey from Prydd. Fierce winds howled through these treacherous hills of Erbyn, shrieking through the trees and rattling the blackened, leafless branches. Her clothes were soaked through and she was chilled to the marrow of her bones. As she stood in the thicket and peered through dripping pine boughs to Castle Erbyn, it seemed as if all the fates were against her.

Erbyn was the largest castle she'd seen in all her years. Like a dragon from one of Isolde's old myths, the keep loomed upon a steep hillside. Rain pelted the wide battlements, and the sturdy walls were built of the same yellow-gray stone as the sheer cliffs on which the castle had been constructed. Somewhere, deep within Erbyn, Leah was kept prisoner. As Sorcha should have been. "I will not fail you, sister," she vowed as a frigid blast of wind rushed through the branches, causing them to sway in an eerie dance.

Sorcha's heart closed with fear and she wondered if Leah was still alive. What horrid tortures had befallen her at the hands of Darton?

"By all that is holy, please give her comfort," Sorcha prayed, her hands blue and trembling as she crossed herself. If only she had learned of the old ways—of Isolde's spells and chants—she would curse the keep of Erbyn forever and call up the dark spirits to strip the baron of his lands as well as his manhood. As for Darton, there would be a place in hell for that maggot. But she, raised as a Christian, had never been allowed to know the secrets of magic, practiced by so many within the walls of Prydd.

Teeth chattering, she tied her horse to a low-hanging branch of an oak tree. Fervently she hoped that the steed wouldn't chill. He was a spirited animal, but she'd ridden hard all night, and now his flesh quivered beneath his hide, and lather flecked his mud-dappled chest. "I'll be back, McBannon," she promised as she patted his sleek shoulder. "With Leah."

From her saddle pouch she pulled the old burnet tunic that Isolde had given her. The fabric was rough and scratchy as she slid it over the shorter tunic and breeches she'd worn.

Next she donned a dirt brown cloak with a cowl. The cloak was in sad need of a needle and thread, but Sorcha was certain she looked like many of the peasant women who lived near the castle. With numb fingers she tied her hair away from her face and pulled the cowl over her head, but never once did she forget the knife tucked into her boot, its cool blade touching her calf.

"Lord help me," she whispered, grabbing her basket and picking her way through the skeletal brambles and dripping ferns. At the edge of the road she waited until two horsemen passed. Once the riders had rounded the bend and the road was empty, Sorcha hurried from her hiding spot and walked quickly in the direction of Erbyn. Sleet tore at her cowl, and her fingers felt like ice around the handle of her basket, but she plodded forward, knowing that Leah's fate was in her hands.

The old midwife's words followed after her. *'Tis ye who are held captive by Lord Hagan himself, 'tis ye who will not return.*

Grimacing, Sorcha shoved aside her fear and gathered her courage. Her plan was simple. With the knowledge gained from the traitor, Robert, she knew how Erbyn's inner bailey was guarded. She also had learned of the keep itself. Robert, once he'd decided to divulge the truth, had been very precise in his descriptions of the great hall. He'd told of a back staircase leading directly to the lord's chambers—cold stone steps for the coward to use if he had to flee the castle, or a staircase used to bring up wenches and unwilling servant girls to the master's bed.

Sorcha gritted her teeth. No doubt Leah's virginity had been stolen, if not by the lord himself, then certainly by Darton and his men. Bile rose in her throat, but she found comfort in the sharp steel of her knife in her boot. Though she'd never killed a man before this night, she planned to take the very life of Darton if she had to.

"God be with me," she prayed, and failing God's guidance, she had, tucked deep in her basket, beneath the linen liner, yet another dagger.

She walked steadily toward Erbyn. The gate to the outer bailey was open, but could only be reached by crossing the heavy timbers of a drawbridge spanning a steep canyon. Flanking the portcullis were two round towers, twice the size of any towers at Castle Prydd.

Though it was approaching dark, people moved freely along the rutted road. Wagons and peddlers' carts, men and women on foot as well as those astride horses, teemed toward the gate. Despite the blasts of frigid wind that ripped the cowl from Sorcha's head and drove the icy rain against her body, she noticed that most of the travelers were laughing and talking among themselves. Already the spirit of the Christmas revels was in the air. Sorcha only hoped that with the holy season upon them, the guards at Erbyn would be less suspicious.

She tagged behind a farmer's wagon, hoping to appear one of the peddlers, troubadours, and minstrels who were making their way to the castle. Stepping around a pile of dung, she slowed her walk as the gatekeepers eyed each of the travelers.

Her heart was thundering and sweat collected between her shoulder blades as she passed by the guard. Without a second look, he waved her on, paying more attention to two on horseback. Her knees nearly gave way in relief and she continued through the outer bailey. Gardens, now choked with weeds, were rivers of mud, and rainwater ran down the thatch of the roofs to drip along the edge of each hut. Cows were penned in one corner of the grassland, and a quintain stood unattended in a marshy field. Several archers braved the weather. With leathery faces and taut bows, they wagered on their skills, then took aim on targets propped against piles of straw. Stables and sheds held horses and pigs while sheep grazed on the wet grass.

"Halt," a guard bellowed as she attempted to walk beneath the portcullis. His face was pockmarked, and his lank hair, wet from the drizzling rain, was flattened to his head. "State yer business."

While her insides quivered, Sorcha forced what she hoped was an innocent smile. " 'Tis with the cook, Ada, I'm wishin' to speak. I got goose eggs to sell, and ivy and mistletoe for the yule." She winked at the guard and offered him a peek at her basket. "And what would the Christmas revels be without a spot of mistletoe, eh?"

Flushing, he laughed. "Ye can pass, then, as long as ye be savin' a bit of the mistletoe fer me."

Sorcha giggled and managed to keep a sharp retort from slipping over her tongue. 'Twould not do to let even a lowly gate guard guess her intentions, so she swung her hips in the manner of a bawdy wench.

Some of the servant girls were lingering near the well, and a boy was dipping his net into a fish pond. Chickens scattered as she passed, and doves flapped near the dovecote.

She knew the inner bailey well, for the traitor had told her much about the workings of Castle Erbyn. The kitchen was attached to the castle, though the bakery was in a small hut of its own. As she hurried by the open door, she felt the heat from the great ovens and smelled the odors of apples and nutmeg and cinnamon.

Her stomach rumbled, but she pressed on, ignoring her hunger. At the door of the kitchen were two broad-shouldered huntsmen, hoisting between them the carcass of a deer tied to a pole. They held the heavy beast while listening to a large woman with a flushed face and fleshy arms and a tongue as sharp as Isolde's magic knife.

". . . for the love of Saint Peter, why ye think I'll be takin' my time to skin that beast, I'll not be knowing."

The huntsmen grumbled, and the cook wagged a fat finger in their faces. "The baron will be back soon, and I'll not be wantin' to complain about the likes of you!"

" 'Tis for the baron that we brought the buck," the older boy proclaimed.

"Then take it to the tanner, see that 'e 'elps you skin the bloody thing, and count yer blessings that I won't report you to the steward. God in 'eaven!" she mumbled as the huntsmen, jaws set, carried their prize along a trail toward the hut. "And me, busy as I am, expectin' the lord any time."

Sorcha's stomach curled in sudden dread. "Lord Hagan is coming home?"

"Aye. One of the scouts said he'll be home the day after the morrow."

Relief flooded through Sorcha. There was still time before the dark one returned.

"Now, then, miss, what've ye got in yer basket?"

"Eggs and mistletoe for the yule."

"Humph." The big woman scowled as she peeked into Sorcha's basket. "Eggs, we got."

"Aye, but these are from me father's geese . . ." Sorcha waggled the basket beneath the cook's nose yet again, and as the big woman looked through the ivy, mistletoe, and holly, Sorcha stole a glance into the kitchen. It was a big room, with two fire pits. In one pit a pig was roasting, its fat melting and sizzling on the coals; in the other, stuffed eels, their skins tightly sewn together, were suspended above the flames. Little red apples filled a large pail by the door. A big scarred table was shoved into a corner, and an arch in the back wall opened to a few steps and the entrance into the great hall. Just as the traitor had forespoken.

"Well . . . I said name yer price," the cook repeated, her piglike eyes squinting suspiciously when Sorcha didn't respond.

"My father sends the Christmas greens as a gift to the lord, and the eggs he'll sell for the same price as hen's eggs."

"Is that so?"

" 'Tis the yule season, sister," Sorcha said, though the words nearly stuck in her throat, "and my father has been blessed to have Lord Hagan as his baron."

Ada grinned a big, gap-toothed smile at the bargain. "Well, come in, come in. We'll empty yer basket without gettin' our 'eads wet." She waved rough red fingers toward the fire. "Warm yer 'ands while I get the steward to pay you." Sorcha followed her into the room and set her basket on the table. "And who is this father of yours?"

"Will . . . Will Carter," Sorcha answered, having concocted the lie on her way to the castle. She opened her palms to the fire where the pig was roasting. Nestled in the coals was a pot filled with eggs and boiling water. Smoke curled through the kitchen, and lard bubbled beneath the boar's thick hide. From the corner of her eye, Sorcha studied the opening into the interior of the castle. She edged closer to the archway. There was a short corridor with stairs winding upward from either end. One set of stairs led to the chambers above the kitchen, the other was the gateway to the lord's room. Another archway opened to the great hall. Sorcha's stomach curdled at the thought that Darton was probably close. And Leah, locked away. But where?

" 'Ere ye go," the cook said, returning with a few coins. "And be sure to tell yer father thank ye from the baron 'imself. 'E'll be pleased to know that 'is man Carter is a loyal servant." She paused as she handed Sorcha the money. "What kind of ring is that?" she asked, eyeing Sorcha's hand where the silver serpent was coiled.

"I know not. An old woman gave it to me mother. 'Twas passed on to me when me ma died."

The cook's brow furrowed, but one of her helpers cried out as she spilled grease on the fire and flames shot up to devour the roasting pig.

"God in heaven, you're a fool, Nellie!" Ada scolded, her attention diverted. She motioned to Sorcha as she turned back to the fire pit. "You, girl, be on yer way."

"Aye," Sorcha replied, stuffing the coins into her pocket. "My father will be pleased to hear that Baron Hagan is returning," she said quickly, and hurried outside. Head bent, she walked across the bailey, as if she intended to return through the gate, but once she was certain the fat cook's back was turned, she veered sharply to the left and found a spot behind a manure cart, near the beehives and untended garden. No one was about, and Sorcha planned to hide in the shadow of the cart's big wheels until supper.

From her hiding spot, she kept fairly dry as she watched the doorway to the kitchen, realizing that though Erbyn was thrice the size of Prydd, the work was the same: Girls tended chickens and ducks, boys split wood and mucked out the stables, the tinsmith tapped with his hammer, and the carpenters shored up a sagging doorway to a hut where candles were made. With a hollow feeling, Sorcha wondered if she'd ever run through the stone halls of Prydd again. Would she smell the sweet lilac-scented rushes, or sneak down to the creek where she swam in water so cold, her blood seemed to turn to ice? Soon, she told herself . . . as soon as Leah was safe.

Slowly the hours passed. Shortly after nightfall there was an increase in activity. Servants hauling water, or carrying goods from the bakery, or laden with firewood, hurried in and out the door to the kitchen.

It was time for her to sneak into Darton's keep. The darkness would help conceal her, and everyone in the castle would be too busy to notice a strange servant boy. Or so she hoped.

She stashed her robe and long tunic behind the beehives, slipped her dagger into a sleeve, then, with her hair tucked in the cowl of her short tunic, she spotted a boy staggering under the weight of a bundle of firewood. "Let me 'elp ye with that, lad."

"Nay. The cook—"

" 'Tis too big a load. Asides, 'tis Christmas."

Sorcha grabbed off the top half of the kindling and offered the boy a smile.

" 'Tis kind ye are."

She followed the boy into the kitchen, where the cook was busy slicing the boar's head from its body and the other kitchen aids were pouring sauces and ladling gravies. Sorcha placed the kindling in the firebox, then, holding her breath, walked through the kitchen as if she had every right to enter the castle. In the hallway she turned right, toward the staircase leading upward to the lord's chamber, which, Robert had explained, was being used by Darton while Lord Hagan was away.

Her heart thundering, she expected someone to yell at her. She stole quietly up the stairs, hardly believing her good luck as no one accosted her. Biting her lip, she let her dagger slide into her palm and sent up a prayer for Leah's safety. She didn't move. Hidden in the shadows in a recessed alcove that once had been used as a wardrobe, she wrapped her fingers around the hilt of her deadly little knife and waited.

Three

"Sir Hagan returns!"

The call echoed through the great hall and plunged a dagger of dread into Darton's heart.

Sir Ives, who had made the announcement, looked as if he might faint. His face was a pasty white, and his sharp little tongue rimmed his lips nervously. Ives was a dullard who was ready to fall apart at the least little change in plan. Darton loathed him, as he detested most of the men whom he'd been able to turn against his brother. Disloyal mongrels, the lot of them, but necessary for Darton's plans.

"Hagan returns?" Darton challenged as he hurried to the stairs, meeting Ives on the landing. "But I was given word that 'twould be two more days—"

" 'Twas a false report. Hagan will be upon the gates of the castle within the hour. A scout has seen the baron."

Darton's fists clenched tightly. "Well, well, we'll have to change our plans a bit, won't we?" he said with more calm than he felt. He did not fear his brother; in truth, he was awaiting Hagan's return, for the capture of Baron Eaton's daughter was but part of a more intricate plan. Unfortunately he'd captured Leah rather than Sorcha and the timing was not yet right, but Darton was quick to alter his scheme accordingly. "See that my things are removed from Hagan's room, and by all means put clean linens on his bed. Instruct the guard of

Lady Leah that he is to let no one into her room. Not even the baron himself. No one is to know that she's being held prisoner."

"He's sure to find out."

"Yea, but not yet." He grasped Sir Ives's shoulder in his strong grip. "You are with me in this, are you not?"

Sir Ives knelt quickly and swore his fealty yet again. Darton smiled. "Good. Tell the men that they are to pretend they are still loyal to Hagan, for he must not suspect that anything is amiss."

"As you wish, sire."

Sir Ives marched quickly out of the solar. Inwardly Darton congratulated himself on his accomplishments. Hagan would be astonished when he found out that half the soldiers in the castle felt no allegiance to the baron, for they were men with wants of their own. Darton, while Hagan was off fighting those bastard Scots for the past few months, was providing well for the men.

Though Hagan had taken a dim view of wenching and drinking and gambling, Darton had encouraged his randy soldiers to find ways to release their energy. He'd staged wrestling matches, bearbaiting contests, and cockfights, and offered the soldiers all the wine and mead they could drink. As for the wenches, there were plenty of girls who would lift their skirts for a taste of wine and a few kind words. Some would even do more and were expert with their hands and mouths and tongues.

"I'll greet my brother myself," Darton decided, though he quickly swooped through the immense castle, going from room to room, making sure that everything looked just as it had on the day Hagan rode away all those months before.

All was well, and within the hour, the thunder of horses' hooves announced Hagan's arrival. A small evil smile crawled across Darton's lips. He'd thought often of killing his brother outright and letting someone else, such as loyal Sir Ives, take the blame, but he couldn't kill Hagan yet. No, he'd rather have Hagan twist in the wind a bit, know the depth of Darton's deception, so that Hagan could, for just a few hours, appreciate the anguish of all the years Darton had lived in his shadow.

Footsteps rang in the great hall as Darton descended the stairs, and he smiled when he saw his brother . . . a pitiful shell of the man he'd once been. Wet and streaked with mud, Hagan was much thinner than he had been when he'd left Erbyn. Though his skin was dark from hours in the sun, there was a haunted look to his eyes. His beard was uneven and matted, and his clothes were mere tatters. Worse than all this, Hagan the proud, Hagan the strong, Hagan the supremely arrogant, was limping slightly as he approached the fire. A pitiful sight and one that warmed Darton's heart.

Flames crackled against pitch and smoke curled lazily upward, scenting the hall with burning oak.

"Brother!" Darton cried with forced delight. "We're honored by your early return."

"Are ye now, Darton?" Hagan said in a voice that was rough as gravel. He cast his brother a suspicious glance, and the insides of Darton's mouth turned to dust. His arrogance fled for a second. Hagan could not have yet heard about the capture of Leah . . . or could he have? Sometimes the man seemed to know in advance what was going to happen. Darton shuddered inwardly.

"You doubt me?"

"I've heard tales, Darton," Hagan said, yanking off his gloves and warming cold-to-the-bone fingers in front of the flames.

"And what kind of gossip has been spread, eh?" Darton

asked, favoring Hagan with a clap on the back. He motioned to a serving girl hovering near the door to the buttery. "Bring the lord some wine, Elfrida, and be quick about it. And call for more firewood."

Hagan's eyes narrowed on his brother. He knew all of Darton's tricks, and his skin crawled as he realized that his twin thought he could fool him. Shoving his wet hair from his eyes, Hagan accepted a cup of wine from a serving girl he'd never seen before. His bones were cold to the marrow and his muscles ached. He didn't want to deal with Darton this night. He was too weary, and his leg, blast it, burned as if hot coals had been buried in the flesh of his thigh. He swallowed back the wine and felt the liquid flow warm and sweet down his throat.

Darton eyed his brother over the rim of his cup and motioned to the page for more wine. Soon Hagan's vessel was full again. "You've had a hard ride, Hagan," Darton observed as Hagan took a long swallow. "Need you a woman?"

Hagan's mouth lifted at one side. "So now you're in the business of whoring, are ye, brother?"

Darton let out an ugly laugh. "There are many here that would please you, Hagan. Elfrida has magic in her hands, I swear." He leaned closer to his brother. "And her mouth . . . sweet wonders, she can do."

"I need not a woman," Hagan said, disgust surging through his blood. He finished his drink and felt the soreness in his muscles loosen a bit.

"Then there's Bliss, and aye, that she is. The smith's daughter, she works in the kitchen." Darton lifted a finger and stroked the side of his mouth. "She'll play any game ye wish. She has the strength of a woman twice her size, yet loves to be mastered. She's got spirit and fire and can handle a whip as well as—"

"Did you not hear me?" Hagan said in a low voice.

With a nod from Darton, the page refilled Hagan's cup. As the boy retreated, Darton said, "Do not be too hasty, brother. Bliss . . . believe me, there is no woman like her in all of Erbyn. She'll disguise herself, torment you, fight you like a tigress, then, once you've proven your strength, open her legs so willingly—"

"Enough!" Hagan whispered harshly. He was sickened at the depths of his twin's perversion.

"But, brother—"

Hagan grabbed the front of Darton's tunic and hauled the shorter man to his feet. Darton's cup spilled on the table, wine flowing between the thick boards to be lapped up quickly by the ever-vigilant dogs. "There will be no wenching, Darton, and if I hear that you've turned any of the serving maids into whores, you'll have to answer to me!"

Darton's face lost color.

Hagan slowly uncurled his fists, but his eyes were still dark with anger, his jaw set and tight. "We'll talk on the morrow," he said as he motioned to a page. "Have hot water brought to my chamber."

"Aye, m'lord." The page hurried out of the hall with swift footsteps.

"Talk of what?" Darton asked, but Hagan didn't reply, just finished his wine and sent his brother a scathing look that was certain to curdle Darton's blood.

Sorcha's ears strained in the darkness. She'd heard the sounds of feasting and revelry and even the sharp noises of an argument, but the words had not filtered up to her, and now the castle seemed asleep. Even the restless hounds who had paced near the kitchen hoping for scraps had settled down for the night.

Though Erbyn was cold, nervous sweat collected over Sorcha's forehead as she crept stealthily to her feet and eased through the partially opened door to the lord's chamber. She'd heard him enter the room hours ago, stoke the fire, and command some poor servant to set a tub of hot water near the hearth. She'd imagined him washing his body, but knew he'd never scrape off enough dirt to cleanse his soul.

In her hand she carried her dagger as she slid into the room and saw the bastard, rolled on one side, snoring softly, his dark hair falling over his face. In the firelight his skin seemed bronzed, his eyebrows thick and black, his nose more hawkish than she'd imagined. His lips, partially hidden, were thin, quite probably cruel, though, in truth, should she let her thoughts wander in so wanton a direction, she would have to admit that Darton was a far more handsome man than she'd heard. Dark, swirling hair covered a chest that was hard with lean muscles. He rolled over, and she stopped dead in her tracks, her heart beating as fast as a sparrow's wings. He cleared his throat, mumbled something, and began to snore again. Sorcha quietly let out her breath and wiped the sweat forming on her lips.

In the firelight, she viewed his backside, and a few old wounds were visible on his shoulders and back—or what she could see of it before it disappeared beneath a coverlet of black fur.

Well, he might be handsome and strong, but he was about to meet his match, she told herself. Fortunately no dogs were curled at his feet, and she had but to stealthily cross the rushes to his bed, seize his hair, and place the wicked little blade of her knife at his throat. Darton was known to be a coward. He would certainly shrivel up and agree to her demands. But . . . oh, Lord, he was so large. She quickly made the sign of the cross over her breasts as she slowly inched across the room. Without making a sound, she prayed that all the saints would be with her.

Just a few more steps.

A quick movement.

She caught her breath.

He rolled over swiftly and his eyes flew open.

Oh, God!

She lunged at him. Her blade sliced downward. A callused hand wrapped over her wrist in a viselike grip that stopped her short. Shadowed, furious eyes assessed her harshly. "So this is what my brother meant when he spoke of games, eh, Bliss?"

" 'Tis not bliss you'll see, but hell," she hissed, struggling and kicking.

To her horror, one side of his mouth lifted into a crooked smile—a grin of the very devil himself. He smelled freshly scrubbed, but the scent of wine was thick in the air. "No doubt."

"Free Leah!"

"Free *who?*"

"You black-souled bastard! Free her!" She aimed her foot at his leg, but he yanked hard and she fell atop him, her hair spilling from her cowl, her body stretched over the hard contours of his. "You bloody bastard, let me go!"

"So you can kill me?"

"Aye, if I have to." Again his smile. Damn the man, had he no fear?

Amusement flickered in eyes the color of purest gold. He released her wrist and stared up at her. She was suddenly aware of her breasts crushed against his chest, of the air that seemed to be lost in her lungs.

"Then kill me, Bliss," he said evenly as he curled rough fingers in her hair, "and be done with it."

Again she raised her knife. "You're a fool, Sir Darton."

"Darton?" he repeated, his tongue a little thick. Was the wench crazy or had he heard wrong? He'd drunk too much wine, and his mind wasn't as quick as usual. He told himself to be wary of Darton's whores, but this one, this little wench, was a beauty, and try as he might, Hagan couldn't deny a fascination with her. As he stared at her thin nose and arched eyebrows, he thought that he'd seen her somewhere, perhaps before he'd gone to war. In the half-light, dressed as a boy, she was beautiful and proud, her stubborn chin thrust forward defiantly, her blue eyes blazing as if she really could plunge the wicked blade of her dagger deep into his heart. A wild thing of beauty; no wonder Darton sang her praises so highly. She was warm and breathing hard, her legs sprawled across his in the most intimate of ways.

His traitorous body responded. Aching muscles cried for the touch of a woman. His groin tightened and he became hard with her weight spread over his.

"You think I jest?" she sputtered, setting the edge of her dagger to his throat. He didn't flinch, though in moving, her breasts, flat, soft pillows, brushed over his chest. A want, hot and deep and murky, flowed through his blood.

"I think you are here for another reason than to kill me."

"Aye, to free Leah. Do so and I will spare you."

"I don't know who she is."

The blade was pressed tighter to his throat, and Hagan wondered just how far the wench would go before she gave up her silly game. Or was she truly half-mad, believing in the words that tumbled so easily off her sharp tongue? He felt no fear, though, only an unholy desire to turn her onto her back and mount her, to triumph over her challenge, to act on pure animal instinct and claim her in the most primal of ways.

"You are holding my sister prisoner."

"Am I?" Both his hands moved upward to take her cheeks in his palms. Gently he shoved the hair away from her face. "You're a strange one, Bliss. Beautiful, but odd."

"I have no patience for this."

"Nor I," he replied, his arms suddenly surrounding her. She tried to slice his wretched throat, but she was thrown off balance as he rolled over, pinning her beneath him. Long legs straddled her ribs, and his hands shackled her wrists to the bed. With maddening ease, he forced the knife from her hand, and as her dagger clattered to the floor and was buried in the rushes, he held her squirming beneath him. His crooked smile of satisfaction was firmly in place as he watched the way her breasts rose and fell, her miserable attempts to kick and claw and roll away from him.

This wasn't supposed to happen! How could she have been so careless? Gulping back fear, she realized that he was completely naked, and quivering inside, she tried to keep her eyes raised to his chest, but her gaze drifted downward to the shaft of his manhood, which protruded hard and thick.

Her throat closed.

"Now, let's have no more talk about killing," he said, sliding down her.

"What're you doing?"

"What you came here for," he said, leaving one of her hands free so that he could work the laces of her tunic.

"No!" she cried, realizing that he meant to take her. "You can't do this, you can't!" she hissed, throwing all her weight into the useless task of trying to push him off her. She pounded at his shoulders, his ribs, wherever she could hit him, and the beast had the audacity to laugh and grab her hand, binding it with the other over her head as she writhed beneath him.

"Come on, Bliss, Darton told me of you."

Darton! "But you are—" She knew her mistake instantly as she stared up at his visage. A strong face, intelligent deep-set eyes, muscles that were strident and lean. "Lord Hagan," she said, her voice nearly failing her.

His lips curved in amusement, as if she were a diverting toy. "Aye, and you're Bliss, the wench sent to serve me."

"Nay!" she cried, struggling harder and watching as his eyes glinted in anticipation.

"Then who be ye?"

It was no use. She had to tell him the truth. To save herself. To save Leah. Only then would he stop this torturous game. *Oh, Leah, I fear I have failed you.* "I'm Sorcha."

"Sorcha?"

"Of Prydd. I've come for my sister."

His muscles tensed and flexed. His eyes sharpened as if he remembered seeing the girl years before. He let out a harsh bark of laughter. "So you're the *savior* of Prydd, are ye?" he teased, his voice low and rumbling, his lips twitching at her proclamation. In the firelight, with red and gold shadows playing upon his muscles, he looked like the very son of the devil. Sorcha's lungs constricted as he studied her. With his free hand he trailed a finger along her jaw, shoving a wayward curl from her cheek. "Why, then, be ye here? At Erbyn?"

Was he deaf? "I told you! For Leah. Darton's captured my sister and brought her here, and I've come to ensure her safe return."

"By warming my bed?"

"By killing you if needs be," she said, breathing deeply. Nervous sweat collected on the small of her back. She knew Hagan to be a fairer man than his brother, but she also believed that he was a great warrior, a fearless fighter, a man who had no qualms about taking any woman in the kingdom and having his way with her. Through her rough clothing she felt his hard muscles, and as she looked up at his face, she saw the determined gleam in his golden eyes.

"You had your chance for that," he said, lowering his head to nuzzle her neck. She twisted away, then, to make her point, bit his cheek hard. With a yelp he drew back, never releasing her, his eyes flashing fire as a ring of teeth marks showed against his freshly shaved skin. "So that's what you want," he whispered hoarsely.

"All I want is my sister freed! I knew not 'twas you in this chamber, Lord Hagan. I was told that Sir Darton would be resting here while you were off fighting the Scots."

He paused for a second, his dark brows drawing into a thick, harsh line. "You truly expected Darton?"

"Aye!"

"Did you not know that I had returned?"

"How could I?"

His eyes narrowed to suspicious slits. "You talk in circles, Savior," he muttered, allowing his finger to dip lower along the neckline of her tunic. He hesitated just a second, looked into her eyes, and frowned.

"I tell the truth. Ask Darton!"

"Sorcha of Prydd is a child. I've met her once."

"Aye, years ago!" she cried. "I was in the minstrel's balcony at the castle when you came for the truce!"

He hesitated a second. "Everyone in Erbyn knows of that."

"Then call Darton!" she insisted.

"And he will tell me of your sister's fate."

"Aye." But she knew it was a lie. If Hagan had returned and already spoken to his brother, why did Hagan not know of Leah? Because Darton had held the truth from him.

Anxiety curdled her stomach. Leah might already be dead. She squirmed. "We must save her."

"You lie. And you call my brother here just to make sport of me."

"No!" What did it take to make him believe her?

He dipped his head, his mouth finding hers, and Sorcha thought she might be sick.

"Nay, Lord Hagan, do not—"

But her words were silenced by the power of his lips moving sensually against her own. Hard and warm, they slanted over hers in a kiss that claimed and overpowered, that caused her mind to swim senselessly.

She tried to turn away. "Please, I beg—"

But his mouth found hers again, and his tongue, wet and slick, rimmed her lips and touched the edges of her teeth. "Beg, Bliss," he whispered into her mouth.

"You son of Lucifer!" she said, and she felt him tense, saw a gleam of sinewy muscles as he ripped her tunic from her body, stripping her of the dirty garment and baring her breasts to his dark eyes. His gaze settled on her necklace.

"The devil, am I? Well, Sorcha—that is still your name, is it not . . . ?"

"Aye."

"Then perhaps you want to bargain with the devil?"

Fear ripped down her spine. "Bargain?"

To her horror, he lowered his head and touched the tip of his tongue to her nipple. Desire mingled with loathing but ran hot in her blood.

"No!" she screamed, struggling.

But the tongue continued its hot, wet assault, causing her nipple to stiffen and her back to arch against her wishes. Her mind was turned against him, but her body was a traitor, a heartless piece of flesh that began to tingle and heat as he ran his callused fingers down her side. He touched each of her ribs, before he held the weight of her breast in his palm while kissing the other dark-peaked globe.

"You will die for this mistake," she warned, her voice low and raspy. "My father will see to it."

"Your father is the silversmith, and he would be pleased to know that you pleasure me."

As she felt his tongue against her skin, she tried to think clearly, to find a way out of this mess. "You said a bargain."

"Would you not lie with me willingly for the safety of your sister?" he asked, eyeing her with an arrogance that bespoke of his authority.

"You jest—"

"Nay, Bliss—er, Sorcha," he replied, obviously enjoying toying with her. " 'Tis a simple request: your sister's life for one night in my bed?"

Heat burned up her neck.

"You are already here," he pointed out.

"My virtue—"

He snorted. "Ahh, Bliss. Methinks your virtue is no longer in question. You need not worry of that."

Why did he seem so amused? " 'Tis not what you think," she yelled in vexation.

"Is it not?" he teased, gently running his hand lower, beneath the curve of her spine to cup one of her buttocks. His breathing was shallow and short as he said, "Tell me now, oh savior of all that is Prydd. What will it be? Your *virtue* or your sister's life?"

Four

Sorcha had no choice. She could not let her sister die. "I will do anything to save Leah's life," Sorcha said, though she thought of the other dagger, the one still tucked in her boot—her only means of escape. Could she go through the disgrace of lying with this cur, or would she, when the time was right, shove her blade into his soulless heart?

'Twould be simple enough to kill him, and yet when she stared up at his rugged features, saw the firelight playing upon the rough planes of his face, she knew she could not take his life.

"You are a strange one, Savior," he whispered, fingering the tiny bundle of sticks that hung at her neck. "Very strange indeed." His mouth found hers again. He kissed her, and she didn't move, just lay waiting, hoping that she could somehow find a way out of his bed, but his fingers, already touching her buttocks, pushed down the clothing that was the only frail barrier between them. His feet worked on her boots, and with a sinking heart she felt the leather stripped from her foot and heard her dagger clatter to the floor.

He glanced back and saw the useless weapon in the rushes. His smile was positively wicked. "You are deadly, are you not?"

"Not deadly enough," she said, inching her chin up defiantly.

"Ah, Bliss," he whispered, and his lips found hers in a kiss that was hot and anxious and spoke of hundreds of lonely nights of battle without a woman, without warmth or comfort, without joy.

Sorcha closed her eyes, refusing to gaze up at him, unable to look at his handsome face. With his free hand he rubbed her skin, touching her slowly, causing an unwanted heat to swirl in her blood.

"Come, Bliss," he murmured against her ear, and she tingled inside. "I'm anxious yet, but I can take all night if needs be."

Sorcha swallowed hard and her eyelids flickered open. Her gaze caught in the liquid gold of his, and she knew that he spoke the truth, that he was willing to give her the pleasure he expected in return.

"Just get it over with," she said, her throat catching.

His teeth flashed white in the darkness before he turned his attention to her breasts and suckled again, as if he were a babe, grunting his pleasure, drawing a sweetness from her that she fought. She would go through with this ordeal, for Leah, but she would not enjoy it.

Oh, but his lips and teeth. She heard a deep moan and realized it was from her own throat. He moved against her, touching her abdomen with his manhood while his fingers delved deeper and found the nest of curls at the apex of her legs.

NO! His fingers probed gently and she nearly screamed. This could not happen, this could not! And yet her body was starting to change, her bones to soften, the middle of her to turn hot as melting wax.

She felt her knees being parted by his and closed her eyes.

"Come, Bliss, is it so bad?" he asked, poised above her, ready to conquer her, his one hand caressing her skin as he drew his fingers slowly from her breasts to the small of her back.

"Just be done with it."

"Not until I know you are ready."

"Never," she said through clenched teeth, though her hips, damn them, lifted off the bed, anxious to give up her virginity to this monster.

"Look at me."

"Nay."

His hand moved to her chin. "Look at me," he commanded, and her eyes flew open to search the golden depths of his. She saw savagery and anger, passion and desire, in his gaze. She was forced to stare at his massive body, his muscles gleaming in the firelight, his expression hard, his manhood ready. She swallowed back her fear and noticed the fresh wound in his thigh. He winced a little as he shifted.

"Finish this, *m'lord,*" she hissed, "or leave me go!"

His body tensed and he glared at her. "As you wish!" Jaw clenched, he moved as if to take her, but instead he hesitated and stared at the charm dangling from her neck. His eyebrows drew together as he yanked and the string broke. Sorcha feared the tiny twigs would be crushed in his big hand. Lips tightening, he leveled his eyes at hers and stared at her face long and hard in the firelight. Recognition slowly dawned in his eyes. "Christ, Jesus," he muttered. "I've seen sacrilege such as this before . . . 'tis the work of a witch."

"Isolde of Prydd, my nursemaid."

"For the love of God—"

"So you finally believe me." Sorcha felt immense relief as she snatched the necklace from his hand.

"What the devil are you doing here?" he said, rolling off and swearing under his breath.

Leaping from the bed and pulling the fur coverlet to cover her trembling body, she sent up a silent prayer of thanks that she didn't have to go through with her part of the bargain, but her silly body felt disappointed and empty. "I told you a dozen times over that I'm here for my sister. Leah." Where were the bloody knives—both of them buried in the rushes? Curse it all. Bending down, trying to cover herself, she eyed her tormentor while her fingers searched the thick rushes.

In the firelight she saw his brows draw together. She took a step closer to the bed, still feeling the floor, cut herself on one dagger, but grabbed the hilt and curled her fingers over the handle.

"But how?" he whispered, his eyes narrowing on her. His expression turned murderous and his eyes grew dark. "How did you—whoever you are—get past the guards?" he asked, and his voice had the deadly ring of a proud man who suddenly realized he'd been taken for a fool.

She stood near the bed, her dagger glinting in the fireglow. " 'Twas easy." Keeping him at bay with the knife, she managed to hold the coverlet over her body as she searched for her clothes with her bare foot.

"Come over here, closer," he commanded, and she saw the gleam in his eyes as he climbed out of the bed and stood naked before her.

So he'd changed his mind. The beast had lied. He had no intention of releasing Leah, he'd only played with her. Shamed to her soul that she'd nearly lain with him, she shuddered as he approached, and warned, "Don't come any closer." She waggled the knife menacingly and saw her discarded tunic.

He ignored her message, moving nearer still.

Her heart thudded with dread and she snatched at the tunic.

He was so near, she could see the ripples of his muscles. Sweet Jesus! Like a snake striking, his arm reached out to take hold of her. Whirling, she drove the blade of her dagger into his shoulder.

Blood spurted.

"You fool," he said through his teeth. His eyes blazed and he sucked in his breath as if in pain.

Writhing, she tried to pull her knife from his body so that she could wound him yet again, but he wrestled her to the bed, pinned her with his legs, and took hold of the dagger.

"God's eyes, you are a witch." He yanked the weapon from his shoulder and dropped the knife to the ground.

Blood flowed freely from his wound. His face was a hideous mask. Anger contorted his features as he twined his hands in her hair, pulled hard, twisting her, and exposing the back of her neck to the firelight.

Upon the pale skin of her neck was the birthmark—the kiss of the moon—that he'd heard about all his life. Old women in the scullery, seamstresses, and cooks, along with tanners and bakers, huntsmen, and peasants who tended the fields, had all spoken in whispered tones of the kiss of the moon, the birthmark coveted and revered by those who still believed that there was to be a Welsh savior for Prydd.

The girl had not lied. She was not Bliss, not a kitchen whore, but daughter of a baron with whom he had a fragile truce. A girl who would have given up her virginity to save her sister—but from what? His teeth ground hard together.

Guilt cut through his soul and he glanced down at her tiny body—naked and inviting—proof that he'd bartered with her to give up her virtue, and nearly raped her as well.

Never in all his life had he taken a woman by force. In all the battles he'd fought, all the villages that had been plundered, he'd never lain with a woman who wasn't more than willing to give herself to him. But this girl had been different; he'd wanted to mate with her to prove that she couldn't thwart him, to best her, to conquer her arrogant spirit. Shame gouged deep in his soul.

"So you are the daughter of Eaton?" he said, his voice low with disgust.

"I told you who I was, and you chose not to listen."

He rolled off her and cast a sorry look at her before turning his back. "Get dressed," he commanded, tossing her the ripped tunic. "I will call for the guard to find something . . . more suitable."

"Just give me my sister and her freedom."

"Your sister is not here." Tugging on his own clothes, he turned to find her struggling into the torn rags that were her disguise. She was a beautiful vixen, with her thick black hair, sculpted cheekbones, and eyes as blue as the Welsh sky in summer. God in heaven, he'd made a vast mistake, the likes of which he'd never seen. How could he not have recognized her? He remembered her as a girl, a mutinous little fox who had the gall to challenge him.

Now she was here, and he'd nearly forced himself on her. Eaton's wrath would be boundless, and the delicate peace between the two castles would surely be ripped apart. How had he been so foolish? He strode to the door and barked an order to the guard—insisting that the man fetch some of his sister Anne's clothes.

"The lady will not like to be awakened," the guard said quietly.

Hagan let out a long, impatient sigh. "True, but I care not what Anne likes, Sir Peter. Tell her 'tis an order, that if she does not comply, I will come down to her chamber myself, strip her of whatever she is wearing, and gladly wring her beautiful neck in the bargain."

He sent the guard hastening down the hall, then turned back to the bane of his existence, the savior of Prydd, the beautiful, stubborn woman who had tried to kill him in his sleep. The fact that she'd tried to slit his throat should have eased his conscience, but he still felt a blundering fool. Why had he thought her initial reaction to his seduction had been the act of a wily whore used to playing upon men's fantasies?

"Where is my sister?" she demanded, still standing in the shadows near his bed. She'd pulled her clothes over her body, but still she trembled. Probably from pure hatred.

"I know not."

"You won't tell me."

"I have no reason to believe that she is in the castle."

"I would not lie, m'lord," she said with a defiant toss of her head. "My sister is here, somewhere, held prisoner by these very walls. Leah was abducted by your men while riding to the village to pass out alms to the poor. The outlaws lay in wait in the forest and sprang upon Leah as she was going to the village. A serving maid and two of our most loyal knights were killed while trying to save my sister and me," she added, changing the story just a little, her throat tightening as she thought of Keane, a man who had loved her, and the horrid arrow that killed him—an arrow from Erbyn.

"You lie," he said, crossing his massive arms over his chest. Blood was seeping through the sleeve of his tunic.

"Why? Why would I dare come here if not for Leah?"

"Darton would not risk breaking the truce—"

"Then one of his men did. Someone bearing the Erbyn

colors has started a war, Lord Hagan, and only you can stop it. Now, shall we find Leah?" she demanded as a knock resounded on the door.

"Lady Anne asks for a word with you," Sir Peter whispered as he handed Hagan a thick stack of clothing.

"In the morning," Hagan growled. He couldn't think about facing his sister's questions until the light of day. His thigh pained him and the new wound in his arm throbbed, but he was bound and determined to yank Darton out of his bed and demand the truth. "Here—wear these," he said, tossing the tunic and mantle onto the bed.

"I'd rather die first."

He snaked a glance at the ripped tunic displaying her breasts. "You might. If my men see you half-dressed . . ."

With a sound of disgust, she snatched up the clothes and tossed them over her head. Her story didn't make any sense. Why would Darton or his soldiers risk breaking the truce by kidnapping one of Eaton's daughters and killing Eaton's men? Head pounding with a blinding ache, Hagan grabbed for her wrists. "Come."

"I'll not be shackled."

"Oh, for the love of Jesus . . ." He had not time for her churlishness. Without a warning he stripped the knife from her hands, hauled her onto his good shoulder, and swearing at the pain, carried her like a sack of grain.

"Let me down," she demanded. "I'll walk on my own."

"You'll do as you're told," he said, and resisted the urge to lay a hand across her rear. She kicked and fought, but he couldn't trust her on her feet. Hadn't she alone sneaked into his castle, his very room, and nearly slit his throat? Chains wouldn't hold her. "Be still."

"You're a beast, Hagan, and you'll pay for this injustice," she cried, swinging her fists. It may have been humorous had it not been for the fact that he'd so recently nearly bedded her.

"Hush, woman," he commanded. He hurried down the hall, kicking at dozing guards as he made his way along the familiar stone hallways of the keep. Rushlights and candles in sconces, burning low, were his guide to his brother's chambers, where he pounded heavily on the door. "Darton!"

Guards, swords drawn, the sleep leaving their eyes, gathered around. Humiliated, Sorcha squirmed, her black hair sweeping the floor as the brute carried her as if she were naught. Aye, he limped a little, from the wound in his leg, but his strength had not faded much.

"Darton, wake up before I kick in the door!" Hagan yelled.

To her misery, she heard the sounds of footsteps in the hallways, servants who'd been awakened with the noise, hidden eyes that watched the spectacle.

With a thick clunk, the door opened, and Darton, hair askew, tunic thrown on hastily, blinked at the ring of soldiers and his furious brother. "What's—"

Hagan dropped Sorcha on her feet in front of a man who looked much like the ogre who dragged her here. The hair was the same, the features only slightly different—a bit softer than the harsh planes of Hagan's chiseled face.

"Who is this?" Hagan demanded, pushing Sorcha toward the door.

"I know not," Darton replied, lifting a shoulder in vexation and running fingers through his hair. "A wench dressed in rags and Anne's old—" His eyes narrowed, and Hagan witnessed the blood drain from his brother's proud face. Darton's mouth closed and his throat worked.

" 'Tis Sorcha of Prydd," Hagan said. To prove his point, he yanked her hair off her neck, turned her backwards, and pointed to the damning birthmark.

At the sight of the kiss of the moon, Darton's lips pinched in annoyance. "I've heard the whispered tales of foolish old women," he said, but there was a darkness in his gaze that betrayed his disinterest.

Sorcha whirled on Hagan, her blue eyes spitting fire as he released her. "How dare you—"

"Just to prove that you're who you say you are, m'lady."

"He knows," she said, pointing a finger in Darton's direction. "He planned all this. I spoke to the traitor, Robert, who is half-dead from the beating my brother gave him, and he told me of your plans."

Hagan added, "This woman sneaked into the castle, past all of our guards, and tried to kill me because she claims that you have taken her sister, Leah, prisoner."

"M'lord, this is preposterous," Darton said, turning his hands, palms toward the ceiling. "I would not dare defy your word and—"

"Liar!" Sorcha lunged forward, ready to kill the bastard if needs be. "She's here!"

"Nay, I—"

"Did you lie with her? Rape her? Kill her?" Sorcha demanded, fear clutching her heart in its cruel fist.

Hagan clamped a hand on the tiny spitfire, who turned on him. "Your brother is a lying cur," Sorcha hissed. "I swear on my own mother's grave, if I find that harm has come—"

"Hush, woman." Hagan grabbed the woman's wrist and held her still. He was beginning to think she was more trouble than she was worth, but he was forced to listen to her ravings as he could not very well banish her. Was she lying? Or was there the hint of truth in her words? He turned his attention back to his brother. "Is she daft or does she speak the truth?"

"Why, Hagan, do you believe her?" Darton demanded. He was beginning to sweat, though the castle was as cold as the bottom of a well. "Look at her. She's either a spy or deranged or—"

"Have you taken any prisoners while I was away?"

Darton's eyes moved swiftly from his brother to the ring of guards standing ready, swords drawn. "Aye, Hagan. You've been gone a long while. There are thieves and murderers, poachers and outlaws, those who refuse to pay taxes and—"

Hagan's patience snapped. "Is the girl here? Leah of Prydd?"

Darton's nostrils flared a bit. "Why would I take a girl—"

"I care not. Is she here?" Hagan said, and when his brother didn't immediately respond, he dropped Sorcha's wrist, ordering a guard to restrain her as he knotted his fingers in the front of Darton's tunic and shoved him up against the cold stone wall. His fingers tightened over the fabric despite Darton's obvious anger and humiliation. "Did I not tell you that there was to be no warring while I was away?"

Darton, his face turning scarlet, nodded and choked. "Yes, brother."

"Did I not make myself clear that there were to be no truces broken?"

Again the clipped nod. "Aye." Darton squirmed beneath Hagan's iron grip.

"Yet you disobeyed me?"

"Would you have Erbyn defenseless?" Darton said, his voice choked, his words strangled.

"Were we attacked?"

"Nay," he said with a rasp, "but our spies had word that Tadd planned to lay siege to Erbyn, and we hoped by —"

"Lies! He lies!" Sorcha cried, lunging forward.

"Is it not proof enough that she crept into your chamber to slit your throat?" Darton whispered hoarsely.

"Sire, please, release him," Sir Ives said, and Hagan, his rage a living beast running through his blood, unclamped his hand. His brother fell into a heap on the floor, clutching his throat and coughing in fits.

Hagan was torn. He knew that Darton would lie to save own skin, but Sorcha had tried to kill him. Mayhaps there was more to the story than either side was telling. Sorcha glared at Darton, and hatred seethed in the air, though there was something else, a glimmer of desire in Darton's gaze, that caused Hagan's gut to clench.

"Tell the truth, you lying pig!" Sorcha cried.

"Enough!" Hagan turned his fury upon her. "If you don't want to be gagged, keep your silence. Now . . ." He turned back to Darton. "Tell me of Leah. The truth. You brought her here, didn't you?"

Darton didn't answer, but his insolence and silence were admission enough.

"Why?"

" 'Twas a mistake," Darton admitted, still kneeling as he rubbed his throat. "I heard of Tadd's plans and decided 'twould be best if we struck first and did damage to Prydd. The men were not to kill anyone, but they were to take a prisoner, that one, the eldest daughter of Eaton."

Sorcha gasped.

" 'Twas she who was supposed to be in the village passing out alms."

Hagan's fingers straightened, then clenched into fists of anger. How could he have trusted Darton with his beloved Erbyn?

"I have only told you the truth. There was no attack planned on Erbyn," Sorcha declared.

"Robert of Prydd disagreed," Darton said.

Sorcha tossed her hair from her face. "Sir Robert was a traitor."

Darton's throat worked. "Against Prydd, aye. He was our spy, and he claimed that Tadd was mounting an army. With you gone, Hagan, Tadd hoped to end the need for a truce once and forever by breaking the truce and taking Erbyn."

"Liar," Sorcha spat.

Hagan glared at his brother. "This makes no sense, brother. Are you telling me that because of some rumor spoken by a spy, you planned to steal Tadd's sister . . . ?"

Darton's lips curved into a hateful smile. "Not just his sister, Hagan. Surely you've heard the old ones whisper between themselves. Think they that the bearer of the kiss of the moon is the savior of all Prydd, and mayhaps all Wales."

" 'Tis foolishness; you said so yourself," Hagan said, shaking his head at his brother's trust in such blasphemy; not that he was particularly religious, but he was certainly not stupid enough to believe in the power of a discoloration of the skin. "You've put this castle in danger and started the feud again. By taking Eaton's daughter, you have thrown down the gauntlet, and we are surely to face bloody battles, losing many men for naught." He shoved the hair from his eyes and resisted the urge to pounce on his brother and beat him within an inch of his miserable life.

"Now we have something with which to bargain," Darton said, and at that particular word, Hagan froze.

"Too many bargains have already been struck and broken. What have you done with Lady Leah?"

"She is safe."

"But kept prisoner."

Darton nodded. "I would not have her escape, even though she was not the woman I sought."

Hagan's head throbbed. "Did you lie with her?"

Darton's eyes flickered with malice. "Does it matter?"

"It matters much. If you've forced her into your bed, then you shall marry her." He ignored the cry from Sorcha's lips. " 'Tis the only way to appease Eaton."

"Mayhap I would rather marry this one," Darton said, motioning toward Sorcha, and Sorcha's blood turned to ice.

"Nay!" she whispered violently.

Hagan glanced at the woman whom he'd nearly bedded and pretended complete disinterest, though the thought of Darton lying with Sorcha burned like a hot ember in his guts. " 'Tis too late. You've made your choice."

"Leah would never marry him!"

Hagan whirled on her. "What if she is with child?"

The joints of her knees seemed to buckle for an instant. The thought of Leah bearing Darton's bastard was a horrid thought indeed, but marriage to this devil's spawn? However, loath though she was to think such vile things, 'twas possible that Leah was already carrying the blackguard's child.

Sorcha inched her chin upward, and her voice was barely a whisper. "My sister would rather die than marry anyone from the house of Erbyn."

"Wench!" Darton whispered. "What she needs is—"

"Where is the sister?" Hagan's voice was as hard as steel, his lips as thin as hunting blades.

Darton, as if sensing the unspoken challenge between Sorcha and Hagan, hesitated. "How did this one sneak past our guards?"

"That, we will discuss later. Now, brother," he said, his lips barely moving, "tell me of Leah."

Darton saw the fury in Hagan's glare and knew that there was no further use in outwardly defying him. If only he'd known that Sorcha had come to Erbyn, if only he'd intercepted her, for she was the woman he wanted, the most powerful woman in all of Wales.

"The lady is in the east wing," he admitted.

"I want to see her. Now." Sorcha didn't trust Darton, nor did she have any faith in his brute of a brother. She would only feel at ease when she saw Leah again. Then, perhaps, they could bargain, if only Hagan would believe her and not Darton's desperate lies. Surely Hagan, who seemed to honor the truce, would free both women and have them escorted safely back to Prydd.

Tadd would be furious with both his sisters as well as with Hagan, but Sorcha was certain her brother would find a way to make this horrid ordeal profitable—without Leah being forced to marry Darton. Tadd would demand payment for the dishonor of Prydd, and Hagan, if he had any shred of decency in his dark soul, wouldn't argue Tadd's claim.

Only Sorcha would know the depths of her own dishonor, for she would live with the memory of nearly giving herself to Hagan. She clenched her teeth at that particular thought as she followed Hagan's swift strides down the stairs through the great hall and to the far side of the castle where the air was dank and chill. This, she understood, was the older part of the keep, used only when there were more guests than could be housed in the western portion. There were cracks in the walls, and she remembered that she'd heard that once, years ago, Erbyn had been scarred by battle, some of the battlements and parts of the hall nearly destroyed. Most of the castle had to be rebuilt.

With its damp smell and dim torches, this part of Erbyn was as much a prison as any foul dungeon. But Leah was strong; she would survive, knowing that Sorcha would come to free her.

They climbed two flights of stairs that led to a narrow corridor lit only by rushlights. A thin guard with a pock-marked face was posted near a thick oak door. "Let us in," Darton said softly, and the grim-faced soldier glanced at Hagan before quickly unlocking the door.

Sorcha's heart pounded. Would Leah ever forgive her for insisting that they change places? Would she understand that she was safe now, and despite the fierce one's plan of marrying Leah off to Darton to balm his guilt, Leah could not be forced into marrying a man she did not love? This wasn't exactly true, of course, but Sorcha was certain she could convince her father that a marriage between the houses of Erbyn and Prydd would be a mistake of hellish proportions.

Sorcha would do anything within her power to save her sister. She stepped forward, following Darton, but Hagan's hand restrained her. "Mayhap you should wait here," he said, and for the first time she noticed lines of strain on his face and worry near his eyes.

"I'll not—"

Darton walked into the chamber. "Lady, you have a visitor from Prydd. Your sister is . . ."

His words faded, and Sorcha could stand the suspense no longer. "Leah!" she cried, wresting her way free of Hagan and nearly tripping on Darton, who stood stock-still near the door. "Leah!

"Thank God I've finally found you!" she cried as her eyes adjusted to the dim light. She didn't see her sister at first, and heard Darton's low voice behind her as she walked to the only piece of furniture in the room—a large canopied bed. "Leah! Wake up!" she said, suddenly anxious as a cool breath of air touched the back of her neck and the wood of the canopy creaked loudly.

"Sorcha, wait," Hagan called.

Her heart froze. Ice filled her veins as she saw the small lump that was her sister. "No!" she whispered, horrified as she saw the blood oozing from Leah's wrists. "Merciful God, no!"

"What in the name of God?" Hagan demanded from somewhere behind her.

Sorcha stepped forward, unable to believe the truth, but in the light of the few candles still waning in their holders, she saw her sister's face, white and unmoving, and the tiny knife that had slipped to the floor.

"By all the gods, I swear . . ." She reached for her dagger, but her fingers encountered only the folds of another woman's tunic. She grabbed part of Leah's tunic, ripped it, and quickly bound the strips of cloth to Leah's wrists. "Please, Leah, do not die," she whispered.

Hagan was beside her, his hand against Leah's chest, his head bent down to her nostrils. " 'Tis too late," he said quietly.

"Nay!" Sorcha screamed, dropping to her knees. "Please, Leah, you cannot die. You cannot!"

A strong hand touched her on the shoulder. "Sorcha, come. There is nothing—"

Sorcha threw off Hagan's hand and turned on him. "She will live!" she proclaimed loudly, her gaze landing on Darton. "Despite the deceit and treachery and lies that infest this castle, she will live! You," she ordered a guard near the door. "Send word to Isolde at Prydd. She is to come here at once." When the man didn't move, Sorcha pointed at him with a long, condemning finger. "Unless you want to see the horrid wrath of the kiss of the moon, you will ride this night."

" 'Tis too late," Hagan said again, and she whirled on him.

"This is your fault, *baron,* and you must do whatever it is that you can to save my sister."

"She's gone—"

"She's not! Her body is warm, and I can feel the beat of her heart. Now, unless you want yet another death in the house of Prydd on your hands, you will find one of your servants who practices the old ways."

"She speaks of sorcery," Darton said.

"I care not what you call it, but Leah needs help."

Hagan glared at her for a second, before telling the guard, "Take Sir Darton back to his quarters—"

Darton waved off the guard. "Hold fast. I'll not be treated like a prisoner—"

"Take him!" Hagan said more fiercely. "Then awaken Rosemary. See that she comes up here, and . . . ask that she bring her daughter, Caitlin."

"Caitlin is not at Erbyn this night, and . . . 'tis said that Caitlin practices the dark arts, m'lord—"

"If not Caitlin, then her mother, but do it. Now!" Hagan snarled, allowing Darton to stay.

Sorcha paid little heed; she was still on her knees near the bed, sometimes praying that Leah's life be spared, other times speaking softly to her sister. "I'm here now, Leah. You're safe; please, please, hear me." Her heart was as heavy as if it had been weighted with stones. She placed the necklace carefully around Leah's throat and retied the broken cords. The red string seemed the color of blood against Leah's pale skin, and the small twigs looked frail and powerless. "Come, Leah. Live!"

She heard Hagan tell one of his men to stoke the fire and light candles before they were banished from the room. Only Darton and Hagan remained.

Darton stood as if transfixed, and Hagan paced restlessly. "This is nonsense," he said.

"Shh . . . she works her magic."

"There is no magic."

Sorcha heard their exchange as if from a distance. She knelt at her sister's side, touching Leah's cool fingers, whispering words of encouragement, willing her life-force into her sister.

The serpent ring felt suddenly warm around her fingers and seemed to possess a pulse of its own. Was it her imagination or did Leah move slightly? Was there a tiny gasp in her shallow breathing? " 'Tis good, sister," Sorcha encouraged, her eyes shimmering with tears.

A woman's sharp voice reverberated down the hallway. "What in the name of God are ye mumbling about—what girl? What sorceress? I swear, Sir Marshall, it's losin' your mind, ye are."

She entered the room, and a rush of wind caused the candles to flicker. "What's this?" she asked as Sorcha turned in her direction, and the woman, big-boned but surprisingly agile, moved to the bedside. Her gaze traveled quickly over Leah's body and wrists. "Lord have mercy!" she said.

"Can you help her, Rosemary?" Hagan asked.

"The poor, sweet child." Rosemary wasted no time and her fleshy hands were on Leah's face, touching her temple, smoothing her skin. "I think ye best be callin' for the priest," she said sadly. "She's nearly gone."

"No!" Sorcha cried. "She can be saved."

"This is the girl's sister. She is called Sorcha," Hagan explained when the large woman glanced at him.

Rosemary sighed and turned kind eyes on Sorcha. "I'm sorry, love, but in all my years I've never seen one so far gone come back. She's sleeping now; her heart is slow, and her breathing . . . I can do nothing but pray for her soul."

"You haven't even tried!" Sorcha proclaimed. "She cannot die!"

" 'Tis not in my hands, child."

Sorcha would not give up. She placed her fingers on Leah's shoulders and whispered, "All that I have is yours, sister. Please hear my prayer. Come back to those who love you." Again the snake ring grew hot, tightening painfully over her finger.

Hagan stood transfixed, staring at the little woman who knelt so proudly near the bed. He almost believed her to be a witch . . . a most entrancing witch. Her black hair, in wild curls, shone dark as a raven's wing in the candlelight, and her eyes, round and surrounded by curling lashes, were filled with conviction. Her cause was futile, of course: Leah was nearly dead and could not be saved.

"Come," he said to Sorcha. "Let Rosemary stay with your sister."

She shrugged off his hand. "I'll not leave until Leah awakens."

Darton started to step forward, but Hagan held him back. "If she wishes to stay, so be it."

She laid a hand over Leah's heart. As the ring strangled her finger, she felt a sudden chill deep in her soul. Though the window was not open, a wind, damp and smelling of the forest, began to blow and circle around her. Candlelight flickered and the fire burned more brightly. "Take not my sister's life," she prayed. "Protect her from all evil and give her back to us." Her own heartbeat thundered through her skull, and as she laid her hand with the ring across the necklace she'd placed around Leah's throat, she sensed a tremor run from her body and through her sister's. Leah's fingers twitched, and Sorcha felt suddenly weak.

"By all that is holy . . ." Rosemary whispered, falling to her knees.

Leah moaned softly, and the world seemed to tilt behind Sorcha's eyes.

"By the gods!" Darton whispered. "She lives!"

Sorcha's heart beat frantically. Her legs were suddenly unsteady, as if all her strength had poured into her sister. Sweat ran down her face and her breathing was shallow—as shallow as that of her sister. A blackness threatened her eyes.

Hagan's voice sounded distant. "Sorcha. Are you . . . ?" The room closed in on her. She couldn't breathe. Hot. She was so hot.

"Sorcha?"

Leah's voice came as if from a great distance. Sorcha tried to respond, to say something of comfort to her sister, but her legs gave way and she began to fall. A strong arm surrounded her as the great black void swallowed her.

Five

Make sure she sleeps," Hagan told Rosemary. "And if she wakes, send for me." He placed Sorcha on a bed in a guest chamber and tucked the cover to her chin.

The old woman eyed her new charge warily. Nervously her tongue rimmed her cracked lips. "I've heard she's a wild one; saw what she could do—"

"There will be guards posted at the door."

"She tricked the cook," Rosemary said, and Hagan found it difficult to believe how fast gossip could race through the keep. "She must be clever as a fox."

"Just tend to her; I'll not be gone long," Hagan said, glancing down at the tangle of black hair that framed a small, white face as beautiful as any he'd ever seen. Sleeping, she looked peaceful and small and vulnerable, though he knew differently. The pain in his shoulder was witness to how deadly she could become, and what he'd witnessed as she'd kept her vigil with her sister was mind-numbing.

"Is it true she is the savior of Prydd?" the nursemaid asked, her lips trembling slightly.

"Of course not. You're a Christian woman, Rosemary. Surely you don't believe in such old wives' tales." He glared at her, daring her to defy him, and she bobbed her old head anxiously.

"Aye. I'm a true believer in the Lord. But—I saw her call

the furies as she brought her sister, Leah, back from the dead."

"Leah was not yet dead, just in a deep sleep. There was no witchcraft, Rosemary. Just prayers."

The old woman seemed disappointed. "But—"

"Rest assured that this woman will not hurt you. She is our guest and shall be treated so."

Rosemary glanced at the blood staining the shoulder of his tunic, but did not argue, and Hagan left Sorcha to deal with his brother. Though it was still a few hours until dawn, half the castle was awake, and the news that Sorcha, the savior of Prydd, had somehow slipped past Erbyn's defenses had traveled like wildfire through the hallways, scullery, and kitchens. The gossip ran fast with the story that Sorcha had laid her hands upon her sister and brought the girl back from the grave. In Hagan's opinion, this was not the case. He had been in the chamber, and aye, the air in the room had been deathly still, then suddenly wrought with winds, but there had been no magic, no conjuring up of spirits, no raising the dead.

However, the rumors were out of control, and the fact that Sorcha had spent part of the night in Hagan's chamber and had managed to wound him had lifted many an eyebrow.

He would tend to the servants and gossip later. First he had to confront his brother, who had started all this trouble. He strode to Darton's quarters, hoping Darton would talk to him and he could begin to sort out the truth from the lies. His twin was furious that Hagan had locked him in his chambers and treated him like a prisoner, but Hagan felt he had no choice.

Darton was waiting for him. Like a penned animal, he paced restlessly between the window and the fire. Glancing up when Hagan arrived, he glared at his brother. "You have no right to keep me locked away, like a common thief," he snarled. " 'Twas I who kept your castle safe while you were off at war, and yet now, because of some daft woman, you would imprison me." His nose curled in contempt. "I'll not be caged like a wild animal, brother," he warned.

"And I'll not be deceived by my own kin." Hagan saw that the guard was listening from his post in the hallway. He motioned for the man to shut the door and waited until he and his brother were completely alone.

"I was nearly killed in my bed tonight," Hagan said as he propped a booted foot near the grate and tried to control his temper. "Sorcha of Prydd sneaked into my chamber and tried to slit my throat."

"I've heard," Darton said, "but it seems you survived."

Hagan wanted to shake him until he'd gained some sense. Instead, he crossed his arms in front of his chest and pinned Darton with his hardest glare. "She says she came here to free her sister, whom you kidnapped and held prisoner."

"I explained why," Darton replied with a shrug. Then, as his thoughts changed their course, he managed a small smile. "Did you not see how she brought her sister back to life?"

"Leah was not yet dead."

"But you cannot deny that something spiritual happened in that chamber. 'Twas as if Sorcha gave up her lifeblood and it flowed into her sister."

"There was no letting of blood."

"Aye—it was magical. Sorcery." Darton rubbed his hands together. "It is true, Hagan, and you, having seen it with your own eyes, cannot doubt that the power exists. She is truly the chosen one. Be thankful that she is now here at Erbyn and no longer with the enemy."

"The enemy?" Hagan said, feeling uneasy. "Who's the enemy? Surely not the Scots—"

"Tadd of Prydd," Darton said.

"We have a truce with Eaton."

"Yea, but the baron's away, and now we deal with his simpleton of a son, a man who is greedy and growing more powerful each day." Darton walked to the fire to stand next to his brother. "Did I not already tell you that there have been rumors, Hagan, rumors suggesting that Tadd is mounting an army the likes of which we haven't seen in years? My soldiers were traveling the road that leads to the village near Prydd. Sir Robert, one of our most trusted men and a traitor to Prydd, told me that Tadd was strengthening his forces while his father was off fighting the Scots."

"There is a truce—" he repeated.

"Aye, and it has been broken many times. Eaton is an old man and far off. Tadd can honor the truce or break it."

"What does this have to do with Lady Leah?"

Darton sighed loudly. "The capture of Leah was a mistake. I told the men to take only Sorcha, that she was worth more."

"You thought to sell her?"

"Nay, to bargain for her. To show Tadd's hand. The exchange would be her safe return for peace."

"You expect me to believe—"

" 'Tis the truth," Darton swore. "She is powerful, Hagan, and tonight was proof of that. Many have whispered that she is the chosen one, the savior of Prydd, a woman blessed by the old gods, and though we may find such beliefs foolish, they exist. Her birthmark alone sets her apart, causes old tongues to wag. We may laugh at the ancient ones and their religion, but many still believe in the old rites. Oh, they hide their blasphemy well by attending mass and pretending piety, but—" he leaned closer to Hagan, conviction etched in his features "—they think of her as their true leader. It matters not what favors Edward bestows upon you, Hagan. Many of the peasants and servants believe that Sorcha of Prydd is the most powerful woman—or man, for that matter—in all of Wales." His voice lowered a fraction and he glanced to the door, as if he was hiding his next words. "There is gossip about her that runs deeper. 'Tis rumored that she was not sired by Sir Eaton, that she's not the seed of his loins. There are many who believe that a true prince of the Celts, a bastard grandson of Llywelyn, raped Lady Cleva, under the watchful eye of a full moon; that Sorcha of Prydd is not Eaton's daughter but is really descended from Llywelyn the Great, that the blood that flows through her veins is from the true rulers of Gwynedd."

Absently, as Darton spoke his nonsense, Hagan rubbed his shoulder, where her knife had found its mark, and Darton sat on a stool near the hearth as he spoke. "The old ones, they believe the prophecy, and they've taught their young the same. Edward may think that he is king of all that is Wales, but he is a fool. Only those with royal Welsh blood can rule the people." Satisfied that he'd convinced Hagan of his prisoner's worth, Darton leaned back and knocked off a bit of mud from the sole of his boot with the toe of the other. "She is a prize, brother. A prize to bargain with."

Hagan's teeth were clenched so hard that he could barely speak. "So you plotted Sorcha's kidnap because of her power over the old people, because she is rumored to be the true ruler of Prydd?"

"Nay. I took her because of the rumors of war." Darton frowned darkly. "Tadd of Prydd cannot be trusted. He has threatened to raise his sword to Erbyn more than once."

"But he's never broken the peace."

" 'Twas only a matter of time." Darton rubbed his jaw and his eyes narrowed. "The mistake was that my men brought the wrong woman and killed two of Tadd's soldiers."

"As well as a lady in waiting."

"Bloody hell," Darton ground out, apparently furious that his scheme had not gone as planned.

"So instead of preventing war, you may have started one. Tadd of Prydd now has an excuse to break the truce. Now he will certainly be looking for trouble."

"Aye," Darton admitted with a lift of one shoulder. "That much is true. However—" one side of his mouth curved upward "—all is not lost. By the fates, brother, we now have Sorcha."

That thought gave Hagan no comfort. "As well as her sister, who may die."

"By her own hand," Darton replied callously. " 'Tis a pity, aye, but there is no way to undo the deed."

"Leah tried to kill herself because you brought her here against her will." Hagan leaned against the warm stones of the fireplace and tried to keep the rage from his voice. This time Darton had gone too far. A woman—Sorcha's sister—was nearly dead. Dead! No amount of chanting would bring her back if she gave up her spirit. Yet Darton acted as if her life made no difference. A cold desperation gnawed at Hagan's guts. "So tell me, Darton, did you treat her well while she was here?"

"She was a prisoner."

"A prisoner? For God's sake, what were you thinking?"

Darton's eyes narrowed. "I was trying to save your barony, that's all, m'lord!"

Hagan's jaw hardened. "As a prisoner, was she beaten?"

Hagan asked, his stomach roiling as he thought of Sorcha's sister being flogged.

"Nay—"

"Raped?" he asked.

A small light flickered in Darton's eyes. "Nay, I—"

"Just tell me this, brother. Did you force her into your bed?" Hagan demanded, though he knew the answer.

"She came willingly," Darton said with a smile that made Hagan's blood turn to ice.

He could stand the lies no longer. Grabbing the front of Darton's tunic, he twisted the fine fabric, making a noose of his brother's clothing as he lifted Darton in the air. "When you are ready to tell me the truth and all of it, I will listen to you. My guess is that you are telling me only what you think I should hear, but I trust you not. That girl tried to kill herself, Darton, with her own knife or else you or one of your soldiers attempted to take her life. You may yet succeed, for she's none too strong. Whether she lives or dies, you will pay, brother, and pay dearly. You've put this castle and all who depend upon Erbyn for safety in danger. 'Tis something I'll not forget." He dropped Darton as if he were a vile piece of meat and strode out the door, stopping only to instruct the guards to keep the heavy door barred.

His leg ached and his shoulder throbbed as he strode down the curved stairs. Damn Darton, damn his bloody schemes and damn him for his whoring.

Tadd of Prydd was not known for his patience. A bully with a mean temper, he would want revenge.

Soon the very gates of hell would open, right here, at Erbyn.

"Bring me the stable master!" Tadd bellowed, his boots sinking into the mud, his fury evident in the harsh lines of his face. Could not anything ever go right? He tapped his riding whip in the palm of his gloved hand impatiently. Guards scurried into the stables and searched the castle.

Finally the bravest of the lot approached Tadd. "The stable master's gone," Sir Prescott said, ducking his head against the fine morning mist that drizzled continually from the gray sky.

"He's gone and my horse is missing," Tadd said, flicking his crop at a piece of dirt on the shoulder of Prescott's tunic. "Think you he took the stallion?"

"I know not," Prescott admitted, showing off the tight wedge of his teeth that bucked prominently over his lower lip. He looked like a frightened rooster contemplating the butcher's hatchet.

"Have you spoken with his wife?"

"Aye, and all she does is wring her hands while her little ones hide behind her skirts."

"She knows not where he is?" Tadd had trouble believing the woman had no idea where her husband had gone.

"If she does, she says nothing."

"*Someone* knows where the man is!" Tadd nearly yelled. He was in a foul mood. The kitchen wench with whom he'd lain the night before had been silly and dull. A beauty, with full breasts and accommodating hips, she was a bore with little imagination, a woman who giggled incessantly until he'd kicked her out of his bed and felt unsatisfied. He'd woken up with the need to go hunting. His blood was up, his temper black, and he wanted only to sight a boar or stag, chase the animal down, and fell it swiftly. Now his horse, his prize destrier, McBannon, was missing. Along with that miserable Tim, the stable master.

"Find out what happened," Tadd ordered, turning on his

heel and feeling a chill as cold as death as Prescott hurried back to the stables.

First the attacks on his sisters, bungled though the one on Sorcha had been, and the murder of two soldiers and a maid, and now this . . . the loss of his finest war-horse. He wouldn't be surprised if Tim, a man who loved mead, had taken off with the great beast. The man was a drunk and a dullard, kept on only because he had a talent with the horses. It was eerie sometimes, the way he could encourage the most headstrong of animals to do his bidding.

Tim had been with Prydd for as long as Tadd could remember and was one of Tadd's father's most trusted men. Though Tadd would love to turn the man and his family out of the castle walls, his father would not hear of it. Should Tadd dismiss the stable master while his father was absent, there would be serious trouble as soon as Eaton returned and discovered the fat pig missing. 'Twas enough to turn a man to drink!

Footsteps approached, and Tadd, who had started up the steps to the great hall, paused. Turning, he saw Prescott running across the wet grass and mud of the bailey. Rain drizzled down his long nose and splattered his cheeks. "M'lord," Prescott said, "one of the guards on duty last night—Sir Michael—said the old woman was out searching for her herbs in the moonlight."

Tadd snorted in disgust. "She's a foolish old hag. She has nothing to do with—" He glanced up at the iron-colored sky, and his eyes narrowed. "Was there a moon last night?"

"Aye." Prescott offered a cruel smile.

"Bring Isolde to me," Tadd said, climbing the stairs with a new sense of satisfaction. He enjoyed baiting the dried-up old crone who had seemed to despise him from the very day he'd been born. Her disgust with him came from the birthright, of course, always the damned birthright. If only Sorcha had been born without that blasted mark on her neck, then no one would question his power. 'Twas he who should have been bestowed with the kiss of the moon. He was the firstborn son of the baron, and therefore heir to Erbyn. No one could question the power that would someday be his—if it weren't for that damned prophecy and Sorcha's birthmark.

Gnashing his teeth together, he kicked at a bench by the fire, yanked off his gloves, and settled into his chair to wait.

Sorcha heard the sounds of the castle coming to life. Girls calling to the chickens, carpenters pounding with hammers, sheep bleating in the distance. She stretched and raised one eyelid. Her heart was heavy with a sadness she couldn't name, and then it hit her with the force of a winter gale: Leah. Sweet, happy Leah was dead. No, that was wrong, she was still alive, or had been when . . . when what?

Why couldn't she remember? She'd seen Leah, the blood, felt the life draining out of her sister, and then . . . the ring. She looked down at her hands and saw the serpent wrapped around her finger. Leah had been alive. Her eyes had opened and she'd breathed a deep breath, but that was all Sorcha remembered before the blackness had wrapped her in its soothing folds.

Stretching and letting out a yawn, she sat in the bed only to find herself in a large chamber with a fire in the grate and a man—a hellish brute of a man—seated on a bench. He glowered at her with an intensity that cut her to the quick.

Hagan of Erbyn! Her insides curdled at the sight of him as the horrible nightmare of the night before played upon her mind.

" 'Tis time you woke up," he said, his voice more gentle than she remembered.

"Where's my sister?"

"She's been moved, to a better room. She is resting."

Sorcha sprang from the bed. "I must be with her."

Hagan shook his head. "She is with Nichodemas, the physician."

"Are you daft? Someone has already tried to kill her." Sorcha, hair flying behind her, bolted for the door, but he grabbed her arm, spinning her back into the room.

"Nichodemas thinks she tried to kill herself."

"Leah?" Sorcha cried. "She had no reason to try and take her life until your brother brought her here. Asides, 'tis a sin, and Leah is devout. She would never—"

"I'm only repeating what Nichodemas told me."

"Take me to her."

"In time."

Sorcha was frantic. "But she's not safe—"

"Rosemary is with her, and the room is guarded. No harm will come to her. I swear it."

"As you swore that she was not here?" she demanded, thrusting out her chin. "You are a pitiful ruler, Lord Hagan, for you cannot control those in your own castle, including your murdering brother."

A muscle tightened in his jaw. His hands clenched and he looked angry enough to spit. "I'll have fresh clothes for you and a bath brought—"

"I want none of your charity."

"You're a guest in this keep and—"

"Make no mistake, I'm a prisoner."

When he seemed about to argue, she closed the distance between them, her feet whispering through the rushes. "Or if, as you say, I am a guest, then let me visit my sister. Surely no guest in the house of Erbyn would be locked in a room far away from the Christmas revels and her own sister."

" 'Tis not possible for you to walk the castle grounds by yourself," he replied, his eyes cold and assessing.

"Why not?"

"Mayhap you have forgotten that you stole into the castle by telling falsehoods, that you tricked the cook and my guards, and that you sought to kill me while I slept."

"Aye, but I had a purpose, *m'lord.* I knew my sister had been brought here. Taken prisoner. The least you could do, as ruler of this castle, is give us our freedom. Let us return to Prydd."

"When your sister is well."

Her heart turned to stone. The beast meant to keep them both here? Didn't he know how dangerous it was for Leah to remain here? Desperation clawed at her. "You must let us leave before someone tries to kill her again."

"Sorcha, Nichodemas found the knife that she used on her wrists. Lying on the floor. There is little doubt that your sister tried to end her own—"

"Last night you tried to convince me that she wasn't here," she said, unable to listen to any more lies. "You know not what goes on in this castle, Lord Hagan. You've been off to war, and many of your servants and knights have sworn their allegiance to your brother." She was guessing now, but she'd seen the same betrayal at Prydd when her father was away.

"You doubt that my servants are loyal?"

"To you? Aye. I know as much."

His eyes gleamed a little. "What else do you know, Sorcha? Hmm? Can you tell the future? Or are your powers limited to bringing those on the brink of death back to life? What kind of woman are you? Sorceress? Witch? One who truly has the power of the kiss of the moon? Or are you a fraud—a cheap magician who has tricked us all?"

When she didn't answer, he stepped closer, his gaze searching the contours of her face as if studying a mystical puzzle. "What was that all about last night? How did you make the wind whistle and the fire dance?"

"I know not," she admitted, her heart beginning to thunder within her rib cage.

"No? And yet your sister, who seems to be drawing her last breath, returns to life; her eyes open and she calls your name."

"Mayhap it was my faith that she would live."

"So now God is listening to you," he said, his gaze lingering in hers.

She could barely breathe. The room seemed to grow smaller.

"Please, let me see my sister."

For a moment he hesitated and his gaze lowered to her lips as if he might kiss her. Her stomach pressed hard against her lungs, and her heart pounded like a hollow drum. "As soon as Nichodemas agrees."

He touched her hand, lifting it so that the silver ring caught in the morning light. One long finger traced the serpent's coil. "What kind of magic is this, Sorcha?" He dropped her hand, and she bit her lip. Seconds passed. His eyes were kind when he said, "Until I can trust you, you will remain in here or with a guard at all times. I can be fooled once, but not a second time. 'Tis your choice whether you are a guest or a prisoner."

Sorcha swallowed the lump in her throat. In truth, she had committed many crimes against Erbyn, be they for a good cause or not. He, as lord, could imprison her as he saw fit. Biting her tongue against challenging him further, she tried to ignore the dried blood on the sleeve of his tunic.

"I'll not forget that you tried to kill me."

She felt a little bit of remorse, for she had never before hurt a man, yet she couldn't stop the words that fell off her tongue. "I only wish I could have slit your miserable throat."

His smile was suddenly cruel. "Mayhaps you'll get another chance," he said, the color of his eyes shifting to a darker shade of gold.

Sorcha's heart thudded painfully. In the thick silence, she knew that he was thinking of their night in his room, and her cheeks flamed hot when she remembered how wantonly she'd behaved.

"Be careful, O savior of Prydd," he warned in a dangerously low voice that touched a forbidden part of her, "for you are at Erbyn now, and here we play by my rules." He turned on his heel and strode quickly out of the room.

The heavy oak bar dropped into place with a thud that echoed to the ceiling. Without a doubt she was doomed to be a prisoner at Erbyn until Hagan the Cruel saw fit to release her and her sister.

Never before had she felt so small and frightened. Crossing her legs, she sat down on the cold floor. If only those who thought she was meant to be their deliverer could see her now, she thought miserably. 'Twas horrid fate that put her in the hands of her sworn enemy.

But she couldn't let him win. No matter what else happened, she would never let the Baron of Erbyn become the man who destroyed her and all that she held dear. He would have to let her visit Leah, and once her sister was well enough, they would escape.

With new conviction she walked to the window of her room and stared down at the inner bailey. The window was set high into the castle wall, far above the bailey, placed too high for her to jump to the ground, and the smooth stones were far too slick to scale downward. She could not escape without help, that much was certain.

But who would help her win her freedom? She leaned against the wide windowsill and eyed the guards standing rigidly at their posts, then forced her attention to a lad carrying a heavy basket of fish into the kitchen. A knight was giving a lesson in archery to several young squires, and still another worked with a stubborn lad at the quintain. Surely someone would help her. The trick was to find out who would be a traitor to Erbyn, who hated Hagan as much as she.

Once she had uncovered a servant's disloyalty, she could use it to her advantage. To do so, she would have to gain access to the castle, and Hagan would not be so foolish unless she deceived him into thinking that she would do his bidding. The thought was like a stone settling deep in the pit of her stomach, but she had no choice. She had to pretend to accept her fate.

Leah's life and the safety of Prydd were in her inexperienced hands.

"What were the herbs that you gathered last night, old woman?" Tadd asked. Seated at the scarred trestle table, a cup of wine cradled between his fingers, he stared at Isolde as if he knew her darkest secrets.

Isolde shivered within her soul, but tried to remain outwardly calm. She noticed one of the scullery maids stringing ivy and ribbons to decorate the great hall. The girl, a gossip with gapped teeth and freckles, worked slowly, her ear trained to the conversation at hand. Isolde cleared her throat. "I found some witches' briar and loveroot," she answered. "Near the edge of the forest."

" 'Tis not the season for flowers or seeds."

"True, but 'tis time to dig roots," she said. "Some herbs

are best harvested while the moon is waning, others while the moon is waxing full—"

"My horse was stolen," Tadd cut in, obviously bored with her. His gaze never left her face. "The deed happened last night, while you were out performing your dark arts. The stable master's missing along with McBannon."

Isolde's insides quivered, but she showed no outward sign of emotion.

"What know you of this?"

"Nothing, m'lord."

His lip curled in disbelief. "You saw and heard nothing, though you were outside the castle gates?"

"I was busy, m'lord, and my eyes are not as strong as they once were."

"You know, old woman, digging herbs for your black magic is frowned upon by Father William and the church. Should the good priest find out that you practice the pagan ways of the old people, you could suffer banishment or worse." Lazily Tadd unsheathed his dagger and, while watching Isolde with his cruel eyes, picked at his teeth.

"I worship not the dark one, Lord Tadd. You know me to be a Christian woman."

He stopped working on his teeth and stuck his wicked little knife into the thick boards of the table. The scullery maid moved closer, and his eyes wandered to the sway of hips before he turned his attention back to Isolde. "Yea, I know of your beliefs, Isolde. I know you still practice the old ways while pretending to have faith in the one true God." He took a long, slow swallow of his wine, then wiped his lips with the back of his hand.

Isolde's palms began to grow moist. Tadd was the least Christian man in all of Prydd. Aye, he attended mass each morn and bowed his head as if in prayer, but Isolde suspected that his piety was false. His heart was black, his soul that of the very devil.

Still watching her intently, he said, "Think hard. I trust you would tell me what happened to my destrier, should you know, should you have seen anything unusual last night."

"Of course, m'lord."

Another slow sip of wine. He swirled the dark liquid in his cup for long minutes, and Isolde felt sweat trickle down her backbone. "You are loyal to Prydd, are you not, Isolde?"

"M'lord, I've been here since the birthing of your own mother—"

"Hush!" He leaned forward so swiftly, he spilled some of his drink. His face was suddenly so close to hers, she could see the small scar near his eyelid where an unhappy maiden had scratched him, cutting deep into his skin. "I know that you believe in the savior of Prydd and the kiss of the moon and all the foolishness of gossiping old women. I know that you would lay down your life for my sister, but not for me." She could smell the foul stench of his breath as he said in a low, evil voice, "If I find out you have lied to me, I will take that knife you use to dig the herbs for your spells and I will use it on you." He smiled coldly, as if the thought of bringing her pain gave him great pleasure.

Isolde's insides knotted, but she bowed her head and bit her tongue. "It hurts me that you have no faith in me, m'lord. Please trust that should I hear anything, I will speak with you."

" 'Tis wise," he said, his eyes narrowing as if he were not quite convinced of her loyalty. "Now, bring me my sister; I should have a word with her."

Isolde's blood turned cold as death, for Sorcha had not yet returned. She nearly argued, but thought quickly, knowing that the only way to beat Tadd was to outwit him. She offered a smile that she didn't feel. " 'Twill please m'lady to leave her chamber. I'll go fetch her at once."

"Said she that she was unhappy?"

Isolde grinned inwardly, but shook her head. "Oh, nay, m'lord. But Sorcha likes not to be penned like an animal. She is one with the wind, her spirit soars to the hills, and being locked up makes her feel tethered and anxious. I will get her—"

Afraid her bluff may not have worked, she started for the stairs, her heart drumming in her chest.

"Wait, old woman! We needs not disturb her just yet." Tadd cleared his throat. "I will call for her later."

Isolde's old knees went weak with relief. "But she may know—"

He waved aside her arguments. "She's been locked up and would know nothing. Leave her be."

"She'll be unhappy—"

"I care not," Tadd said. "Because of her, Leah is held prisoner and two knights and a maid are dead. Let her sit and think about her actions. I'll talk to her on the morrow."

Isolde scurried out of the great hall, and with a prayer to the Christian God, she planned a few special runes and spells for Sorcha's safety.

"I need no assistance," Sorcha told the quivering maid standing before her. A large tub of fragrant water had been delivered to her chamber by two stout guards. They'd returned to their posts, and this frail simpleton of a maid was left holding soap and towels and the finest tunics and mantles Sorcha had ever seen. Though she'd promised herself to do Hagan's bidding, thereby earning his trust, she couldn't help the sharp words that sprang from her tongue.

'Twas not her nature to be subservient, and doing so seemed impossible.

"Lady Anne asked me to tend to you."

"As I said, I need no help."

"The lady will be offended."

"Not if you do not run back to her chamber and tell her."

The girl set the clothes on the bed. "You must be tired, m'lady, and sore." She let her eyes wander down Sorcha's body, lingering on her matted hair and dirty face. "Please, let me assist you."

In truth, the bath, smelling of lavender, looked inviting. But Sorcha wanted privacy and time alone to grieve for Keane. For Henry. For Gwendolyn. Sorcha's throat threatened to close and she blinked rapidly against hot tears building suddenly behind her eyes. If only she were back in Prydd, she would cry a thousand tears for those who had trusted her and given up their lives, but not here, not when she had to find a way to escape with Leah.

" 'Tis my duty to tell the baron that you are disobeying him." Her fingers moved restlessly in the folds of her bliaut. " 'Tis not wise to go against Lord Hagan."

"I care not."

"He will be displeased—"

"As I am."

The maid sighed loudly and dropped the towels and clothes on the bed. "As you wish. But I heard the baron tell the guard that if you refuse the bath and bed, he will come in here himself and bathe you. As for the bed . . ." She let the sentence trail off and a dark blush stained her cheeks.

Sorcha swallowed hard. She had a vision of Hagan, so furious his face was mottled, his strong hands surrounding her waist before he stripped her of her tunic and tossed her into the tub of hot water. In her mind's eye she saw herself sputtering as he shoved her head under the water and lathered her hair until her lungs felt as if they would burst. Then as she sat mortified, he ran his callused hands over her body, cleansing her in the most intimate of places. "God be with me," she whispered, and she felt herself no better than a wench because her vision was not entirely unpleasant.

The girl managed a sly smile. " 'Tis your choice, m'lady."

Furious with herself, Sorcha stripped and stepped into the tub, feeling the hot water caress her skin, just as Hagan's hands had touched her the night before. Shame seared through her and she closed her eyes and dunked her head, scrubbing the dirt from her body and rinsing the lavender-scented water through her hair.

When she'd finished, the servant girl handed her a towel. Glancing over her shoulder to see that they were still alone, the girl whispered, " 'Tis said that you saved your sister's life, that you brought her back from the dead. Tell me, Lady Sorcha, are you truly the savior of Prydd?"

Suddenly Sorcha realized that escaping the thick walls of Erbyn would be easier than she'd first thought. Many of the servants here still believed in the old prophecy. She wrung her hair in the tub, careful so that her birthmark was visible to the girl. "Aye," she said with a smile as she shook out her black curls. " 'Tis true, but this must be our secret. No one else in the castle is to know."

"My word of honor," the girl said, her eyes round as she stared at the dark crescent on Sorcha's skin.

"Good." Sorcha wrapped herself in the towel and shivered. "Now, tell me, is my sister well?"

Six

"The girl, Leah, will live," Rosemary predicted as she rubbed ointment into Hagan's wound and cast a glance at Anne, who was sitting near the window stitching embroidery. "Leah's restin' now, and Nellie is watchin' over her." She crossed her heavy bosom quickly. "Lord, that was somethin' to see when the girl came back from the dead."

"She couldn't have been dead," Anne said.

"What of Nichodemas?" Hagan grimaced as Rosemary cleaned the cut and blood began to flow again.

"That old bloodletter, he left sayin' there was nothin' more he could do. I wasn't one to argue with him, not after I saw with me very own eyes the magic of Sorcha of Prydd. Lord in heaven, did you ever see the like?"

Anne's gaze lifted to meet that of her brother. "I heard that she casts magic spells."

Hagan snorted.

"I'll not have witchcraft in the castle—"

"Worry not. There was no witchcraft, only the clever tricks."

"Darton, too, says she brought the girl back from the grave."

Hagan was tired of the argument and didn't bother answering. Sorcha had tricked them all, including him, but he didn't believe that a few sticks and some red thread tossed around a dead person's neck would bring her back to life.

Anne's lips pulled into a frown and her forehead furrowed as she drew her thread through her hoop. A few curling brown strands escaped her wimple, and from the set of her chin, Hagan knew she was vexed. He shifted on the bed.

"Be still, m'lord," Rosemary commanded. A hefty woman, she'd raised Hagan since he was a boy. "I'll be stitchin' ye up 'ere and I'll not be 'aving you wiggling like a sucklin' pig searchin' for a teat."

"Just be careful."

"Always am. Been sewin' this family together as long as I can remember."

Anne tossed down her hoop impatiently. "You can't keep Darton locked up like some common thief."

"He is a common thief," Hagan replied as he felt Rosemary's needle prick his skin. "He stole a woman. A lady. Daughter of a rival baron. You think he should not be punished?"

"He made a mistake, aye. But he's your brother and it's the Christmas revels."

"He's lucky I didn't kill him," Hagan said.

Anne rolled her eyes to the coved ceiling.

"A woman nearly died, Anne," Hagan said.

"But she didn't. Rosemary said she'll be fine."

"I said she was restin'," Rosemary clarified.

As if feeling a sudden bone-chilling draft, Anne rubbed her arms and cast Rosemary a look to put the woman in her place before training her eyes on her brother again. "I'm not saying you shouldn't punish him, but please, for the sake of our family's name, don't make Darton a joke to his servants."

Hagan winced as Rosemary tugged on the thread binding his wound. "Trust me. This is no joke."

"Just remember that Darton is your twin." Anne, who had never had a stomach for seeing blood spilled, kept her eyes averted from the nursemaid's handiwork. She stood and turned, her back as stiff as a scepter, her arms folded under her breasts. Hagan knew that she detested public displays of emotion and she would go to great lengths to keep any hint of scandal from touching her family. Anne and Darton had been close as children, though Hagan suspected that she knew of Darton's temper and his ambitions. However, his sister had been blessed with the uncanny ability to delude herself into believing that if she denied something long enough, it didn't exist.

"I'll not tolerate Darton's disobedience," Hagan said as the nursemaid drew hard on her thread again. Gritting his teeth, he added, "Our brother is not above the law, Anne."

"Don't you see what's happening here? It was all a mistake, a tragic, unfortunate mistake. Surely you know that Darton didn't ask her to slice her wrists." As if she could read the protest forming on his lips, she held up a hand to keep him still. "I know that Darton is . . . well, not like you. He sometimes bends the rules. But he's not a murderer, for God's sake," she declared, though Hagan guessed she was trying to convince herself.

"I pray you're right."

"Of course I am. He's our brother, Hagan. Your twin. The same blood that flows through your veins, runs through his. What I find hard to believe is that you, as baron, won't stand by him and put an end to this nonsense."

"I think she tried to kill herself because she couldn't stand being held prisoner, because she couldn't allow herself to be used by Darton as his wench."

Anne's fine lips clamped into a firm line, and Hagan felt that he'd finally struck a chord.

"Darton held her prisoner and used her for his own pleasure, did he not?"

Swallowing hard, Anne shook her head, but without much conviction. "I know not, Hagan. He . . . well, he's always fancied the women, and they find him attractive." She let out a long, unhappy sigh. "I knew not that he had taken the woman prisoner. I learned of it later."

"Did you not speak with her?"

"Nay. She was only here a short while, and Darton would not allow it."

"Still you trust him?"

She shifted from one foot to the other and walked to the window. "He is my brother. That is all that matters."

Hagan lifted a dark brow. " 'Twas his men who brought the girl here. On his orders."

"Darton's . . . ambitious," she said, walking to the bed and trailing a finger along the posts that supported the canopy.

"To a fault. Ouch!"

He slid a glance over his wounded shoulder to the nursemaid, but she only muttered, "Be still."

Growling an oath, Hagan fixed his stare on his sister once again. "Darton will stay in his chambers until I've contacted Tadd of Prydd and told him . . . God's teeth, I don't know how to explain—" With a grimace, he shot a look at the nursemaid. "Aren't you finished yet?"

The nursemaid grunted, then clipped the thread with her teeth. "There ye be, m'lord, but I'd be advisin' you to see the physician—"

"There's no need to bother Nichodemas."

Rosemary carried her towels, thread, and water out of the room, and Hagan pulled on his tunic.

"Ona told me the girl will not come down for meals, and only agreed to bathe when she was threatened," Anne said.

"Threatened?" Hagan repeated, his eyes fixing on his sister.

"Oh, do not worry. 'Twas not by beheading or torture or anything so vile, brother," she said with a laugh. "Ona told her that if she didn't get into the tub herself, you had vowed to do it for her."

Hagan's jaw tightened in silent fury. "Ona makes trouble. I know not why you decided she was to be Sorcha's maid."

"Ona may have a bit of an imp in her, but she's trustworthy, Hagan, and she will tell me everything that . . . What is it they call her? The chosen one . . . ?"

"The savior of Prydd."

Anne's nose wrinkled in distaste. "Aye, the savior. Ona will tell me everything, and that is good, for the savior is a sly one." With a lift of her eyebrows, she added, "She was clever enough to pass through our gates, was she not?"

Hagan didn't answer.

"Then she hid herself in the castle and what . . . ? Waited until nearly dawn to try and slit your throat." Anne look pointedly at the sleeve of his tunic. Though Hagan had washed and changed, the wound was bleeding again, despite Rosemary's efforts. "Her aim wasn't so good, though, was it?"

"You give me no credit, sister, for being able to disarm her."

"And get yourself cut in the bargain."

Bargain. The word held new meaning for Hagan, but he held his tongue. Anne guessed enough as it was. "Should you not be supervising the feast?" he asked. "We have many guests arriving."

"Aye, but I have avoided the kitchen. The cook is fit to be tied. Because she was tricked by the little savior, she feels as if everyone is laughing at her. Oh, her mood is foul, Hagan. She has already boxed the ears of two boys who didn't tend properly to the kitchen fires, and gave a tongue lashing to a scullery maid so fierce that the girl ran out of the keep in tears." Anne sighed. "The steward is in a black mood because the wardrober has lost some valuable spices, and the wardrober insists they were stolen. Last week we ran out of salt, but fortunately a peddler came by. The gutters overflowed just before the revels, and the buttery roof is falling in. You should have stayed with Edward to fight the damned Scots," she said. " 'Twould have been easier and mayhaps safer."

"Amen," Hagan muttered under his breath.

Anne, her mission in telling him the problems of the castle accomplished, started out of the room.

"Wait. Send a seamstress and some of your clothes to Sorcha's chamber."

"*My* clothes?" Anne asked, her eyebrows lifting with new interest.

"Aye. They will have to be altered, but—"

A small smile tugged at the corners of her mouth. "Why not some of the servants' tunics? Surely there is someone her size—"

"I will not have her wear russets when she can dress in silk."

Anne's eyes danced with a merry light. "You dress your little savior like a princess rather than the traitor she is."

"She is a lady," he said, as if that ended the subject, but Anne's gaze darkened with interest.

"Aye, but she came here to kill you." Anne's smile turned curious. "What happened in this chamber, Hagan, that you would treat a traitor like royalty, hmmm?"

"She is a guest."

"Oh, my mistake." Anne made a great show of crossing the room and warming her palms on the fire, but her eyes never left the bed. "I thought she was the chosen one—ruler of all Wales—and that was why she took it upon herself to kill you."

"She came to free her sister," he growled, tired of his sister's teasing.

Anne laughed at her brother's vexation. "Am I to send some clothes to Leah's chamber as well?"

"Aye."

"What are you going to do with those women—the patient and the savior?" she asked.

Hagan reached for his sword. "I wish I knew."

"Please, m'lady, be still," the tiny seamstress said, keeping her eyes averted as she pinched another tuck in the scarlet tunic.

Sorcha frowned as she stared at the stack of gowns, bliauts, and tunics that had already been marked for altering: more clothes than she owned. Why would Hagan insist she have such a large wardrobe? The answer was clear. He intended to keep her here, and though she would be a prisoner, he would treat her as if she were a guest.

Her fists clenched in silent rebellion. She wanted to shove the poor girl away from her and run out of the castle. Her horse was still hidden in the forest . . . but she was guarded every second, and if she were to escape, she knew, she would have to trick the guards and deceive Hagan.

Her spirit warmed at the thought of playing Hagan of Erbyn for a fool. 'Twould serve him right.

"Now, please, m'lady, turn round," the girl suggested, and Sorcha did as she was bid. She wondered what Hagan had in store for her. First there had been the bath with that twit of a maid, and now this seamstress. "If you could hold your hair up so," the girl said, lifting Sorcha's curls off her neck. Sorcha complied, inwardly seething.

"Almost done . . ." A needle pricked the back of Sorcha's neck, and the seamstress gasped.

"What the devil?"

"Mother Mary preserve us! Sweet Jesus!" Stumbling backward, the girl dropped her sewing basket and fumbled with her fingers, making a hasty sign of the cross over her bosom.

Sorcha was shocked for a moment before she realized the wide-eyed maid had seen her birthmark. Without finishing her task, the girl ran from the room, scurrying away from Sorcha as if she were the very daughter of Satan.

So more than silly Ona had heard the prophecy. Some of the servants probably believed in the old tale. Good. This could work to her advantage when she tried to escape with Leah.

With each hour she was away from Prydd, the chances increased that Tadd would discover that she and his prized horse were missing. As Isolde had foreseen, she'd been foolish taking the most fleet horse in the stables, her brother's favorite mount. Had she stolen her own palfrey or an old jennet, mayhaps the stable master would not have noticed.

In her haste, she'd made a vast error in judgment, not considering the fact that she might be caught. She'd only contemplated the need for a strong horse that could travel great distances carrying two people. McBannon was strong and fast, the best in the stables. Sorcha had stolen him to insure that she and Leah returned to Prydd swiftly.

Her insides felt like jelly when she considered Tadd's wrath. Coward that he was, he could certainly take out his fury on poor old Isolde, who, for as long as Sorcha could remember, had done nothing but care for her.

Chewing on her lower lip and plotting her escape, she stared out the window to the grounds below. Erbyn was nearly inescapable. Surrounded by a great wall, the bailey was complete with pond, well, stables, barns, and various sheds for the baker, candlemaker, carpenters, tanners, and other peasants. She could see part of the gardens, now dreary and covered with old weeds in the winter rain.

Guests arrived through the open gate, as she had, but the soldiers greeted each wagon and horseman more carefully than before. A hunter arrived with several pheasants, quail, and a large boar. The dead pig had been lashed to poles and was being dragged toward the kitchen.

Erbyn was larger than Prydd, but castle life was much the same. Carpenters were shoring up the roof of the stables, and the armorer, under his covered porch, was polishing shields and helmets in sacks of bran. Swords and crossbow bolts were cleaned as well, and Sorcha's heart turned cold as she gazed at the weapons that could be used against the people of Prydd. The truce that had been observed for years was always feeble at best, and now that both daughters of Eaton were imprisoned, there would surely be war. Because of Darton's ambitions.

Damn him and damn his brother. Hagan, if he were indeed a ruler, could surely have controlled his twin.

As if she'd conjured up the very devil himself, she saw Hagan, limping slightly, as he strode along the well-worn paths of the bailey. He stopped and talked with the carpenters, congratulated the hunter on his kill, and even paused to speak to a small boy who was catching eels in the pond. The people he spoke with smiled up at him and there was no fear on their faces, not like the servants at Prydd, who rarely dared speak with Tadd. When they had, their expressions had always been brittle, like old candle wax, and their smiles were forced. But not so with this ruler of Erbyn.

Her gaze narrowed on Hagan. He was a handsome devil,

she'd give him that, but his good looks did not atone for his arrogance and pride. His hair, so brown as to be mistaken for black, gleamed in the pale winter light, and his angular features looked as if they'd been hewn from stone. Hollow cheeks from months at war, skin weathered by the elements, thick, dark eyebrows, a nose shaped like a hawk's beak, and eyes the color of liquid gold.

She should have killed him when she had the chance, she thought, though a small part of her knew that she could never have taken his life. That piece of knowledge bothered her sorely, and she realized that heretofore she'd believed part of the myth of her birth, that she was the savior of her people. How foolish! How could she save a castle when she couldn't even slit the throat of a sworn enemy?

Maybe her mission was to heal rather than kill, for surely something magical had happened in Leah's room last night. She twirled the serpent ring around her finger and considered her plight. Though she'd saved her sister, she'd failed all of Prydd by letting herself be captured. Mayhap the old rumors surrounding the mark on the back of her neck were as false as Father William had preached they were. Oftentimes at mass the chaplain had pointed out the frailties of his congregation, noted that their beliefs in God were not strong. Father William had stared openly at Sorcha when he'd begged the congregation to give up their pagan rites and blasphemous ways. She'd sat in her pew, her back stiff, her cheeks burning, as she'd endured the condemning weight of everyone's gaze sliding in her direction.

Father William despised her; he made no effort to hide his feelings, and Sorcha had often worried of his dissatisfaction. She'd once confided her concerns to Isolde.

"Ahh, don't be bothered by that jackass," Isolde had remarked.

"But he hates me."

"Nay, child, he *fears* you."

"Why?"

Isolde's weathered face had wrinkled into a smug smile and her eyes had gleamed with devilment. "Because he doesn't understand you and the power you've been given. He's afraid that the mark on your neck, the kiss of the moon, is the work of his God, or worse yet, the work of the gods of the old ones—the gods he denies."

"But he says he believes not in the story and calls it the idle thoughts of gossiping old women."

"Aye, but he will not let the prophecy die, will he? Time after time, he brings it up himself, and there is fear in his faded eyes. Believe you me. You have challenged his own faith, and that frightens him."

Sorcha had always taken comfort in Isolde's words, and a part of her wished to be the true savior of Prydd. But now, imprisoned by a man she hated, she realized that she wasn't much different from any other captive.

She eyed the ring surrounding her finger. The only difference was that there might be people, servants, merchants, guards, and even part of the baron's family, who believed in the old tale. Hadn't silly Ona thought her magical? The seamstress had fled in terror at the sight of her birthmark. Those people would fear her. There was a chance that she would be able to convince them that she was picked by the gods and therefore sacred. Mayhap they could be persuaded to help her. Curse it all. If only she'd taken the time to learn some of Isolde's spells; if only she'd paid attention to the runes that the old woman drew in the sand. But no. She'd been much too practical to study the old ways.

What had Isolde said? *Listen to your heart; the magic will be with you.* Hadn't magic happened last night?

Hearing excited shouts, she forced her eyes away from Hagan and the hunter to see a peasant man leading a horse—Tadd's destrier—through the gates.

Her heart dropped like a stone as she stared at the stallion, who reared and pulled at the bit and was lathered in sweat. Hagan walked over to the peasant. "Oh, McBannon," she whispered.

Fists planted firmly on his hips, Hagan studied the animal carefully. The charger whistled shrilly, pulling away, but Hagan wasn't afraid. He dodged a swift kick. Running experienced hands over McBannon's mud-spattered hide, he cast a glance to the castle and the very window of Sorcha's room. For an instant their gazes locked, and Sorcha felt the warm air in her lungs turn to crystals of ice. Fury radiated from Hagan and he muttered something to the peasant, who put his shoulders into the task of leading the balking stallion to the stables. Sorcha didn't move, and again she was rewarded with a glance that could cut through steel.

Again the bay tried to bolt, and Hagan barked an order to a lanky blond stableboy who said some soft words and calmed Tadd's stallion. The boy led the horse toward the stables, and Sorcha smiled to herself in the knowledge that at least McBannon was with her and, if needs be, could soon provide means for escape.

Somehow she would have to convince Hagan that she had accepted her fate, make him trust her so that she could have some freedom within the castle walls. So that she could visit Leah.

It had been easy to sneak into Erbyn. Surely stealing away—even with Leah wounded—would prove less a task. Now that she had the stallion, escape was possible . . . She rubbed her hands together thoughtfully and wished Hagan hadn't taken her daggers from her. Aside from a fleet horse, she needed a sharp weapon, a lot of courage, and twice as much luck. Still, the towering walls of Erbyn weren't invincible, and Sorcha would find a way to break free. Or die trying.

Bang! Bang! Bang! The knock at the door was so loud, Sorcha jumped from her seat at the window. The door swung open before she'd recovered, and Hagan entered. "'Tis time for dinner. Come."

She expected to see fury in his eyes as he held the door for her, but his face was a mask without emotion, his stare penetrating but unreadable.

She did as she was bid, for only if she lured him into believing that she was obedient would she gain his trust, which was very important were she to succeed in escaping. Linking her arm through his, she had a momentary vision of lying with him in his bed, their bodies entwined and naked, sweat glistening on his skin.

She swallowed hard. A deep flush warmed her cheeks.

Hagan took her elbow and guided her down the stairs that curved into the great hall. Tables and benches had been placed facing the baron's table. Servants and commoners gathered together. There was much laughter and gossip, and the spirit of Christmas was in the air.

As Sorcha descended the stairs, a hush rolled over the crowd and every pair of eyes turned in her direction. She held her head aloft, her chin raised, as they walked through the throng.

"That's the one," she heard whispered. " 'Tis said she's got magic in her fingers—saved her sister's life, she did."

"That little mite of a thing?" Disbelief and a cackle of nervous laughter.

"Aye . . . they claim she's got the bloody kiss of the moon printed on her backside."

"The savior of Prydd is a *girl?*" Heartier laughter. "Well, I'll be buggered."

"I'd give me right eye to have a look-see at that mark."

"On her rump, ye say?"

"Aye." A snort not unlike a boar rutting. "Maybe me left eye, as well."

Sorcha's back stiffened and she wished by all that was holy that she had her little knife in her fingers. She felt the hot gazes upon her, heard the whispers and laughter, and wondered how she'd get through the meal.

They sat at the head table, she at Hagan's side, her head held high despite the curious stares cast her way. On Hagan's other side was a tall, stately woman with brown eyes and a long, slim nose. Hagan's sister, no doubt, the owner of the clothes she was wearing.

"My sister, Lady Anne," Hagan introduced. "Lady Sorcha of Prydd."

"So the savior of Prydd is our guest," Anne said as she lifted one elegant eyebrow. "The whole castle is speaking of you. I've heard you've been busy."

"That I have, Lady Anne, and now all I want is for my sister and myself to be set free to go back to Prydd." Mayhap Hagan's sister wouldn't turn a deaf ear on her request.

Hagan sent her a warning glare.

" 'Tis not much to ask," Sorcha insisted.

Lifting a shoulder, Anne agreed. "I see no reason why you can't—"

"When your sister is well enough to travel," Hagan interrupted, pinning Sorcha with his angry glare, "I will return with you myself." Sorcha could hardly believe her ears. Her spirits soared for an instant. Mayhap Hagan was not the beast she believed him to be. "However, we first must hear from your brother. I've sent a messenger telling him that you are here and that we want peace."

Her elation gave way to despair. Knowing Tadd as she did, she was certain that he would use Leah's kidnapping and her capture to his advantage. He would demand payment of some kind—retribution for the slaying of Gwendolyn, Henry, and Keane. Her heart twisted when she thought of Keane and how he had wanted to marry her. She hadn't loved him and suspected he was more in love with her wretched birthmark and the stories that surrounded it than he was in love with her, but he hadn't deserved to die.

A thick lump filled her throat and she glanced at Hagan, handsome and proud, baron of all that was Erbyn, a cruel and arrogant ruler.

Yet her traitorous heart already had found a soft spot for him, and though she experienced more than a little shame when she remembered how she'd nearly given herself to him, she still felt a spark of desire, a betraying want that coursed through her blood. Shameless desire she'd never felt with Keane.

Startled by the turn of her thoughts, she glanced up and found him staring at her, as intently as a hawk searching the ground for mice. For a horrible second she wondered if he could sense her thoughts.

"I'll keep you from your sister no longer," he said, his voice so low that the hounds beneath the table growled. "After dinner, you may see her." For a second, kindness touched his features and he didn't seem so threatening.

Pages brought bowls to wash their fingers and linen cloths to wipe them clean. Another page carefully filled the wine cups. From the hallway near the kitchen, a trumpet blared, announcing the first course of boiled mutton and spiced sauce. Ada, the cook, sending Sorcha a blistering glare, carried a huge platter of the mutton while other servants brought in more food: huge dishes filled with brawn and pike, pheasants and custard. Though her stomach rumbled, Sorcha could barely eat.

She forced a bite of jellied eggs and pretended not to feel the interested gazes cast in her direction.

Two gray dogs lay behind Hagan, their great heads resting on their paws, their yellow eyes watching each piece of meat in hopes that a tasty morsel would drop into the rushes.

She heard snatches of several conversations and learned that outlaws infested the forest surrounding the castle. "Two guests have already been attacked and robbed," Anne told her brother around a mouthful of pike. "Word has it that to the east, a group of Osric McBrayne's soldiers were beaten and their horses stolen. The men were more embarrassed than hurt, but McBrayne is ready to go to war."

"No doubt he blames Garrick of Abergwynn," Hagan said, knowing of the age-old feud between the powerful barons.

"Or us."

Hagan lifted a shoulder. "I care not what McBrayne thinks."

"You should. He's become powerful again and has an army twice the size of ours. He's sworn to find the outlaws and bring them to justice."

"As well he should," Hagan said, though he seemed worried, probably because Sorcha had claimed she was attacked by outlaws, and those lawless men were somehow linked to Darton and therefore Erbyn. Hagan scowled into his trencher. "Who is the leader of this riffraff?"

"No one knows. But the sheriff has been unable to stop him."

"Mayhaps you should ask your brother," Sorcha suggested. "I see that Darton is not at the table."

Hagan reached for a silver salt shaker sculpted into the shape of a stag and salted a piece of venison. "Darton is to remain in his room until I have settled this matter of your sister."

"This matter of my sister," she repeated, feeling the color drain from her face. "My sister nearly died, and the blame lies at Darton's feet."

"We do not know this yet," Anne said, her gaze moving quickly about the room, as if she were afraid some of the guests would overhear Sorcha's accusations.

"She was kidnapped. Held against her will and Lord knows what else. Of course it was Darton's fault."

She felt a big hand clamp over her arm. "Not here," Hagan said through lips that barely moved. "I said I will settle things as best I can. You will have to trust me."

Trust him? After what had happened? Was the man daft? "Never," she vowed, knowing that she should simply bow her head and nod, pretend to accept his wisdom, but it was not in her nature to quietly turn a blind eye to deceit and treachery. She took a bite of bread and felt it swell in her throat.

Oh, that she'd been granted patience instead of a quick tongue, it would have served her well.

"More wine, m'lord?" A serving girl wedged herself between Hagan and Sorcha.

He nodded. "Aye, Lucy, a little," he said, gesturing toward his cup. Lucy had hair like spun gold and she took her time as she filled the cup slowly, bending low, offering the baron a healthy glimpse of her abundant bosom. Like two plump pillows, her breasts rose above the edge of her bliaut.

"And you, Lady Sorcha?" Lucy asked, though her voice

had gone flat and she barely moved to pour the wine into Sorcha's cup.

Sorcha had never before felt jealousy, and yet her blood ran hot as Lucy turned back to Hagan, silently offering him much more than wine. What did it matter how many wenches he bedded? Just because he'd nearly lain with her, almost forced himself upon her, gave Sorcha no right to his affections, not that she wanted his attention. He was a liar, a devil, a murdering beast! Though he'd not slain Henry or Keane, his men had, and as baron, Hagan was responsible.

So why didn't she want to rip his heart out? Why did her fingers not itch for her dagger so that she could wound him still further? Why did she still think of his lips on hers and the desire shining in his eyes when she'd surprised him in his bed?

She managed to keep still throughout the dessert of plum pudding, and after the pages had brought clean water and towels, Hagan turned to her. "Come," he ordered, his expression revealing nothing. "I will show you the castle."

"You said I could see Leah."

"We will end in her chamber."

"But I want not to waste time by—" She cut off her wayward thoughts and managed a thin smile. "As you wish."

Hagan's face was grim. "Understand this, Lady Sorcha. I will allow you the privilege of freedom within the castle walls. As I said, you are my guest, not my prisoner, but if you disobey me and try to leave Erbyn before I have settled things with your brother, or if you make mischief with the servants, or if I hear of any small argument that arises from you, I will do with you as I have with Darton and confine you to your room."

"I will never be kept a prisoner—"

He whirled on her then, and his face, so impassive

through dinner, was suddenly red with fury. "You shall do as I say, Sorcha. Forget you not that I am still the baron of Erbyn. While you are here, you will obey me!" He yanked on her arm. His boots rang loudly across the floor of the great hall as he forced her to keep up with him.

Seven

Bjorn had never seen such a magnificent animal. The horse had spirit and fire and allowed no one close without tossing his great head or kicking with enough force to snap a strong man's leg. Aye, this new animal found in the woods was a fine steed, better than any animal in Erbyn, the first horse that could outrun any of Darton's soldiers' mounts, the only horse capable of bringing Bjorn his freedom.

"Come, boy," Bjorn coaxed, his voice low and soothing as the horse, tethered in the stable, shifted in the straw and rolled his eyes. "For you . . ." He held an apple in his fingers, but the stallion snorted and pawed the floor.

"What do you think you're doing? Get away from that beast!" The stable master's voice echoed to the rafters, and the horse reared as far as the tether would allow. "Christ Jesus, Bjorn, I don't know what goes through that stupid 'ead of yers!"

Every muscle in Bjorn's body tightened. A shovel was propped against the wall, and it would take nothing to snatch it up and club old Roy over the head. The thought was pleasant, like forbidden wine.

"Get back to mucking out the stalls, and be quick about it," Roy insisted, muttering under his breath about good-for-nothing peasants. "Lazy Viking or whatever the hell you are." He snorted and spit. "I've 'eard the stories about you, laddie. Think y're somethin' y're not. What is it? The son of a princess from the North and some German soldier who raped her?" He snorted and wiped his nose with the back of his hand. "That's a good one, it is. Face it, son, y're a bastard, boy; that's what ye are and it's all ye'll ever be."

Bjorn clamped his jaw shut. He picked up the shovel and again thought about bashing Roy's skull. The old goat's eyes would pop out of his head, but Bjorn resisted the urge and held on to the handle of the scoop until his knuckles showed white. At eighteen, Bjorn was taller than Roy, though not as heavy, and he was quick on his feet and stronger than anyone in the castle imagined.

Soon the time would be right. Bjorn glanced at the horse again, then threw his shoulders into his task and scooped out the dung. Some day old Roy would see the fire of his wrath. Viking! Ha. If the old man only knew.

". . . and these are the stables. You are not allowed use of any of the horses without my approval." The baron's deep voice filtered through the open door. Bjorn glanced through the crack and looked into the bailey to see Lord Hagan, who was showing the grounds to the most beautiful woman Bjorn had ever seen.

She was small, a full head shorter than the baron, but she tilted her fine chin up defiantly and she glared at him with fierce blue eyes. Her tiny mouth was turned down at the corners. "You promised I would see my sister."

"You will. First I thought you might like to see the keep."

"Where I am to be kept prisoner?" she spat, tossing back her witch-wild hair.

"You are a guest."

"Ha! At Prydd I am allowed my freedom. I go where I please and ride any horse I want and—"

"You're not at Prydd any longer," Hagan cut in, his jaw tense, his lips flattened against his teeth. Obviously this tiny woman vexed him, and that thought brought the hint of a smile to Bjorn's lips. Though he didn't despise Hagan, not the way he hated Darton, Bjorn still enjoyed seeing the baron bested, and this little woman was doing a fine job of it.

"As you said, I am your guest, and as such—"

"Do not push me, woman," Hagan said in a voice that made all the peasants in the castle tremble. However, this woman didn't appear to be afraid of him or any power he had over her. She tossed her thick mane of black hair over her shoulders and held him in her imperious gaze.

"What will you do to me that you have not already?" she demanded as she crossed her arms under her full bosom, lifting her breasts slightly in her ire. "Will you hold me prisoner? Kill my family? Steal my virtue? What?" She inched her way closer to him, her blue eyes slitting. "I saw my horse being led into the stables this morning—"

Bjorn's heart nearly stopped. He glanced at the stallion. This great horse was hers? This *woman's?*

"—and I remind you that he belongs to Prydd. I'll not have him mistreated or ridden without my knowledge."

Bjorn sucked in a quiet breath. For the love of Jesus, did she not know to whom she was speaking? Had she not heard of Hagan of Erbyn's savage temper? True, Hagan was not as cruel as his brother, but he was stubborn and used to being obeyed without question.

Hagan grabbed her roughly and seemed as if he wanted to shake some sense into her. "Here you are a guest . . . a very treacherous guest. You are not the savior of Prydd, nor are you the enemy, but I warn you, Sorcha, while you are here you will do as I say." A muscle ticked violently near his eye as he took hold of her arm and forced her to turn and walk back toward the great hall.

Bjorn leaned on the handle of his shovel. That little mite of a woman was the savior of Prydd? She was the enemy who had tricked the guards and the cook? This slip of a woman had nearly killed the baron with her wicked little knife? Bjorn had already heard the gossip that was racing through the castle as fast as frightened horses.

" 'Ey, you! Get to work!" Roy yelled as he poked his head through one of the windows. "By the gods, you're a lazy one!"

Bjorn didn't mind. He smiled to himself and scooped a shovelful of dung. From the corner of his eye, he watched through the crack in the door and saw the great baron shepherd Sorcha up the steps of the keep, treating her as if she were a wayward child.

So the grand animal was her horse, eh? Good. Finally it seemed as if his patience was to be rewarded. Not much longer would he have to suffer at the hands of Darton or Roy.

Bjorn whistled softly under his breath and started plotting his revenge.

"What do you think you're doing?" Hagan demanded, his hand firmly on her elbow as he half shoved her up the stone steps to the keep. "Arguing with me in front of my men?"

"I'm only speaking my mind," she replied. "I want to see my sister and— Oh!"

He turned abruptly, kicked open the door, and hauled her up the stairs. For a second she thought they were going to see Leah, but he shoved her into a room she recognized—his chamber. Her heart nearly stopped. The huge bed where she'd nearly lost her virtue mocked her, and she inwardly shivered.

Hagan's face was the color of wine, his eyes dark with fury. Both of his hands were clenched. "While you're here you will do as I say, Sorcha. You will not argue with me, nor will you disobey me." Frustration etched his features and he stared for a second at her lips before dragging his gaze back to hers.

The room seemed to grow still, and all she could hear was the thunderous beat of her heart. She licked her lips, and his skin stretched taut over his face. The fingers around her arm tightened for a second, and as she gazed into the golden embers of his eyes, her breath caught in her throat.

They were all alone in his room, and because of his power and strength, he could do anything he wanted with her. No one would care if he threw her on the bed and took her by force. No one would help her if she screamed. To lie with him was considered a privilege and an honor. She swallowed hard and forced words from her suddenly breathless voice. "You said you would take me to see my sister. Are you now a liar as well as a kidnapper?"

He ground his teeth as his patience shredded. "I will take you to Leah."

"And you promised to contact Tadd."

"A messenger has already been sent," he said curtly. "I expect his return within the week."

"What if he does not return alive?"

"You borrow trouble, woman."

"Have you no plan?" she asked, determined to be mistress of her own fate.

His eyes flashed like lightning. "I will wait a few more days; then, should he still not appear, I will assume he has been captured and we are at war with your beloved Prydd."

Her stomach turned to dust. "You will mount an army?" she asked.

"Aye."

So Prydd's fate rested on the shoulders of one messenger. She sent up a prayer for the soldier's quick return.

"Now, if you will keep your sharp tongue to yourself, we shall see your sister."

Leah's room was at the other end of the corridor, a small chamber with a huge fireplace, whitewashed walls, and tapestries that hung on the wall over her bed. Pale as death, her chest barely rising, Leah lay beneath covers, her eyes closed, her lips dry.

Heart in her throat, Sorcha approached the canopied bed. "Leah?" she whispered. "Can you hear me?" She touched her sister's hands. They were warm, but lifeless. Sorcha had hoped that her eyes would flutter open and she would smile up at her, but Leah didn't move, and Sorcha sat on the edge of the bed, tears gathering in her eyes, fear twisting her heart. *Live, Leah,* she silently prayed, hoping to see some signs of life in her sister. *You must live!*

The room wasn't empty, but Sorcha, in her worry, barely noticed. Nellie was changing the rushes, keeping a distance between herself and Sorcha. As she scooped the old straw, she tossed worried looks in Sorcha's direction. Hagan propped himself near the door, arms folded over his massive chest, eyes trained on his "guests."

Time moved slowly and still Leah didn't move. Sorcha fell to her knees, still holding Leah's hand, praying to a God who didn't appear to be listening.

When her prayer was finally over, she stared into the still, white face of her sister. "Leah?" she whispered. "Oh, please wake up."

Nothing.

"Please. Lord Hagan's sent a messenger to Prydd, and we are allowed to go home," she added, not caring if Hagan heard her lie. Desperately she rubbed the backs of her sister's hands. "Wake up, Leah. I need you."

Still nothing.

Her heart was a weight. She linked her fingers through her sister's. "You can do it, Leah."

" 'Tis time to go."

"Not yet."

Hagan's voice was gentle, but firm. "You can do nothing for her. Let her rest."

"Nay. 'Tis my fault she is here, and I will stay with her."

"Why is it your fault?"

"Had I not begged her to take my place and give alms in the village, she would be safely at Prydd."

"You forced her to go for you?" He was skeptical.

"Nay, but—"

Leah's eyes fluttered open for a second, only to close again.

"Dear God, please . . ."

Sorcha felt a moment of triumph, then experienced a wave of defeat. Oh, if she could only hear Leah's laughter, or see her green eyes sparkle with mischief. Never again would Sorcha think ill of her sister, or consider her a ninny for not being able to keep the castle records or shoot an arrow straight. She sent up a silent prayer and stayed at her sister's side.

"Come, we should let her sleep," Hagan said softly, but Sorcha didn't budge.

"Not yet."

He didn't argue but stood by the door. Only when Rosemary entered with fresh linens and a bowl of stew did he become restless.

Clucking her tongue, Rosemary walked to the bed and set the food and sheets on a bedside table.

"She doesn't wake when I speak to her," Sorcha complained.

"Give her more time," Rosemary said, touching Leah's forehead and brushing a dark curl from her brow. "She is healin' well. There is no fever and—" she looked at Leah's bound wrists "—her wounds are healing. She will awaken," Rosemary predicted, "and soon. I will call for you when she does." Her kind gaze met Sorcha's. "Remember, child, it has not been long since she . . . since her wounds were new."

Sorcha knew the nursemaid was right, yet she felt useless and guilty and wished that God would hurry up about this healing. There was much to do, and she needed to know that her sister would be well again. Her fingers closed over Leah's hand and she willed Leah to open her eyes and smile. "Leah, can you hear me?"

No movement.

"It may be best if you leave her be," Hagan said, his voice surprisingly gentle.

"I'll not leave her," Sorcha whispered. Dejectedly she stared at the blood-soaked strips surrounding her sister's wrists. If only she hadn't begged Leah to take her place, if only she hadn't been so desperate to meet with Keane and tell him she loved him not, if only they were both alive and well! Oh, wretched, wretched fate!

"Well, brother," Darton said when Hagan strode into his chamber. Seated on a ledge at his window, one leg drawn up, he finished his wine in one gulp. His eyes gleamed with satisfaction—much like a lion who knew his prey had no way to escape. "What think you of our little savior now?"

Hagan tried to keep his temper, though he was still furious with his brother.

"Is she not the most beautiful woman ever to walk this earth?"

Hagan shrugged. "I see not that it matters," he said, though in truth, he could not wedge her from his mind. Beautiful did not begin to describe her. When he was around her he was torn between a desire so deep, his blood seemed to singe his veins, and the knowledge that had she had more time, she would have killed him. The memory of her lying naked in his bed seared through his brain, but he knew she was still treacherous and could not be trusted.

"Ha! Of course it matters. But not as much as the power that surrounds her." Darton walked to the fireplace, where his sheathed sword was mounted, and yanked the weapon from its resting place. "Last night when she stood over her sister and began to chant, Christ, Jesus, I swear the power in that room could have destroyed a hundred castles."

Hagan shook his head, still disbelieving. "I know not what happened last night—"

"She called up the spirits. The gods of the old people. Don't try and deny it, Hagan. I was there. I *felt* it. That empty room was filled with the souls of dead Welshmen—an army of Cymru!" Darton's eyes gleamed in anticipation. "Last night when she drew back the spirit of her dead sister—"

"The girl was not dead."

"Nearly so. And you admitted that you, too, felt the power in the room. As if the eye of the storm was in that chamber. By the gods, I have never seen anything like it." Darton's mouth curved into a cruel smile. As if anxious to reach out and grab that power for himself, he paced the room, his strides swift. "You remember the prophecy, do you not?"

"She is a woman. How can she be savior?"

"Ah, 'tis a trick of fate. She should have been born a man."

Hagan thought of her naked body beneath his, the play of firelight upon her skin, the rise and fall of perfect breasts with dark nipples. His throat tightened as he remembered her nest of black curls and the slender whiteness of her thighs. His groin began to throb. " 'Tis hard to think of her a man."

"But she is the savior, trust me. She holds in her palm the most wondrous power on earth, brother," Darton said as he buckled the belt that held his sword into place.

"I don't know that there was any force working—"

"By the gods, Hagan, you have eyes and ears. You saw what happened when she placed that damned necklace of twigs around her sister's neck and the serpent ring seemed to glow in the darkness. There was magic in the room."

"Or trickery."

Darton snorted, shaking his head. "How can you doubt when you were there?"

"Is this why you wanted to kidnap her? For her power?"

"I told you—"

"I know what you said, brother," Hagan cut in swiftly, "but none of my scouts has reported an army being gathered at Prydd. Only you and a handful of your men seem to think there will be an attack."

"You think I lie?"

Hagan thought long and hard. " 'Tis no secret that you have plans, Darton. There are new faces in the castle, men who are loyal to you."

"You think I've plotted to wrest control of Erbyn from you?" Darton said, one brow lifting. "Aye, I'm ambitious, brother, and there is nothing I would like better than my own keep, you know this, but I'm also loyal to Erbyn and the lord thereof. I would be satisfied with a castle somewhere to the north, Benwick mayhaps."

"Benwick?" Hagan wasn't sure he'd heard correctly. "But it's occupied by—"

"Father's whore. I know. Lady Aileen. But she is old and I've heard she's ill. She will not last much longer." His eyes held Hagan's. "I would be glad to be lord of Benwick . . . or of Prydd."

"Prydd?" Hagan repeated, though he finally understood the reasons behind his brother's behavior—why he stole the girl, why he wanted the savior of Prydd.

"When Tadd attacks, and surely now, with his two sisters prisoners here—"

"They are not prisoners."

"Guests, then. Call them what you will. But they cannot leave, and Tadd has his pride to consider."

"You *want* this war?"

"Nay, brother, but 'tis nothing we can stop, and when the fighting's done and we're the victors, I see no reason that I shouldn't become the baron of Prydd."

"What of Eaton—off fighting the Scots? He has only to tell Edward, and Longshanks will send hundreds of men to give Prydd back to its rightful baron."

"Eaton is old. 'Tis unlikely he will survive the war," Darton observed.

Hagan was astounded at the depths of his brother's deception, and he knew with a sudden vision into the future that Darton would stop at nothing to get what he wanted. Benwick wouldn't be enough to satisfy him, nor would Prydd. Until Darton ruled all of Erbyn, he would be dangerous. However, Hagan had no proof, only suspicions. "I'll consider giving Benwick to you," he said, buying time, "but Lady Aileen would be allowed to live out her days there as the castle is her home."

Darton didn't respond.

"However, when Lady Leah awakens, I will hear how she was treated." Hagan frowned as he stared at his brother. "If she wasn't cared for like the lady she is, you will be punished, Darton. Tadd will demand it, and I will see that it's done."

"She was not hurt."

"And yet she nearly died."

"At her own hand."

"Because of you." Hagan raked furious fingers through his hair. "I'll not keep you in your chamber like a wayward child," he said, though his eyes narrowed on his brother, "but, Darton, I warn you, if I find out you've mistreated Leah, or if you have done anything disloyal, there will be the very devil to deal with."

"The girl will be fine," Darton said, slowly withdrawing his sword and watching the reflection of the fire's flames on the smooth steel. "And to prove to you that I want to make up for the mistake of kidnapping Lady Leah, I'll agree to marry her sister." He slid the sword into its case.

"Her sister?" Hagan repeated, trying to keep his temper under control, although his blood thundered through his brain. The thought of Darton and Sorcha . . . His stomach turned over, but he managed to remain outwardly calm. "You want to marry Sorcha?"

"Aye, as I said, she is a beautiful woman with a power that is rare. I think her passions are deep and she would be a tigress in a man's bed."

Hagan's guts twisted painfully as he envisioned his brother tearing off Sorcha's chemise and mounting her. It was all he could do to keep his voice from shaking in rage. "You'll not marry Lady Sorcha."

"Certainly Tadd would be satisfied with a marriage that would link Prydd with Erbyn."

Hagan's jaw tightened. "There will be no marriage,

brother, until it is certain that Leah does not carry your child."

"What if she does?"

"Then you shall marry her and give the babe his birthright." Hagan noticed the whitening of his brother's skin.

"Suppose Leah is not with child and I convince Sorcha that she and I should be wed."

"She hates you," Hagan replied, but knew of his brother's power over women. There were several bastards already toddling around the castle, the result of Darton's seductions. Two kitchen wenches, a laundress, and the armorer's daughter had borne Darton babes that he didn't recognize as his own. When called to claim the children, he'd laughed. "Those wenches have lain with half the soldiers in this castle, brother." His smile had turned wicked. "Do not blame me for their births. Asides, could the babes not be from your own seed?"

Hagan hadn't bothered to reply, but he was certain the children were Darton's.

Now his brother seemed unconcerned about Sorcha's feelings for him. "There are ways around hatred, brother." Darton straightened his tunic.

"Be careful, Darton, she is not a woman to anger."

"I have no intention of angering her, brother, but I do plan to lie with her."

Hagan's temper exploded. He grabbed Darton by the scruff of his neck and carried him back into the room. His blood was boiling, and jealousy, a new and hated emotion, flexed every muscle in his body. Suddenly he wanted to snap his twin's foul neck. "Stay away from Sorcha," he ordered, his eyes thinning upon his brother. "You have caused enough trouble as it is."

Darton reached for his sword, and Hagan dropped him onto the floor. Hagan swung out of the room before he did further damage as Darton stood watching his retreating back.

The scent of sizzling meat drifted upward in a cloud from the spit where the rabbits were roasting. Several of the outlaw band had taken cover in the dense foliage, wrapping their fur coverlets and thick cloaks around them. Mead was passed from one man to the other from a heavy jug. There was laughter and bawdy jokes, but Wolf, the leader of this ragged group, kept his distance, sitting upon a log, his thoughts dark and far away. He'd been in his own private hell for years—an exile he'd imposed upon himself—and yet none of the men knew his Christian name. 'Twas best that way. As his band had grown, he'd taken in strangers, not asking more from a man than a single name. He cared not what crime any man had committed; his only demand was each man's complete loyalty.

There were no questions about families. No curiosity about the lives that his men had led before they became outcasts and scavengers of the forest. A man pledged his loyalty and became part of the band. There were no women, no children, no ties of any kind.

Wolf licked his knife and felt the cold December fog cling to his skin. Through the rising mist came the sound of hoofbeats and snapping twigs, brush being slapped aside. A horse was running as if the devil himself were on his tail. The men scrambled for their swords and bows. Wolf leaped to his feet, his instincts wary, his fingers curling over the hilt of his own weapon.

"Don't shoot! 'Tis only me: Odell," a high-pitched, wheezy voice proclaimed, and a ghost of a smile curved

Wolf's cynical mouth. "Put down yer bloody weapons! God's teeth, Jagger, it's me!"

"Hey, Wolf. He's got a bloody prisoner with him," Jagger called through the dark forest.

Wolf shoved his sword back into its sheath. The men knew they were to bring no captives to their camp. Even though this spot was only a temporary resting place, Wolf planned to use it again. That would prove impossible now. Damn Odell and his headstrong ways.

Odell, riding his old brown hack, emerged from the shadows. Both horse and rider were splattered with mud. Smiling as if he'd won the war against the Scots single-handedly, Odell held the reins of a handsome animal, a gray courser who balked at the sight of the fire, rearing and nearly losing his rider. Astride the stolen horse was a huge man with his wrists bound behind him and a blind over his eyes. He was muttering and cursing and attempting to stay astride. "Down, you bloody beast," Odell ordered.

"What nonsense is this?" Wolf demanded as Odell dropped to the ground, his boots sinking into the mud near the fire.

" 'Tis not nonsense. This one—" he tugged on the prisoner's arms, and the captive fell hard to the ground "—is worth much ransom."

"I'll kill ye, I will," the prisoner snarled from behind his blind.

"Ah, sure ye will, and I'm shakin' in me boots." Odell landed a swift kick to the man's back, and the captive fell forward, face-first into the dirt.

"Stop! No prisoner is beaten!" Wolf ordered, standing between Odell and the man struggling to his feet.

"Who are you?" the prisoner demanded.

Odell spat on the ground. "Ah, shut up," he commanded

before turning to Wolf. "This here's a messenger from Erbyn, one of the baron's most trusted men." Odell smiled at his captive. "Isn't that right, piggy?" He made hoglike grunts, and the rest of the men laughed.

"You dirty cur, I'll kill ye with me bare hands!" the prisoner yelled.

" 'Cept yer hands are bound now, piggy, ain't they?" Odell chortled, pleased with himself.

"Enough," Wolf ordered. "From Erbyn, are you?"

The messenger turned toward Wolf's voice. "Aye. Mindin' my own business, on my way to Prydd, when this old man at the side of the road begs for my help—says his horse is crippled."

Odell cackled, and the hooded man snorted at his own foolishness.

At the mention of Castle Prydd, Wolf's head snapped up. He had his own private war with Tadd of Prydd, though no one, not even his most trusted man, knew the truth.

The messenger was prattling on like an old woman. "When I stop and get off my horse to offer some assistance, he sticks a knife in my ribs and—"

"Oh, y're a fool, that's what ye are," Odell crowed, grinning wickedly, enjoying his moment of triumph.

"Let him speak," Wolf commanded, his eyes slitting on the frightened soldier.

"Your man binds me wrists and plops a hood over me head and brings me here."

"Why were you on your way to Prydd?" Wolf asked, annoyed at Odell's jeering.

"I have a message from Baron Hagan to Lord Tadd."

"Hagan's returned?" Wolf asked, his muscles tightening at the thought of an old acquaintance. Hagan once thought he might turn outlaw himself, but he changed his mind, all for the love of a silly woman. "The message, from Hagan; what is it?"

"I know not—"

"It's in his pouch," Odell said, pointing to the leather bag on the courser's flank.

"Don't!" the man yelled from behind his mask. " 'Tis sacred—"

Wolf reached into the bag and without a qualm broke the seal on the scroll with the blade of his knife. Of his band of outlaws, only he could read. The information contained in the letter was his alone. He could tell his men that the words contained anything he wanted, and they would believe him. Bending on one knee, he held the letter close to the firelight, letting the red-gold shadows play through the parchment.

Trouble was brewing between the houses of Prydd and Erbyn, and since his personal feud with Sir Tadd was not over, he was interested in how the armies would ally. A cunning plot stole through his mind, and he couldn't help but smile inwardly as he rolled the parchment back into a scroll and pointed at the prisoner. "Sit him down," he told Odell. "Remove his hood and offer him food and drink."

"But then he'll know—"

"We have naught to fear from him," Wolf replied.

Odell slid the hood off the man's head and kicked him toward some logs surrounding the fire.

The soldier stiffened. " 'Tis important that I take this news to Lord Tadd."

"Worry not about that," Wolf said as the man's hands were cut free and he was given a shank of rabbit and a cup of mead. "There has been word of trouble at Erbyn."

The messenger regarded his captors mulishly and silently but finally took a long swallow from the offered cup.

"Bloodshed and trickery are rumored," Wolf said.

There was no answer.

Wolf sat next to his prisoner and stared long at the young face. Though the temperature was near freezing, the man was sweating; long drips drizzled down the side of his face. "I can make your stay with us comfortable. Even pleasant. Or I can make it more painful than the fires of hell. 'Tis your choice." He leaned back on an elbow and waited. "Either way, you will not leave with your message tonight—"

"But I must—"

"Worry not." Wolf's mouth stretched into a silent leer that caused the messenger's blood to congeal. "I will see that the letter is delivered."

"By who?" Odell asked.

"I'll visit Tadd of Prydd myself," Wolf said with an inward grin of satisfaction for finding a way to best his sworn enemy. "I'll go when the time is right. Now, tell me of Sorcha of Prydd—Lord Tadd's sister."

The captive swallowed.

"She's the bloody savior!" Odell said. "I've heard that—"

"Savior?" Wolf had not heard this piece of gossip, and he silently cursed himself for not listening to the rumors that were brought back to the camp by the men when they ventured into the villages in search of women or drink.

"Aye. Born during a tempest, with hair as black as a raven's wing and the kiss of the moon upon his skin, the savior of all that is Prydd will arise—"

"*His* skin?" Wolf asked. "But she is a woman, is she not?"

"Aye," Cormick, one of the older men in his band, whispered. "But 'tis said she can conjure up the winds, and talk to the spirits—"

"A woman?" Wolf said, scoffing, though he felt a premonition of dread, as if a phantom had walked with cold footsteps upon his spine. Memories, long dead and buried, swam to the surface of his mind. "Does she talk to the wind?" he asked, his heart beginning to beat a little faster. Was it his mind playing tricks on him or did the icy breeze stir the branches overhead in a sudden rush?

"Yea, she speaks to everything: The wind. The gods. The animals. She is Mother Earth, born of woman but sired by one of the true rulers of Gwynedd," Odell said, his voice filled with respect.

"Llywelyn?" Wolf asked as he studied the faces of his men. Some were cast in awe; others, doubt.

"Some say she is the bastard of his bastard," Cormick said, obviously a believer. "Maybe even his grandbastard."

" 'Tis rubbish!" Jagger, the silent one, said. He was a huge man with a black beard and the scars of many battles on his face and body. He carried a rosary with him always and prayed often. Wolf knew not whether he'd once been a priest and had somehow been banished from the church, or if he'd simply stolen the string of beads from a man of the cloth. As they spoke, Jagger rubbed the worn beads between his fingers.

"Tell me more about Sorcha of Prydd," Wolf encouraged, and when the man did not comply, Wolf unsheathed his sword and heated it on the rocks that glowed red around the fire.

"He'll cut out your tongue if ye don't talk," Odell said.

"And I'll cut off your balls if you don't hush!" Wolf warned.

Odell sulked, and Wolf waited as he watched drips of perspiration slide down the captive's face. Swallowing hard, the prisoner watched as his tormentor took up his sword and laid the hot blade against his tunic. Steam rose in the foggy air.

"What's your name?"

"Frederick. Frederick of—"

"We use only one name here, Frederick. I'm Wolf; these others will introduce themselves if it becomes necessary."

Frederick's Adam's apple bobbed as he swallowed hard.

"Now, either you give us the information we need or . . . I'll let the men decide what to do with you."

Frederick glanced at the eager, mud-smeared faces surrounding the fire, and his shoulders slumped. All of his courage seemed to disappear on the wind. "All right," he said, finally realizing he had no choice. "I'll tell you of Sorcha of Prydd. But you'll not believe me."

"I'll be the judge of that."

" 'Tis said she can raise a man from the grave."

Jagger snorted. "No one but the Lord can—"

"Hush! Let him speak." Wolf sheathed his sword deliberately, then settled back on his rock. Overhead he thought he heard the eerie whisper of the wind. "Speak, soldier," he commanded in a voice that no one in the forest dared dispute. "Speak to me of Prydd, the savior, and Lord Tadd."

"I come from Erbyn. I know not Prydd."

"Yes, but there must be plenty of gossip. Come. Drink some wine and tell me all you know."

Isolde carried a trencher of mutton into Sorcha's room. " 'Ere ya go, m'lady," she said, making sure the guard did not get a peek into the chamber. As he was instructed, the sentry bolted the door, for Tadd was certain Sorcha would escape and cause him great misery.

Inside the room, Isolde worked fast, keeping up a steady stream of conversation with herself, mimicking Sorcha's voice as best she could, for the guard would only hear muted sounds from the door. She kindled the fire, ate the mutton herself, drank from the pail, and relieved herself in the other bucket. Oh, if only Sorcha would return quickly, for soon Tadd would become suspicious. If not for his interest in drink and women, he probably would have discovered Sorcha's deceit before this.

She made sure the window was open, so that the breeze could enter the room and toss whatever was about to make noise, then she said a quick prayer and picked up the remains of her last meal so that the guard would think that Sorcha had been nibbling at Cook's food.

"Good day, m'lady," she said, knocking on the door for the guard and slipping through as soon as the bar was lifted.

"Still not feeling well?" the dullard of a sentry asked.

"Aye, she's still in her bed. Resting. But I think she's on the mend."

The guard smiled, and Isolde was thankful that Sir Geoffrey was a trusting soul not known for his wits.

"Leah!" Sorcha could hardly believe her eyes as, with a moan, Leah stirred, her lids opened, and she stared up at her sister.

"Praise the Lord," Rosemary said.

"Or the devil," Nellie muttered under her breath.

Sorcha didn't care what the simple woman thought. It was enough to know that her sister was going to survive. For three long days she'd kept her vigil, sitting for hours at Leah's side, waiting for word from the messenger, and plotting their means of escape if Tadd refused Hagan's terms and started a war.

She was worried, for she'd seen the armorer and his sons working from daybreak until long into the night, cleaning and preparing weapons and mail. The stableboys, too, had been grooming the horses and repairing broken saddles and bridles.

Soldiers eagerly practiced against the quintain or spent hours shooting arrows at targets, and troops from other castles seemed to be amassing. Aye, there was more than the spirit of the Christmas revels in the air, there was the smell of war.

"Sorcha?" Leah's voice was faint and raspy, barely more than a whisper. "What? Where?" Her confused gaze traveled over the room. "I've had such horrible dreams . . ." Her voice left her as her gaze settled on Nellie. "Oh, God," she whispered. "We're at Erbyn."

"Yes. But not for long."

Leah's green eyes filled with sudden tears and terror shook her voice. "Oh, please, you don't know . . ."

"Shh. 'Twill be all right."

Leah tried to scramble to a sitting position, winced in pain, and noticed for the first time the strips of linen binding her wrists. She let out a pitiful moan, then clamped a hand over her mouth, as if she was afraid of being overheard. "Darton?" she whispered, her eyes like mirrors.

"He's here, but not allowed in this chamber. Lord Hagan has returned."

Leah didn't seem relieved. She clutched Sorcha's hand with cold fingers and amazing strength. "Do not let him near me, Sorcha."

"Worry not."

"Oh, but you do not know!" Leah's voice was desperate, her pretty face lined with strain.

Sorcha held her sister's hands between her own, and a great joy filled her heart. Leah was alive. She'd survived. She leaned close to her sister and kept her voice low. "Worry not, Leah," she said with more conviction than she felt, "for our days here are numbered. I have found a way to escape."

Eight

Lying on her bed, listening hard, Sorcha heard the changing of the guard. She knew from talk in the castle that it was well past midnight when the soldiers changed posts. Ears straining, she heard a few words of greeting, then, holding her breath, listened as they walked past her door. One guard was posted at each end of the hallway, but she guessed, from the sounds she'd heard within the castle every night, that there was a little time when they both talked at the head of the stairs, and now, because of the Christmas revels, they'd drunk more mead and wine than they should and would soon be dozing at their posts.

She slid into the black hooded cloak that she'd inherited from Lady Anne, then soundlessly made her way to the door. It was not locked, as Hagan had insisted she was a guest, and she'd spent most of the evening greasing the hinges with the mutton fat she'd sneaked from the table.

Without a sound she opened the door, and then, spying the guards with their backs to the hallway, she hurried noiselessly in the other direction to the back stairs past Hagan's chamber. It was dark; she felt the rough wall with her fingers as all along the hallway the rushlights had burned down to soft red embers.

She held her breath as she passed Hagan's door and slipped down the stairs, careful not to fall. The kitchen was empty, but a dog guarded the back door. She couldn't see the hound, but heard him growl ominously.

He was joined by another with an even lower and more threatening rumble of his throat.

"Now, now, boys," she whispered, hearing the hounds start to get to their feet. "See what I've got for you." She tossed the scraps of the mutton fat to the animals, who snarled and fought for the prize as she opened the back door and felt the cold breath of winter against her face.

Only thin light from the moon sifted through high clouds, but Sorcha had spent her days committing the features of the dark bailey to her memory. Without hesitation, she dashed along a muddy path that wound past the cobbler's hut and the closed doorway of the candlemaker.

Hens clucked anxiously as she passed their coop, and farther away, the lowing of a cow filled the night, but Sorcha didn't hesitate. The stables weren't far now, and she gathered her skirts and ran through the shadows, certain the soldiers at their posts on the battlements couldn't see her.

Upon the wind the acrid smells of urine, leather and sweat, dung and horseflesh, combined to meet her hungry nostrils. She found the stable door and sent up a quiet prayer that she wouldn't be discovered. With a groan the door opened and Sorcha slipped into the dark interior, unaware that Hagan, restless from a night filled with dreams of her warming his bed, had walked out of the keep himself and was standing near the well, watching as she dashed furtively within the walls of the inner bailey. He followed Sorcha's path and decided she was more trouble than he needed.

Yet he was fascinated and he wondered what he would do when he caught up with her. Grab her roughly and toss her back into her room and bar the door, or yank her to him and kiss her until the passion that roared through his blood disappeared?

"There you are," Sorcha whispered as she saw McBannon tethered near the doorway. She would recognize the stallion anywhere, even in the stables illuminated only by the frail light from the windows. Other horses had snorted at being awakened, but McBannon nickered softly, guiding her with his voice.

"Miss me, did you?" Though the horse was Tadd's, Sorcha had befriended the animal when he was only a colt hiding behind the flanks of his mother. She'd offered sugar, apples, and kind words to the long-legged animal and had ridden him often until Tadd had declared the destrier to be his.

Though he was Tadd's favorite mount, the horse had never forgotten Sorcha. "Look what I brought." She withdrew a piece of apple from her pouch and felt the velvet softness of McBannon's lips whisper upon her outstretched palm. "Are they taking care of you well?"

"Aye, m'lady, the best of care," a deep male voice asserted.

Sorcha visibly jumped and McBannon snorted, twisting against his tether.

"He's a fine horse, he is," the voice, unfamiliar to her ears, continued. "Lord Hagan fancies the animal."

"Who—who are you?"

There was a long pause, and though she stared into darkness from where the voice had boomed, she heard nothing, saw nothing. Her skin prickled with fear. Finally she heard a rustling of straw and a tall, lanky man appeared at McBannon's flank. In the darkness, she couldn't recognize him.

"I work here," he finally said.

"You're . . ." What was that unfamiliar name? "Ben?"

"Bjorn."

"The stableboy?"

Again the hesitation, and she sensed an anger, burning deep and hot, radiating from him. "For now."

"You don't plan to stay at Erbyn?"

He didn't answer.

"I will tell no one of your plans."

"I have no plans," he said quickly. "What're you doing here?"

"I . . . I couldn't sleep. I needed to take a walk."

"You weren't planning to steal the horse?" he asked, suspicion and something else—pleasure perhaps?—ringing in his voice.

"Nay!"

"Good, because 'tis impossible to leave this castle at night. Guards are posted and the portcullis is down." He moved, shifting a little, and Sorcha felt a second of fear. She turned, hoping to face him, not wanting him to have the advantage of being at her back.

"You think I intended to leave," she said, hoping that her plans weren't so visible to others.

"I *know* you want out. I can see it in your eyes. You have only not made good your escape because of your sister."

"You don't know anything about me."

A second's pause, then a sigh laced with disappointment. "So you, too, consider me a simpleton, a stableboy who's half-witted and can do nothing more than scoop horse dung and spread straw?" he said, and within his voice she heard a sudden tone of nobility, as if the job he'd been given were far beneath him.

"Nay, but—"

"I know that you sneaked into Erbyn, Lady Sorcha," he said, his voice coming from yet another direction. "It is said that you lied your way past the guards and the cook, then tried to kill the lord."

"If I had wanted to kill him, he would be dead." She whirled, trying to keep up with him as he moved in the darkness. He was quick and silent, and she could barely see.

"I also heard that you brought your sister back from death. This . . . I find hard to believe." He paused, and when he spoke again, he was so close to her, she could feel the heat of his body next to hers. "If you do plan to escape, m'lady," he said so quietly, she barely heard the words, " 'twould be best if you spoke with me. I can help you—"

The door creaked and he stopped speaking altogether. His hand clamped over her arm and he attempted to pull her away from McBannon, but he was too late. Hagan's voice cut through the quiet. "What the devil are you doing here, Sorcha?" he demanded, and Sorcha shriveled inside. She held her breath. " 'Tis no use to hide; I saw you enter and heard you speaking with someone."

Oh, Lord, no! How could he have seen her? Her heart pounded so loudly, she was certain he could hear it.

" 'Tis me, m'lord," Bjorn said suddenly, the hand around her arm tight.

"No—" she cried, but he clamped his hand across her mouth.

"Come forward. Outside."

Bjorn pressed her back against the wall, silently telling her to remain hidden. "Be still," he whispered against the shell of her ear. "I am used to his punishments." He left suddenly, following Hagan, and Sorcha drew in a long, shaky breath. True, it would be less suspicious if Hagan didn't find her, but he'd already seen her enter the stables, and she couldn't let Bjorn take the brunt of the baron's wrath.

Squaring her shoulders, she followed Bjorn. At the doorway, he turned and hissed, "Stay," but she didn't heed his command.

They both ventured out of the darkness of the stables, and their eyes adjusted to the weak light cast by a shadowed moon.

Hagan struck fear in her heart. Taller than Bjorn and much broader, he seemed to tower over the stableboy. In the dim light she could barely make out his features, but they were hard and set, his anger visible in his stance. "What kind of treachery goes on here?" he demanded.

"I could not sleep," Sorcha said.

"So you sneaked past the guards and ended up here."

"Aye, to see about McBannon."

"In the middle of the night?" he said with a disbelieving sneer. "Why not wait until morn?"

"As I said, I couldn't sleep and needed to get some fresh air."

"Did you tell the guards?"

"I bothered no one."

"Had you plans to leave?"

"As you pointed out, *m'lord,* 'tis the middle of the night. I doubt the tower guard would let me pass."

"You've done it before," he said, deep, angry grooves surrounding his mouth. "And you—stableboy, what of you?"

"He was guarding the steed," Sorcha said before Bjorn could answer.

"I sleep in the stables and heard her enter."

"And what did you tell her?"

"To go back to the keep," Sorcha answered again, too quickly.

"The boy has a tongue, does he not? Let him speak for himself." Hagan didn't bother to hide his irritation.

Bjorn stiffened, his eyes slitting in hatred. " 'Tis as the

lady says. I told her I would look after her horse and that 'twould be best if she returned to her chamber."

Hagan looked from one to the other and finally grabbed Sorcha by the arm. "Make sure no one disturbs the animals," he said to Bjorn. "I'll see to it that the stable master knows what happened."

Pulling hard on Sorcha's elbow, he started back to the keep. His blood was on fire, his pulse thundering in his brain. Did she think he was stupid enough to believe her lie? She'd either been plotting her escape or she'd taken a fancy to the handsome stableboy. Either way, 'twas trouble. In truth, he'd rather think she was trying to find a means to leave Erbyn, but he doubted she would risk escape while her sister was still ill. No, but if not for the horse, then why? For the boy. They'd been speaking in whispers when he'd thrown open the stable door, and Hagan felt jealousy course through his blood.

How could he have been so blind? Bjorn was handsome and had a way with horses as well as women. Many a young maid had dallied near the stables, hoping to draw his attention. Rumor had it that he claimed a birthright to nobility or royalty from the heathens of the North, but until now, Hagan had thought the gossip just the idle dreams of a poor stableboy.

But Sorcha had gone to him in the middle of the night, risking her very life to be with him. Hagan's teeth ground together and his fingers tightened over the muscles of her arm.

"What do you think you're doing?" she demanded as she trotted beside him.

"Taking you back where you belong. 'Tis not safe for you to be out here at dark."

"Have you no faith in your men-at-arms?"

"Aye, I've faith enough. Faith that some of them have had too much to drink and would find a woman alone fair game."

"No one saw me."

"*I* saw you. *The stableboy* saw you. But that's what you wanted, was it not?"

"What?" she asked as he opened the back door and forced her up the stone steps to the upper floor.

"Don't bother lying to me," he growled as she stumbled upon the stairs. "You and he have either plotted together for your escape or you've become lovers."

"Lovers?" she repeated, her voice low. Was he jesting? He thought she and the stableboy had fallen in love. The thought nearly made her laugh, but she held her tongue. If Hagan believed that she and Bjorn had met to be together, he would be less suspicious of her true plans. " 'Tis only been a few days, m'lord. What think you of me—that I be no better than a common wench?"

He didn't say a word, but his lips compressed into a thin, angry line.

"Trust you no one?"

"Certainly not a woman who tries to kill me in my sleep."

"I don't even know the stableboy," she said, but didn't sound convincing.

"Don't you now? Yet you were alone with him in the dark, defied my orders and sneaked out of your chamber to meet him." He kicked open the door to his room and threw her inside. Embers from the fire reflected bloodred in the angles of his face, and the smell of burning wood singed the air.

Sorcha nearly lost her footing, but turned, intent on running out of the room, when he closed the door firmly and turned the key. "Now, savior of all that is Prydd," he said, advancing upon her with even, sure strides. "You had best be telling me what it is you were doing with the stableboy."

"I told you—"

"Liar! From the moment you set foot in this castle, you have lied and argued and *bargained* for your release. You tricked the guards and the cook and tried to thrust a knife into my ribs." She'd inched backward, her heart thundering as he closed in on her, and finally her back was pressed hard against the smooth stones of the wall. "And now, when I find you with the stableboy and hear you whispering, you tell me that you hardly know him." His face was fierce, his eyes slits. "You've made a fool of me and a mockery of this castle, and now you think that I should believe that you were only restless, unable to sleep, and you just happened to meet Bjorn as if you were on a summer stroll through the gardens."

"That's the way it was."

"You would lie to save him, just as you would have slept with me to protect your sister?"

She tried to slap him, but he was quick. Years of training had prepared him and he caught her wrist and curved it backward, catching her arm around her back.

"I've tried to trust you, Sorcha. I've treated you as my guest, and for that you've betrayed me."

"Nay, I—"

" 'Tis time I collected on my part of the bargain," he said through tight teeth as he slammed his body hard against hers and crushed her breasts.

"Please, Lord Hagan—"

But he wasn't listening. His lips crashed down upon hers. With fierce possession, he kissed her. She tried to push away, but couldn't, and though she willed herself to kick him, he pinned her with his larger, stronger body. His thigh muscles pressed against hers, and his mouth, hard and eager, slid easily over hers.

She felt her bones begin to melt, as if they were as soft as candle wax, and when his tongue pushed against her teeth, her jaw unlocked to allow him entry. With brutal strokes, he touched and teased, his tongue flicking against the roof of her mouth, and thrusting against her own.

She heard a moan and realized it came from her own throat as he lifted his head to stare down in her eyes. "So what be you, Sorcha? Lady or wench?"

"I'm not—"

He kissed her again, his lips hard and supple, his tongue slick and wet as it mated anxiously with hers. She felt a tingle that centered deep in her insides. One of his rough hands moved forward to capture the weight of her breast. "Ahh, that's right. You're neither, are ye? Not a lady. Nor a wench. Just the damned savior of Prydd."

"Please . . ." she whispered as he tore open her cloak and found the strings of her tunic. "Do not . . ."

His fingers scraped her flesh, and she dragged in a sharp breath. Somewhere deep within her, a murky cloud of desire began to swell. Her blood turned to liquid fire and his lips sought hers again.

Though she knew she should fight him, beat against his chest, she couldn't, and the lust that invaded her body was a living, breathing being that was all-consuming. She wanted more of him and didn't stop his hands from dipping into her chemise and touching her skin.

Her nipple tightened and her suddenly aching breast filled his palm. He teased the dark point with his fingers, and again the beast of desire rolled hot within her, causing her bones to soften.

"Aye, Sorcha, you feel it, too," he said, holding her against him, breathing across her neck as he slid her cloak from her shoulders and pushed the sleeve of her tunic down her arm. He kissed her neck as he shoved her chemise away from her skin and bared one breast to the firelight. " 'Tis beautiful you are, and treacherous," he murmured, stroking her and kissing her bare skin.

Her flesh tingled, and as he drew her to her knees, she couldn't stop him. He wound his fingers in the tumble of her hair and kissed her with a passion that made the earth shift beneath her. She couldn't think, couldn't catch her breath, and losing all will, gave herself up to the passion that burned bright in her soul.

Slowly he dragged his lips from hers, tracing the slope of her jaw and the length of her neck with his tongue. He rimmed the circle of bones at the base of her throat, his tongue dipping into that soft recess to play with her pulse. Sorcha made a low sound that came from the back of her throat, and her body turned, anxious to know more. Still he slid down her body, kissing her flesh as he lowered his head to her breast. She groaned, a deep primal sound that came from her very being. His tongue tickled and laved as he teased her nipple, then drew his lips around the puckering point.

She cradled his head against her, her back arching to meet his mouth. Though her mind denied him, her body acted of its own accord, shaming her in its wanton display.

He kissed her again and his hand moved lower to cup her buttocks and rub across her lower back. In her mind's eye she shivered as she saw herself, acting like a shameless whore, anxious for the feel of his skin against hers.

Somewhere in the distance she heard the hoot of an owl and she forced herself to grab the shreds of her dignity.

"Nay," she whispered, grabbing his wrist with her fingers. "Hagan, please, not here. Not like this." She turned pleading eyes up to his.

His jaw was clenched tight, and tiny dots of sweat broke out on his skin. Staring down at her, he hesitated, but his hard expression slowly vanished, and instead of arguing, he gathered her into his arms and buried his face in her neck. For a second she thought that he had ignored her request, that he still intended to claim her, but he didn't move. Instead a shudder ripped through him as he regained control and continued to hold her close.

Shoving the hair off her shoulder, he traced her birthmark with his finger. "What are you, Sorcha? Woman or witch?"

"Woman," she said, her breath still shaking in her lungs, her voice a mere whisper.

"Yet still you bewitch men. None, it seems, is free from your spells."

"That's daft," she said as he moved away from her but stared at her bare skin as if savoring every second. She covered her breast with fumbling fingers, and he clamped his hand over hers. Then, before he placed her cloak around her, he leaned forward and took her nipple into his mouth one last time. Her heart raced unevenly as he suckled and rimmed the nipple with the tip of his tongue. "Sweet are you, but dangerous," he finally said as he lifted his head and covered her nakedness with the rough black wool of her cloak.

"Dangerous?" she repeated, shame heating her cheeks.

"You can turn a man's thinking round." Without further explanation, he stood and refused to offer her his hand. "Come, then; if you know what's good for you, you'll hurry back to your room before I change my mind. I'll take you there."

"I know where to find—"

He placed a finger to her lips. "Aye, but I trust you not. Should I let you go, you might not return to your chamber."

"Where would I go?"

"Back to Bjorn?" he suggested with a cruel twist of his mouth.

She couldn't believe her ears. "Nay, I swear—"

"Come, Sorcha," he said tightly, the passion in his eyes replaced with distrust. Again taking hold of her elbow, he opened the door and shoved her down the hall past a guard who was dozing, but scrambled to his feet as he heard their footsteps.

"Halt!"

" 'Tis only I," Hagan said as he kept walking furiously. "See that you don't sleep the rest of your shift."

"I was just . . . As you wish."

"And see that this one does not wander around the castle at night. If needs be, post a man at her door."

Sorcha yanked her arm free. "You bastard."

"Not me, m'love," he mocked. " 'Tis your other lover, the stableboy, who is the bastard." He kicked open her door, and she breezed past him, certain that no part of her touched him. The door slammed shut behind her, and she kicked at the bed in vexation. Horrible, horrible beast! He thought little enough of her to nearly bed her, then accuse her of lying with someone else.

But when you asked him to stop, he did. He did not force himself on you.

She flung herself across the bed and cursed her luck that Hagan had returned before she'd freed her sister. She would have had an easier time dealing with Darton, for he was a man she could hate without a trace of guilt.

But Hagan was different; hateful one instant, loving the

next. She never knew what to do or think around him. She wanted to detest him, to spit on his soul, to betray him and his castle, and yet there was something in him that called out to a very dark and forbidden part of her spirit.

She closed her eyes and refused to think that she could care for him; no, she would rather think of escaping the thick walls of Erbyn.

Tadd kicked at the gray cat who was lying in a patch of sunlight and thereby blocking the doorway of the kitchen. "Miserable, lazy puss," he muttered as the cat, with a startled cry, scrambled out of the castle and scurried from harm's way.

"Be careful, Lord Tadd," Mab, the cook's helper, said, then nearly bit her tongue when Tadd stabbed her with a look as vile as a serpent's glare. "I mean, er, beggin' yer pardon, m'lord, but the cat, she helps keep the rats from the flour and grain."

"Does she now?" Tadd said, advancing on the silly kitchen wench who would dare defy him.

"Go out and pluck the feathers from those geese, Mab," Lynn, the cook, ordered quickly. He was a short, wiry man with a shiny bald pate and lips that didn't quite cover his prominent teeth. " 'Tis nearly time to start roasting."

"Wait a minute." Tadd took hold of the wench's arm and squeezed hard enough to bruise her white skin. His gaze slid down her front to her small breasts, nearly hidden in the folds of her old tunic. He curled his lips in disgust. "I thought mayhaps I'd want you to warm my bed, but you've no bosom, have ya, lass? Nay, you're flat as the cook here, and I like women who don't look like boys."

Mab gasped, but didn't say another word. She turned her head away, but not before he felt the satisfaction of seeing fat tears glisten in her eyes. Served her right for upbraiding him. His fingers gripped her forearm even tighter and he shook her a bit, just enough to show her he could do anything he wanted with her. "Mayhaps I'll strap two pillows over your chest and pretend that you've got what I want while I'm bedding you."

"Nay, Lord Tadd, please . . ." Her lower lip trembled in pain and fear, and he felt his member begin to swell. The thought of taking her, mayhap coloring her small breasts with sheep fat and rouge to display them and abase her further, pleased him. Perhaps one of his guests would like to join in the fun. Old Osric McBrayne enjoyed slight women, and there was gossip that he liked young boys as well. Surely he would have a go at this skinny wench.

"Be ye a virgin, girl?" he asked.

"She needs be plucking the geese," the cook said, his bald pate wrinkled in worry.

"But tonight I will send for you," Tadd said, running one hand over the tiny mounds that were her breasts and watching as a tear slid down her cheek. "Mayhap all these need are a little more attention, eh? Perhaps then they'll grow big and soft and you'll finally be a true woman, able to satisfy a man."

She swallowed back a sob, but her skin turned the color of flour. Tadd was pleased. Aye, he'd have her tonight and let one of his men or one of his guests join in the fun of deflowering her if she was a virgin and mounting her as others watched. Just the thought of it caused a swelling between his legs and spit to gather in his mouth. He tweaked her breast through her tunic, and she cried out in fear and shame. Aye, 'twould be fun. He didn't know if he could wait. Why not have her this afternoon?

As soon as he released her, the girl scampered out of the room, dashing the tears from her eyes.

"She is young," the cook said as he cut the head off a salmon and slit its silver belly. Entrails slid onto the table.

"I like 'em young. You can have the old dried-up women, Lynn. I'll take a fresh girl any day."

Lynn scowled at his work, gutting the fish quickly and tossing the entrails into a pail.

Tadd started into the keep when he heard the porter shout. Turning, expecting to greet a neighboring nobleman, maybe Osric McBrayne, Tadd walked through the kitchen and outside, where the winter sun was trying vainly to warm the cold, wet ground. The porter was talking to a tall, straight-shouldered soldier astride a sleek gray courser.

". . . as I said, I must speak with the lord of the castle."

The guard caught Tadd's eye. "This man claims to be a messenger from Erbyn, but would not let me bring you the baron's letter."

"Nay, I am to deliver it personally." The soldier slid from his stallion and walked to Tadd with long, even strides. He stood taller than Tadd by nearly two inches and somehow gained an advantage in that, staring down his nose imperiously. "You are the baron here?"

"Aye," Tadd said without a qualm. While his father was away, he'd inherited all the power of a baron. "Tadd of Prydd," he said, surprised at the messenger's tone. His shoulders were wide, eyes a cutting shade of blue. His face had probably once been considered handsome, but had been altered slightly; his nose was not straight and one dark eyebrow was split, as if cleaved by a sword earlier in his life. For a second Tadd thought he recognized the soldier, but the feeling passed quickly. "What news do you bring?"

The messenger stared at Tadd's crimson mantle and shiny boots for a second, then, with a slight smirk, seemed to decide that Tadd was who he claimed to be and reached into his leather pouch. "This is word from Hagan at Erbyn."

"Hagan?" Tadd whispered. "I thought he was at war and Darton was . . ."

Did a sense of satisfaction steal over the messenger's face?

Tadd stiffened slightly, his jaw tight as he took the scroll and, in his hurry, didn't notice the altering of the wax seal. He unwound the parchment, read it slowly, and turned a shade of red to match his mantle. "This is a lie!" he finally said, his voice a low growl.

"No lie."

"One sister is missing, aye, that much I'll admit, but the other is locked in her room . . ." His voice faded as he thought about Sorcha's long silence, which was in direct contrast to her sharp tongue. Then there was the matter of McBannon; few could ride the beast, but Sorcha had trained the destrier from a colt. A new, cold fear clamped its claws around Tadd's soul, and he knew that he'd been betrayed.

"You, messenger, are to stay here," he told the tall soldier. Lips flattening in anger, his mantle billowing after him, he stalked back to the keep and took the steps two at a time. He threw open the door and knew with a chilling certainty that he'd been played for a fool.

"Curse and rot her," he muttered. Coming upon one of his men, he grabbed the fellow by the throat. "Bring me the old hag, Isolde, at once," he growled.

"Aye, m'lord!"

He dropped the man and swept up the stairs in a blind fury. How could he have trusted the old woman? How? His boots rang on the stones, and at the door to Sorcha's room he found the listless guard, leaning against the wall, his head nodding forward.

"Open the door!" Tadd demanded.

"Aye, m'lord!"

The key jangled loudly and the bar was lifted. The door flew open to bang against the wall of the hallway, but the room was empty, though a half-eaten trencher of brawn sat upon a stool and there was refuse in the pail. But no one was within the chamber.

"Bloody Christ, why didn't you tell me she was missing?" Tadd yelled as he stepped into the room only to whirl on the lazy guard.

"I knew not—"

"You were guarding an empty room, you fool!" Tadd slapped the man so hard, his head spun. "Where is the old woman?"

The man touched his cheek. "I know not."

"Did she not bring up the morning meal?"

"Nay . . ." Again he was slapped, so hard the sound echoed from the rafters.

"Fool! Why wasn't I told?" Then, not waiting for an answer, Tadd drew his sword. "I want every soldier in this castle to search for Isolde. She alone knows of Sorcha. She's lied to me, tricked me, and betrayed me, and she'll pay. As for that messenger from Erbyn, lock him in the dungeon with Robert the traitor!" Spinning on his heel, he ran down the hallway, intent on finding the hag and cutting out her tongue if she dared lie to him again.

Wolf saw the commotion and knew there was serious trouble afoot. From the way men were scrambling, reaching for their weapons, shouting, and laying blame on one another, Wolf was certain Tadd was in a rage. No doubt Hagan of Erbyn's letter had proved distressing.

"Isolde! Find Isolde!" one man said as he came up to the porter. "We're to bring the old woman to the lord and throw this one in the dungeon with Robert."

"I am but a messenger," Wolf argued, pleased that Hagan's missive had destroyed Tadd's peace.

"Aye, but the messenger of evil." The porter lunged at him, but Wolf reached up his sleeve and grabbed the knife he had hidden there. Sidestepping the porter's blade, he jabbed his would-be attacker quickly, sending the man howling and clutching his side as he fell to the ground. Blood pooled on the wet blades of grass.

Spinning, Wolf leaped upon the courser, yanked the reins from a surprised page's hands, and whirled the stallion toward the gate. With a quick kick to the ribs, the horse broke into a gallop.

"Stop him!" the porter yelled. "Close the gate!"

"What? Oh!" The boy at the portcullis worked the ropes to the gears, but Wolf spurred the fleet horse through the opening just before the heavy grate fell into place. Several men in the outer bailey stood in his way, but as he tucked low against the courser's neck and showed no fear in running them over, they dodged out of the way and scrabbled for their useless weapons.

Arrows whizzed past his head.

"Run, you miserable beast," Wolf cried as the horse raced through the outer gate and across the bridge, his hooves thundering as people screamed and scattered, dropping onions and silver and sacks of grain. Wolf felt the thrill of deceit course through his blood; he enjoyed besting Tadd, his old enemy. He'd waited long for this moment, and seeing Tadd again brought back all the old hatred.

Tadd of Prydd had slit his eyebrow years ago, and now 'twas time to pay the bastard back.

His heart pounding with revenge, Wolf guided the courser ever forward, along the road that curved through the woods. He followed the muddy path for nearly a mile before suddenly yanking on the reins and turning in to the dense woods, where he could hide in the shadows.

From the road came the sound of his doom. Horses' hooves thundered. Wolf peered through the bracken as men, wearing the crest of Prydd, rode by, shouting and cursing as they passed in a flurry of flashing hooves and mud-splattered hides.

His smile curved into a wicked grin. He knew he was out of danger. Breathing hard, he rode deeper into the thicket of oak and pine and stopped only when he was well out of the way of Tadd's wrath.

So the rumors had proved true. Erbyn and Prydd would soon be at war. All because of some woman who claimed to be the savior of Prydd. Good. The time was right. Wolf did not doubt Sorcha's powers; he'd seen too much in his life to convince him otherwise.

Long ago he'd been the son of a nobleman, groomed to someday have his own barony if not for his older brother. He'd seen much in the way of magic and sorcery then and didn't doubt that Sorcha of Prydd might have been blessed with the "sight," as he'd heard it called so many years ago.

He gritted his teeth and refused to think of his home. He'd spent too many years away and he felt comfortable with his life the way it was now—on the other side of the law. He'd been accused of harboring a rebel spirit, and it had served him well.

Asides, before he could ever go back, he had a few more duties to perform as Wolf, the leader of his band of outlaws.

He took off his gloves and tucked them into his belt as he cut through the forest to another road that was overgrown and seldom used. Though it was cold and damp, he was warm from his journey. He would have liked to ride to the next village and buy a cup of mead and find himself a woman, but he dared not. He had to return to his men, decide what to do about the messenger they held prisoner, and plot how the war between Prydd and Erbyn would benefit him.

So caught up in his plans was he that he didn't notice the old woman propped against the trunk of an oak until she shouted at him.

"Wolf of Erbyn Forest, I know you!"

His heart grew cold and he wheeled his horse to look at a crone with wrinkled skin and sunken eyes. Like a witch, she seemed, until he stared more closely and saw the spark of life in her faded eyes.

"Who are you?"

"Isolde of Prydd." She stood slowly as if her joints ached. "I knew you would come today, I saw it in my vision, so I left the castle early, before you arrived. If I go back, Tadd will kill me."

He didn't doubt it. "But how did you know my name or that I'd come this way?"

"Sometimes I'm given the gift of sight. You've seen it before, have you not? Before you changed your name to that of the forest creature that you hold dear?"

His mouth was suddenly dry as hot sand. She was a witch.

"Do not fear me, for I need your help," she said, her voice steady and sure as she picked up a bundle that lay at her feet. " 'Tis your destiny, Wolf—outlaw and murderer, son of a man most noble—to take me to the savior of Prydd."

Nine

Sorcha watched from her window. The men, armed with bows and arrows, were talking and laughing, their breaths fogging as they stood near their mounts in the bailey. The sun was barely up, and a slow mist crawled over the ground. The hunting party was anxious to be off.

Sending up a prayer that Hagan would lead the party, Sorcha held her breath. It was time to set her plan into motion, and it would be safer for everyone if Hagan was out of the castle.

Fidgeting, she drummed her fingers on the window ledge until she spied him, and her heart did a strange little flip. Dressed in an emerald-colored mantle and brown leggings, he waited as Bjorn led a sleek black destrier into the bailey.

Hagan mounted, and the other men, some his soldiers, others his guests, climbed upon their horses. With a trumpeting of horns and the baying of dogs, the hunt was underway. Hagan tugged upon the reins, whirling his horse as he led the party out of the bailey. Hooves clattered and men shouted, the smell of the hunt heady in the air.

Sorcha waited until Hagan disappeared through the gates, then reappeared far away, on a distant hill that was visible over the castle walls. His horse ran effortlessly up the grassy slope toward the edge of the woods.

Oh, if only she could ride with him and feel the wind stream through her hair, feel the strength of a horse running through the woods, watch sunlight and shadow play upon Hagan's face as he rode . . . Her heart stopped at the thought and she reminded herself that he was still her sworn enemy.

She bit her lip as he, along with the men following behind, entered the gloom of the forest.

She waited a few minutes, her heart pounding loudly in her chest. If Hagan ever got wind of her plans, he'd make her suffer, and yet she had no choice. Patience, though a virtue, wasn't a part of her.

Her plan was not foolproof, but it was the best she had. Because the tunic she'd worn to mass needed further alterations, she'd had to strip it off, hand it to Ona, and find something else for the rest of the morning.

Now, hurrying to the wardrobe, she chose one of Anne's castoffs, a tunic the color of ripe plums.

She knew that she'd found in Bjorn the man who would become her accomplice. She could tell that he felt a vast hatred for all that was Erbyn and was only waiting until the right moment to flee. Hadn't he nearly said so much himself? However, his anger, from what Sorcha had observed on her walks in the bailey, was not directed so much at Hagan, but at the stable master, Roy, a huge, pockmarked man who loved to belittle his charge.

Yanking the tunic over her head, Sorcha smoothed the soft fabric over her hips. Hagan had never returned her daggers, and she felt naked without a weapon strapped to her belt. Curse the beast, why couldn't he trust her?

For the very reason that you're planning to defy him and escape, using one of his trusted men to help you.

Scowling, she tightened the belt. Just this morning she had learned from gossiping Ona that Bjorn considered himself some kind of prince, a direct descendant of a Viking king from the far North.

" 'E's a bloody fool, 'e is," Ona had told her as she'd braided Sorcha's hair before mass this morning. "Believin' 'is mother's stories. She was a fool, that one was, all those silly dreams in her 'ead." Ona stopped working and thought a moment. "Even claimed she was a princess, kidnapped by a German soldier, then raped and left for dead. Baron Hagan's father, Lord Richard—God rest 'is soul—'e found her and brought her to Erbyn. Turned out she was the best seamstress ever. 'Tis her work 'angin' in the great 'all above the lord's bed. I'm tellin' you, no princess would know how to work a needle the way that woman did. She was messed up in her 'ead, if you're askin' me. Got herself with child and came up with some story about a German soldier to make 'erself feel good. Probably her man just up and left 'er. No shame in that, I'm thinkin', but Bjorn, he believes everything she said. Thinks 'e's got noble blood runnin' through 'is veins." Ona tugged on an unruly handful of hair, smoothing out the curls.

"Does Bjorn's mother live here still?"

"Naw." Ona tied off the braid. "She died. When Bjorn was but a lad. Lord Richard kept him on out of the goodness of 'is heart, and the boy turned out to 'ave a way with the 'orses. Poor luck, that. Got 'im 'is job with old Roy."

Sorcha had listened to the gossip, learning about the man who she hoped would help her escape. She planned to offer him a reward for her safe return to Prydd not in money, but horseflesh, for Bjorn was taken with McBannon, and Sorcha felt no qualms about giving him Tadd's destrier in return for her freedom. Tadd would be furious, of course, but she had always been able to turn the tide of her brother's anger. 'Twould be a simple matter.

Yes, Bjorn would be the most likely man to approach, she decided as she tossed the mantle over her head and pinned a gold brooch—another gift from Anne—at her throat. She needed Bjorn's help to return to Prydd, and he needed her as he owned nothing and could scarcely leave the castle without anything of value.

Sorcha had said nothing of her plans. She allowed everyone, except for Leah, to think that she'd accepted her fate. Even Hagan seemed to believe that she was content to wait until the messenger from Prydd returned. She tried to fall into the routine of Erbyn and pretended interest in the Christmas revels.

For the past few days she'd spent much time in the castle, and though most eyes that were cast in her direction were hostile, she was no longer the center of attention. She was able to walk through the keep and grounds at her will, although she was forever watching for Hagan, wondering where he was and praying that she wouldn't chance to stumble upon him. The delicious and shamefully wanton sensations he'd aroused deep within her were a bother. She didn't want to think of him as a man; 'twas easier to consider him the enemy.

This proved more difficult than she imagined. As the days passed, she felt her heart melting toward him. She'd caught glimpses of him dealing with his servants and the peasants who resided in the keep. Except for a few soldiers who seemed to distrust him, the residents of Erbyn seemed to want to please him. He was a fair lord, asked only that his men obey him, but he often showed a spark of humor or more than a passing kindness to the children and women of Erbyn. No one was mistreated, and no one said a word against Hagan, though when he was disobeyed, his temper could turn dark and deadly.

More often than she would admit, she'd let her thoughts wander to him. His eyes were the color of a purest gold, and those gilded depths fascinated her. When he caught sight of her he scowled hard, his glare unforgiving . . . unless she glimpsed him from the corner of her eye, when he didn't think she'd noticed him. Those few times his gaze was softer, full of smoky desire, warm with promise, and she felt her body tingle, though she wouldn't even glance his way.

Once, near the archery range, she'd come across him helping a squire learn how to restring a broken bow. He'd been so involved in instructing the boy that he hadn't heard her footsteps, and when he'd finally looked up, his gaze had gotten lost in hers for a fleeting second. The breath had seemed to stop in her lungs. She'd hurried on, ignoring the sensation, but she'd felt as if she'd just run a great distance and couldn't breathe regularly for long moments.

Silly.

Now, as she left her chamber and walked past the guards in the hall, she thought of the times that he'd touched his mouth to hers and the promise of passion that had caused her lips to throb and her heart to thud. Even now, just thinking of the kiss, she felt new, unwanted sensations that frightened her. Her body trembled at the memory, and a dark heat, liquid and warm, seemed to swirl deep in her most private parts. Never had she felt so wanton—so eager for more of his touch. Certainly never with Keane . . . Dear God, was she no better than a kitchen wench? Wanting a man she'd sworn was her enemy?

Steadfastly pushing those wicked thoughts from her mind, she still couldn't make herself hate him. Aside from the two times she'd been with him in his private chambers, he'd been kind enough to her and Leah. Though he'd refused to let them return to Prydd, he hadn't treated them as prisoners.

"When the revels are over," he'd promised, just after supper the other night. "If we haven't heard from my messenger by then, I'll ride you and your sister to Prydd myself. Both Nichodemas and Rosemary agree that Leah's recovering well and should be able to withstand a journey soon."

"How can I be sure that you're not lying?" she'd asked, staring up at him.

"You can't be. Just as I can't trust you, Sorcha," he'd said on a sigh.

"But—"

"You have my word."

They had exchanged a dark, secret look, and though he'd said nothing more, she was certain that he, too, was remembering that she'd been in his room not once, but twice, since she'd arrived at Erbyn, and each time he'd come close to stealing her virginity; no, that wasn't quite right. The last time she had nearly given it to him willingly.

"You're a goose, Sorcha," she muttered under her breath as she stalked along the hallway.

"M'lady?" a small guard asked, standing to attention. "Is there something I can do for you?"

"Nay, 'tis only my idle tongue, Sir Winston."

This soldier was one of the few in Erbyn Sorcha trusted. Small of stature, with brown eyes too big for his face, he had always treated her with respect and fondness.

"If I can be of help—"

"I'll let you know," she said, hurrying past him toward Leah's chamber.

Since this was the first day of the celebration, Sorcha decided it was time to set her plan in motion. The messenger whom Hagan claimed to have sent to Prydd hadn't yet returned, and she was beginning to worry that the man had lost his way, had been captured by Tadd, or, worse yet, had never existed at all. Hagan could have lied to her about the messenger, and she would have eagerly believed him.

She had been at Erbyn nearly a week, and each day, when Hagan told her that there was no word from Prydd, her heart had settled a little deeper in her chest.

When she'd heard that Hagan was leaving the castle to go hunting, she knew she couldn't let this opportunity pass.

With a soft knock, she pushed open the door to Leah's room. Nellie, Leah's serving girl, was bustling around the room, straightening the bed and kicking at the rushes while Leah was seated near the window, staring down at the bailey. Leah's face was still pale and her hands were clasped in her lap and she looked startled when the door opened wide. Fear registered in her eyes until she recognized Sorcha.

"Thank God it's you," she said, exhaling a long breath.

"Who else would it be?" Sorcha asked.

"Lord Darton, 'e came this mornin'," Nellie said.

"Has he been bothering you?"

Leah's smile was grim. "Nay, he was being kind, asking about my health, pretending that he cared." Her lovely face turned into a mask of stone as if she remembered Darton's cruelty to her. "I would gladly cut out his heart if I could."

"Hush!" Sorcha hissed.

"I didn't hear a thing," Nellie said, removing an empty cup and, with a sly wink, slipping through the open door.

"Be careful," Sorcha warned. "Trust no one in this keep."

"Nellie can keep a secret."

"You think so?" Sorcha said, closing the door behind the serving woman. "My guess is that she tells everything to Lady Anne, as does Ona."

Leah lifted a shoulder. "I care not."

"Of course you do."

"What can they do to me that they have not already?" she asked, her eyes suddenly lifeless.

Sorcha grabbed hold of her sister's hand. "What did he do to you?" she whispered, and Leah shuddered as if an icy blast of winter wind had cut through her small body.

"What did he not?"

"Did he beat you?"

"Nay." Leah shook her head.

"Touch you?"

Tears sprang to her eyes.

"Lie with you?" Sorcha asked gently, and Leah swallowed, tears drizzling down her cheeks.

"He . . . He was angry when he discovered that his men had captured me. He wanted you. I thought he would leave me alone, but he was so . . . filled with wrath that he tore off my clothes and . . . and forced me . . . oh, God . . . There were other men nearby, for they met up with us in the forest, and then . . . though I was naked and he was fully dressed, he tied together his breeches and ordered me upon a horse." She sniffed and touched her fingers to her eyes.

Sorcha's blood ran hot with fury. "The ride. 'Twas painful."

"Aye . . . but not the worst. Later, he brought me to that horrid room and left me there, coming and going, taking me whenever he was angry."

Sorcha's heart twisted, for she imagined how brutal Darton could be.

"I meant nothing more to him than an animal or a piece of meat. Though I would scream, he would . . . tell me to do the most vile . . ." Her stomach wrenched and she shook her head. "When I could stand it no longer, I stole the knife I was to eat with and, praying to God, cut at my veins. I wanted not to live."

Sorcha blinked back her own tears. "You will be avenged, sister. He will hurt you no more."

"He could not," she said without inflection, and Sorcha

realized that Darton had taken more than Leah's virginity, he'd stolen her dignity as well.

"I promise you, he will suffer," Sorcha vowed, and Leah's color came back a little. She had been recovering slowly, her appetite had increased, and she had even smiled once in a while, though she never left the chamber, certain that if she did, she would run into Darton. Her wrists were still bound, but her hands moved freely.

"I only hope I am the one who will inflict his pain," Leah said. She took the necklace of twigs from her neck. "I think I'll need these no longer."

Sorcha stuffed the cord and sticks into the pouch hanging from her belt.

"There are many guests arriving," Leah said, looking out the window.

"Just like home."

"Aye." Her voice quivered with sadness. "Have you time for a game?" she asked, and Sorcha, though she was anxious to find Bjorn, agreed, hoping to raise her sister's sagging spirits.

They often played dice, something her father frowned upon but Hagan encouraged. Outwardly he seemed to want to do anything to help Leah's recovery. All her meals were sent to her room, and her clothes were the finest the seamstress could sew together.

Sorcha sat near her sister on the window ledge. They passed the dice between them and talked, their voices muted by the rattling cup as Nellie returned with fresh linens.

"Has there been news from Prydd?" Leah asked, her gaze wandering to the servant girl, who couldn't help but overhear part of the conversation.

"None yet." Sorcha tossed out the dice. "Lord Hagan thinks 'twill not be much longer."

Their eyes met. "Good."

"Today I planned a walk in the bailey. Mayhap you could join me?"

"I don't think—" Leah caught the gleam in her sister's eye. "You know I don't like to leave this room."

"But you can't stay here forever. Asides, there is much to see with the revels upon us. Come." Sorcha scooped up the dice and left the cup on the sill. " 'Tis not too cold today, and you needs see the rest of the castle." She took her sister's hand in hers and felt the tremor of fear in Leah's touch.

Leah paled, but walked to the wardrobe and, with Nellie's unwelcome help, selected a gray wool mantle trimmed in squirrel fur. Sorcha guided her sister through the dark hallways and down the back stairs past Hagan's room. Leah followed along, though she nearly jumped at her own shadow.

Outside, Sorcha hurried along the path that led past the candlemaker's hut through the gardens near the bakery. A chill wind swept through the grounds, but it was fresh and brought with it the scents of baked goods and spices as they walked along the paths through overgrown rosebushes and mulberry trees.

The clang of the armorer's hammer, the creak of the bucket being drawn up the well, and the shouting of thatchers who were repairing a hole in the tanner's roof were only a few of the sounds filling the air. Children laughed and played, and the rattling of bridles and creak of the wheels of carts was ever present.

Leah slipped the hood of her mantle over her head. "You were right," she admitted, breathing deeply of the cool air, " 'tis good to be out of that room. Oh, if only we were at Prydd again!"

"We will be, and soon." They passed the dovecote and followed the trail to the stables, where Bjorn was brushing a small chestnut mare. He looked up when they approached, his gaze colliding with Sorcha's for an instant, his blond hair ruffling in the breeze, before he turned his attention back to the horse's muddy hide.

Sorcha cleared her throat. "I wanted to check on my horse," she said, ignoring the stiff back turned in her direction. Her heart turned to stone. He had to help her, and yet all friendliness had disappeared and he was treating her as if she were an enemy. "My stallion's the big—"

"I know which one is yours," he said swiftly. "Your charger's fine." Again his eyes met hers for just a second before he turned back to his task and ran the comb through the mare's coarse mane.

What had gotten into him? Was he so afraid of Hagan or had she read him incorrectly? "If I could see for myself."

"No one is allowed near him. He's a wild one, that."

"I rode him here from Prydd. I'm not afraid." Annoyed, she felt her fists clench and stared at him boldly. "Please, get him for me—"

"Hey, what's this?" The stable master, squinting against the daylight, appeared in the doorway of the stables. Covered with filth, with a belly that hung low and eyes nestled in a puffy face, he hitched up his belt and hung his whip on a peg near the door. "Well, well, well." He dusted his big hands together and grinned widely, showing off a mouth with few teeth. "I'll be buggered. What can I do for you, m'lady?"

"I just wanted to check on my horse."

"A devil, he is," Roy said.

"But surefooted," Sorcha replied. "He belongs to my brother."

Bjorn looked up quickly, his eyes meeting Sorcha's over the back of the mare.

"Sir Tadd's charger, is he?" Roy asked, his pig eyes slitting a bit.

"Aye, he's taken my brother into many a battle." This was a lie, of course. Tadd had not yet seen war, but Sorcha wasn't above stretching the truth if it served her purpose.

Roy rubbed the stubble on his chins. "Bjorn, can't you tell that the lady is worried about her charger? See that he's fed and watered. A bit of exercise wouldn't hurt, either."

Every muscle in Bjorn's body flexed. His jaw clenched tight as if he were trying to hold his tongue, and for a second Sorcha thought he might disobey. He snapped the mare's reins from the post to which she'd been tied, then led the docile horse back to the stables, as if he were following Roy's orders.

"We'll take good care of the animal; you've got no worries of that," Roy said with a smile that made Sorcha's skin crawl.

"Well, if it isn't the savior of Prydd and her sister, Lady Leah." Darton's voice reverberated through the bailey. Leah gasped softly, and Sorcha turned, wondering how long he'd followed them. Wearing polished boots, a dove gray surcoat, and purple mantle trimmed with black fur, he smiled easily, as if pleased to have found them. "What brings you to the stables?" he asked amiably, though Sorcha read suspicion in his eyes.

Leah looked at the ground, refusing to meet his gaze.

"I was checking on my brother's horse."

"I'm sure Roy will take good care of him."

"If only I could see for myself—" she said just as Bjorn reappeared holding the tether to McBannon. The stallion's eyes were wild, as if he sensed danger, but he was following the lead, nervously mincing as Bjorn spoke soft words to him.

Roy spat on the ground. "What in Christ's name do you think y're doing?" Wiping his sweaty hand on the front of his tunic, Roy swaggered toward Bjorn. The stallion reared.

"Move slowly," Bjorn warned as the first few drops of rain fell from the sky.

"Don't tell me what to do, you stupid bastard! I've taken care of more horses than you'll ever clean up after. They just need to know who's boss! Come here, you!" Roy stripped the reins from Bjorn's fingers.

"Be careful!" Bjorn yelled.

"Shut up!"

Whistling, the horse reared. Heavy hooves pawed the air.

"No, please . . ." Sorcha said. "McBannon, please . . ."

The huge stallion paid her no mind. Neighing loudly, he lunged, then reared again, his front hooves flailing the air.

"You bloody bastard." Roy threw his weight into the reins and pulled hard on the lead, nearly snapping the leather.

The wind seemed to rise. Peasants and servants abandoned their tasks and inched closer to the stables. A group of children playing near the well stopped to watch. People were whispering, others shouting, some even laughing as the fat horsekeeper tried to calm his charge.

"Give me the reins," Sorcha said, her eyes fixed on McBannon. "Slow, boy—"

"No!" Bjorn stepped forward. "Let me—"

"Get the hell away from me!" Roy snarled, his puffy face flushed and straining. "Bring me my whip."

"Nay. I will calm him." Sorcha reached for the bridle, but Roy jerked hard on the reins. McBannon stepped backward, the muscles in his great neck bulging as he strained against the tether.

Despite Roy's strength, the stallion began to drag him forward. "This bloody animal needs to learn a lesson, and

I'm more than willing to give him one." The muscles in Roy's arms flexed. He leaned back against the reins, digging in the worn heels of his boots.

McBannon reared again, twisting in the air, trying to rid himself of the horrid man.

"Who's teaching who a lesson?" one of the carpenters yelled. Loud laughter erupted as a group of men gave up work in favor of watching the battle between horse and man.

"That's it, Roy, give 'im bloody 'ell!" a guard yelled from the tower.

"Yeah, show 'im who's boss!" another guard called, laughing at the fat man's vain attempts to quiet the stallion. The children who had been near the well moved closer to the stables, three boys and a little girl with a smudged face.

"Let me hold him," Sorcha commanded, fearful for the nervous stallion and unaware of the interested crowd. Sweat flecked the great beast's hide, and his nostrils flared into the wind. His ears twitched anxiously, and blood colored the spittle that ran from the corner of his mouth. "He's frightened. Give me the reins!"

"And have the beast kill you?" Roy spat on the ground. His forearms bulged with strain, and the cords in his thick neck stood out. "Bring me my damned whip!"

When Bjorn didn't move, Roy inched closer to the stables, to the whip coiled on the peg.

Sorcha was frantic. "I can calm him—"

Roy sneered. "I'll quiet the bastard!" With one hand he reached for the whip.

McBannon's flesh quivered. Lather appeared on his great chest.

Fear curdled Sorcha's insides. Without thinking, she ran forward. "Don't—"

"Watch out!" Darton tried to grab her, and McBannon kicked hard. The blow landed on Darton's knee with a sickening crack.

"Christ!" Darton wailed to the heavens as he dropped to the ground, writhing and clutching his leg.

"Almighty God, now look what you've done! Get back, woman!" Roy snarled. He wrapped the reins around one meaty fist and yanked hard, intending to reach the stables and the whip.

"No!" Sorcha flew across the ground, grabbed hold of the whip, and backed up. Her eyes were on fire, her heart hammering above the rising wind.

"Let him go!" she commanded.

"Are you daft? He'll tear the damned keep apart."

The crowd hushed as Sorcha uncoiled the whip. "Give the reins to Bjorn, you idiot, or I'll give you a sting from your own strap!"

Darton pulled himself to a stance. His face was white with pain and rage, his eyes murderously dark. "I'll handle that devil." He made a move for the reins, and Sorcha, reacting, snapped the coiled whip over her head. Crack! The leather lashed out and the tip of the whip flicked against the stable master's butt. With a roar, the man danced, nearly dropping the reins.

"Hey!"

Darton's mouth was tight with fury as he struggled to stay on his feet. "Stop!"

"Give the reins to Bjorn!" Sorcha commanded again, the whip drawn back and ready. Her fingers began to sweat around the handle as she saw the rage on Darton's features. He took an uneven step toward McBannon, and she cracked the whip over Darton's head.

He ducked and covered his head. "You bloody wench!"

The little boys and girl giggled nervously.

"Take the stallion, Bjorn," Sorcha ordered, unaware of the whispers of milkmaids and the silversmiths and even the cook, who had stepped out of her kitchen to watch the drama in the bailey.

"God help us," Ada whispered through the spaces in her teeth and she crossed her ample bosom.

Bjorn walked toward the beast, but Darton grabbed hold of the stableboy's tunic. "I'll handle this!" he said, pushing the younger man backward. The horse wheeled, yanking his head with renewed strength. The reins slid from Roy's sweaty fingers and McBannon, sensing freedom, whistled and kicked.

"Oh, God," Sorcha murmured. "McBannon . . . whoa . . ."

The horse was loose. For a stunned second, even he did not realize his freedom.

Sorcha walked quickly forward, trying not to frighten the nervous stallion. "Easy, McBannon, there's a good boy." She dropped the whip as she advanced on the horse, who wasn't moving, though his coat was gleaming with sweat and his muscles quivered. "You're going to be all right."

From the corner of her eye, Sorcha saw Darton grab the vile piece of leather from the ground. "Don't!" she said under her breath as she tried to grab the free-swinging reins.

Without warning, Darton snapped the whip against McBannon's rump. The horse neighed wildly and Darton struck again. McBannon tore away, hooves flying, barreling toward the crowd of children who had gathered near the stables. Screaming in fear, the boys scattered, but the tiny dirty-faced girl stood frozen on the spot, her skin paling to the shade of snow.

"No!" Sorcha yelled. "McBannon—"

Bjorn lunged for the child, throwing himself in front of

the enraged animal. He shoved the girl out of the way. McBannon's deadly hooves came down. Bjorn screamed, a horrid wail that would wake the dead.

"No!" Sorcha cried, running forward as Bjorn was trampled. "No! No! No!"

The horse sped for the gate.

"Christ Jesus!" one soldier whispered, and a woman howled with grief and fear.

The tiny girl cried pitifully.

"Oh, Lord," Leah whispered, running to the child, but Sorcha could see that the girl was unhurt—saved from certain death by the stableboy.

Several women crossed their breasts as Sorcha dropped to her knees to sink into the mud where Bjorn lay, his chest crushed, his eyes at half-mast. Blood stained his tunic, and a jagged rib poked through his skin.

"Oh, please, God, no," Sorcha whispered.

"Get him, you fools!" Darton pointed at the fleeing stallion. Chickens flew, scattering feathers; men and women alike hid in their shops.

Bjorn didn't move. Dread coiled around Sorcha's heart. His eyes were closed, his lips pale. Blood trickled from the side of his mouth. She dropped to her knees and felt for a sign of life. His breath was shallow, the beating of his heart faint. "You must not die," she said, placing a hand upon his cheek. "You must not."

A few drops of rain began to fall, and the wind whipped through the bailey, tugging at her hair.

"Take 'im inside," the cook said, but Sorcha didn't move.

As if in a trance, she reached into her pouch and pulled out the necklace that had once surrounded Leah's neck. "May the gods be with you, Bjorn," she whispered as she placed the red, knotted string over his head. She laid her hands upon his chest and closed her eyes, oblivious to the men who had finally captured her horse, or the crowd of peasants who stood a safe distance from her and yet stared in awe, or the commotion at the gates where Hagan and his hunting party had returned early.

"Save him," she whispered, willing Bjorn to live. He had acted with noble valor, throwing himself in front of the horse to protect the child. He didn't deserve to die. "Please . . ." she prayed, her voice soft on the rising wind. Cold rain drizzled down her neck and fell upon her hands as she touched him. "Don't give up," she said, and the earth seemed to tremble. Somewhere in the distance she thought she heard her name, and then the serpent ring began to warm her finger. With one hand she clutched the twigs of the necklace. "Live, Bjorn," she commanded as the breeze tossed her hair in front of her face. "Please, live."

She didn't know how desperate she sounded, didn't realize how she appeared, on her knees, in the mud, her hands caressing the bloodied tunic of the stableboy.

Hagan watched in silence. He slid from his destrier and stood a short distance away as the day seemed to turn to night. The wind shrieked through the castle walls and rain lashed the ground, but the peasants and soldiers, who could easily have run into the castle or huts for warmth, stood transfixed, as did he, fascinated as Sorcha leaned over the boy. Her lips moved silently with the words of love, her hands offered warmth and comfort. Jealousy cut Hagan to his soul.

Lightning sizzled across the sky.

" 'Tis the sign of the devil!" Ada, the cook, cried.

Thunder cracked across the hills.

Still Sorcha didn't move.

"Saints preserve us!" one of the seamstresses whispered.

Bjorn's eyes blinked open and he moaned.

" 'E's alive! By Christ, 'e's alive!" Ada said, gripping the doorway for support. " 'Tis a bloomin' miracle!"

To Hagan's horror, Sorcha smiled and pressed her cheek to that of the stableboy. She clutched the twigs around the boy's neck, then whispered so softly, no one but Bjorn could hear.

Anger and awe surged through Hagan's blood. His throat was dry, his joints didn't want to move, but he strode through a puddle and called to his men. "Take him inside—to my chamber."

"But, m'lord, 'e's just a stableboy," a soldier said in protest.

"Take him!" Hagan roared, and the soldier, along with three other men, lifted Bjorn from the mud and carried him away. "Call Nichodemas—see that the lad's cared for. As for you—" his gaze settled on Sorcha "—I think there are things you need to explain."

She swallowed hard as he grabbed her arm. "The child . . ." she began to protest as he marched her toward the keep. Looking over her shoulder, she watched as Leah gave the little girl to a slim peasant woman with lank, damp hair and eyes still gripped in fear for her child's life.

"Baby, oh, sweet, sweet baby," the woman whispered, kissing the muddy curls and holding her daughter close to her tattered dress. The girl clung to her mother's neck.

With Sorcha in tow, Hagan approached the woman. "Does Marna need care?"

"Nay, she is but scared," the mother replied, smiling at Hagan as if he had saved her himself.

"If she needs the physician . . ."

"I know, but she will be fine, won't you, sweet?" With tender lips she kissed the child's muddy crown, then bowed quickly and carried the girl into a hut near the well.

"Get back to work!" Hagan yelled at the peasants, servants, and soldiers who were still standing around, whispering among themselves. Several of the women were pointing at Sorcha and eyeing her with either awe or fear. The men, too, cast worried looks in her direction.

Darton, still holding his leg, fixed Hagan with a glare. He'd been right, curse him, Hagan realized. Whether Sorcha was blessed with special powers or not, the people of Erbyn believed her to be unlike any other. His fingers clenched more tightly over her wet arm when he heard the guard shout.

A company of horsemen and women passed through the gates.

His stomach tightened as he recognized the coat of arms emblazoned upon a banner—the colors of Nelson Rowley. Rowley climbed off his mud-spattered destrier. A short, stout man with a fringe of gray hair and a thick beard, he waited for his wife to dismount. Astelle, Nelson's wife, was helped to the rain-washed ground. A stately woman who stood three inches taller than her husband, she was slender and seemed to forever wear a smile.

"If you'll excuse me," Sorcha said, ready to take her leave. "I must see to Bjorn—"

"You'll go nowhere."

"But—"

His fingers dug deep into the muscles of her arm.

"There you are!" Rowley spied him, and Hagan realized that he was still gripping Sorcha's arm as if he intended to break it.

"Welcome, Nelson . . . Astelle."

Darton, limping painfully, joined them. His face was white, the skin across his nose and cheekbones stretched tight. "Nelson," he said through a grimace. "I was hoping you'd be here for the revels."

"We wouldn't have stayed at home, now, would we have?" Nelson clapped Darton on the back. "What happened to you?"

"Trouble with a horse." Darton's eyes flicked toward Sorcha for just a second, and Hagan felt the unlikely urge to protect the damned woman who had been the bane of his existence from the moment she'd stepped into his chamber. " 'Tis over now."

"Good to see you, Lord Hagan," Astelle said with a soft smile.

"This is Sorcha of Prydd," he said. "Nelson Rowley, the Baron of Pennick, and his wife, Astelle."

"The devil you say!" Nelson whispered.

"Glad to meet you." Astelle offered her a smile.

"I, as well," she said, but shot Hagan a look begging for him to release her. Even now Bjorn might need her.

"Perhaps we should go inside." Astelle's gaze slid down Sorcha's muddy tunic.

"Yes, inside . . ." Hagan said, motioning to guards to help with the horses.

"Just made our way through a hell of a storm," Nelson muttered. "Came up out of nowhere. Lightning and thunder, the wind whistling as if Satan himself were screaming." He shuddered and frowned as he stared at Sorcha. "Near scared the horses to death."

"Frightful," Astelle agreed, and Hagan shot Sorcha a hard glare.

"Please, Lord Hagan, if you would but let me attend to Bjorn," she said again as they walked toward the great hall.

"Hush!" he growled out of the side of his mouth. "Your precious stableboy will live."

"But—"

"In time!"

They started up the steps of the keep and Sorcha said, "Other than the storm, I trust your trip was safe."

"Aye, though we expected to be set upon by outlaws at any moment. My scouts told me that there's a particularly nasty band that haunts the road between here and Castle Hawarth."

Sorcha half listened to the conversation, and though she stared straight ahead, she thought of Bjorn and her escape. She sent up a prayer for the noble stableboy and watched Hagan from the corner of her eye.

Her heart turned to stone at the thought of leaving him and she silently told herself that she was being foolish. It had been barely a week since she'd been captured. Outlaws had changed her life, outlaws whom she'd thought had been paid by the treasures of Erbyn. But now old Rowley was discussing the band of thugs as if they had nothing to do with Erbyn.

Hagan opened the door to the great hall, and they walked into the interior and out of the damp rain.

Sorcha told herself she couldn't think of the outlaws now; she had other worries. Bjorn was injured, perhaps mortally, and wouldn't be able to help with her escape. McBannon would probably be considered a wild animal and kept separate from the other horses, and Hagan's messenger to Prydd was nowhere to be seen.

A chill as cold as the sea settled in her heart, and she shivered as Hagan handed his guests to his brother. Darton, still limping, helped Astelle to a bench near the fire. Without any notice, Hagan turned on Sorcha and dragged her into an alcove that led to the chapel. "Meet me in your chamber," he ordered through gritted teeth.

"But—"

"Just be there." Angry fire leapt in his eyes.

"Why?"

Fury pulled his brows into a single, dark line. "There are things you need to explain, oh savior of Prydd," he mocked, his face set in anger, his breath warm as a summer wind against her face. "Things that seem mystical and have disturbed my men. Half of the peasants are ready to get down on their knees and pray to you, and the other half are ready to cut out your heart. Now, as soon as my guests have found comfort, rest assured I will come to you, and this time," he said, holding up her hand so that the serpent ring seemed to glitter in the glow of the rushlights, "I'll not take anything less than the truth."

Ten

Rain lashed at the battlements, and Sorcha, sick with worry, paced from the hearth to the window and back again. Now Bjorn was hurt, Hagan was furious, and . . . the whole castle thought she was some kind of sorceress or mad-woman.

The door banged open. "*What* was that?" Hagan's face was a mask of fury. Suspicion glinted from his eyes as he walked into the room and kicked the door behind him. "Out in the bailey—with Bjorn, what was that?"

Outside, the wind still howled and rammed the battlements, and inside, the air in the room was thick. "I cannot explain—"

"Try, damn it."

Her throat tight, her hands wringing with worry, Sorcha bit her lip. "Bjorn—is he all right?"

"Nichodemas is with him."

"That old man knows nothing. He'd put leeches onto a man who had already bled to death."

Hagan's eyes narrowed. "And what would you know about it?"

"Only that it makes no sense to suck a man dry of the very lifeblood that flows through his veins." She wrapped her arms around herself. "I must go to him." She started for the door, but Hagan was swift, his hand reaching out to capture her arm with deadly aim.

"Do not worry. Your precious stableboy is safe."

"*My* stableboy?"

"I've seen how you look at him, Sorcha."

Sorcha wanted to laugh aloud; so Hagan thought she fancied Bjorn. Fine. Let him think that. 'Twas better than him knowing the truth.

"Now, tell me, what happened out in the bailey? What kind of magic is it that you spin?"

"No magic."

"Then you would not care that Nichodemas removed this . . ." He reached into the folds of his tunic and withdrew the red string necklace.

"Oh, no . . ." She reached for the knotted twine, but Hagan snatched it away.

"Nichodemas sees no need for charms from the devil, as he calls them."

"Nichodemas is a fool. He's not fit to stitch up a wounded dog." To her surprise, a touch of a smile wavered over Hagan's cruel lips, as if he knew that old man's failings. "How did you get this?" she asked, pointing at the necklace. Though she told herself she did not believe in magic, in truth, she placed more than a little faith in Isolde's runes and spells and herbs, and she worried that the stableboy would die without the old remedies.

Her throat was dry as sand. 'Twas her fault Bjorn was injured, Bjorn, whom she felt was her only ally in this castle filled with enemies.

She yanked her arm free, ripped the necklace from Hagan's fingers, and pulled open the door. Ignoring Hagan's shout of outrage, she ran out of the room and through the dim corridors. Rushlights flickered as she turned a corner and found herself at the top of the back stairs at the door to Hagan's private chambers.

A short guard with greasy hair and dark eyes blocked her way. "No one's allowed—"

"Let me pass," Sorcha ordered, and when the man seemed unmoved, she stepped closer to him. "I could cast a curse on your family, tell the gods that—"

"Nay, m'lady, please. I've been given orders not to let anyone inside."

Sorcha placed her hands on her hips. "I'm warning you, let me pass—"

" 'Tis all right, Matthew." Hagan reached over Sorcha's shoulder and shoved open the door to the chamber. Candles were lit and a fire blazed in the hearth, but rain still beat against the exterior walls. Bjorn was sprawled across Hagan's bed. His eyes were open and he slid a glance toward Sorcha as the old physician touched him with practiced fingers.

Bjorn winced.

"Be still," Nichodemas, his bald pate shining in the candlelight, ordered. "Looks as if you lost your fight with the beast," he said, shaking his head and clucking his tongue as if at the boy's foolishness.

" 'Twas an accident," Sorcha interjected. "Bjorn tried to save a little girl."

"Aye, but he got himself trampled in the process." He bound Bjorn's chest with strips of cloth.

"He saved the girl's life." Despite a warning glare from the old physician, she walked closer to the bed. "For your nobility, please take this gift, Bjorn." She placed the knotted string in his callused fingers.

"Bjorn is no nobleman, just a common dung sweeper

who wasn't smart enough to jump out of harm's way," Nichodemas said as he tied the strips and wiped his hands on his soiled tunic.

Hagan said quietly, "He saved the child."

Nichodemas lifted a shoulder, then, for the first time, he seemed to notice Sorcha's gift. "Red string. Knotted in a special manner? 'Tis the work of Satan."

Sorcha shook her head. "It will help him heal."

"And he'll owe his life to the devil. The old ways are dangerous . . ."

Sorcha ignored the old man's warning and curled Bjorn's fingers over the string. "Wear this until you are strong again."

Bjorn stared up at her, and his big fingers curled over the necklace, but there was not the hint of a smile in his blue-green eyes, and his color washed grayer than usual.

"I will wait for you," she whispered quietly, knowing that he probably didn't understand, but wanting to give him some hope.

Hagan heard her promise, and the muscles in his neck twisted into painful hard knots. So Sorcha and Bjorn were lovers. His stomach coiled at the thought, but he watched in silence and told himself that hatred of the stableboy was a waste of time, though the thought of Bjorn wrapping his arms around Sorcha caused Hagan's fists to clench. He looked away from the tender scene at the bed and tried to concentrate on his other worries. The messenger from Prydd had not returned, and soon he would have to ride to visit Tadd himself.

Again Sorcha whispered some kind of endearment to the boy, and Hagan gritted his teeth. Unable to stay in the chamber a minute longer, he turned on his heel and stalked along the corridor, barking at a guard to make sure Bjorn was kept comfortable, though his own thoughts of the stableboy were murderous. Jealousy raged through his blood.

Damn that woman. She truly was some kind of sorceress, the bloody savior of Prydd, because she had found a way to turn his head around so completely.

The steward approached him with news of a squabble between the silversmith and the armorer—some argument about metal—and Hagan yelled at the man, sending him cowering in the opposite direction. Several serving maids scurried out of his way, presumably from the scowl that blackened his features.

He told himself that he had guests and couldn't be bothered with worrying about a beautiful woman with a damned birthmark, but still her image of silken black hair and eyes as blue as a mountain lake filled his mind.

He'd come back to Erbyn hoping to take a wife, to father children, to settle into the steady life of a baron here at the castle, but never had he intended to come across a wild, half-daft witch-woman like Sorcha of Prydd.

The sooner he could send her back to her brother and her precious Prydd, the better for all concerned. She could do whatever she thought she had to as the bloody savior behind the stone curtain of her own castle. Soon he would wash his hands of her.

"We've looked everywhere in the keep. Isolde's vanished," Sir Prescott said as he approached the dais.

Tadd gritted his teeth in vexation. "She's old. She couldn't have gone far." He drummed his short fingers on the clawlike arm of his chair. "What about the messenger?"

Prescott frowned. "He's missing as well. Our men searched the woods and the roads and found no trace of him."

"The dogs?"

"Couldn't track him."

Tadd closed his eyes against the headache that burned behind his forehead. A tic jumped beneath his eye, and he couldn't stop his cheek from twitching uncontrollably.

"There is some good news, though," Prescott said, his mouth curving into an evil leer. "Some of the soldiers talked with the traitor again, Sir Robert. We described the messenger to him, and Robert swears he's certain there was no tall knight in Erbyn with black hair, a broken nose, and cleft brow."

Tadd wasn't convinced. He fingered the buckle of his belt thoughtfully. "Robert's a liar and a traitor, and the messenger could be a soldier who returned from the war with Hagan."

"Aye, but he might be an outlaw."

Tadd sat up a little straighter.

"There's talk of a band that lurks in the forests between Hawarth and Erbyn. The man who leads the band is called Wolf, though no one knows his true name. He talks as if he was once a nobleman, and he knows how to read."

"There are many outlaws."

"But this man rides tall, with shoulders as wide as an axe handle. It is also said that one of his eyebrows has been split, as if from a previous battle."

Tadd remembered the messenger—the way he carried himself, the smirk in his harsh blue eyes, and the curl of disapproval in his thin, cruel lips. There was an arrogance about him, a pride that had made Tadd uncomfortable. Without a qualm, the messenger had disobeyed Tadd and whirled his swift horse through the castle gates.

"You think the letter from Hagan was a fraud?"

"I know not; but something's amiss."

Clapping loudly, Tadd ordered a cup of wine from a page

who stood at attention near the table. "Find the outlaw," he said to Prescott as the boy brought him a cup, "and bring him to me." He took a long swallow and felt the wine burn a warm, welcome trail to his stomach.

"What about Isolde?"

Tadd considered. The woman had lied to him and made him look a bloody fool.

"Kill her."

"Your father—"

"Is away. Kill her, and be done with it."

Prescott swallowed so hard, his Adam's apple bobbed. "And what of Lady Sorcha? When she finds out—"

"She won't."

"But she has ways. She's the—"

"Don't even think it, Prescott," Tadd warned, sick to death of his sister's birthright. "I'll handle Sorcha. Now, be off."

"Some say Isolde is a witch," Prescott persisted. A drip of sweat slid down the side of his face.

The coward! Tadd was on his feet in an instant. "You are a Christian man, are you not?"

"Aye."

"Then kill Isolde and worry not. God knows 'tis good to get rid of someone who worships false gods." He took a long swallow from his wine and eyed the nervous knight over the rim of his mazer.

"As you wish," Prescott said. With a quick little bow, he turned and quickly took his leave.

Sorcha be damned, Tadd thought as he rested the heel of his boot upon a bench. 'Twas the revels and he'd been celebrating for days. Hence the pain in his head. The musicians had entertained him, the jugglers and minstrels had been amusing, and afterwards, long into the night, he'd lain with several women, the most interesting having been the shy little kitchen wench with the sharp tongue. He tingled at the thought of her and knew she couldn't refuse to warm his bed yet again.

She hated him, he was sure of it, but she was frightened as well, and mounting her like a stallion had been a pleasure that he intended to share with his guests . . . but not just yet. For the time being, while she was still frightened and trembling, he would have his way with her, teach her how to pleasure him further, then, once he was tired of her, he'd cast her off to his soldiers for sport.

Just the thought of her caused an aching hardness to swell between his legs, and he could barely think beyond the night's pleasures. As for his sisters, he wished they'd stay where they were. Leah was too pious for his tastes, always frowning down her short little nose at him, then quoting Scripture as if in hopes to redeem him. Then there was Sorcha. She had the gall to outride and outshoot him, and took great pleasure in making him appear a fool to his friends.

Another gulp of wine.

Why not leave them both at Erbyn? This thought warmed his heart as the wine warmed his belly, but he knew he'd eventually have to go and retrieve his sisters and bring them back to Prydd. 'Twas a matter of pride.

Unless they were not at Erbyn.

What if the message was part of a trick to lure him from Prydd, to make the castle defenseless? What if that cur of an outlaw already had his sisters and was waiting to capture Tadd? Worse yet, what if Hagan and the outlaw were working together, plotting the downfall of Prydd?

God's eyes, 'twas all a mess. His gaze slid to a slit in the curtains that led to the kitchens. He spied Mab hauling a basket of eggs into the kitchen. She was scurrying quickly, as if afraid that he might see her. That pleased him and he smiled to himself as he rubbed his member with the palm of his hand. He'd worry about his wayward sisters tomorrow.

"I don't like it," Jagger said, tugging on his beard as he glared at Isolde.

Wolf felt the dissent of the men as they sat around the fire, passed a bottle of mead, and chewed on tough, burned meat. He saw the glances cast between the members of his band. For the first time, they didn't trust him. Because he'd broken one of their sacred rules and brought the old woman back to the camp.

They felt betrayed.

Wolf didn't blame the men.

"Jagger's right. I don't like it neither. What do we need 'er for?" Cormick asked. He picked at his teeth with a small bone.

"She knows the ways of the old ones and she was Sorcha of Prydd's nursemaid." Even to Wolf, the excuse sounded weak, and he couldn't afford to be weak with his men, but he didn't want them to know of his private feud with Tadd. That was one of the secrets that he kept close to his soul.

" 'Ell's bells, just what we need, a nursemaid!" Odell spat into the fire, causing the flames to hiss as he turned the four fat pigeons on the spit and the meat sizzled and rent the air with the smell of burning fowl.

"I say she stays. She could be of much help." Why he was convinced that she would help him, he didn't know, but there was something compelling about the old woman. He stared into her lined face as she sat in the shadows, away from the circle of men at the fire, and felt as if he could trust her. "Asides, no doubt Tadd of Prydd would like nothing better than to find her and take her back to the castle to punish her."

"So what?" Odell asked, his nostrils curling a bit. "The rule is no women."

Wolf's temper snapped. He focused his harsh glare on Odell. "So this time I bend the rule."

The men grumbled, but as Wolf eyed them one by one, no one dared question his authority. He was ready for it. Some of the younger men were anxious to take over leadership—like young bucks vying and butting heads for the right to mate with a female deer.

Someday one would challenge him, and he'd be ready. All in good time.

"All right, I say she stays," Peter, the one-eyed soldier, finally agreed. He oftentimes was the single member of the group who could straddle both sides of an argument, pulling two warring factions together.

The men growled and whispered among themselves, but their conversations stopped when Isolde stood slowly and walked closer, her weathered face seeming more lined and ghostlike in the shifting light from the flames. "I only want to get to Erbyn," she said quietly as her gaze moved slowly from man to man. "I mean none of you harm."

"Humph!" Odell snorted as he stood and swaggered up to her. His face was crumpled into a disbelieving scowl. "Y're just like all women, and when ye gets to the castle, you'll be talkin' to the maids, tellin' tales about yer night with the outlaws. What we do, who we are, where we camp—"

"Nay!" Isolde's old eyes glittered. "Do not doubt me," she said in a tone so low, the forest seemed to grow suddenly still. The wind died, the fire no longer crackled, and even the horses were silent, no longer restless.

Odell gulped. His eyes narrowed on Isolde for a second, and he licked his cracked lips before falling back to his spot near the campfire and resting his buttocks on a large, flat rock where his knife lay. His grubby fingers surrounded the carved bone handle of his weapon, and he hastily made the sign of the cross over his chest.

"Then she stays," Wolf said, uneasy with the situation, but feeling that he could not let her out to wander the dark forest alone.

"What do we do with 'im?" Odell asked, pointing his dirty blade at Frederick. " 'E's seen our camp, and we can't very well just let 'im go, can we?"

"You should have thought of that when you brought him here," Wolf said, his body tired from a day's journey, his mind weary of the arguing.

"Aye, but then you wouldn't know what was goin' on between the 'ouses of Erbyn and Prydd, now, would ye?"

Wolf saw the gleam in the older man's eyes. "You're right, Odell. 'Twas good that you brought him here. We'll keep his horse and send him back home."

Frederick's back stiffened. "Nay, my steed—"

"Is now mine," Wolf said decisively. He offered the messenger a cold smile, guaranteed to put fear into the hearts of many a brave man. "You're lucky, Frederick, to be leaving with your life."

" 'E'll tell the baron about this camp, I'm warnin' ya!" Odell shouted, not satisfied with Wolf's reluctant praise. Cutting a strip of dry pigeon from a small bone with his dagger, he glowered at the prisoner.

"By the time he gets to Erbyn, we'll be gone." Wolf leaned closer to the fire. "It matters not; the message was delivered to Tadd at Prydd."

"How can I trust you?" Frederick demanded angrily, though he was no longer shackled and he was drinking the outlaws' mead and eating their sorry dinner.

"You can't." Wolf grabbed the spit and tossed four small

pigeons onto the stones. He left the stick in the ground, grabbed one of the birds, and tore off a chunk of seared flesh from the pigeon's breast. "But I have no reason to lie."

"You have no right sticking your nose into the baron's business."

With a lift of his shoulder, Wolf chewed the tough meat and glowered at the fire.

"What care you?" Frederick demanded.

"Old scores to settle."

"With Lord Hagan?"

Wolf grinned and reached for the jug of mead. Hagan was a formidable foe, one he would have gladly challenged, but it wasn't Erbyn with which he had a feud.

No one knew of his plans. Odell thought him a common criminal, running from justice for killing a man or raping his wife. Jagger thought him a thief of the lowest order. Cormick believed that he was the son of a nobleman who was at odds with the king. The rest believed what they would.

Wolf didn't care.

But he was interested in Sorcha, for the woman had power, more than she probably guessed. Wolf could use some of that power—as well as a lot of luck. However, the woman was Tadd's sister and therefore a mortal enemy. He wondered if he would be able to hurt his old foe by stealing away his sister.

"You will be free to leave in a few days," he said to Frederick. Before he gave the soldier his freedom, Wolf wanted to learn more of Sorcha and the ties that bound her to her brother. He bit off another chunk of meat and stared at his prisoner. "If you prefer not to return to Erbyn you could throw in your lot with us."

"Nay!" Odell cried. "He is a prisoner—"

One corner of Frederick's lip lifted a little, as if the

thought disgusted him. "Mayhap I will," he said, but Wolf knew the man to be a traitor. Frederick's eyes were dull, as if he was deliberately hiding his thoughts. No, he couldn't be trusted.

Well, fine. 'Twas just as well. Wolf leaned back upon the ground, propping himself up with an elbow. When it was time to set the Judas free, Frederick would be in for a surprise the like of which he had not witnessed in all his life.

Sorcha had no choice but to wait. Her patience was wearing thin as each day the messenger didn't return. The revels were full of merriment and laughter, but she only endured them, counting off the days until she could return to Prydd.

Each day guests arrived at Erbyn. They were always tired and weary from their journey, but dressed in finery and always anxious for celebration. Several young women, in the company of their fathers and mothers, seemed interested in gaining the attention of Lord Hagan, and he spoke and laughed with them, danced with them and smiled down at them as he held them in his strong arms. They seemed to melt at his touch, nearly swooning if he favored them with a word.

Sorcha told herself she didn't care. Though her blood seemed to boil when she saw them together, she half convinced herself he could marry the whole lot of silly girls and she wouldn't be bothered.

She, too, danced and laughed, and surprised herself by sometimes forgetting that she was only waiting, biding her time, until she could return to Prydd. Though none of the men were as handsome as the lord, they were amusing, and more than one man had encouraged a smile from her lips.

Erbyn was festive. Fresh rushes scented with chamomile and lavender had been strewn across the floor, and the whitewashed walls had been strung with mistletoe, ivy, and holly. A fire crackled over a huge yule log, and on the trestle table a large candle, with tallow dripping down the sides, the yule candle, was always lit, giving off a warm, soft glow.

During the day, the gates of the castle were thrown open to peasants and noblemen alike, and there were people everywhere, laughing, talking, working.

Each evening Hagan walked easily among his guests, sometimes with Sorcha, and he introduced her to neighboring noblemen and ladies. Often he stopped to laugh at a peasant's bawdy joke or inquire about a newborn babe. He knew all the peasants and servants by name and seemed adored by most, though there were a few soldiers who, when he passed, cast him looks of pure hatred. Sorcha was sure of it. Though not a harsh word was spoken, there were silent currents in the air, secret glances and tight lips that bespoke of hostility.

She told herself she was imagining the dark looks, that she was reading more into passing glances than was meant. Surely Hagan didn't seem to notice.

Food and ale were plentiful, and if the baron had worries, he usually hid them well. Only once in a while did Sorcha see his eyes shadow and his forehead wrinkle.

As for her, the servants treated her with respect, though there was a new fear in their eyes. Many had witnessed the storm that had appeared as she revived Bjorn, and the gossip about her was running fast and wild through the castle, to servants, peasants, and guests.

More than once she'd caught people openly staring at her, and one of the serving girls had crossed her bosom in fear as Sorcha had passed her in a corridor.

'Twas silly, really. Yes she knew that what had happened with Leah and Bjorn appeared unnatural, and she couldn't explain the sudden rush of wind and rain that had appeared when she'd tended to them, but 'twas no miracle, only a chance of fate. She was convinced that Leah had responded to her voice, knowing deep in her near-death sleep that Sorcha had come to save her. As for Bjorn, his wounds were not as serious as they first appeared, and he was young and strong. He would have survived without her.

But she couldn't explain the warmth of the serpent ring, which nearly glowed on her finger, nor did she understand the rising wind and storm.

Not that it mattered. All that concerned her was that she received a new respect from those who lived in the castle. A few, including two serving girls, thought she was a daughter of the devil, but the rest seemed to think she was blessed.

So let them. At least she no longer feared for her life, and the hatred she'd felt in more than one glance when she'd first arrived at Erbyn seemed to have vanished . . . or was well hidden.

Even Lady Anne, at first distant and cold, had become friendly, oftentimes drawing Sorcha into conversation.

Sorcha's most worrisome concern was Darton. She was forced to talk to him, to pretend that she didn't loathe him, and he, more than anyone in the castle, seemed convinced that she was magical, that she had some gift of healing. He'd drawn her into conversation twice at mealtimes and once after mass. Her skin had crawled during the conversations, which she'd kept short, and it was all she could do not to accuse him of trying to murder her sister. But she'd held her tongue, knowing that with Darton she would have to be careful. According to Isolde, he had planned on capturing her rather than Leah.

Darton was hateful, but Hagan . . . oh, her feelings for Hagan were in such a jumble, she couldn't think straight.

He was the enemy, to be sure, but there was something about him, something powerful and male and commanding, that she found fascinating. Telling herself she was a silly goose, and silently condemning herself for any fantasies at all with the black-heart, she tried to keep her distance from him. But even in a castle the size of Erbyn, avoiding him proved impossible, and the foolish little catch in her heart when he gazed at her wasn't easy to ignore.

On the fifth night since the messenger had been dispatched, they were seated at the table and finishing a course of quince pie, perch, and little lost eggs. A nest of stag antlers rested before them, with long white candles affixed to the entwined branches of the horns. Hagan, as he drank wine, watched her over the rim of his cup. He had spoken very little to her since McBannon had trampled Bjorn and she'd used her "magic" to help the stableboy recover, but now he turned toward her. His eyes were still wary, but not unkind. For the first time he seemed amused by her.

He jabbed a piece of fish with his knife. "You have not told me how you brought the storm upon us."

"I didn't," she said, unable to eat another bite. Leah was seated next to her, picking at her food as she shared a trencher with a lord from a neighboring castle, but she only nibbled at the tasty food and kept her eyes downcast, for Darton, too, was at the head table.

"You did something," he insisted, watching her intently.

"I prayed for Bjorn's health."

"As you did for your sister's?"

"Aye." She took a sip of wine and managed a confident smile. "Truly, there was no magic involved."

"The servants believe that you called upon the spirits of the old ones."

"The servants believe what they want to believe."

Hagan salted his fish, but his eyes never left hers, and he waggled his knife at her. "The wind changed, as it did the night you . . ."

"The night I brought Leah back to life; that's what you were going to say, wasn't it?" she asked.

"That's the way it appeared."

She offered him a smile that caused his heart to stop. Mysterious and coy, her eyes catching the reflection of a hundred candles, she had the nerve to laugh at him. A soft, tinkling sound that should have enraged him, but didn't. She was dressed in a gown of blue silk with silver threads that sparkled in the candlelight. Her cheeks were the color of rose petals, and her lips a tiny pink bud. "Do I look like the Lord Christ Jesus?"

He snorted a laugh and dropped his knife back to the table. "I hope not, or all of Christendom is in dire jeopardy."

Her eyes shined in merriment. "Well, m'lord, unless I'm greatly mistaken, He's the only one who can raise the dead."

Darton, seated farther down the table, turned his head in her direction, and she felt a cold as bitter as the north wind sweep through her soul.

"Something happened," Hagan insisted. But he wasn't demanding, and he held his wine cup loosely between his fingers, as if he half expected her to jest.

"What you saw was God's will," she said, believing that God, either with the help of the old pagan gods or by His own hand, had saved Leah and Bjorn. She was but His vessel. She cleared her throat and shifted uncomfortably under the intensity of Hagan's stare. "Have . . . have you heard from the messenger?"

"Nay." Hagan shook his head, and his eyebrows drew into a knot. He rested his elbows on the table and supported his chin in his big hands. "Frederick is a good man; I cannot understand why he has not yet returned unless he was delayed at Prydd."

"For the revels," Sorcha guessed, though, from Hagan's expression, she knew otherwise. Her throat was suddenly dry and she took a long gulp of wine.

"Mayhap he was held captive by your brother," Hagan suggested.

"I don't think—"

"Would not Tadd want revenge?" He shoved aside their trencher. "I should have sent more men. 'Twas my mistake."

"Perhaps he'll return on the morrow," she said, though her heart was sinking quickly. She finished her cup of wine and felt a little dizzy, for she'd drunk more than was her custom. But the gaiety of the revels and the unsettling manner in which Hagan stared at her seemed to bring on her thirst.

She wanted to return to Prydd, to take Leah back to safety, and yet a part of her was beginning to feel at home at Erbyn, and she would hate to leave Hagan . . . Oh, but that was foolish and disloyal. *Prydd! You must remember Prydd!* Yet when she stared up to Hagan's chiseled features, she could not for the very life of her conjure up memories of her home.

Hagan's gaze lingered in hers, and her insides felt as if they had suddenly turned to jelly. He seemed about to ask her something when the minstrels in the gallery at the far end of the hall began to play a lively tune.

"Come." Hagan took her small hand. " 'Tis time to dance," he said, and though she wanted to back away, she was trapped. He was the lord of the castle, and to deny him would be unthinkable. Still, she felt awkward as the tables and benches were quickly cleared away and Hagan's arms surrounded her.

Others joined in, but she couldn't stop the wash of embarrassment that climbed up her neck as they twirled around the floor. Even Leah joined in the celebration by dancing with a dark knight Sorcha didn't recognize. Lady Anne was on the arm of a nobleman from Castle Hawarth, and Darton, his gait uneven, danced with a woman who was his guest and was easily one of the most beautiful women in the castle. Sorcha felt a jab of jealousy when the woman, in a shimmering gold tunic trimmed in fox, swirled by. Her face was flushed, her lips drawn into a smile, her eyes flashing merrily. Hagan, too, glanced her way, and Sorcha died a little, though she told herself it mattered not.

But the strength of Hagan's arms around her, the tickle of his warm breath against her neck, the touch of his body to hers, caused her head to spin. She couldn't help but feel an inward joy to be dancing with him, and though she told herself she was being foolish, she let herself laugh and talk and pretend that she wasn't a prisoner in an enemy castle. She swirled and let the music play upon her ears and leaned against this man who could be her enemy. He wore a white tunic with a rich brown surcoat trimmed in tooled leather and fastened with metal studs. His boots flashed as he danced, and he held her with a possessiveness that caused her senses to swim.

If she let herself, she could lose her spirit to this strong man who held the power of her life and death in his hands.

Only when she looked up to the top of the stairs and saw Bjorn, tired and drawn, holding on to a pillar for support, was she reminded of her purpose. In Bjorn's pale face she was reminded of others—Keane, Gwendolyn, and Henry. Her throat grew suddenly tight and she spied Leah, smiling and laughing and dancing with the unknown knight.

What was she thinking? Her silly fantasies were deceiving her. She glanced up to the landing again, but Bjorn had disappeared.

"He'll be all right," Hagan said, his voice without a trace of merriment.

"Who?"

"Bjorn. He's well enough to walk, thanks to you, so he'll be returning to his hut."

"Oh . . . good."

She glanced up at Hagan, whose eyes were thoughtful, his mouth thin and white as the music stopped for a second. "What is it that fascinates you about the stableboy?"

" 'Tis only his health—"

"Would you do me the honor?" Darton flashed his white smile and bowed to Sorcha, expecting her to dance with him. Hagan's grip on her tightened and the music began again.

"She's with me this night, brother," Hagan said before Sorcha could reply.

"You have not shared her."

Hagan's mouth curved wickedly and the fingers around Sorcha's waist gripped her hard. "You are right, Darton. As I said, this night she is with me. 'Tis my right. As lord." Without another word, he swept Sorcha into the middle of the hall, and she settled into his arms again.

"Darton has offered to marry you," he said against her ear, and she nearly lost her breath.

"Nay!" *Darton? Marry Darton? Become his wife? Warm his bed?* Her stomach rolled and she glared up at Hagan. "I would rather roast in hell for eternity than marry into the house of Erbyn."

Hagan's eyes flashed and his nostrils flared slightly. "I know, you have more noble intentions. If 'twas up to you, you would marry the stableboy."

"I will marry whom I choose, Lord Hagan." She tossed her hair defiantly. "Make no mistake."

"And what if I decree that you will marry my brother?"

Though she felt cold inside, she managed a thin smile. "Do not test me, Hagan, for the next time I sneak into your chamber, I'll certainly do more than wound you."

He laughed and glared down at her. "Careful, Sorcha, or I might demand payment on that bargain." With a laugh, he twirled her in his arms and didn't notice Darton's eyes following his every move.

The knight's clothes were in tatters, his face streaked with mud, and he looked as if he hadn't eaten in a week. Tadd barely recognized Bayard, his father's most trusted soldier, one of the men who had ridden off to battle with him.

The castle was cold, the fires of the new day not yet lit, and Tadd thought of his warm bed and the wench, Mab, who was waiting for him there. He had no worry that she would flee as he'd secured her to the bed with leather straps. Aye, he'd much rather be next to her frightened warmth than in the dark listening to an old man whose ribs stuck out.

"I come with grave news," Bayard said, his voice a bare whisper. They were in the great hall, alone, as it was before dawn when Tadd had been roused from his bed. Only a few servants were about, getting ready for the day, though some of Tadd's men were lying on the floor wrapped in their cloaks and snoring noisily or standing guard and trying not to doze off.

The yule log had burned down to red embers, and only a few candles had been lit. In the darkness, Bayard's face appeared nearly fleshless, little more than a bony skull. He coughed and his chest rattled. He was not long for this world, Tadd decided, but felt no pity for the loyal knight.

"What is it?"

Another horrid cough rattled through Bayard's lungs,

and Tadd curled his lip in disgust. " 'Tis the lord, Baron Eaton," Bayard rasped, and his lip quivered a bit. "He . . . he was killed in battle."

Tadd stopped fidgeting. What had the old soldier said? His father was dead? His heart began to beat crazily and he had to repress a smile. "What?"

" 'Twas a horrid battle and your father fought bravely, putting his life before the king's, but—" Bayard's voice cracked with the strain "—he took an arrow near the heart, and the wound was mortal."

Dear God, the old man was actually crying. Bayard's eyes were filled with tears and he sniffed loudly before lapsing into a coughing fit that nearly tore out his lungs.

" 'Tis a shame, m'lord, and I'm sorry to bring you such bad tidings."

Tadd forced a frown and let out a long sigh that he hoped sounded riddled with grief. " 'Tis not your fault, Bayard," he said, his thoughts spinning ahead. With the old man dead, he was truly the baron of Prydd; the castle and lands were his. His! He wouldn't have to worry about his father's return; there would be no recriminations for anything he'd do. He could get rid of the lazy stable master, kill Isolde if he ever found her, and marry off his sisters! That thought pleased him immensely. Both Leah and Sorcha would be off to run their own castles, and there were barons who would be willing to pay for young women—old men who were widowed and would like a fresh flower, silky skin against their old, tired bodies. Men who wouldn't demand dowries, but would pay for the honor of sleeping with such young, healthy wives.

For years Tadd had dreamed of being lord. He dropped his head into his hand as if he could no longer bear to hold it by his own neck. " 'Tis a tragedy," he whispered gruffly, "but we will have to move forward." Clearing his throat and blinking as if against tears of grief, he motioned to a guard near the stairs. "Take Sir Bayard to the kitchen. See that he's fed and offered a bath and bed." Forcing a sad smile to lips that wanted to curve in glee, he clapped Bayard hard on his thin shoulder. "Thank you for returning in haste. You will always have a place here, in my father's castle."

The guard led Bayard away before Tadd let himself have the pleasure of a wicked grin. What good fortune! Now he was ruler of all of Prydd. As he climbed to his feet, another thought struck him: He could demand much from Hagan of Erbyn for the kidnapping of his sisters, and if either of the women had been hurt, the payment would be high. Perhaps a piece of the baron's estate . . . a small castle or fiefdom. As soon as the revels were over, he would travel to Erbyn himself as the new baron of Prydd. He wanted to shout and scream and laugh his head off. All that he'd wanted was within his grasp! Racing up the stairs, he took the steps two at a time. Yes, things were going well.

Tossing open the door to his chamber, he saw Mab, half-asleep on the fur coverlet, her wrists bound to the posts of the huge bed. In truth, she was a pretty wench despite the fact that her breasts were too small to satisfy him. Still they fit into his palm easily, and when he suckled from her teat, he felt a surge of desire like none other. Even now he grew hard at the sight of her. Aye, she was a hot little wench.

As if she felt the air stir, she opened her eyes and stifled a short scream. Tadd closed the door with a thud, watching her jump a bit. Ah, he loved the fear etched across her face. Slowly he took off his tunic and hose, and she closed her eyes, resigned to her fate.

"You are in for a treat, little one," he said with a deep-throated chuckle that brought goose bumps to her flesh.

Climbing onto the bed, he stood on his knees, towering above her, his member hard and wanting. "You are the first woman to lie with the new lord of Prydd."

"What?" she whispered, those beautiful brown eyes widening in horror as he caressed her breast and watched it pucker despite her obvious distaste for him.

"My father is dead," he said, his hand a little rougher. "Killed by a lucky Scot's arrow. 'Tis a pity, is it not?"

"No!"

" 'Tis true."

"I don't believe it!"

His grin was evil. "I am lord of all of Prydd now. My word is law."

"Merciful God," she whispered, and all the life seemed to drain from her, for in Baron Eaton she knew a fair man, a kind man, a man who cared for his servants and the peasants who worked for him. In Tadd there would only be cruelty.

With Sorcha and Leah gone, no one would stop him. She shuddered as he stroked the side of her face with his long finger. "Come, Mab," he said, his eyes glowing with hot lust, " 'tis time to please your lord."

Eleven

You want only one 'orse?" Roy hitched up his pants and attempted to hide his displeasure at Hagan's request. One horse or ten, Roy didn't like putting out the extra effort it would take to saddle and bridle the beast. Ever since Bjorn's injury, Roy had been forced to work harder than usual, and Hagan had heard him grumbling to some of the other men.

"Aye. For myself. 'Tis not a hunting party," Hagan said before he turned back to the keep. In truth he was tired of the revels, the guests, the noise of the castle, and his thoughts had been gnawing at his brain all morning, ever since the pale winter sun broke through the clouds. He planned to go riding, and he'd been foolish enough to consider taking Sorcha with him, though he'd fought the urge just as he'd fought his wayward desires for over a week. His lust for her was something he had to control, but it entered his mind whenever he gazed at her and kept him awake long into the nights.

Seeing her each day was beginning to affect his mind. He found himself staring at her during mass and looking forward to the meals, when she would be at his side. He made excuses to watch her, telling himself that it was just to make sure that she was doing as she was told, but in truth, it was because he couldn't help watching her.

She'd gotten into his blood, no doubt of that, and he'd woken up on more than one night with the ache between his legs so hard that he thought he might go mad. Even now, in broad daylight, he wanted her. But he would deny himself. Until he was certain the truce with Prydd was still intact.

The truce worried him. His messenger, Frederick, should have returned days ago, and yet there was no word from Tadd, no sign of Frederick's return. If Darton was telling the truth and Tadd was mounting an army, Erbyn could easily fall. True, Hagan had taken some precautions. The armorer was laboring over weapons and mail, the tanner had new saddles for the horses, the steward had been told to buy extra supplies in readiness should Hagan have to call his men to battle or, worse yet, should Erbyn be besieged.

This morning the armorer had stacked crossbows and maces alongside polished swords. Several men were oiling the portcullis, and a wagon bearing sacks of milled wheat rolled into the bailey. Behind the wagon a peddler's cart jangled with his wares. Near the fishpond, the son of the cook was chasing down geese while his mother waited with a hatchet near a bloodstained stump.

" 'Ere ye be," Roy said, leading Hagan's favorite mount, a sleek black destrier named Wind, into the yard. Roy, glad his task was over, managed a grin. " 'E's ready for a little run, methinks."

"Good." Hagan swung into the saddle and caught movement out of the corner of his eye—a dark cloak billowing behind a small woman who hurried along the path leading to the stables. His gut tightened as he watched Sorcha.

Her eyes were downcast and she clutched the hooded cloak about her, as if she were wearing a disguise. Rounding the corner of the stables, she saw the horse and rider and drew up short.

"Oh! I, um, didn't expect to find you . . ." Her cheeks darkened scarlet. "I—"

"You were looking for Bjorn," he guessed.

"To see how he's doing . . . and to check on my horse." She tossed her head defiantly and her hood blew off. Untamed raven black hair caught in the breeze.

She was lying. No doubt she was plotting with her lover. Hagan's fingers curled over the reins. "Mayhap you would like to go riding."

She glanced up at him sharply, to see if he was playing with her, but she saw no mockery in his gaze. His jaw was set harshly and his lips were blade-thin, but it seemed as if his offer was genuine. Her silly heart skipped a beat.

"I would love it, m'lord," she said, her spirits soaring. She'd not ridden since her flight away from Prydd upon McBannon, and the thought of feeling the wind stream through her hair as a horse raced beneath her was too tempting to turn down. True, she'd come to the stables hoping to find Bjorn, to make him the offer of escape, but that could wait. Would it not be better to ride outside the castle gates, to see for herself the lay of the land, search the forests and hills and roads of Erbyn with her own eyes? She had traveled from Prydd on the main road, but if she and Leah and Bjorn were to escape, they would have to use other routes to avoid capture.

Muttering under his breath, Roy lumbered back to the stables, and within a few minutes, he returned with McBannon. The powerful horse was tugging on the lead, prancing and snorting, trying to rear.

Roy jerked hard on the reins, then danced quickly to escape a sharp kick. "Stop it," he commanded the horse, then muttered, "Bloody devil."

Bjorn, who was able to do some of the lighter chores,

appeared in the doorway, and when his gaze touched hers, Sorcha couldn't help but smile. "You are healing well," she said as she took the reins from Roy and the stable master gave McBannon wide berth.

"Aye." Bjorn returned her grin and touched the knotted string that still hung from his neck. "Some say I have you to thank."

Sorcha felt Hagan's gaze heavy on her shoulders. " 'Twas God's will," she said. "You should thank Him."

"I will," Bjorn replied, but his blue-green eyes were filled with jest, and without words he told her he wasn't a believer in the Christian God.

"Get back to work," Roy ordered, and Bjorn slanted the stable master a hard glance before turning and disappearing into the stables.

"Let's be off." Hagan's voice was hard.

Sorcha needed no more urging; she climbed onto McBannon's broad back and lifted the reins. The stallion's dark ears pricked forward in anticipation. With mincing steps he followed Hagan's steed to the gate. Nostrils flared, pulling at the bit, McBannon was anxious to stretch his legs.

She managed to hold him into a light trot until they were through the gates, but then, with the black horse in the lead, McBannon took the bit between his teeth and stretched out, his long legs eating up the steamy earth, his muscles stretching and bunching in a smooth rhythm.

Sorcha had the urge to laugh. She felt free and wild and lighthearted.

"This way!" Hagan called over his shoulder as his own horse was running full out, galloping along the road until the path forked. Without hesitation, Hagan yanked on the reins and headed through the forest. Sorcha followed his lead, watching as the play of sunlight filtered through the leafless trees and pooled on the cold ground, causing mist to rise. The air was fresh and the forest silent except for the labored breathing of the horses and the occasional chirp of a winter bird.

Hagan pulled on the reins and his horse slowed. McBannon, sweating and blowing hard, fought the bit but gradually fell into step beside Hagan's charger.

"Where are we going?" she finally asked as the road split yet again and Hagan turned north.

"Someplace quiet."

"That could be anywhere."

"Aye, it matters not, as long as we are away from Erbyn."

"Tired of castle life already, m'lord?" she said, unable to keep the teasing lilt from her voice. "Ready for yet another battle?"

"War is noisy as well," he said, frowning. "And bloody. A waste."

She was surprised. "I thought men enjoyed the battle."

He offered her a half smile, one filled with a newfound wisdom. "Young men spoil for fights. They thirst for blood and lust for women."

"But you do not?" she asked, lifting a mocking dark brow, for she knew how lusty this man was.

He snorted and shook his head. "I've seen enough bloodshed. Enough pain."

"Enough women?"

His lips curved and his eyes glinted. "Women are trouble. Sometimes only one woman is more trouble than she is worth."

"But men—they are worth much?" she taunted as the horses continued to pull at their bits, anxious to run yet again.

"Some are."

"As are some women," she said, tossing her head and sighing while the wind tugged at her curls.

"Aye, as are some women." He lapsed into silence, and Sorcha did not disturb him. 'Twas enough to be free and unconfined by the castle walls. They rode for nearly an hour before he turned onto an overgrown path where the ferns and berry vines crept over the seldom-used trail. Wide enough for only a horse, the path wound deeper into the woods, through the leafless trees and into the gloom of the dank forest.

"Where are we going?" she asked, but he didn't answer, and she had to duck to avoid hitting a branch that hung over the trail. She watched his horse's even gait and the way he swayed just a little in the saddle. His hips were flat, his shoulders broad, and his hair near black in the dark forest. He rode a horse well, and she sneaked a peak at his buttocks moving with the animal. His legs, tight against Wind, were long and muscular, and an unwanted heat settled somewhere in Sorcha's belly. She felt her cheeks warm to crimson and forced herself to drag her gaze from his strong thighs. Instead she concentrated on the land, and wondered if this path would be a wise choice for escape—probably not since Hagan himself knew of it. She chewed her lip in vexation.

Eventually the woods gave way to a clearing, a tiny meadow with a stream slashing through the trees. On the far shore was a stone house, long in ruin, with moss growing upon the chimney and the thatched roof having disappeared to show rotting rafters and walls that were beginning to crumble. Stones, once attached to the building, now littered the ground.

"What place is this?" Sorcha asked as they crossed the stream and left their horses to pluck at the weak blades of grass that grew near the banks of the brook.

" 'Twas the home of a witch." Hagan stared at the walls and rubbed the back of his neck.

"You brought me here to frighten me?" she asked, thinking he was teasing her.

"Nay."

"Then why?"

He dismounted. "I know not. It seemed like the right thing to do."

"Tell me of her." Sorcha climbed off McBannon.

Hagan studied the ruins. "Her name was Tullia and she was born of noble blood, the daughter of a Welsh prince, or some such nonsense. She was related to Enit of Wenlock, who herself professed to know magic. Anyway, Tullia was banished by her father for the practice of witchcraft and she settled here years ago, becoming a medicine woman—one who seemed more comfortable in the isolation of the forest than with men and women. People, peasants and noblemen alike, came to her if they were ill, or if they wanted to know the future, and she would help them.

"My mother visited Tullia," he said, finally turning to face Sorcha. His expression was thoughtful as he tugged off his gloves and rubbed one hand over the smooth stones of the walls that had yet to fall down.

"She was ill?"

"Barren," Hagan replied. "She could give my father no heirs, and worried that she was not pleasing him, she went to great lengths to get with child. So she finally ended up here, at Tullia's doorstep, with her lady in waiting sworn to secrecy. Tullia listened to her troubles and, for a few pieces of gold, gave her a potion, which my mother drank."

Sorcha was enthralled by the tale. "And your mother conceived."

"Aye. Ten months later she gave birth to twin boys. Heirs. My father was so pleased, he even gave up his other woman . . . well, at least for a while. But two boys were not enough for my father, he wanted more sons, and so my mother visited Tullia again. This time the cost for the herbs was more, but still my mother paid, and though she did not conceive, she went back yet again and insisted upon a stronger potion. By this time she knew my father was keeping another woman, and Mother was desperate to get with child."

"Did she?"

"Oh, yes. Anne was born the next year, but the birth was complicated and infection set in. Mother died a horrid death within weeks after Anne's birth."

Sorcha felt her throat grow hot. Her mother, too, had died young, during the birthing of Leah.

Hagan's forehead furrowed and his eyes darkened. "From Mother's lady in waiting, my father found out about Tullia. He came here, accused her of killing his wife, and forced her to drink some of her own potions."

"Oh Lord," Sorcha whispered, fearing the rest.

"Aye, she, too, died, and no one has lived here since. My father ordered the cottage destroyed, but the soldiers who came to burn it and tear it down were set upon by outlaws and killed. Rumor had it that the forest was infested with ghosts and demons and that the spirit of the witch Tullia still walked between these old walls."

"Yet you come here," Sorcha said.

He frowned. "I find it comforting. There was an uprising soon after—with Prydd—and my father turned his hatred away from here."

"And to Prydd?"

"Aye." He leaned against the bark of an ancient oak and

gazed up to the sky through the leafless branches. "There has been little peace between our castles."

"Where is Tullia buried?" she asked suddenly, glancing around for a gravestone.

"She was burned."

"What?"

"No Christian burial for a witch. Her body was laid on a pyre and consumed by flames, for her soul would surely go to hell; at least that was my father's thinking. I've tried long and hard to understand him, but failed. He died years ago, and I only know that he could be a kind man or he could be unreasonably cruel." Hagan's features turned hard and he threw an angry glance at the rubble of the old house. "Mayhap we should leave."

"Why did you bring me here?"

"I had no intention of bringing you anywhere. I planned to ride alone. Come." He started for his horse, but she touched him on the sleeve and he stopped short, his expression pensive.

"But you wanted me to see this place. There was a reason."

"Because you vex me, Sorcha," he said, his eyes the color of ale. "Some say you're a witch, others claim you speak with God, still others expect you to be the savior of Prydd, as if Prydd needs a savior, and others . . ."

She waited, and when he didn't continue, she twined her fingers into the folds of his tunic. "Others . . ." she prodded.

"Others claim that you are not the true daughter of Baron Eaton, that—"

She let go of his sleeve as if his tunic were on fire and she shrank from him. "I know what they say, Hagan, but 'tis a lie," she hissed, the old fury burning bright in her breast. She'd heard the rumors herself, knew that some of the servants at Prydd whispered and laughed among themselves over the lie, but Sorcha would never believe the horrid tales. "My mother would never have lain with another man. She was true to my father until the day she gave up her life!"

"What of the rest of the stories?"

"I'm no witch, Lord Hagan; I've told you so myself," she said as she lifted her chin at a defiant angle. Tossing her head, she turned away from him.

His insides turned dusky with want. In the dark woods with only the soft rush of a breeze stirring the branches of trees and the quiet lapping of the brook as it rippled over stones and the occasional snort from one of the horses, Hagan stared down at Sorcha and intended to haul her back to the castle. He took her arm and twirled her to face him, thinking he would push her toward her steed and they would be off.

She gasped, her hair fanned away from her face, and in the instant when her blue eyes met his, he lost all control. Instead of shoving her away, he pulled her closer still, until her breasts were crushed against his chest and her startled breath whispered over his face. She gulped, and the air was tight in his own lungs. Though he knew he was being a traitor to his very soul, he couldn't stop himself and his lips settled eagerly over hers—warm and wet and wanting.

She didn't push him away as he expected, but quivered at his touch, and when he pressed his tongue against her teeth, she sighed, slowly opening her mouth to him, like a bud opening to sunlight.

He held her fast, feeling the softness of her body and hearing his own thundering heartbeat. Lust flowed hot through his veins and pooled between his legs.

With featherlight strokes, his tongue dipped and touched, as if lapping sweet nectar, and a low moan escaped her throat. Fire flashed through his blood and he couldn't stop.

Pulsing desire swept through him and he ground his mouth over hers, wanting, taking, demanding more from her.

She responded with a reckless hunger. Her arms wound around his neck, and there was no ounce of struggle in her bones.

Soft, warm, pliant. His hands spanned her small waist and he slowly dragged them both to the ground. She didn't make a sound of protest. When his tongue touched hers, she eagerly responded, that sweet, slick little beast touching and playing with his teeth and the roof of his mouth until he was blinded with desire. He snapped open the brooch at the base of her neck, and her black cape spread upon the forest floor like a blanket.

Kissing her was sweet ecstasy. He no longer fought with himself and gave in to the demons in his mind that told him she was his for the taking; all he had to do was strip her of her clothes and claim her body with his. Ah, 'twould be paradise to feel her hot warmth wrap around him. But he wanted more than her supple body, he wanted her mind as well.

She moaned into his open mouth when he unlaced her tunic and let his fingers trail against her skin. Beneath the soft layer of her chemise he felt her breast, warm and ripe, waiting for his touch. Her heart beat rapidly, her pulse jumping as he scraped a long finger against her throat.

"M'lord," she whispered.

"Shhh . . ."

Sorcha closed her eyes as he touched her. She knew she was wading in dangerous waters, but she couldn't stop herself. The magic of his touch made her feel weightless, and his rough fingers stoked fires of desire that grew hotter with each stroke of his hand.

As he kissed her, she felt her clothes being pulled away from her body, knew that parts of her skin were naked to the cool air and shadows of the forest, but she didn't care. Her own fingers found the clasp of Hagan's mantle and slid beneath his tunic. He sucked in his breath when she touched his skin.

His muscles were hard and strong against her fingers, and she felt the scars of battle on his flesh, the wound in his shoulder which she herself had inflicted. Though it was cold outside, his skin was dewy with sweat and his breath was shallow.

His eyes darkened seductively.

She felt him brush aside her chemise and growl deep in his throat as her breasts were bared to him. She had trouble breathing and her heartbeat thudded in her brain as he rubbed her nipple between his thumb and finger, watching the dusky bud grow tight, nearly painful with want. New sensations carried her away on wave after wave of pleasure, but she wanted more. He placed his lips around her nipple and gently tugged.

Her back arched off the ground and he caught her buttocks with his hands, pulling her against him, bending her like a bow, forcing her closer still so that she felt hardness swelling between his legs. The dark heat within her turned liquid with desire, and when he laid her gently back on the ground and parted her legs, she shivered with need and flushed with embarrassment.

He kissed her again and she became liquid inside. "I will not hurt you," he vowed, and she believed him as he kissed her eyes, her cheeks, her throat, and moved lower to tease her breasts with his tongue and teeth until she writhed beneath him, wanting more, feeling empty and not really understanding the aching void that seemed to pulse with desire deep within her.

Again he slid lower and his hands moved to her back,

fingertips touching her spine as he lifted her close to him. His breath was hot on her stomach and abdomen as he lowered himself slowly, his tongue rimming her belly button as he moved toward her legs.

What was he doing?

A finger slid down the inside of her thigh and she cried out.

"You want me?" he asked, his breath ruffling the nest of curls between her legs.

"I—I—"

"You want me?"

"Yes." She closed her eyes in mortification. She was behaving like a wanton, a common whore, and yet she couldn't help herself.

"And I want you, little one. So much." His breath fingered up her belly. "Be you witch or woman, I want you more than I've ever wanted a woman."

Why his words brought tears to her eyes, she didn't understand, but when he moved one hand around her waist and held up her buttocks with the other, she cried out. " 'Tis good, Sorcha," he said, his words rippling over her skin as he gently opened her with his fingers, touching her in the most vital of spots, causing candlelight to flash behind her eyes. His hand was slow and sure, and her throat turned to dust as her hips moved with his wondrous rhythm.

She felt as if she were drowning in a sea of warm water, but when he pressed his lips to her flesh, she stiffened. What was this? she wondered but for an instant before his tongue and lips wove a special magic upon her, and soon she was twining her fingers through his hair, twisting and panting, feeling wave after wave of desire until her heart seemed to stop for a moment and she bucked up against him. Of its own accord her body squeezed tight and then exploded. The forest seemed to spin, and the sun, somewhere above the trees, danced wildly. She could barely catch her breath, and when Hagan came to her, lying atop her and wrapping her in his sinewy, sweat-stained arms, she clung to him and listened to the wild beating of his strong heart.

Words of love formed on her tongue, but she held them back as the spinning slowed and her mind seemed to work again. Just because she'd acted like a common wench was no reason to embarrass herself further with silly claims of love. While the act of lovemaking was new and frightening and awe-inspiring to her, no doubt it was commonplace to him.

Despite her embarrassment, she looked into his eyes. Her heartbeat had not truly slowed when he kissed her again, and she realized the act was not finished. With bold hands, he took her fingers and guided her to the bulge in his breeches. His lips found hers and to her astonishment, the desire so recently fulfilled began to burn. His hands caressed her, and she worked at the laces of his breeches.

A twig snapped.

He stiffened and quickly rolled away from her. She began to protest, but he cupped his hand over her mouth and shook his head silently.

McBannon nickered and pricked up his ears. Snorting, the stallion turned to face the woods and his coat quivered nervously.

Sorcha's throat turned to sand. She listened, and over the quiet lapping of the brook she heard the sounds of voices—men's voices, muffled but drawing near. Without a word, Hagan quickly donned his mantle. He strapped his belt with his sword in place, then sneaked to the horses. Sorcha slid into her clothes, her fingers fumbling with the catches, as Hagan snatched the reins in one hand and motioned to the woods on the far side of the hut. Sorcha, heart thundering, followed. As quietly as a cat stalking prey, he led her deeper into the shadows, past scrawny trees and bushes to a spot behind a blind of berry vines.

They were barely hidden when Sorcha, swallowing against her fear, peeked between the thorns and saw a group of men appear on horseback. The ragged band with tattered, stained clothes and weapons strapped to their sides hovered near the edge of the forest before urging their horses into the clearing. Only one man rode tall, the leader of the band, it appeared, for all the men followed him and listened to him as they let their horses drink from the brook. The leader's courser was a sleek stallion, unlike the other horses, which looked like little more than plow animals. But the gray was a fast horse . . . a soldier's horse.

Hagan's eyes thinned on the leader and his breath swept into his lungs in a silent hiss. His lips drew tight and his hand clenched Sorcha's arm in a grip of death.

Sorcha's heart was a hollow drum, beating with fear, for she recognized that the men had to be outlaws, thieves and murderers and heaven only knew what else. She bit her lip and prayed that their own horses would not nicker and give them away. As she eyed the riders, she noticed that one kept his horse away from the rest and deeper in the far edge of the forest. The rider, in a brown cloak and hood, was hunched, perhaps old, and obviously not considered part of the inner circle of the band. There was something familiar about the solitary horseman, and yet Sorcha knew not who he was.

The moments passed in agonizing slowness, and the men, as if sensing danger, stayed alert, watching the undergrowth, until the horses had their fill. Without a sound, the leader motioned his ragged band back to the overgrown path and they urged their sorry mounts forward. The singular rider followed last on a horse that looked nearly crippled, and Sorcha felt a familiar tug on her heart as she was reminded of Isolde . . . kind Isolde.

Her throat went suddenly dry and she nearly shouted. Could it be? Her pulse raced wildly. Isolde and the robber band? Impossible. And yet . . .

She stared after the horsemen.

Only after long minutes did Hagan stir. "Christ Jesus," he whispered.

"Who were they?" she demanded, still certain her mind was playing tricks on her.

"Come, we must return to Erbyn," he whispered.

"Who were they?"

"Outlaws. Led by a man who calls himself Wolf, though I doubt that is his given name. Now, hurry."

"Why?" she demanded.

"Why?" His expression turned as dark as the clouds beginning to gather over the hills. He swung into the saddle and stared at the trail where the outlaws had so recently passed. "Wolf was riding Sir Frederick's horse, and yet Frederick was not with them. So Wolf has killed my soldier or left him for dead." Hagan's jaw clenched so hard the bone showed white beneath his skin. His enraged gaze held Sorcha's for an instant. "Either your brother never got my message, so he probably thinks you and your sister are being held prisoner, or . . . Tadd and Wolf have allied themselves against Erbyn."

"You cannot believe . . ." she said, but her heart turned to stone when she knew that Hagan was probably right. By now, Tadd would have found out that she'd tricked him, and Isolde . . . oh, poor Isolde would bear the brunt of Tadd's vicious wrath. Her insides knotted. If the messenger had not gotten word to Prydd that she and Leah were safe . . . Her world seemed to crumble around her.

"There will be war, Sorcha."

"War—nay . . ." she whispered, but a cold, certain fear gripped her heart in its clawlike grasp.

"Aye," he said tersely. "War between Erbyn and Prydd."

"We must strike early," Sir Brady said, finishing his cup of wine and eyeing the serving wench as she moved between the tables in the noisy little tavern set on the edge of the village. The interior was dark and filled with men who sat at tables, drank mead, and rolled dice. They were a raucous bunch, bellowing insults and laughing at one another.

"Hush—we trust no one," Darton said with a harsh glance at the men at other tables.

" 'Tis time!" Brady insisted, pounding his fist upon the scarred table. "If we wait much longer, fewer soldiers will turn away from Hagan. He has come back, and those who had said they would turn their allegiance to you are now wavering. Like it or not, m'lord, Hagan is well loved."

"Bah! He's a bastard."

"But a kind one," Marshall said, disgust threading through his words. Marshall had no use for men who were not strong and cruel. Kindness was a sign of weakness.

The others seemed to agree with Brady that some of the soldiers they'd hoped to use to start their rebellion were now doubting the wisdom of rising up against Hagan. Sir Marshall touched his neatly trimmed beard with strong, bony hands. "The longer Hagan is back, the harder it will be to wrest his power from him." He was the thoughtful one of the group. The others—Brady, Elwin, and Ralston—were known for their strength rather than their cunning. They were burly men who had hungry appetites for gambling, drink, and women. Greedy by nature, they'd cast their lots with Darton on the promise of riches—riches

Darton could only give them when he was the true Baron of Erbyn.

And of Prydd. For he still planned to take Sorcha for his bride. Her two miracles at Erbyn had convinced the peasants, servants, and soldiers that she was, indeed, powerful—the savior of all that was Prydd.

"I say we lure Hagan out of the castle and kill him. Blame it on outlaws." Marshall's plan was simple.

"Others can't be trusted to do the deed," Darton replied, thinking of his earlier plan and the archer whose deadly aim was supposed to have killed his brother in the battle with the Scots. But Hagan, by a stroke of luck and the careful eye of his loyal knight, Sir Royce, had escaped with only an injury to his leg—the very injury that had sent him back to Erbyn early. By God, it just wasn't fair, as it wasn't fair to be born scant moments after his brother and thereby lose all his inheritance. He swallowed some of the sour-tasting mead. All his life Darton had been forced to endure the indignation of being born second. What a cruel, vile twist of the fates, for only he was destined to be ruler of Erbyn.

"There's a cockfight round back," the serving wench said with a swing of her wide buttocks. "Big Henry, he's takin' bets."

"Ye like cocks, d'ye?" Brady asked with a gleam in his eye.

"Only big ones," she replied with a toss of her brown hair. She poured more mead into the cups. "And good fighters. That's what I look for."

All of the men except Marshall laughed loudly.

Brady tugged on his belt and grinned broadly at his companions. "If it be cocks y're lookin' for, I'll be glad to show ye—"

"I'm sure ye would, darlin', but it would cost ye more than what y're payin' for the drink." With a slow wink, she turned to another table of men and switched her rump close to Brady's florid face. He clambered to his feet, but Darton grabbed hold of his arm.

"There's time for wenching later," Darton said. "We've other things to discuss."

Brady looked about to argue, but caught the determination in Darton's gaze and sat down reluctantly, his eyes following the serving wench as men pinched her fleshy arms, joked with her, and patted her on the rump.

"There must be a way to flush Hagan out of the castle and into a trap," Marshall was saying. "All we need is a little bait—something to entice the good lord to go out on his own." Marshall took a sip of his mead, and his gaze locked with Darton's.

" 'Twill be a simple matter," Darton said, though his stomach curled a little at the thought. Sorcha. He would use Sorcha to lure Hagan into the woods alone. "As soon as the revels are finished."

"In two days' time?" Brady asked.

"Aye, then you can go back to your whoring and gaming."

Brady grinned wickedly, and Darton settled back on the bench, propping up a knee as he drank of the poor man's ale. He'd been restless since he'd seen Hagan leave the castle on horseback. Darton had watched in silent rage as Sorcha had joined his brother on a ride far from the walls of Erbyn. Darton had felt it, too, whenever they were together, the passion that they both so vainly tried to hide.

The revels were winding down. Some of the guests were already preparing to leave, and soon, unless the coward had not an ounce of courage in his body, Tadd of Prydd would ride to the castle walls and demand his sisters be returned to him. No doubt he would ask for much more as compensation, and being the hot-tempered ruler he was rumored to be, would never be satisfied. There would be arguments, perhaps even swordplay. Darton hoped so, for his plan was that while the soldiers of Erbyn who were loyal to Hagan were engaged in battle with the warriors from Prydd, he and his band would take over the castle. Aye, it could work. He waved the wench over and motioned to his cup.

The men were right. It was time to attack.

Hagan rode as if Satan were on his tail, but McBannon wasn't to be outdone and he managed to keep stride with the fleet-footed Wind. Sorcha followed Hagan's lead, watching the road, learning the countryside that flashed by in a blur. They ran through fields, loped across marshlands, and trotted more cautiously through the forests before they came to the road again and spied Erbyn, that vast and yellow gray dragon curving up the hillside.

To her surprise, Sorcha felt relief, almost as if she were home again, as she watched the banners of Erbyn snapping in the wind. But her feelings were silly. Prydd was her home. Erbyn was the enemy castle, yet she rode through the gates eagerly, glad to be away from the outlaw band and anxious to forestall the war that Hagan thought would so surely be upon them.

Hagan drew up his destrier at the stables, and men surrounded him. He tossed the reins of his steed to a page. "Make sure he's walked and cleaned before he's fed," he ordered sharply.

"I'll see to it myself."

"And to Lady Sorcha's horse as well."

"I'll take care of McBannon." From the doorway of the stables, Bjorn appeared. His gaze was even when he took the reins from her hands.

"Thank you."

" 'Tis an honor," he replied as Sorcha turned and saw a deep flush crawl up the back of Hagan's neck.

"Where have you been?" Lady Anne hurried down the stone steps of the great hall. "We still have guests," she admonished her brother, and sent a searching look in Sorcha's direction. "And you go racing off to God only knows where."

"I've no time for this," he growled.

"Lord Rowley plans to leave tomorrow morning and—"

"No one enters the castle or leaves without my permission." To Anne he added, "There are outlaws about. Sorcha and I came across their band, and I have reason to believe that they may have killed Frederick."

Anne gasped and one hand flew to her throat. The color drained from her face. "I thought Frederick was sent to Prydd." She slid another meaningful glance in Sorcha's direction.

"He was. But I doubt he made the trip. Come inside . . ." He spied his most trusted knight. "Royce, post double guards on the battlements during the day and at night as well. Tomorrow, at dawn, I want a party of men to ride through the forest and search the roads."

"You expect trouble, m'lord?"

Hagan's nostrils flared slightly. "I'm sure of it." He started up the stairs, but the guard's voice caught his attention.

"Lord Hagan . . . your messenger returns!"

Sorcha whirled, hoping that all the worries were for naught and Frederick would appear riding his gray courser with news that Tadd was not mounting an army and wanted only the safe return of his two sisters, but as she saw the messenger, her heart sank.

The man looked near death. Wearing only an old feed sack tied about the waist with a piece of twine, he stumbled into the bailey on bare feet. His teeth were chattering, his skin a worrisome shade of blue, and mud covered him head to toe.

"Lord Hagan," the man said, gasping.

Hagan ordered Anne to fetch Frederick hot soup and wine as he threw one of the messenger's cold arms over his shoulders and helped him into the keep. "What happened to you?" he asked once Frederick was seated near the fire, a fur blanket tossed over his shoulders and a cup of wine resting between his palms.

"I was set upon by outlaws, m'lord," Frederick said in a voice that was a hoarse whisper. "Ten or twenty of them." His gaze shifted away from Hagan's, and Sorcha, who had followed the men inside, felt as if Frederick was stretching the truth a little. "They captured me before I got to Prydd and stole my horse."

"Did you see Lord Tadd?"

Frederick shook his head and his shoulders slumped. "The leader . . . a man called Wolf, he took the letter, read it himself, and decided to take it to Prydd. He returned the next day, all puffed up like a rooster, and claimed to have bested Sir Tadd. When he came back to the camp he didn't have the letter with him, but in truth, I do not trust him and I cannot be certain that the letter was delivered."

Hagan swore softly under his breath and ran a hand through his hair.

"Where are your clothes and your horse?"

"Stolen."

"By the outlaws?"

"I tried to escape," Frederick said, his face turning a deep shade of scarlet, "but failed, and the leader told me that I could leave, but without a possession. The men, they found great sport in taking my things." His face hardened in the firelight and hatred gleamed in his eyes.

Boots rang unevenly on the stone floor, and Sorcha looked up to see Darton stride into the room. He walked with a slight limp but still hung on to his dignity. His gaze touched hers for a fleeting second, and she shivered when she saw a spark of smugness in his eyes, as if he knew a great secret.

"What happened?" he asked, his frown deep as he spied Frederick.

Again the messenger had to tell his embarrassing tale. This time there were at least thirty outlaws who had attacked him. Robbers and murderers who were excellent marksmen and were equipped with grand weapons, much more deadly devices than he'd described earlier.

"Think you that the outlaw and Tadd of Prydd have joined together?" asked Darton. He crossed his arms over his chest and studied the messenger intently.

Frederick shook his head and accepted a mug of soup, which he quickly devoured. The hounds moved closer, hoping for a morsel, and several servants and guests listened to Frederick. If Erbyn was attacked, no one would be safe.

Nelson Rowley scowled thoughtfully. "I had planned to leave in the morning."

Hagan's mouth twisted into a scowl. "I'll have my men search the road and woods, but I myself saw the outlaws in the woods today."

Frederick's back straightened a bit, but he went on with his meal.

"The leader is indeed Wolf; I met him years ago. The men who were riding with him were fewer in number than Frederick reported, and less well armed, but if they join with Prydd—"

"They will not!" Sorcha said, tired of all the gossip of her home.

"You know not what your brother has planned."

"He would not deal with outlaws," she said, but even as the words passed her tongue, she knew she was lying. Tadd had no loyalty.

"Ha!" Darton rubbed his thumb over the nails of his fingers. "Tadd is not so pure, Sorcha, and we all know that he thinks the truce between Erbyn and Prydd little more than a yoke which strangles him. He's no prince, m'lady, and I think you know it as well."

"You do not even give him the chance to prove his good intentions."

Hagan tossed his gloves onto the table. "I have ordered no attack on Prydd."

Sorcha wasn't convinced. "Not yet."

"In good time," Darton said.

"And I will go to Prydd myself, seek counsel with Tadd." Hagan motioned for more wine, and the serving maid complied.

Sorcha felt herself begin to smile. "Then Leah and I can return."

Hagan's gaze turned thoughtful. He rubbed the back of his neck and felt the weight of everyone's gaze on his back. "If I take you home, what's to prevent Tadd from tossing me in his dungeon and demanding ransom?"

Her heart sank and her small fists clenched. "You're a coward."

"Nay, woman, just not the fool you take me for."

"But—"

He whirled on her, his fury as dark as a midnight storm. "Don't argue with me, Sorcha," he hissed. He loomed above her, a horrid, hateful beast who would imprison her. How silly she was to think that she was falling in love with him.

"I will not be held captive, and don't even argue and say

that I'm your guest, for we both know much differently, don't we, Lord Hagan?" Without waiting for her leave, she swept up the stairs.

Hagan caught her halfway and dragged her up the remaining steps.

"Don't you ever defy me in front of my men!" he ordered.

"Your men are all cowards like your brother."

"Keep still—" Hagan warned.

But she could not. Instead she glared up at him. "Do you know what your brother did to Leah?" she demanded. "Did he tell you that he tied her to the bed and raped her? That he allowed his men to watch? That he would have killed her if he didn't enjoy the sport of torturing her?"

"He admitted that he took her to his bed."

"Against her will! And the things he did to her, 'tis no wonder she tried to take her life! Don't tell me about your men or their honor. Or yours. As baron, Lord Hagan, you are responsible for the actions of your men—including your cur of a brother!" Furiously, she turned and stomped away from him toward Leah's room.

Hagan watched her go. Her back was stiff as a scabbard, her shoulders braced as if she intended to fight and her hips swung with each of her angry strides. She was a hellcat and a liar. She'd stolen into the castle, lied to his men and the servants. Aye, she would lie to him as well. About Darton. About his men. About anything to get what she wanted.

Stroking his chin thoughtfully, he glanced down the stairs and watched Darton. Would he have raped Leah? Defiled her in front of his men? 'Twas his nature.

A rage deep and black and fierce roared upward through him, but he forced it back. At least for now. Until he could find out the truth. Then, if Sorcha was speaking honestly, Darton would pay for his sins and pay painfully.

* * *

Leah was busy with her embroidery and pricked herself with a needle when Sorcha slammed the door behind her. "Ouch! Where have you been?" She sucked at her wounded finger.

"Come," Sorcha insisted, ignoring the interest in Nellie's face as she hemmed the sleeve of a tunic. "I will speak to you outside." Sorcha found a mantle, tossed it in Leah's direction, and started for the door.

"Where are we going? Hey, wait a minute—" Leah called after her as Sorcha rushed her down the corridor and hastened down the back stairs. Only when they were outside in the bailey where the air was fresh and the men more interested in their tasks than in the conversation of two women did she slow down. They walked near the well and watched fish rise in the pond.

Leah touched Sorcha's tangled curls and plucked a thorn from her ripped tunic. "You've been out of the castle."

"Aye, with the beast himself."

"Hagan?"

"The bastard."

Leah laughed and clucked her tongue. "I thought you couldn't wait to be free of the castle walls."

"But not with that fiend. He's a devil, that one," she said, blushing a little when she thought how easily he could turn her bones to jelly and her mind to mush. It had been so easy for him to kiss her and touch her and turn her skin to fire. Even now, with fury coursing through her veins, she remembered the magic, the wicked warmth of his fingers on her flesh, and her skin tingled with want all over again.

"What happened?"

Sorcha wrapped her arms around her middle and told of their ride, leaving out that which she thought was best left unsaid. She spoke of the cottage, but not of Tullia's magic nor of Hagan's lovemaking. She did explain about the outlaws and Frederick's story of being attacked by half an army of the best soldiers in the land, finishing with the news that she and Leah were again to stay within the castle walls.

"So nothing's changed."

"Nay, and nothing will until Tadd appears."

"And when he does, there will be war."

Sorcha felt her insides churn. War. Death. She saw no reason for the houses of Erbyn and Prydd to destroy each other. Some savior she turned out to be. If not for her, Prydd would be safe.

"We must warn Tadd," Sorcha said, glancing over to the stables, where Bjorn was brushing McBannon.

"But how?"

"We have to escape," Sorcha said with conviction as she eyed the great curtain wall that surrounded the bailey, "and we must make good our escape tonight."

"But Hagan has doubled the guard," Leah protested.

A tiny smile played upon Sorcha's lips. "Then we'll just have to be smarter than he is, won't we?"

"It won't work," Leah predicted.

"Oh, it will work, all right," Sorcha said, though in her heart she felt dread. When Hagan the Horrible found out that she had deceived him, he would risk anything, even the safety of his own castle, to find her again. And when he did, there would be hell to pay.

Twelve

As Hagan stalked to Sorcha's chamber, he told himself that he couldn't wait until she was safely back at Prydd. He was anxious to rid himself of her, for she and her sister created far too many problems for him and everyone at Erbyn. War seemed inevitable, and Darton had offered once again to marry her. Hagan's blood had boiled at the thought and he'd shoved his brother up against the castle wall and told him there would be no marriage.

Leah could be with child—Darton's child—and if she was, Hagan intended that Darton marry her, though that, too, caused him grief. Leah quivered like a frightened rabbit every time she was within touching distance of his brother. Hagan knew what had caused her to be so timid and the thought of Darton forcing himself on her made him gnash his teeth.

When Baron Eaton found out, he would demand that the two get married, or take the law into his own hands and murder Darton for deflowering his daughter.

And what of you, Hagan? Are you so noble? If not for the robber band that had come trudging through the woods, you, too, would have lain with the daughter of Eaton.

"Damn it all to bloody hell," he growled under his breath as he reached Sorcha's chamber and pounded on her door. " 'Tis time for dinner, savior," he said, his voice riddled with sarcasm.

She threw the door open and stood imperiously before him. Her raven hair was braided loosely, allowing a few black curls to escape, and her gown was of some fine silver silk that rustled and caught the light as she moved.

His throat closed in on itself as he gazed at her beauty. With eyes as blue as a summer sky and lips so soft he wanted nothing more than to taste them, she tossed her hair over one shoulder and started to breeze past him.

His hand reached out and he clamped it over her elbow. "Together," he said, and she didn't respond, just inched her fine chin up a notch and waited for her next command. "You're angry with me."

"Me? Angry?" She let out a taunting laugh. "Is it any wonder when you treat me as a child?"

He felt the corner of his mouth twist into a cruel smile and his gaze slid from her face to the pulse throbbing at the base of her throat and lower still, to the sweet bosom that lifted with each of her sparse breaths. "I assure you, Lady Sorcha, the last thing I consider you is a child."

Scarlet invaded her face as they walked toward the stairs. Her heart hammered loudly and she remembered all too vividly how wanton she'd been. As they descended the time-worn steps, she felt a hundred pairs of eyes following her every movement. Everyone else had been seated, including Darton, Lady Anne, and, some distance away, Leah. Sorcha's stomach twisted into knots as she felt the stares, some curious, some kind, others condemning. There were whispers, of course, and she heard a few of the phrases, much as she'd heard before. Holding her head high, she took her place near Hagan and told herself she would only have to endure the curious stares of the common folk and servants of Erbyn one more day, for tonight she would leave the castle forever. And that thought tore her apart inside.

Beneath the sweep of her dark lashes she cast a glance in Hagan's direction and found him gazing at her, as if she were a great puzzle he had yet to solve.

Nervous at the thought of defying Hagan, she barely tasted the venison with spiced corn or suckling pig stuffed with forcemeat. The food seemed flavorless, and she felt as if she might be ill.

When the minstrels began their music, Hagan again took Sorcha's arm. She wanted to tell him that she wasn't in the mood to dance, that she had no interest in pretending to be friendly to him, and yet she couldn't. For if her plan was to work, she had to act as if nothing were wrong. Gritting her teeth, she forced a smile and followed him to the main floor as tables were hauled out of the way.

Soon they were dancing with other couples, twirling in the light of the yule candle, avoiding the children playing games near the stairs.

At first Sorcha was stiff and unyielding in his arms, dancing as if her legs were made of wood, but soon she could not help herself and her bones seemed to melt against him. He held her as if she were a priceless possession that he wouldn't give up, and through her clothes she felt his heat.

He didn't say a word, and yet, when his gaze touched hers, she heard a stirring deep in her soul, and in her mind she saw him as he had been in the forest.

Her breathing became difficult. When he took her by the arm and led her away from the great hall and through the door to the bailey, she didn't protest, didn't make a sound.

Outside, the night was clear, and the moon cast thin silver shadows upon the ground. Her breath fogged in the air as they hurried to a corner near the chapel.

He stopped near the silversmith's hut and turned her in to his arms. She lifted her face to the moon, and he pressed hot, anxious lips to hers. His hands spanned her small waist, dragging her close, forcing her hips against the swelling that was so ripe in his.

She opened her mouth and felt his tongue touch and quiver against hers, and all her doubts seemed to flee into the darkness. She kissed him hungrily and felt his hands move upward to hold her breast and rub long fingers over the silky fabric of her dress.

"What kind of woman are you?" he asked when he finally lifted his head. "A lady? A girl? Or a witch?"

She laughed at the question. "What kind of man are you? Baron? Friend? Or enemy?" Her eyes shined in the pale light of the moon. "We are all many things, Hagan, and those things change."

"So now you're a prophet?" He kissed her again and sighed loudly. "I have told myself that I should lock you in your room, bar the door, and let you sit there until I deal with your brother."

She nearly gasped. Not now! Not after all her plans were in place.

"But instead I find ways to be alone with you, and I cannot seem to stop myself."

"Nor can I," she admitted when he kissed her again, and his hands slipped the buttons of her dress open and cool air drifted across her skin.

His lips found hers again as he shoved the dress over her shoulder. Bending lower, he kissed her milky white skin, the back of her nape, his tongue rimming the damned birthmark.

"Ooh," she groaned as his mouth slid lower, over the mound of her breast . . . searching. Deep inside she began to ache and throb for the want of him. She sucked in her breath as he took her nipple into his mouth and teased the bud. Her fingers cradled his head, holding him close, and she bowed her back so that he could take more of her into his wickedly sensual mouth. Lips teased and nipped, teeth scraped, and he growled against her, his hands twining in the thick curls of her hair.

"Hagan?" Anne's voice swept across the night.

Sorcha froze. Hagan groaned deep in his throat.

"Are you out here?" Again the horridly sweet voice.

A near-silent curse escaped Hagan's lips. Sorcha, dying a thousand deaths, scrambled into her dress and prayed that she wouldn't be seen.

"I must see what she wants," he said. "Wait for me."

"Nay, you go in first. I'll follow."

"But—"

"Please, m'lord. For my dignity," she whispered.

His eyes narrowed a fraction and he grabbed her and kissed her so fiercely, she turned to liquid heat inside, then he released her and turned to disappear around the corner near the great hall.

Though she felt a jab of guilt, Sorcha wasted no time. Gathering her skirts, she ran across the bailey and along the path leading to the stables. She wanted to shout to Bjorn, for she didn't have much time, but she held her tongue, in fear that Roy would be about. Though he usually drank himself into a sound sleep by this time of night, she couldn't be certain that he wasn't lurking in the shadows.

"You've come." Bjorn's voice was soft, his footsteps muffled in the straw. She couldn't see him in the darkness but felt his presence.

"I have not much time, but I have a bargain for you, Bjorn, a bargain for your freedom. Along with that freedom, I will give you my brother's favorite stallion."

His intake of breath was swift. "Go on."

"I must leave Erbyn tonight, and I need your help."

When he didn't say anything, she told him of her plan.

"You need clothing and a way out of the castle?"

"Aye. When you take the horses out to run and graze in the meadow, that is when we will escape," she said, anxious for his response.

"And for this you will give me the horse?"

"Yes, yes! McBannon. Now, what say you?" she asked breathlessly as her heart hammered in her chest. "I have not much time."

He hesitated, blew out a long breath, then said, "I will have the clothes put in your room—"

"And my sister's."

"Yes. You must meet me here before the first light of dawn."

She didn't pause for any further conversation, and though she thought she saw a movement on the other side of the hayrick, she convinced herself she was jumping at shadows, that she and Bjorn had been alone, their words heard by no one.

Holding her skirt high, she dashed across the bailey to the other side of the keep. Music and laughter still filtered through the open windows, and Sorcha hurried up the steps and slid through the door. The noise inside was great, the flames of a thousand candles bright against her eyes. She smoothed her hair and took long breaths, to calm herself. Then, wiping her sweating palms on her skirt, she entered the great hall. Within a few hours she would be free of Erbyn and Hagan forever.

The moon had settled low over the hills when the castle was finally asleep. Sorcha tightened her belt over the baggy clothes Bjorn had stolen from some of the stableboys. The leggings were too long and the hooded tunic would have held two of her, but she couldn't complain. At least 'twas a disguise, she thought as she moved swiftly along the hallways, stopping only at Leah's door and slipping quietly inside.

"Thank God you've come," Leah whispered, her voice shaking. "I don't know if I can do this." She, too, was wearing the scratchy and smelly clothes that Bjorn had somehow sneaked into her room.

"Of course you can."

"But if we're caught—"

"We won't be."

Together, without another word between them, they hurried silently along the corridors to the back staircase. Sorcha was tempted to pause at Hagan's door and slide it open a crack. Would he be sleeping? Or making love to a kitchen wench? That thought was decidedly painful, but not as frightening as the idea that he might not be in his bed at all, but somewhere in the castle, waiting for her. Her throat felt suddenly filled with sand, and the skin at the back of her scalp crinkled in fear. Hagan didn't trust her and would expect her to flee. But it was too late to change her mind.

Leah tugged on her sister's hand, silently urging Sorcha forward. Biting her lip, she stayed near the wall and walked quickly down the stairs and into the kitchen, where the banked fires gave off a thin smell of smoke and a hazy red glow. From the darkness a sleeping cat stirred and hissed, sending goose bumps racing up Sorcha's arm, but she walked carefully along the wall, banging her toe on a basket of apples before she shouldered open the door and the rush of cold air caused the embers to glow with fiery sparks.

"This is madness!" Leah whispered, but her voice had an odd edge of excitement to it as they hurried into the baily.

"Would you rather stay here, with Darton, waiting for Tadd to free us?"

Leah shuddered. "Nay."

"Then come on." They kept close to the wall surrounding the bailey, walking quickly in the shadows until they reached the stables. Their plan was simple. At the crack of dawn, Bjorn would talk to the porter, who would open the gate as he did sometimes to let the horses graze on the grass on the other side of the bridge. Often Roy or Bjorn would exercise the horses outside the castle walls early in the morning, and it was then that Sorcha hoped to leave, when the darkness and dawn had not yet split and they could disappear into the forest.

Sorcha knew that Leah was worried about riding the horses without saddles, but she was willing to chance escape rather than stay any longer in a castle with Darton. Sorcha suspected that Leah had not told her all of the evils Darton had forced upon her, preferring to keep those dark secrets to herself. Sorcha knew enough of the horrors that Darton had inflicted. Leah's torment had been no less than walking through the ghastly gates of hell. For his sins, Darton would be forced to pay. Once they were back at Prydd and Leah was assured of her safety, Sorcha would find a way to make Darton atone for Leah's torment and the deaths of Keane, Henry, and Gwendolyn, if indeed it had been his men who had killed them.

But what of Hagan? Surely if Darton was made to pay for his sins, his brother would be involved. Mayhaps Hagan had been right when he suggested that there would be war between the two castles.

As they sat in the stables waiting for dawn, Leah prayed silently and Bjorn stood at the window, studying the night sky, waiting for the right moment, while Sorcha thought of Prydd and returning home.

Hagan would be furious, but by the time he discovered her missing, she would be far ahead of him. She wondered if he would follow after her and decided it didn't matter. If he chased her, 'twould be because of his great pride and nothing more. He felt naught for her but simple, ugly lust.

" 'Tis time," Bjorn said suddenly, though Sorcha could see no difference in the dark, star-studded sky. "The guards have changed and Sir Nolan is at the gate."

Sorcha peered through the window. Though darkness still prevailed, somewhere in the distance a cock crowed loudly, anticipating the dawn. A few candles offered light in two of the huts, and the kitchen fires were being rekindled. Young boys ran through the darkened bailey carrying kindling and firewood, and a girl was out early gathering eggs.

"Wait." He rummaged in his pouch. "Here." He pressed a fine dagger with a sharp, curved blade into Sorcha's palm.

"How . . . ?"

Bjorn's smile flashed white in the darkness. "A gift from the tanner."

"You stole this—"

" 'Tis nothing compared to the horses."

"I know, but—"

"You needs protect yourself. You, too . . ." He tried to give a knife to Leah, but she recoiled.

"I would not," she whispered.

"No? What if Darton comes searching for you? Would you not like a weapon?" Sorcha asked, irritated a bit at her sister's disapproval.

Swallowing hard, Leah took the wicked little knife.

"Come. We waste time." Bjorn handed each woman the reins of two horses. "Just follow me." One after the other they walked into the bailey, heading slowly toward the main gate.

"Halt!" a young voice called from the tower.

" 'Tis only me, Nolan," Bjorn replied. "With Tom and Jack and Lady Anne's jennet and a few other animals that need grazing."

"You usually go alone."

"But there are outlaws about, and Roy thought it best to have more men to protect the animals, just as there are more guards in the ramparts."

"I was not told—"

"I'm telling you now." Bjorn's voice rang with annoyance. "Would you like me to wake Baron Hagan or Anne or maybe the stable master . . . ?"

There was a moment's hesitation, and Sorcha felt a drizzle of sweat slide down her spine. Though it was cold enough for mist to rise from the ground, she was nervous, her fingers slick around the leather reins.

"As you wish," Bjorn said, his voice filled with misgiving as he clucked his tongue and, to Sorcha's horror, turned his two horses back to the stables. "But Hagan does not like to be disturbed, nor does Darton. If they be with women, they will want to take their wrath out on someone, and I assure you, Nolan, 'twill not be my hide that will be strung from the towers. Hagan, he fancies the Lady Sorcha, the one who calls up the storms and furies and some say is a witch—"

Sorcha drew in her breath.

"Enough!" Nolan said quickly, his voice faltering a little. "Do not disturb him. Gatekeeper—let the stableboys pass." With a shriek of metal on metal, the portcullis slowly opened. Leah and Sorcha kept their horses between themselves and the guards as they began to move. Sorcha's heart was galloping as she kept her eyes downcast and her fingers tight over the reins.

Leah's animals shied and reared for a moment, sending

the gatekeeper into the tower. Sorcha's heart dived. She was certain all was lost.

"Here!" Bjorn, still holding two destriers, grabbed the reins. "Be strong with the horses, Tom," he reprimanded Leah, his voice harsh. "How many times do I have to tell you!" He smacked the reins back into Leah's hands and continued through the gate.

Hooves echoed dully on the bridge as they led the horses to the green in front of the forest. To the east, the sky was turning a lighter shade, and the mists that crept along the ground swirled around their feet. Sorcha heard the sound of the huge gate being lowered again, and when they were finally near the woods, she let out her breath.

They didn't say a word until they were at the edge of the forest, and Erbyn, the sleeping dragon, was still lifeless as it loomed at their backs. " 'Tis time," Bjorn said, climbing astride McBannon. "Within the hour Roy will discover me gone, and the guards will notice that there are but three horses still grazing here, with no one watching over them. Baron Hagan will surely follow us."

They had planned to ride together for several miles, then split up, Bjorn heading north, and Leah and Sorcha taking the road to Prydd. Sorcha helped Leah onto Lady Anne's bay jennet, then she climbed onto the sleek back of a white palfrey.

Leaving three horses grazing in the meadow, they rode carefully into the forest as the early light had barely pierced the woods.

Slowly night became day and they turned onto a little-used road and let out the reins. "I can't believe we're doing this!" Leah said as they galloped easily, putting much-needed distance between their horses and Erbyn.

The plan had been simple, but Sorcha felt pleased with herself. Bjorn had proved a worthy ally, not only in providing their disguises and weapons, but in his knowledge of the area. It was he who had come up with the route to Prydd and had handled the guard at the gate as if he'd been lying to sentries all his life. He'd earned his compensation, and though Sorcha would miss McBannon, Bjorn would treat the horse well.

As the sun climbed in the sky, it was partially hidden by clouds, but the mists parted and it was soon easy to see far ahead. The horses loped until they were breathing hard, and Bjorn signaled for them to slow.

Sorcha didn't question him, for her palfrey was laboring and flecks of lather stood out on McBannon's dark coat. She noticed the lines of strain surrounding Bjorn's face and knew that the ride was difficult for him. His ribs, though healing, were still not knit, and the jarring ride was surely painful.

"If you want to rest—" she offered, but he shook his head. " 'Twould be death to stop."

Sorcha agreed. "I want to thank you for helping us."

"Wait until you're safely back to Prydd," he said without a trace of humor. "Then you may thank me."

Prydd. She smiled as she thought of her home and the happy memories of her childhood. Absently patting the mare's white neck, she considered the conversation she would have with Tadd. He would be furious with her for eluding him, and his temper would grow black when he heard that she'd given McBannon to a stableboy. But he would be pleased that she had freed Leah, tricked Hagan, and come away with two fine horses. They were not nearly as valuable as McBannon, of course, but they were worth much. *And they are stolen. Do you think Hagan will not track you down and demand them back?* She couldn't think of Hagan, not now. Her images of him were too confused. One second she thought of him as Hagan the Horrible, the beast of Erbyn, her sworn enemy. The next moment she was remembering the way he smiled at her, or the feel of his arms around her when they danced, or the tingle of excitement that slid down her spine when he slowly removed her clothes. Oh, she was a hopeless wanton, fantasizing about a man who no doubt, at this moment, would like to strangle her.

They had just turned a sharp corner in the old road when Bjorn pulled up. McBannon's ears twitched nervously, and Sorcha's heart leaped to her throat.

Bjorn's eyes were trained on the road, and he slowly urged his mount forward until he came to a fork in the path. He hopped lithely to the ground and studied the animal tracks, as if reading his future in the trampled grass and mud.

"What is it?" Leah asked, but the cutting glance he sent her stopped further questions.

Kneeling, he touched the cold earth, and Sorcha, who couldn't stand the suspense a second longer, dismounted and followed him. She saw the curved impressions of horses' hooves along with tracks of roe deer and boar. A badger had passed this way, as well. She knew, for she could read tracks as well as any page. Years before, her father had shown her the footprints of the forest creatures, and she'd placed them unerringly in her memory. Also, wheel marks, as if from a very heavy cart that had passed, were carved into the mud.

Several piles of dung littered the road. "Many horses have passed this way, and recently," he said, his frown deepening. "The tracks and dung are fresh."

"So?"

He rocked back on his heels. "An army?"

Sorcha's throat closed in on itself. "Mayhap just a party going from one castle to the next for the revels."

"Mayhap," he said, but a smile didn't touch his eyes. "But these tracks, they come from the direction of Prydd."

She'd already thought of that and wondered if her brother had finally come to free her.

They climbed back on their horses.

"What is it?" Leah demanded as they rode into a shadowy thicket of oak.

"We don't know. Maybe an army. Maybe guests for—"

An arrow hissed, splitting the air and burying deep in Bjorn's shoulder. "Son of a dog!" he growled, sucking in his breath as he nearly toppled off his horse. He managed to turn McBannon away from the attack. "Run!" he yelled through gritted teeth.

Sorcha yanked hard on the palfrey's reins and kicked the little horse hard. The mare broke into a gallop, and Leah's frightened horse was close behind. Their hooves pounded the ground, their breathing nearly as loud as the thunder of Sorcha's heart in her ears.

Another arrow sliced through the air, landing in the gnarled bark of an ancient tree.

Oh, God!

"Run, you devil!" Sorcha said as her game little mare stretched her legs, extending muscles that bunched again and again. Tears blurred Sorcha's eyes.

Over the whistle of the wind she heard men's shouts and knew her little horse would soon give out. The palfrey had been ridden hard already, and against fresh horses, she would be no match. Still Sorcha urged the mare forward, glancing over her shoulder for only a second. Leah was right behind her, and Bjorn, hunched over McBannon's shoulders, brought up the rear. Blood stained his tunic and drizzled down his arm.

Farther behind were riders. She only saw glimpses of them through the trees, but it was enough to drive a stake of fear into her heart.

"Get off the road!" Bjorn yelled as McBannon raced beside them. "Take to the forest and follow me."

Her heart clattering as fast as the horses' hooves, Sorcha watched McBannon disappear into the forest. Leah followed and Sorcha gave chase, though she felt her little horse falter. "Come on, girl," she said as she heard the voices grow louder behind her.

McBannon's rump was only a flash through the trees, and Leah's bay seemed to melt into the woods, but her white horse would be visible, a bright target.

"We got 'em now!" The harsh voice rumbled through the forest, and Sorcha knew she couldn't outrun the bastards.

"Think," she told herself as Leah's horse jumped over a fallen tree. Her own horse, a few strides behind, gathered for the leap, sprang wildly, and Sorcha held her breath as hooves grazed the old log and the mare stumbled on the far side only to regain her footing.

"That's it! Good. Good." She heard another arrow sizzle through the air over her head and ducked low on the mare. The horse was breathing hard, her strides no longer fleet, and it wouldn't be long before she was overtaken. The thought of the cutthroats behind her chilled Sorcha's blood, and she knew she had no choice but to try and hide; lead her pursuers away from Bjorn and Leah, and hope to win this battle with her wits. She didn't think they were far from Tullia's cottage by the stream, and by sheer instinct she turned her little mare in the direction of the rising sun.

Chancing a glance over her shoulder, she saw the horsemen follow her, peeling off from the trail that led them to Bjorn and Leah. "Come on," she yelled at the horse, her voice rising on the wind. "Run!" Slapping the reins against the tired mare's sides, she hugged low against her shoulders, urging her up a hill that the poor beast could barely climb.

Again an arrow hissed by her ear, and another landed in the mare's hip. With a scream, the horse went down on her knees only to scramble to her feet. "You can do it!" Sorcha whispered, though by now the palfrey's breath was whistling and her legs were unsure. Twice she stumbled, and the horses behind her, galloping through the trees, came closer. The huntsmen were not always in sight, for the forest was a shield, but their hooves echoed through the canyons, and the riders' shouts sent shivers down Sorcha's spine.

At the top of the hill, the mare gave out. Sorcha tried to encourage the beast over the ridge and down a steep embankment, but the white horse refused. "You've done well," she said, patting the mare's quivering shoulder. Voices, muffled and savage, floated through the trees. Sorcha had no choice. She hopped off the horse and slapped the animal hard with the reins. The little horse broke into a run, cantering atop the ridge. Sorcha scrambled down the other side of the hill, into the shadows of trees, and prayed that the men chasing her would follow the horse for a while before they realized that she was no longer astride.

She still had the knife Bjorn had given her, and she clutched it in her fingers. "Please let them be safe," she said, thinking of Bjorn with a horrid arrow lodged in his shoulder and Leah frightened out of her wits. Even her mare was injured and might not survive the wound of the arrow that had found her white coat. "Godspeed," Sorcha whispered as her boots slid over the mud and rocks.

Far in the distance she heard men shouting and she realized that her attackers, whoever they were, had discovered the riderless mare. Now it was only a matter of time before they doubled back and found her. She scrambled down the hillside, her tunic ripping on the thorns of berry vines, her ankle twisting as she tried to keep her balance.

In the canyon, the forest was darker still, providing her with more shadows to hide within. She heard the lapping of a creek and stumbled through the brambles and ferns until she spied the sliver of cool water cutting through the forest floor. Her muscles ached, her head pounded, and she had to spit the metallic taste of fear from her mouth. She fell onto the bank and drank huge gulps of the water, splashing some of the cool liquid over her face and arms. Though the day was cold, with winter winds rushing through the gorge, she was sweating from her wild ride and race down the hillside. But she could not pause too long. The men who were chasing her did not seem inclined to give up, and it was only a matter of time before they found her.

She followed the stream, keeping her boots in the water, making sure that she left no footprints as she started upstream. She wasn't certain where she was going or who the murderers were who were attacking her, but she knew she had to keep running. Eventually, God willing, she'd find the road to Prydd.

"What do you mean she's gone?" Hagan's temper turned white-hot at the news.

"Just what I said, m'lord." Ona, the silly girl who had been Sorcha's maid, wrung her hands. Looking for all the world as if she expected to be beaten, she kept her eyes downcast and bit her lip. "She wasn't in her bed this mornin', and I talked with Nellie, the girl who's with her sister, and Lady Leah's missin', too."

"Anyone else?" Hagan asked, a tic leaping near his eye.

"It looks as if the stableboy, Bjorn, has taken flight as well." Darton, his skin drawn taut over his features, strode into the room. "And several horses are missing. The horse from Prydd, a white palfrey, and Anne's courser."

"What?" Anne had been hurrying down the stairs.

"It looks as if the savior of Prydd has escaped," Darton said.

"How'd they get out?" Hagan asked. "The guards were to be doubled."

" 'Twas that twit Nolan at the gate. Bjorn claimed that he was going to let the horses graze."

"Was anyone with him?"

"Two pages, but it was dark yet, just before dawn, and Nolan wasn't quite sure . . ."

As Hagan listened to his brother, his teeth ground together. Sorcha had given him her word that she would wait until after the revels and the messenger had returned. True, the revels were now over and Frederick had walked back through the gates, but the wench hadn't waited until he'd decided how to approach her brother.

Well, now, it seemed, it didn't matter. Anger aimed at his own foolishness as well as the scheming woman raged through his veins. "Get my horse," he ordered a page who was hovering nearby. "I'll ride after them myself. Tell Royce, Kennard, and Winston and a few of the other guards that they are to go with me."

"But you know not where they are," Anne said.

"Of course I do," he said with a snarl as he reached for his sword mounted high on the wall. A fury, black as midnight, stormed through his soul, and betrayal burned through his veins. "Sorcha planned this all along." He slammed his weapon into its scabbard. "She's on her way to Prydd, and whether she knows it or not, she's about to start a bloody war."

Thirteen

"You're sure of this?" Darton eyed the stable master, because Roy was known to lie. A shrewd pig of a man who smelled of horses, filth, and dung, Roy sat on the hearth in Darton's chamber, one muddy boot resting on his other knee, fingers with grimy nails drumming against his leg. He was proud of himself, the fat little spy, and Darton was grateful for his watchful eyes, loose tongue, and easily bought loyalty.

Sir Marshall was also in the room, upwind of Roy and standing near the window, surveying the bailey with narrowed eyes. He showed no interest in the conversation, but Darton knew he was following every word that the fat man spoke.

Roy took off his hat and ran thick fingers through his coarse, oily hair. His fleshy chin jutted stubbornly. "I'm just tellin' you what I 'eard, there in the stables with my own damned ears. The witch-woman came to 'im, I tell ya." His lower lip was thrust forward in indignation. "Look, if ye don't believe me, I'll ride after the baron and tell 'im what I seen."

"No reason, no reason," Darton said hastily. With a nearly invisible nod from Sir Marshall, he reached into his pouch and handed Roy two gold pieces. "Asides, Hagan's already gone. 'Twould do no good."

Roy grinned, and Darton didn't doubt for a minute that

the stable master knew that the two brothers were at odds. He'd chosen his side. Good. Darton appreciated a man with a greedy streak.

"I just thought ye'd like to know that the witch has stolen off with Bjorn." Roy's eyes, deep in the puffs of his skin, slitted with evil intent. "Been plannin' it for days, I guess. Anyway, when I get me hands on Bjorn's skinny neck, I'll gladly wring it meself." He grinned broadly, pleased with himself, and he rubbed the pieces of gold that Darton had handed him between his fleshy fingers.

"Don't worry about Bjorn just yet. Only listen to the gossip and tell me what you hear from the peasants and servants. You've done well, Roy."

"I 'ave, 'aven't I?"

He seemed about to settle in for a spell, so Darton helped him to his feet.

"But the job's not done, now, is it? Not until Lady Sorcha is found and safely back in the keep. So you must be off, with your eyes open and your ears to the ground." Darton shepherded the stable master out of his chamber and closed the door.

Marshall wrinkled his nose. "You think he can be trusted?"

"Nay," Darton said with a grin, "but he can be bought, and that serves me just as well."

It was as if fate had played into Darton's hands. True, he was still missing Sorcha, but she would be found, and when she was, he would force her to marry him, just as he planned. In the past few weeks he'd been thwarted by his brother, but now Hagan was off chasing her, taking with him his most trusted knights, leaving the castle to its lesser defenses.

Most of the guests, including Nelson Rowley, had already left, so the timing couldn't be more perfect. He gloated inwardly at this stroke of fortune. Now no one, not even his sister, doubted his authority, and soon he would be the true baron, for, unless things turned unexpectedly against him, outlaws would kill Hagan and the barony would fall neatly into Darton's waiting lap.

"What if the plan goes awry?" Marshall, ever the doubter, asked.

"What can go wrong? Ralston and Brady are the best archers in the castle. They will see to it."

"You thought that once before," Marshall reminded him. "One of your paid assassins was to have killed him in the war but Hagan returned with barely a scratch."

"That was my mistake. But Brady will not fail. He, like Roy, enjoys his gold." Darton felt more confident than he had in days. Things had turned around in his favor. With his ever watchful eyes, Darton had seen the friendship growing between Sorcha and the stableboy, suspected that she would use Bjorn to help her with her escape. Ever since the day that her devil horse had nearly shattered Darton's knee and Bjorn had saved the child, Darton had known that the bond between the stableboy and captive lady was strong. He'd watched with interest as she'd laid her long fingers over his wound and whispered into his ear.

Hagan had seen the friendship forming as well, but he'd thought her concern for the boy was due to the stupid notion of love. What a fool his brother was when it came to women. Hagan still believed in romance of the heart, in loving a woman until the end of his days, when it was painfully obvious to Darton that women were simply put on the world to service men and bear their children. Only once in a long while did a woman come along who was more than a warm body on which to rut.

Sorcha of Prydd was such a woman. Because of her special powers. That she was beautiful meant nothing. The fact that his fingers ached to strip away her clothes and touch her in the most intimate of places wasn't in and of itself so all-compelling. But a woman who had the power to raise the dead, to heal the wounded, to cause a storm to rise from a listless wind; now, that was a woman worth binding oneself to. Her other attributes would give him much pleasure, but 'twas her power that seduced him. Oh, to unleash that power on the world, to use it for his own gain. Darton's mouth fairly watered at the thought. Kings had been crowned for less.

Clouds blocked the sun, but the cold that cut through Hagan's surcoat and mantle had nothing to do with the raw January wind that whistled through the canyon. His chill came from within. From fear. From the knowledge that out here somewhere in these damp, gloomy hills, Sorcha was riding.

He hoped she'd returned to Prydd safely, but his fingers tightened over the reins as he thought of the outlaws who prowled these woods. Many of his guests during the Christmas revels had told stories of being attacked on the less-traveled roads. The noblemen had all lived to tell their tales and mayhap they had embellished the truth, heightening the excitement, but several knights had been killed, two women raped, a peasant beaten near to death for his cart of milled wheat.

If Sorcha had managed to get herself safely to the walls of Prydd, there might possibly be war, but at least she would be secure, and her safety, he discovered, was more important than the threat of battle.

Tadd of Prydd was not known for his bravery, and unless his pride was stretched thin, Hagan suspected he could be bought. If not, there would be war.

If Sorcha or Leah were taken by outlaws, there would be war.

If the women remained his prisoners, there would be war.

But it mattered not. As long as they were safe. He sent up a prayer for their safety when the first arrow struck. Thwack! It pierced the tough bark of a yew tree. His horse reared. The air whistled and arrows rained. Thwack! Thwack! Thwack!

Holding on to the reins in one hand, Hagan drew his sword.

His men scattered through the woods.

Another arrow screamed past his ear.

"Bloody Christ!"

With an agonizing wail, Jacob, one of his men, fell from his horse. Sir Benjamin stopped to help and was felled as well.

Hagan yanked hard on the reins, guiding Wind into the woods, searching the leafless cover of brambles and vines, squinting in the darkness. The two men were dead, two trusted knights, and his heart ached. He could not see his attackers, yet they were there in the woods, waiting, suddenly silent, their weapons, no doubt, at ready.

An eerie breeze rattled the branches of the trees overhead. The horses pranced nervously, coats shiny with sweat, eyes white-rimmed and wild.

Silently Hagan motioned to his men, spreading his arms and telling them without words to split into two groups in hopes of surrounding the attackers. The men did as they were bid, with Hagan leading one group and Kennard leading the other. Silently they moved through the black-barked trees, ears straining, mouths spitless.

Another arrow zinged past Hagan's head, and still another. Kennard yelped as one of the deadly missiles ripped through his leggings. "God's eyes," he growled, yanking the damned arrow from his leg as he fell to the ground. Blood oozed up from the wound as more arrows screamed through the air.

"I'll get him," Winston said, and Hagan, knowing that he had to face his attackers, to unmask the men who were trying to kill him, agreed.

"Put him on his horse, get Jacob and Ben as well, then return, all of you, to Erbyn and wait for me."

"Nay, we will not leave you—"

"And find the others!" Hagan ordered, his voice harsh. He would accept nothing less than complete obedience. "Tell Kennard to take his men and return as well."

"But—"

"The outlaws will think I've gone with you. Now, go, before they find us."

"I will not leave you," Winston said, as Hagan sheathed his sword and dismounted.

Angrily, Hagan grabbed him by the front of his hauberk, the mail rattling between his fingers. His face grew fierce. "'Tis an order, Sir Winston. Do as I say."

"I cannot—"

"You will, Winston!" Hagan growled. Another arrow sizzled through the air, and Hagan's nostrils flared with impatience. "Now!" He didn't wait for his command to be answered, and took up the reins of his horse. He swung into the saddle and turned in to the deepest woods, through the shadows, racing against the faceless forest murderers who dared attack him. Gritting his teeth, he yanked suddenly on the reins, turning in to a gully where a creek washed over smooth stones. With the noise of the brook as his cover, he rode back in the direction from which he'd come, the horse wading through the water. Hagan held his bow at ready, in one hand, and his dagger, hidden in his boot, pressed cold and deadly against his leg. He hoped to come up behind those who had ambushed him, grab the leader by his hair, and press a knife to the black-heart's throat. 'Twould be sweet vengeance.

Carefully he picked his way through the trees, pausing every few steps to listen, hoping to hear the quiet jangle of a bridle, the clearing of a throat, the plop of a heavy destrier's hoof in the mud. But the noises and the men seemed to have vanished as quickly as they had come. He heard no shouts of victory, so he hoped that his men had been able to elude their attackers and return to Erbyn safely.

He rode along the creek bed when he noticed the footprints that appeared on the edge of the shore. Not often, but once in a while, as if someone had purposely tried to keep his tracks hidden, an impression of a boot was visible.

Hagan jumped down from his steed and touched the mud. The tracks were fresh; whoever he was following had been here not long before. A cruel smile played upon his lips. No doubt he'd found one of the outlaws. Who else would wander through this dense part of the forest? His fingers tightened around his bow as he walked the horse forward. Soon he would get some answers. Maybe then he'd learn of Sorcha. His heart twisted at the thought, for even now she might be in the hands of the outlaws. Would they treat her as a lady? Ransom her, but not harm her? Or would they be captivated by her beauty and, having not been with women in a long while, torture her and force her to lie with them?

His teeth gnashed together and he swore on his very life that if she was harmed, he would return that pain to her captors a hundredfold and they would beg for his mercy before he killed them slowly one by one.

It was fitting that he was in the woods near Tullia's cottage, he thought. If needs be, he could rest and find shelter in the stone house, sharing it with the rats and vermin and ghosts of witches who, some claimed, lived within the crumbling walls.

He circled up the hillside again, but found no one lurking in the forest, no sign of Sorcha nor the outlaws who had attacked him. He rode for several hours until what little sunlight there had been filtered away in the evening gloom.

Silently praying that Sorcha and her small band of rebels had made it to the gates of Prydd and were now safely tucked within the thick stone walls, he rode through the gorge. He had almost convinced himself that she was certainly fine when he came upon the horse—a white palfrey that had been stolen from the stables of Erbyn. The hairs lifted on the back of his neck as he walked up to the animal. Covered with mud, the mare had been through much. There was an arrow in her haunch and dried blood on her matted coat.

Hagan felt as if his world had stopped. They'd been captured or killed. He knew it as certainly as he knew his own name. Bloody Christ, what a waste. Grief swallowed him and he felt as if his soul were being ripped from his body. "Sorcha," he whispered, his eyes hot.

He tore the arrow from the mare's hip, and she squealed; rearing back, blood oozing again.

Hagan whispered to her and held on to the reins, but she didn't trust him and her eyes were wild as he led her behind Wind. Night closed around him, and the forest became so dark, he could barely see. He had no choice but to follow the stream and hope to find shelter.

"There is death in the forest." The old woman's voice was sharp as a crow's caw and caused his skin to prickle in fear.

"Death? Whose?" Wolf asked as they made camp for the night. They'd had to keep moving, for surely by now Frederick had made his way back to Erbyn, and Hagan had sent out his soldiers. Wolf wasn't worried about the warriors from Erbyn, he was more concerned with Prydd and Tadd's reaction to the letter.

Wolf wanted just one chance at Eaton's son.

" 'Tis not clear," she said, obviously vexed. Isolde sketched upon the ground, using a sharp stick and reading her own scratches as if they were the very words of God. She muttered to herself, cast some herbs into the wind, and frowned at her marks in the mud.

"Surely not my death," Wolf said, not concerned. It mattered not a lot whether he lived or died, though he would like to finish a few deeds before he crossed to the other side, whatever that might be. Mayhap there was a God; then again, mayhap not. He wasn't certain, and he was sure if there was a heaven and a hell, he would be more likely to enter through gates of brimstone and fire rather than gold and splendor. He hadn't been a saint, but he wasn't about to change his ways. Not when vengeance against Tadd was at hand.

The old scar splicing his brow seemed to tingle, and he scratched at his beard.

"You are too stubborn to die," Isolde said. Biting her lip, she mumbled something in the words of the old ones, the language of the Welsh of which he understood little.

He felt a gasp of wind against the back of his neck, though the air was still. Turning, he half expected a beast with breath as cold as ice to be standing behind him, but there was no one near him. Nothing stirred.

"What of Sorcha?" he asked finally, for he knew she was on the old woman's mind.

"I wish I knew," Isolde said, and stared up at the black sky. A few billowing clouds moved across the half moon, and in the darkness Wolf saw lines of despair and worry deepen upon Isolde's forehead. "I fear she is lost."

"Lost?"

"Aye."

"Is she not at Erbyn?"

Isolde rubbed her fingers together, as if they itched. Closing her eyes, she lifted her face to the pale light of the moon. "She is alone and afraid, though she pretends not to be. She is hiding in a place of great power and waits for the dawn."

"What will happen then?"

The old woman's fingers curled into fists so tight the knuckles bleached her old skin white. She trembled slightly, as if a shaft of fear sliced through her. "She is in danger."

Wolf took a step closer. "From whom?"

The old face wrinkled. "I know not."

"Hagan?"

One of Isolde's arms began to shake more violently. "Nay. The brother."

"Tadd?" Wolf asked, his hatred of his old enemy turning in his stomach like a snake shedding its skin.

"Nay . . ." Her other arm shook as well. " 'Tis the brother of Hagan who would destroy her."

"Darton." Wolf's lips thinned as he stared at the old woman. Was she to be believed? Her eyes were round with fear, her frail body spent from looking into the mirror of the future, and yet she could be just an old woman, one who wanted to fool him or one whose mind was already half-gone.

Whichever she was, Wolf could take no chances. Sorcha of Prydd was much too valuable.

* * *

Sorcha rested her back against the damp wall. Her entire body ached, and muscles she hadn't known existed throbbed from her hours on the horse, the scramble down the hillside, and long walk in the icy water of the stream.

Her feet were numb with the cold, and she huddled in a corner of the old house, hoping to sleep until morning, when she could set off on foot toPrydd. She prayed that Leah and Bjorn had escaped the huntsmen, whoever they were, but fear was her constant and only companion.

The thought that even now Leah might be captured worried her. Had she saved her sister from the evils of Erbyn only to lure her into more danger, where Hagan didn't rule and couldn't protect her? Somehow, through any means possible, she had to save Leah. If she wasn't dead already. Oh, Lord, surely she couldn't be responsible for more deaths, she thought desperately. Keane, Henry, and Gwendolyn were more than enough to bear in her heart, but Leah and Bjorn as well . . .

Tears filled her eyes and she blinked them back. This was no time to cry. This was time to plot how to find the men who had attacked them. She thought they were part of the robber band she and Hagan had seen earlier, but she hadn't noticed the leader, nor had she seen Frederick's horse. However, she hadn't spent a lot of time looking over her shoulder.

Somewhere in the faulty rafters an owl, or other roosting bird perhaps, flapped its wings loudly, and she held her cloak around her more tightly. She shivered and closed her eyes, only to open them again at the noise. The scrape of a boot.

Heart in her throat, she reached for her dagger, but cowered silently in the corner, hoping whoever was outside would pass. Her heart stilled and she swallowed against a throat as dry as winter leaves. Fear tasted like metal in her mouth as she saw him enter, a big figure, dark and tall, with wide shoulders and long legs.

Despite the cold, her hands began to sweat as her fingers curled over the hilt of her knife. She hardly dared breathe and stared in awe as he dropped his sword on dirt that had once been the floor. Biting her lip, she watched him take something from a pouch, then leave. Her stomach rumbled at the thought of food, and yet she didn't move. Whatever was in the pouch would have to stay there for a while.

He returned with sticks, and her heart dropped clear to her knees. He was going to build a fire! Though she longed for the warmth of flames, she would be discovered in the glow of the blaze. For all she knew, this man could be one of the men who had chased her down, or if not, the light from the fire would attract her enemies.

She had to escape or stop him.

He placed the bundle of sticks in the hearth, then worked with his flint.

Sorcha barely dared breathe as she slowly advanced. His back was to her, and the distance was not great, and he seemed absorbed in his task, so she stepped forward, her dagger raised, her eyes centered on the back of his neck. She'd grab him there, fling herself onto his shoulders, and lay her blade at his throat. If he valued his life, he wouldn't dare move. She could then tie him, rob him of whatever food he had with him, steal his horse, and be off.

One more step. She sprang, and at that moment he turned, grabbing her around the middle with one arm and capturing her upraised wrist with the other.

"Oof!"

"Damn you to hell," he roared, and she nearly laughed aloud as she recognized his booming voice.

"Lord Hagan?"

"Bloody Christ. Sorcha?" Was there relief and joy in his voice? "By the gods, I found you!" His arms tightened possessively around her, and suddenly his lips captured hers. He kissed her wildly, as if he couldn't stop, and she clung to him, refusing to give way to the hot tears of relief that burned against her eyelids. Hot, hungry, breathless kisses that didn't stop. The warmth of his body invaded hers and she sagged against him.

His voice was rough. "I thought I'd never see you again."

"I guess, m'lord, you're not that lucky."

He snorted a laugh, but his arms didn't loosen, and when he pressed his lips to her grimy forehead, she wanted to melt inside, so gentle was the kiss. "Tonight I feel as if the fates have cast good fortune to me. I thought you might be dead."

She shuddered thinking how close he was to the truth. Her teeth chattered and he held her tight again. "You must tell me what has happened." Then, as if suddenly realizing that she was chilled to the bone, he said, "Here, talk while I build a fire."

Relieved, she settled on one of the stones that had fallen from the walls and told him of the attack.

"I warned you not to leave the castle," he said with a sigh. "Yet you disobeyed me, turned the stableboy against me, stole my horses with the intention of running back to Prydd and starting a damned war."

"I do not think—"

" 'Tis the problem. Sometimes you act before you think." He rubbed the flint, frowning deeply as he tried to start a spark.

"You were keeping me prisoner."

"I was only waiting until I'd talked with Tadd."

"Which might have been a long while." Finally a spark

sizzled and caught on some dry moss. Carefully he set the burning ember atop some twigs in the fire.

"You needs learn to be patient," he reprimanded as the flames crackled against the dry wood. Golden light reflected on the decaying walls.

"Think you not that our fire will attract the huntsmen?"

" 'Tis too late. They have already made their own camp," he said. "Asides, no one comes here. 'Tis rumored to be haunted."

"By Tullia?"

"Aye."

"But you are not afraid?"

He snorted in contempt. "Were it not for Tullia, I would not have been conceived. I feared her not alive, so if her spirit still lingers, I doubt she will do me harm." He cast a glance over his shoulder and his gaze settled upon her. Deep in the pit of her stomach something warm and wanton turned over. "Come closer. You're wet. Warm yourself by the fire and tell me where are Bjorn and Leah."

She sighed and shook her head. Dread settled in her soul. "I know not," she admitted, her eyes clouding over as she wondered where they were.

"Think you they were captured?"

Lifting a shoulder, she stared into the growing fire and her teeth began to chatter. "I pray not."

The wind whistled through the open rafters, and she shivered.

"Take off your clothes."

"What?" She couldn't believe her ears. *Now* he wanted to lie with her?

"Dry your boots and leggings by the fire." He unclasped his mantle, which was only slightly damp. "Wear this. 'Tis long enough for you to use as a wrap until your clothes dry."

She thought of undressing in front of him, and the idea was not unappealing, but she shook her head. "Nay, I cannot . . ."

His fingers tightened into fists and he inched closer until his face was so near, his breath was warm and angry against her skin. A furious pulse jumped in the side of his neck. "You disobeyed me and tricked my guards so that you could leave the castle. Like a common thief, you stole my horses. I've spent the day looking for you, and two good men may have given up their lives in my quest, while another has an arrow lodged in his leg. Leah and Bjorn could be captured or killed—"

She shivered, biting her lip.

"—all because you were too stubborn to listen to me." His words were fierce and seemed to ring through the forest, though he spoke in a rough whisper. "For once, you bloody savior of Prydd, you will do as you're ordered, or by the gods, I'll strip you myself!" He swept the mantle off his shoulders and held it out to her.

With shaking fingers she took the fine wool cloth and then turned her back, quickly working out of her boots and leggings and tunic. She used the large mantle as a shield, to hide her nakedness, but she could feel his eyes upon her back and she blushed deeply.

"That's better," he said, his voice low and silky when she was finished. A satisfied grin slashed white in the darkness and she felt wanton, like a common strumpet. Without saying a word, she placed her wet clothes in front of the fire, watching the steam rise from the damp fabric.

Hagan kicked off his boots and set them next to hers. The remains of the cottage walls seemed to close around them. She half expected soldiers or outlaws to be drawn like moths to the fire, but no one appeared.

"Come," he said softly, "you need sleep." He patted the ground next to him.

"I'll stay awake."

" 'Tis foolish. Come over here."

"Really, I—"

"Sorcha." His voice was more harsh. "Come lie beside me. For warmth. I promise that I won't harm you." His eyes were dark but sincere.

She hesitated, knowing that being alone with him was dangerous enough, but pressing her body against his with only the mantle separating them . . . 'twas madness. Her skin tingled as she remembered the other times she'd been with him, how her traitorous body had quivered for his touch, how his kisses had ignited secret dark fires deep within her, how she'd been so willing to give herself to him. 'Twould be better to freeze to death.

"Come here." His expression had turned harsh, and she, arguing with herself, slid closer to him. He wrapped an arm around her, holding her body close to his. "Sleep. Morning will come soon enough."

"I can't—"

"For the love of God, close your eyes and quit arguing," he growled, yanking her closer still. She realized then that he wasn't going to kiss her, that he had no intention of trying to claim her body with his, and she felt a tiny shaft of disappointment pierce her heart.

She did as she was bid, snuggling closer to him, resting her head on his chest, and closing her eyes. The wool mantle scratched her skin when she moved, but along with the heat of Hagan's body, provided warmth. The smell of him invaded her nostrils, leather and smoke, mud and rainwater. All male and so, so, hard. With a yawn she felt sleep overtake her and wondered why this crumbling haunted house located in the middle of a forest inhabited by outlaws felt so safe.

All his life, Hagan had kept his code of honor concerning women. He enjoyed women, dreamed of women, and had lain with more than he would like to remember. But he'd never taken a woman by force, nor had he tricked one into sleeping with him. When a lady said no, he didn't argue and left. His need for sex had always been strong, but he'd never allowed himself to lose his emotions and had always kept his passion in check.

Losing one's control, even while in the throes of lust, could be a death sentence. Never had he lost his heart and his self-control. No woman had touched him to his very soul.

Until now. The feelings he had for Sorcha, the savage desire that swept through his blood like a desert storm, was tenfold to the passion he'd ever felt before. Holding Sorcha so close, listening to the gentle rhythm of her breathing, sensing the steady knocking of her heart, having her pressed so intimately against him, caused fire to burn through his veins. The swelling in his groin was painful, and though he tried to ignore it and hoped that the hard ache would disappear, it didn't. As the minutes dragged into hours, he tried to stay alert, to listen to the sounds of the night, to be at the ready should anyone stop by the tumbledown cottage. But as each second slowly passed, her warmth, the deep lilac scent of her hair, the gentle whisper of her breath across his chest, brought images to his mind that he couldn't dislodge. He remembered the first night when he had nearly forced her into submission, when she'd bargained with her body, and times thereafter when her kisses, sweet and innocent, had turned lusty and wanton. How jealous he'd been of Bjorn . . . God's eyes, she'd turned his thinking all around.

She moaned low in her throat and nestled against him, so that her black hair rubbed against his neck. His gut tightened, and the lust burning through his body turned to liquid heat. He gritted his teeth and tried to think of the coming day and how they would have to return to Erbyn for more soldiers before giving chase to the faceless enemy in the woods, but even as he concentrated, she moved again, her small hand touching the base of his throat. His wayward manhood stiffened tighter still.

Somewhere near dawn, she stirred, and blinking in confusion, she opened those glorious blue eyes to stare at him. The smile that was forming on her lips froze and she grew rigid for an instant before memory assailed her.

When she tried to pull away from him, he couldn't stop himself, but kissed her, long and hard.

Sorcha felt his powerful arms surround her and the sweet pressure of his lips on hers. Her own mouth opened and his tongue slid gently between her teeth, touching and probing, creating feelings within her as magical as this crumbling old building.

A gray light began to invade the forest, and mist rose toward the trees, cloaking the cottage in its thin lacy veil.

Hagan's body was warm and inviting, his lips possessive, and though she knew she was wading in dangerous waters, she could not stop herself from taking the next step, through the ripples and over the ledge if needs be. Her mind was already swimming when he reached beneath the mantle and felt her skin.

Goose bumps rose on her flesh and he touched her breast, causing the nipple to stiffen. He took in a swift breath as his thumb grazed the dark bud, and a liquid warmth rolled deep within Sorcha. She felt the mantle being stripped away, shoved beneath her as a blanket, knew that she was naked beneath him and didn't care. He kissed her eyes, her cheeks, her throat, running his slick tongue over her skin, tasting of her and making her shiver with desire.

She knew she wouldn't stop him, they'd come too often to this precipice only to pull back, but this time, alone in the woods, with the embers of the fire glowing red and the forest coming alive with the morning, she couldn't resist.

He took her breast into his mouth, teasing with his tongue, nipping gently with his teeth, until she arched upward, her spine bowing as she strived to get closer to him.

He kissed her and ran his hands along her body. "Not yet, little one," he whispered as skilled hands skimmed her rump, then grazed the inside of her thighs.

Something hot and moist blossomed within her and she bucked. Her eyes were open and she watched while with one hand he caressed her, and with the other he tore off his own clothes. His body, hard and sinewy, gleamed in the firelight, and a thin sheen of sweat covered hard muscles.

Her throat felt as if a noose were slowly tightening over her neck as she watched him. Though her own body was screaming for more and she was shivering in anticipation, her eyes devoured every inch of him, seeing the slick muscles, the dark hair beneath his arms and at the top of his legs, the long shaft of his manhood, anxious and ready.

She closed her eyes, certain he would pierce her, but instead he settled over her and kissed her breasts and stomach, moving lower, making her squirm with a need so fierce, she could think of nothing save loving him.

"Please," she whispered.

"Not yet." He parted her legs and breathed on her in a way that made her hips lift from the ground. His hands grabbed her buttocks and held her near as he pressed his face even closer and he tasted of her.

Sorcha gasped, her heart thundering, her body moving of its own accord as he loved her with his mouth. She writhed and cried out, wanting more until, in a steamy moment of heat, the earth shattered and her soul rocked. With a cry as primal as that of the forest, her body wrenched and convulsed, and stars grew bright in the early morning light.

He laid her gently back on the mantle, and she sighed. "I don't understand," she said.

"You will," he promised, and he spread her legs with his knees.

"But—"

"Kiss me."

"What?"

"Kiss me."

She lifted her face to his, pressed warm lips to his mouth, and felt his arms surround her. She'd thought she was finished, that he'd wrung every emotion he could from her, but she was wrong, for the loving started all over again.

His tongue worked its magic, his hands brought her to dizzying heights of desire. Her blood, so recently cooled, ran hot again, and soon, as his fingers touched and probed her, she was moving anxiously beneath him, wanting more. So much more.

It had taken all Hagan's determination to go slow with her, for he'd wanted to thrust into her hard and fast, pouring his seed into her and rearing back his head in a triumphant male mating call. He could think of little else but burying himself in her sweet lush body, but he'd held off, digging his fingers into the dirt, silently cursing his need to think of her, feeling the sweat run down his spine as he'd loved her with his mouth. Not that he hadn't enjoyed it, she'd tasted sweeter than any fine wine, but it hadn't been enough.

But now, as she writhed beneath him, begging him to end her agony, he knew giving her what she'd needed first was worth it. He wrapped his arms around her and, with his lips claiming hers, pressed into her. He felt the resistance, the tightening of her abdomen, the swift intake of her breath, but he couldn't stop and he thrust past the thin barrier of her maidenhead, feeling her warm and oozing, hot and steamy, surrounding him.

She cried out and he tried to be gentle, taking it slow, gritting his teeth against his own desire as he sheathed himself in her silken warmth and waited a heartbeat before slowly withdrawing again.

She whimpered at the loss of him, and he entered her yet again. She was tight and frightened, but slowly her body opened to him, joining him in his rhythm.

Her fingers delved into the deep muscles of his shoulders, touching the very wound that she had inflicted, and she stared up at him and watched his skin gleam with sweat, the sinewy muscles tightening as her mind began to spin a private tapestry of color and light.

A force built within her, hotter and hotter, pulsing with need, thundering in her ears until, with an earth-shattering cry, he thrust himself into her one last time and an exploding of sweet pleasure caused her to arch up and accept the seed he spilled from his body to hers.

"Sorcha, sweet, sweet Sorcha," he whispered hoarsely as he fell upon her, crushing her breasts and twining his fingers in her hair. He sighed loudly and stared into her eyes. "So you were a virgin."

She felt as if the earth had truly moved, as if life itself had changed, and she kissed his chest, tasting salt and man, clinging to this warrior whom she'd thought her enemy. "Aye," she said.

"No other man?"

She managed a naughty smile. "Nay, m'lord, not even the stableboy, Bjorn."

Jealousy caused a tic at the side of his face. "What of someone at Prydd?"

She thought of Keane, and her throat worked. "I cared for someone once, though I loved him not," she admitted, seeing Hagan's eyes turn dark. "He was a good man, though . . . he seemed more interested in my birthmark and the gossip surrounding the silly thing than he did in me."

"Where is he now?"

"Dead," she admitted. "Killed the day that Leah was abducted to Erbyn."

His mouth grew grim. "By my soldiers?"

"By outlaws, but I know not that they weren't bought by Darton. Seems it not strange that on the very afternoon Leah was captured, that Keane was killed?"

"Odd, yes," he admitted, his thick eyebrows drawing together. "If I find out an innocent man was slain by my men, everyone involved will pay."

She sighed. "Be careful, m'lord. You may have just condemned all your soldiers to an early death."

"My soldiers are loyal," Hagan argued, and touched a long strand of her hair. "Much more loyal than you, I fear."

She stared up at him innocently. "Oh, you are wrong. I am very faithful and true."

"To Prydd."

"Aye," she said.

"Just as I feared." With a crooked smile, he pushed a lock of her hair away from her cheek and stared down at her with his liquid gold eyes. "Well, now, little savior of all that is Prydd, tell me, what the devil am I going to do with you?"

Fourteen

"Where is the woman?" Darton demanded, his patience stretched thin. Seated in the lord's chair on the dais, he drummed his fingers. His companions were a nearly empty cup of wine and the dark fury that roiled through his blood.

He took a long swallow from the silver-rimmed mazer and watched as two of his best soldiers, Sir Ralston and Sir Marshall, exchanged worried glances. They stood next to the fire, warming their backsides.

Ralston spoke. "Lady Sorcha escaped us."

"She escaped you," Darton said with flat condemnation. "A mere woman and she escaped two of the finest knights in the entire castle."

"Aye," Ralston said, ignoring the bite of sarcasm in Darton's words. "We lost her in the gully that runs by . . . the witch's house."

"The what . . . ?

"Tullia's cottage," Marshall interjected as he took off his gloves, tossed them on the floor, and opened his palms to the warm golden flames. "Some of the men are superstitious."

"Of course they are." He couldn't keep the annoyance from his voice. *These* were his best men? God help him. His rebellion would surely fail if he had to depend upon the likes of these morons.

" 'Tis haunted," Ralston said, nodding his head rapidly. "The house. 'Tis haunted. And 'twas dark by the time we got to the gully. We thought we'd find her in the morn, then came Hagan and his men and . . ."

"And you failed me," Darton said, so angry, spittle collected behind his teeth. Fools. He kept company with fools!

Ralston had the decency to appear contrite. He looked down at his grimy fingers and avoided Darton's condemning gaze.

"Why isn't Hagan dead?" Darton demanded. He drained his mazer and checked over his shoulder to see that none of the servants might overhear. The great hall wasn't the best place to discuss this, as the walls seemed to have ears at times, but he had no choice. Ralston and Marshall had returned with disturbing news. Now all of his plans, the plot that had seemed so perfect only hours ago, were suddenly crumbling to jagged pieces that he might be unable to fit together again. Curse and rot his bloody luck. When this was all over, he'd remember those who obeyed him without question and those whose own fears controlled their actions. He had no use for knights who wouldn't ride willingly into the very gates of hell if commanded.

Marshall, damn his calm, waved off Darton's worries with his bony fingers. "Hagan will die. By the end of the day." With a knowing glance at Sir Ralston, he added, "Brady and Elwin are still in the forest tracking him. 'Twill not be long before we have news of his death."

"You'd best be right, Marshall, or we'll have anarchy on our hands." In vexation Darton kicked a bench away from the table and paced restlessly before the fire. He couldn't hope to become baron without news of Hagan's death, for there were far too many people in the castle who were perversely loyal to his brother.

"Did we not detain his troops?" Marshall asked in that silky voice of his.

"So you say."

"They are shackled in the old mill, along with their horses, waiting for word from you. A few are dying already from their wounds, and the others are bound. Would you like them killed? Or do you hope to turn them into your own soldiers?"

Darton was in no mood to discuss anything so trivial. With Hagan loose, nothing else mattered. He rubbed the knotted muscles at the base of his skull. " 'Twill be difficult to turn them away from Hagan. His damn knights are stupidly loyal to him. Since they've seen your faces, they must realize that I am behind the attack against my brother and will resist accepting me as their liege." He plowed two sets of fingers through his hair. "We need other ways to convince them to join us."

"A bribe, if it's large enough, might work on a few of them," Marshall said thoughtfully as he stroked his beard. "And for those who can't be bought outright, we might be able to find secrets that they'd rather keep to themselves and offer to maintain our quiet only if they meet our demands and turn against Hagan."

"You know of such secrets?" Darton was impressed. Maybe he'd underestimated his second-in-command.

"A few," Marshall said, his cold smile causing a chill to drip into Darton's blood. Marshall wasn't loyal. He was only interested in his own greedy ambitions, and Darton knew that someday he would have to get rid of the knight, elsewise Marshall would be plotting Darton's death. As soon as the rebellion was successful, he would find a way dispose of the cur.

"There's always torture," Ralston said. His faded blue

eyes gleamed deep in their sockets. Ralston's cruel streak was well known throughout the castle. More than once Darton had been forced to reprimand him for his mistreatment of a horse or hound or whore. Darton, too, enjoyed his sex rough, but even he had limits. Ralston had none. "A few lashes of the whip can convince a man that he needs to think in a new way," Ralston suggested. "Or take away 'is food and water for a while. Turns a strong man into a simpering, crying puppy who would run after you on all fours and lick yer arse to boot." He laughed and eyed Darton's empty cup greedily.

Darton wasn't swayed. "Keep Hagan's men locked up for now. Until we hear of his death. Then we can decide." Darton sat back in his chair, frowned into his empty cup, and clapped for a serving wench just as a soldier, his boots ringing against the stones, joined them. A plain girl scurried in with more wine, filling Darton's cup before hurrying away.

"There is news?" Darton asked the sentry. He tried to keep his willful heart from leaping in anticipation. Surely this was it—the word that Hagan was finally dead.

"An army approaching," the stone-faced guard said without a trace of emotion.

"An army?" Darton repeated, sliding a suspicious glance at Marshall. This was a complication he hadn't expected. "Whose?"

"The colors are those of Prydd."

Darton's heart sank. Was it possible that Sorcha had returned to her home and found a way to convince her brother to mount an army against Erbyn? But the timing wasn't quite right. It was nearly a day's ride to Prydd from here, and Tadd would need time to equip and ready an army. Again Darton was on his feet. He bit his lip as he strode with a gait that pained him, and his thoughts whirled ahead of him. He was at a disadvantage, not knowing what to expect. He hated for anyone, friend or foe, to have the upper hand. "Is the lady with them?" he asked, though he knew it to be a stupid question. Even if Sorcha demanded to return to Erbyn, Tadd would have forbade a woman on the journey. Any woman, including his powerful sister.

"I know not."

"Allow in only the leader . . . and one of his soldiers, I suppose. Swear that he will have safe passage."

"Aye." The soldier turned on his heel and clipped out of the room. Darton fingered the knife at his belt as his gaze met Ralston's. "If Tadd of Prydd gives me any trouble, you are to kill him at my signal," he said.

"What signal?"

"I'll call for more wine and ask for the jug to be left at the table rather than having it returned to the kitchen. You then draw him into battle with an insult or two and slay him."

"What of his guard?"

"I'll handle him," Marshall said.

"Good." Darton was pleased with Marshall's act of allegiance. Maybe he wouldn't have to kill the pensive knight after all. "I'll see that only my men are around, and they will swear that Tadd struck first."

Ralston's smile stretched beneath his red beard. "Just give me the signal and I'll run 'im through."

"From the front. The wound must be in his chest, for it must appear a fair fight."

" 'Twill, my liege," Ralston assured him as Darton made ready to receive Sorcha's brother. "Have trust in me."

Astride a tall stallion, Tadd led his party around a final bend in the forest road. The gloomy trees gave way to a trampled meadow, a deep chasm, and the sharp cliffs supporting Erbyn. Tadd's guts twisted at the sight of the huge keep. In comparison, Prydd seemed small and of no consequence, but this . . . this was truly a castle. Thrice the size of those at Prydd, the battlements and towers crawled along the steep cliffs, rising above the ground with thick, impenetrable walls and a drawbridge wide enough for four carts abreast. Banners in the forest-green and gold colors of Erbyn snapped in the breeze from poles mounted on the highest towers. Envy coursed through Tadd, and he suddenly wondered why he'd been satisfied to be baron of Prydd—a tiny fiefdom with a small keep. The missive from Hagan of Erbyn told him that both his sisters were within the strong fortress that was Erbyn, and Tadd suspected he could command much for their imprisonment, for though Hagan said the women were his guests, Tadd would choose to call them prisoners and insist that he be paid much for his worry.

That thought pleased him, and he grinned inwardly.

As Tadd's party approached the main gate, a horn sounded and guards appeared at every post. Archers stood at ready as if expecting an enemy. Aye, this was a fine castle . . . a castle fit for a king . . .

Scratching his crotch, he squirmed in the saddle. He'd been riding for hours and was weary. His muscles and back ached clear to his bones, but the thought of bargaining over his sisters' future brought a smile to his face. Sorcha—his tormentor. Now, at last, he could be rid of her and be paid a handsome price as well. As for Leah, he was glad to see her off, as far away as possible. Let her preach and pray at another castle; Tadd was tired of her piety and glances of disapproval. Yes, he'd take whatever he could for her as well.

From the looks of the castle, the Baron of Erbyn was a very rich man. He could let go of a few pieces of gold and a smaller castle somewhere near Prydd, a castle where Tadd could keep several whores, women who would take care of him in ways his wife would never.

He planned to marry soon, get his wife with child, and become father to a son, but he knew that whatever noblewoman he chose, she wouldn't excite him in bed. She'd do her duty and bear children, but would probably disapprove of the wenches he would need to satisfy his lusty appetite.

Yea, a small castle for drinking, gambling, bearbaiting, cockfighting, and whoring. *Mab.* He'd take Mab with her small breasts and quivering lips and round, fearful eyes. He'd keep her until she no longer trembled at the sight of him. Then, as was his original plan, he'd loan her to his friends; by then she would learn that by pleasuring a man, she would receive gifts and kind words. Yea, in time, she would make a fine whore.

At the outer gate his party was stopped, and he argued with a guard. Eventually he was allowed into the castle with two of his knights, though the guard wasn't happy about the second man. But Tadd insisted and rode proudly into the inner bailey. A fat man with suspicious eyes and a belly that hung over his belt grudgingly took their horses to be fed and watered.

The guard was a man without expression, and he led Tadd and his two men, Christian and Gower, into a great hall that was as grand as it was immense. Huge beams crossed beneath a ceiling that was high and coved, tapestries decorated the whitewashed walls, and the lord's dais was two steps above the smooth stone floor. Sweet-smelling rushes had been scattered over the floor, and a huge fire crackled in the hearth.

Servants scurried out of their way as they walked through a wide corridor and past a staircase toward the dais, where the cur Hagan . . . nay, Darton of Erbyn sat in a huge chair, looking for all the world as if he were the baron. Two were with him, a tall, gaunt-looking man and a shorter fellow with red hair and mean eyes. The hairs on the back of Tadd's scalp lifted in warning, but he showed no trace of fear.

"Welcome," Darton said, rising. His hands were outspread in a gesture of greeting and goodwill. "Come sit at the table. Have food and drink and find comfort."

A serving wench appeared carrying a tray laden with six mazers of wine and a basket of apples. She was a comely girl with big breasts that seemed about to spill out of the top of her tunic. "Lucy, give Sir Tadd whatever he requests," Darton said warmly, and the girl, flashing large brown eyes in Tadd's direction, smiled. Tadd's loins tightened as he took a cup of the wine, stared at the deep cleft of the wench's incredible bosom, and drank heartily. Oh, to bury his face in those warm, supple pillows. He watched Lucy retreat. Her hips were wide and swung as she walked, and he imagined himself mounting her. A big woman, she could endure much and might spend hours satisfying a man. His breeches were suddenly painfully tight and he had to force his gaze back to his host. He gritted his teeth and hoped his passion didn't show.

"You like her?" Darton asked, his eyes flashing as he picked up an apple, polished it on the end of his tunic, and tossed it in the air. "You may have her. I'll arrange it." He caught the apple deftly and took a bite. "Or . . . if you would prefer, there is Bliss . . . None sweeter, I assure you. Here, drink . . . and eat." He motioned to all the soldiers.

Tadd's throat constricted and his mouth was dry with lust, but he forced his thoughts away from whoring for the moment and picked up a cup. "I am here about my sisters." He took a long swallow, quenching his thirst. The others joined in.

Darton smiled warmly. "I expected as much."

"Baron Hagan has promised their safe return along with payment for the trouble and grief I've suffered." Importantly, Tadd plucked Hagan's letter from his pouch and laid it on the table near Darton, who scanned the words and shook his head.

Sighing, Darton said, "I'm afraid I have some disturbing news."

His sisters—were they dead? Already killed by Hagan's men? Tadd's muscles tightened and he was glad he still had his sword with him. "News?"

"Hagan is missing. As are your sisters."

"What?"

"Oh, don't fret," Darton said with a wave, as if swatting away a bothersome insect. " 'Tis only a matter of time until all are found." Setting his elbows on the table, he leaned closer to Tadd, as if to confide a great secret. "Sorcha and Leah decided to return to Prydd on their own and convinced a stableboy to turn traitor. Then they stole some valuable horses to accomplish their escape." He clucked his tongue as if the plan were silly and foolish. "Hagan, of course, was incensed at their disobedience. He gathered together a few of his men, left me in charge of Erbyn, and took off after the traitors. We expect them back any time."

Traitors? "My sisters were not traitors. It sounds as if they were treated like prisoners." Tadd was uneasy. He didn't trust anyone from Erbyn, and this story seemed a convenient lie guaranteed to make him sweat. Well, he was worried, but he hid it well. "Leah was kidnapped," he reminded his host, "brought here and held against her will."

Darton's lips tightened a bit, but he didn't argue.

"Hagan admits to the deed."

"Yes, well—"

"And Sorcha only came here to free her sister," Tadd continued, smiling to himself as he defended the woman who had been the bane of his existence from the moment of her birth. "I will expect compensation." Tadd decided to press his advantage. "But, of course, I should discuss this with Lord Hagan."

Darton's smile froze. "I've spoken with Hagan about this and I know his plans. You will be compensated well, Sir Tadd, and as for your sisters, they will be provided for. Sir Marshall has offered to marry Lady Leah—" from the corner of his eye he saw Marshall stiffen, but if he was inclined to argue, he held his tongue "—and I myself will take Lady Sorcha as my bride. We will expect no dowries, of course, and in truth, I think Hagan will want to keep the peace."

"Three people were murdered during the kidnapping."

"A mistake. Those responsible have already been imprisoned," Darton said, lying easily. Tadd was so easy to read—a mere boy. "Justice at Erbyn is swift."

"I lost two soldiers and a woman servant."

"For which you will be paid."

It was Tadd's turn to inch closer. "I want a small fiefdom; a castle not far from Prydd."

Darton seemed to pale a bit, and Tadd felt a sense of satisfaction. From the moment he'd stepped into the great hall, he had felt manipulated, but now he had the upper hand.

"Your father would demand this?" Darton said, recovering a bit.

"My father is dead," Tadd said firmly. He managed a thin smile and drank Hagan of Erbyn's choice wine. Things were going better than he'd hoped because he'd finally understood Darton's motives—oh, he'd hidden them well, but Darton of Erbyn was not the first man entranced by Sorcha. Nor was he the first man to ask for the hand of the savior of

Prydd. 'Twas foolish. And to Tadd's advantage. "I am now the Baron of Prydd, and my honor as well as the honor of both my sisters has been trampled upon, and the truce has been broken. For this I demand payment of the castle. 'Tis not too much to ask. Sir Darton, you will end up not only with peace, but my sister as well. Yea, you will be married to the savior of Prydd, and that's truly what you want, is it not?"

" 'Tis time," Hagan said, lifting her onto his destrier and climbing behind. Dawn had broken, and through the claw-like branches of the trees overhead, Sorcha saw the sky, dark and somber. Gray clouds with purple bellies rolled across the sun, threatening rain, causing the forest to close around them.

With one arm wrapped possessively around her waist and the reins clenched tightly in his other hand, Hagan urged his horse forward along the seldom-used road. The white palfrey followed behind, content to stay with the stallion.

Sorcha tried to ignore the heat of Hagan's body and the intimate fit of her buttocks as they wedged against his thighs. She didn't think about the strong band of his arm surrounding her just below her breasts, but as the horse cantered and she rubbed up against him, she felt her blood stir with desire and she was reminded of their lovemaking within the cracked walls of the old cottage.

She told herself that her heart wasn't involved, that though she was attracted to him, she hadn't fallen for this man she suspected to be her enemy, but deep in her soul, she knew differently. Though she hated to admit the horrid fact, she was beginning to care about this dark baron and his gruff ways. She'd been fighting her feelings of love for days, and now, in the gray light of morning, she could no longer lie to herself. She loved him. 'Twas simple and foolish, but the truth. She could deny it to everyone else, but deep in the most secret recesses of her heart, she knew that she would never feel the same about another man.

'Twas a curse; just like the damned birthmark that had gotten her into this mess in the first place. *Yes, but had you not the birthmark, you would never have met Hagan.*

Her throat closed in upon itself, for she could not think of being without him.

She should hate him. Hagan had left his castle to be guarded by his twin, and Darton had only wreaked havoc. 'Twas under Darton's orders that Henry, Gwendolyn, and Keane had been killed, and Darton had kidnapped Leah and raped her. No matter how Sorcha's wayward heart felt about Hagan, she could not forget the pain his brother had caused her family and Prydd.

"We'll be home soon now," he whispered against her ear.

Home. Erbyn was not her home. And yet she'd begun to feel at ease in the yellow stone walls of the great keep. The peasants and servants, once suspicious, had grown friendly, though some who had heard of her powers still viewed her with a wary eye. Her heart filled with anticipation of seeing the stone dragon of a castle standing proud on the ancient cliffs.

The horse raced through the woods and the wind shifted, blowing cold against her face in an icy blast. The stallion's black ears pricked forward, and Sorcha felt the slightest hesitation in his gait. The mare whinnied nervously, and when Sorcha looked over her shoulder, the palfrey stood nose to the wind, nostrils extended, and didn't budge.

"Hagan . . . ?" A premonition of dread slithered down her spine, and Hagan tensed, his fingers pulling back on the reins, his other hand reaching for his sword.

Wind slowed to a trot.

An arrow whistled through the air.

Instinctively Hagan wrapped his body over hers.

Thump!

Hagan flinched, his body bracing against a burst of pain. "Christ Jesus!" he swore, yanking hard on the reins, forcing the beast to wheel.

Oh, God, he'd been wounded! "Hagan—"

"Run, you demon," he cried, kicking the horse so desperately that the destrier took flight, his great legs stretching into a hard gallop, mud flying from beneath his heavy hooves. The air sang past them, cold and dry, blinding Sorcha as the bare trees flashed by.

A horrid, blood-chilling whoop erupted from somewhere in the shadows. More arrows sizzled through the air, and the startled white mare galloped through the woods.

Thwack! Hagan's entire body convulsed, and she knew he'd been hit yet again.

Where were they? The attackers—where were they hiding? Sorcha felt the rigidity leave Hagan's body. He slumped against her. *Please God, don't let him die!*

"You must go on," he said, his voice a wheeze, his breathing shallow and labored against her ear.

He was leaving her? Not as long as she had a breath of life in her body. "No, Hagan—"

"I cannot stay. 'Tis not safe for you—"

"Hang on!" she insisted. What was he saying? That he was going to give up? She felt his body slipping off the horse and she clung to his arms, forcing them around her. "I will get you to Erbyn. The horse knows the way."

Another horrid whoop curdled the air.

"Leave me now, Sorcha. I'll stand and fight."

"Never!" She kicked Wind with all her strength.

"For once in your life, woman, obey me!"

"I can't . . . Hagan . . ." Her eyes filled with tears and love, and she clung to him, unwilling to let him go, to let him die.

"There is no other way."

"I'll never leave you—"

Thwack! A deadly arrow sizzled through the air and pierced Wind's haunch. The horse reared and screamed, and Hagan slipped to the ground, leaving Sorcha to scrabble for the reins. She started to dismount, but her foot tangled in the long stirrup.

"Ride to Erbyn. Get help!"

"Nay!" she cried, desperate. She thought for a fleeting second of riding to Prydd, but the journey was much longer than to Erbyn, and she could not leave Hagan.

Tossing his great head and whinnying in terror, Wind bolted. From the corner of her eye Sorcha saw Hagan crawl into the gloom of the forest. No! No! No! She couldn't leave him! She had to return and save him. Only she had the power to heal, and for the first time in her life, she was grateful for the damned curse of her birthmark.

She groped for the reins, but the terrified horse lunged forward, racing down the road. Trees and light flashed by, and Sorcha, determined to return for Hagan, gritted her teeth and clawed at the stallion's neck, straining to reach the leather straps that flapped in the air and slapped against Wind's lathered coat. His hoofbeats thundered through the forest, and with each stride he carried her farther away from Hagan.

"Whoa!" she screamed, her lungs burning. "Damn you, stop!" She could barely breathe, but she couldn't give up. Even now Hagan could be set upon by the outlaws, his blood staining the forest floor. Her throat was dry, her heart hammering with fear. With one hand she knotted her fingers in the animal's thick mane and grabbed for the reins with her other. "Stop, you bloody beast. Stop!"

The reins were just out of reach, slipping away each time she caught hold of a strap.

Determined not to lose this battle for Hagan's life, she lunged and her fingers captured one thin strip of leather. With all her might, she wound the rein through her fingers, feeling the leather cut into her skin as she pulled back with all the power in her shoulders. The horse nearly stumbled as he slowed and turned in a tight circle. "Now, you damned animal, we go back!" she commanded, though the horrid arrow still protruded from his rump. "Hiya!" She kicked him in the sides and started back.

Hagan, oh, Hagan, hold on. I'm coming. Don't give up, my love!

He had to be safe! He had to! But pictures of him lying in a pool of blood tortured her mind as the stallion raced through the dead leaves and mud. He couldn't be dead. Oh, God, what would she do without him? She sent up prayer after desperate prayer for his life. Her heart twisted as wind coursed through her hair and tears streamed from her eyes. So blind was she that she almost didn't see them—a strong line of soldiers blocking her path.

Tugging hard on the reins, she felt a moment of gladness, for she recognized these men—they were Hagan's soldiers. "Thank God," she whispered as Wind skidded to a stop near a rider on a bay stallion. "Oh, Sir Brady! You have to help me! Hagan's been struck down by outlaws and he's here, in the woods . . ."

Brady grabbed the reins, stripping them from her frozen fingers. His smile was cold as the North Sea, and his eyes glinted with an evil light.

Sorcha's breath died in her lungs, and dread, that black monster, settled deep in her heart.

"I have terrible news, m'lady," Brady said as Sorcha's heart pounded with the rhythm of doom.

"No!" she screamed before the horrid words found her ears.

Brady's mouth pinched a bit. "I'm sorry, Lady Sorcha, but I fear Lord Hagan is dead."

Fifteen

"I won't believe it!" Sorcha regarded Darton with hate-filled eyes. The great hall was nearly deserted and felt dreary and dank without the revelry of Christmas, without the laughter of the peasants, without Hagan. She shivered and rubbed her arms, but her gaze never left Darton's. "Hagan's not dead! He can't be!"

"You saw him fall yourself," Darton said with a smile that was meant to be kind but shredded Sorcha's insides. He motioned quickly to Lucy. "Hot soup for the lady and a cup of the best wine. She's had a long journey and needs—"

"Nay!" Sorcha had no time for these comforts he offered. Each minute wasted precious seconds of Hagan's life. "We must go back," she insisted, restraining herself from lunging at Darton and shaking the very life from him. What was the matter with him? His own brother, his *twin,* was lying in the forest, his lifeblood seeping out of his body, and here Darton sat, in the baron's chair, drinking wine and talking with his men, as if an attack on Hagan's life happened each day.

There was something amiss, but she wasn't sure what. "Take me to him. Send his soldiers . . ."

"I'm afraid you're asking the impossible," Darton said, and she suddenly had a glimmer of the truth—that Darton, and not outlaws, was behind the attack. Her throat tightened in fear, for Darton was far more dangerous than unknown cutthroats.

"Where are all of Hagan's men?" she asked, her mouth feeling as dry as sand. "Sir Kennard and Sir Royce and Sir Winston . . . Where are they?"

"They left with Hagan yesterday. No one's seen them since." Darton let out a long, unhappy sigh that Sorcha didn't believe for an instant. " 'Tis feared that they, too, were set upon, and none survived."

"This I cannot believe. So many strong knights—all perished?"

" 'Tis a tragedy," Darton said with a sad lift of his eyebrows, though he seemed bored and flicked a bit of dirt from his blue tunic. "I've sent men looking for them, of course, but so far no one has been found. Ah, Lucy! You're an angel." Blushing, Lucy placed the cup of wine and bowl of soup on the table, but Sorcha ignored Darton's offer. She was cold inside and numb all over. Hagan couldn't be dead. She was sure of it. If he'd died, she would feel it. A part of her would have died with him. No! No! No!

She didn't trust Darton; never had. Today he was too calm. Too . . . satisfied and smug, as if he knew a dark secret he would share with no one.

"What of Bjorn and Leah?"

"The traitors?" He plucked an apple from the bowl on the table and slowly slid the blade of his dagger under the fruit's red skin.

"They were but following my plan," she insisted. "If anyone is a traitor, 'tis I."

"That isn't the question." He sliced a bit of apple and carried it to his mouth with his blade. "Bjorn and Leah are thieves and traitors, and should they be found, will be treated as such." He chewed the slice of apple slowly.

"And me?" she asked, sensing that there was something more—something hideous that he'd left unsaid. Unspoken words hung like ghosts in the air.

"You . . . I can forgive." He lifted a shoulder and sliced off another piece of apple.

"What have you to do with it? Hagan is lord of this castle, and he has forgiven me."

Darton's flesh tightened over his face and he pounded his knife, blade first, into the table. His eyes turned black as night. "Hagan is no longer baron. He is dead, leaving no issue, and therefore I am the rightful heir to Erbyn."

So that was it. Her heart thudded painfully, but she would not give up. "I want to go back," she said, shoving aside the soup and wine, sloshing broth onto the table as she leaned forward, pressing her face closer to Darton where he sat so imperiously—so self-righteously—in Hagan's chair, as if he were truly lord.

"To Prydd?" he asked, setting the apple aside.

She was surprised at her own reaction, for the mention of her home brought back none of the bittersweet memories that had been with her since her arrival at Erbyn. She no longer dreamed of returning to Prydd, nor of escaping to her home; no, something had changed in her heart on the night, the one fateful night, that she'd spent in the forest with Hagan. Hot tears stung the backs of her eyes. "Nay, Sir Darton," she said, "I want not to return to Prydd, but to the forest to find Hagan."

Darton's nostrils flared and the small lines around the edges of his mouth turned white. "He is dead, Sorcha. You must accept this."

"Have you his body?" she asked, her voice rising as if she were a madwoman.

"Nay, but—"

"Has any one of your men seen his body?"

"Not yet, but 'tis only a matter of time."

"He's alive!" she screamed. "We must find him."

" 'Tis too late, I'm afraid."

"Too late?" A sick feeling knotted her stomach and she hardly dared breathe. "Why?"

"There are other, more important matters to deal with."

"More important than Hagan's life?" she said.

Darton's smile was pure evil. He snapped his fingers, and a page scurried up the stairs. Dread stole up Sorcha's spine and prickled her scalp. What had he done? Within seconds she heard a shuffling of feet in the hallways above. She turned her eyes upward toward the noise, and her heart nearly stopped.

Tadd!

Dressed in a russet tunic trimmed in gold and a mantle of sleek sable, her brother appeared at the top of the stairs. He favored her with a gentle smile, and fear as dark as a moonless night entered her soul.

"Sister!"

She could barely breathe as he descended the stairs. Something was wrong, vitally wrong, and her insides churned. Why was he here, and so obviously treated like a royal guest? Her stomach curled as she saw the deceit in his eyes. Though he was smiling and reaching toward her as he walked swiftly down the steps, she didn't trust him for a minute, and it occurred to her that he might have been behind the attack on Hagan.

She felt as if her soul were scraped raw.

"I was worried about you." His voice rang falsely through the hall.

Liar!

"Thank God you've returned safely." As he reached the

bottom of the stairs, he squared his shoulders, then swaggered toward the dais. Inside, Sorcha cringed.

She'd always been able to read his thoughts and knew that this day he had a secret—a great secret that pleased him, a secret he savored.

Her hands turned to ice.

"Sir Darton has told me that you stole horses and tricked his men, just as you did with me at Prydd." He clucked his tongue and smiled a cunning little grin as Lucy reappeared with more wine. For a moment his attention was distracted and he hesitated, sending the serving girl a look that fairly sizzled in the air. Lucy grinned back, coloring a little, and Sorcha realized that Tadd had been at Erbyn long enough to bed at least one of the women of the castle. Tadd's tongue rimmed his lips before his gaze returned to Sorcha.

"I tried to escape," she said, though she doubted he cared. Already he had allied himself with Darton, and that foreboded ill for everyone at Prydd as well as Erbyn. "Leah and I were being held prisoner."

"By Hagan?" Tadd asked.

"Yes, but Darton kidnapped Leah and—"

"They were guests," Darton corrected.

"Leah was never a guest! Your men carried her off to Erbyn, where you locked her into a room and forced yourself upon—"

"Sit!" Darton commanded in a voice that shook the rafters. Then, speaking more softly, he said, "Please, Lady Sorcha, sit here at the table and have some wine, for we have much to discuss with you."

She wanted to argue and stand her ground, but she knew that opposing them would serve no purpose, for they had thrown in their lots together, that much was clear as glass. Instead of enemies, they acted as if they were fast friends.

Sorcha was certain that their friendship was more deadly than any battle that had ever been waged. Her legs trembled slightly as she took the chair Darton offered, the chair next to his, the one in which she'd sat during meals when Hagan, lord of the keep, was at her side. *Hagan . . . please, please be safe!*

Tadd sipped his wine. "Lord Darton has acknowledged his part in the kidnapping of our sister."

"*Lord* Darton?" she whispered.

"As I've already said, m'lady, you must accept that Hagan is dead," Darton said.

"Never!" She tried to stand, but he pulled her roughly back to the chair, his fingers punishing as they manacled her wrist.

Tadd's expression turned murderous, his eyes dark with a silent rage. "Lord Darton has been most generous in offering to pay for any losses we at Prydd have felt."

"You mean for the lives of Keane and Gwendolyn and Henry? For the rape of our sister?" she said, horrified. "There is no payment that can begin to atone for his crimes!"

Tadd continued, and though his voice was even, a vein began to throb at his temple and his fingers clenched tightly as if he wished he could place his hands around her neck for arguing with him. "Darton has forgiven Leah for stealing from him, for escaping Erbyn and turning the stableboy into a traitor."

"He's turned this all around, don't you see?" she said, sick with disgust. "He raped Leah, Tadd! Forced her into doing the most vile of acts, and when he was done with her, she was so humiliated and desperate that she attempted to take her own life!" She was shaking and tried to stand yet again. "For this she is *forgiven?*" Darton muttered something low in his throat and again forced her back to her chair, but she wasn't finished with her brother. "What kind of man are you that has no pride, no sense of loyalty to your own kin?"

Tadd's jaw tightened. "I came here with an army which is now unnecessary. My men are now loyal to Erbyn and joined forces with Darton's as Lord Darton has agreed to end the feud."

"How?" Then it hit her, as if suddenly her mind opened to the truth. "He bought you, didn't he? Gave you gold for your sister's virtue and the lives of your most trusted men." Tadd didn't argue, and Sorcha's eyes narrowed. He must have hidden his soldiers—the ones she would recognize as part of his scheme. "When Father learns of this, he will see you hanged."

Tadd had the audacity to chuckle. "Oh, I think not."

"I will tell him myself," she vowed.

This time Tadd laughed out loud, and Darton grinned wickedly.

Sorcha's mouth went dry and all her worst nightmares became the soul-wrenching truth. *Oh, God, no! Please, please . . .*

" 'Tis not possible, sister. For, although it grieves me sorely to have to tell you the dreadful news, Bayard returned to the castle alone. Near death himself, he'd ridden home to deliver the sorry word that our father was killed in battle—"

"No!"

"—trying to save the king—"

"Nay! Nay! Nay!" Sorcha felt as if her soul had been ripped from her body.

"—protecting us all. 'Tis a pity."

"You lie!" With all her strength she pulled her hand free and struggled to her feet. Before Darton could restrain her, she rounded the table and looked down on her brother with furious blue eyes. "You lying bastard—"

"Oh, not me, sister. *I* am the true issue of my father's loins. Now, your legitimacy has always been in question. Rumor has it that our mother was not faithful to Eaton and that she gave herself to some soldier claiming to be the grandson or great-grandson or some relative of Llywelyn."

Sorcha lunged and wrapped her fingers around her brother's throat. Oh, if she only had her dagger, she'd cut out his lying tongue. Rage surged through her blood. "He is not dead," she screamed. "He is not!"

Tadd sputtered and shoved, but she was like a burr on a long-haired cat and couldn't be moved. Tadd was lying as he'd always lied.

Tadd's face turned red with rage and fury. He coughed and kicked, but still Sorcha wouldn't give up until strong hands peeled her from her brother and she was restrained by Sir Brady.

"You'll pay for this," Tadd swore, his voice rasping as he gulped air. Rubbing his neck, he grabbed his mazer, raised it to his lips, and drank so fast that wine slid down the sides of his mouth, leaving purple stains that drizzled into his beard.

"I'll not believe that my father's dead!" she cried, her world spinning crazily.

"Believe it. Eaton died in battle. I am the Baron of Prydd."

She felt as if a thousand knives had been thrust into her soul.

"And Hagan is dead, as well. Killed by outlaws. Now Lord Darton is ruler of Erbyn, sister." Tadd's eyes gleamed with a malevolent light, and he wiped his mouth with the back of his hand. His slick little tongue rimmed his lips. "He's been generous, I think. He's given me a castle—a small one that is not a day's journey from Prydd."

"And what have you given him in return?" she spat.

His smile was pure evil, and a thousand ghosts seemed to tread on her spine. "You, sister," he said, patting his fingers together. "I've given him you. You are to become Darton of Erbyn's bride."

Pain burned in Hagan's back and screamed down his legs and the taste in his mouth was putrid. Spitting, he tried to move, but felt as if his muscles had been rent from his bones.

"Be still!" a woman's harsh voice ordered. Fingers as cool and dry as parchment touched his body, sending a searing agony that ripped through his skin. " 'Tis only ointment of thistle and ash; 'twill help you heal."

"I doubt anything that causes such a burn will help," he muttered, trying to keep his mind from spinning. He remembered the attack and falling from the horse. He'd dragged himself into the forest, his sword drawn, ready to kill at least a few of the murderers and take them with him to hell. But as he'd waited, night had fallen, or blackness had overcome his mind; he knew not which. Now he was awake and in an enclosure . . . a dark place, mayhap a dungeon. He forced the dizziness to stop and saw that he was not in a prison, but a tent of some sort. 'Twas dark inside except for candles burning in a corner and the reflection of restless red flames from a campfire on the other side of the tent's flap.

Again he asked, "Where am I?"

"You are safe, Lord Hagan."

"You know who I am?"

"Does anyone who lives near Erbyn not?"

Again the pain, but he fought the urge to flinch and forced the blackness around his eyes to recede. He needed his wits about him.

"Trust me," the old voice whispered.

He had no choice. He couldn't move. Lifting his head to

hazard a glance over his shoulder, he saw an old crone with gray hair, deep grooves on her face, but kind eyes working over him. He winced and sucked in his breath as she applied more of her painful remedy. He smelled smoke from the campfire and heard the wind sigh in the trees. So he was still in the forest, mayhap with the thugs who had tried to kill him. So why the old woman? "How long have I been here?"

"Two days. 'Twas time you woke up."

Two days? Two bloody days? He tried to push himself upright, but agony throbbed through every inch of his body and seemed to explode behind his eyes.

"You are healing well."

He tried to move, but the blistering pain stopped him cold and he felt helpless and weak.

"Be still. You are with friends."

What friends? It seemed as if no one could be trusted. His mind spun with memories. Sorcha. What had happened to her? Was she, too, in this camp? Her beautiful face swam before his eyes, and he nearly smiled at the thought of her tangled raven hair and mischievous blue eyes. Her lips, so sweet and turned into a little pout . . . Oh, Jesus, where was she? His guts coiled and he nearly retched at the thought that he had failed her. Even now she could be in enemy hands . . . beaten, raped, tortured . . . He slammed the door shut on those painful thoughts and forced the words over his tongue. "There . . . there is a woman."

"Sorcha of Prydd," the old crone said with sorrow deep in her voice, a sorrow he felt to his bones. "I know."

"How?"

"I was her nursemaid."

Sorcha's woman servant? Here in the forest? With a band of men whose voices and laughter drifted into the tent? Hagan tried to disguise his doubts. "What is your name?"

"Isolde," she said.

The name was familiar.

"I raised the lady from a babe, I did," the woman said, and a trace of fondness lingered in her voice.

"She is here?"

The hands stopped moving for a minute. "She was not with you when the scouts found you in the forest."

"Scouts," he repeated. "Whose scouts?"

"Ours," she answered, and he knew she would say no more. He felt as if she wanted to tell him something more, to ask him questions, but she remained silent for a while, and fear began to drip slowly into his heart.

"Where is Sorcha?"

"We know not."

"She is in grave danger," Hagan insisted, and rolled upon his side to gaze at the old crone. Her wrinkled skin was weathered from hours in the wind and rain and sun. Her mouth was without lips, and her eyes were sunken deep but kind. She looked ancient. He grabbed at her hands. "I must find her!"

She glanced anxiously at the flap of the tent. "Our leader, Wolf, will want to talk to you."

"Wolf?" So he was with the outlaws.

"Aye, I will tell him you have awakened," she said quietly. Again he moved, but pain stayed him, and he cursed under his breath as the old woman ducked beneath the flap and disappeared.

Sorcha. What had happened to her? He thought they'd been beset by outlaws, Wolf's band or another company of cutthroats, and yet here he was, alive, being tended to. His head pounded, but the pain in his back and leg seemed to lessen as if the old woman's remedies had begun to help. He reached for his sword and found it missing. His quiver and arrows, too, were gone. Mayhap he would be ransomed, and that thought left a bitter taste in his mouth. How foolish he would appear to his men—to be set upon by outlaws. Never again would his pride be the same, and yet he found it didn't matter. Nay, all he cared about now was Sorcha and her safety.

He heard footsteps and a rush of wind as the flap was opened yet again. A tall man with broad shoulders and a savage, rough-hewn face walked inside. Carrying a torch, the light of which played eerily across his bladed features, he strode to the pallet where Hagan lay. "So the mighty Hagan of Erbyn finally awakes."

Hagan's jaw tightened.

"My men found you in the forest, near death." He shook his head, and raven black hair brushed his shoulders. "This is no way for a ruler of Erbyn to act."

"You did not try to kill me?" Hagan doubted the rogue.

"If I wanted you dead, you would be."

Hagan had no choice but to believe him. "What is it you want, Wolf? Name it."

The leader smiled, a twisted grin that held not a glimmer of humor. "You know," he said, placing the torch on a stand near the pallet and crossing his arms in front of his chest, "I thought a nobleman might sleep for weeks."

"What do you want?"

Wolf leered. His face had probably once been handsome. But his nose had been broken and grew slightly crooked, and one of his dark brows bore the scar of a sword or knife. His lips were thin and cruel, his eyes as cold and blue as the sea. Dressed in black, his hair the same raven color, he seemed evil and sinister.

"Did you bring me here to ransom me?"

This caused a mirthless laugh. "You think your brother wants you returned to the castle?"

Hagan didn't answer.

"Who do you think tried to kill you?"

Again silence, and again Wolf's mouth spread into a wicked smile that showed long white teeth. He was enjoying this. "Oh, so you blame us, do you? Think you that my ragged band would attempt to kill the baron?"

"I know not."

Wolf unsheathed his knife and insolently ran the sharp blade under his nails, dislodging dirt and filth. "I've thought of it, yes," he admitted, frowning a little. "But it seemed foolish. Asides, my friend, we have no reason to quarrel. That you did not join with us long ago is forgiven. You betrayed us not."

Hagan's head pounded, but he remembered nearly becoming one of the outlaw band. He had detested his father and he'd wanted to rebel, to go against all he'd held dear, to lose himself in the woods. He'd been young enough to think that joining a company of thieves and turning his back on his home would anger and wound his father, make the old man understand that Hagan was his own man, but in the end he'd realized his best revenge was to inherit Erbyn.

But he'd changed his mind yet again as he lay on the pallet, his back on fire. He would give up everything he owned—aye, his very life if needs be—for Sorcha's safety.

"If you keep me not for ransom, what then?"

Wolf sheathed his dagger and his smile faded. "Vengeance."

"Against whom?"

"Tadd of Prydd." Wolf's cleaved brow lifted. "He is now at the house of Erbyn with the new lord."

"The new lord?"

"Yea." Wolf appeared amused. "Sir Darton has proclaimed your death and has assumed your title." Wolf darted a quick glance at Hagan. " 'Twas his men who were chasing you. He had given orders to have you killed."

"You lie."

Wolf snorted. "Are you so blind?" he asked, and Hagan decided there was some truth to his words. "Even now, as we talk of this, *Lord* Darton is entertaining Tadd of Prydd, and the castle is preparing for the wedding."

"Wedding?" Hagan repeated, his soul turning black as death.

"Aye. The houses of Prydd and Erbyn are to be united at last. Baron Darton has asked for the hand of Lady Sorcha."

Hagan's guts twisted and he wanted to jump up and call the outlaw a liar of the worst order. His blood turned hot with jealousy and he thought of slitting the lying thug's throat. But he couldn't. Like it or not, he had to trust this man. Slowly he said, "Lady Sorcha would never agree to this marriage; she loathes my brother."

Wolf shrugged. "Tadd has agreed, and he is the Baron of Prydd as Eaton died in battle against the Scots. It matters not what the lady wants."

With more strength than anyone would have guessed possible, he lunged forward, grabbing the outlaw's tunic. "How do you know this?"

"A spy, of course."

"Who?"

Wolf's eyes gleamed. "I'll not say."

Hagan cursed but knew he would not be able to beat the truth from the outlaw. "We must stop the wedding," he ordered as the image of Darton marrying Sorcha burned through his brain. His fingers twisted into the dirty folds of Wolf's black tunic. "You must help me."

This time Wolf's smile was wide. "Oh, I shall help you, Hagan of Erbyn, if you agree to my terms."

Hagan's fingers tightened and yanked on the tunic, pulling the outlaw close. "You want Erbyn?"

"Nay," Wolf said, his eyes narrowing to slits that reflected the torch's flame. In the flickering shadows of red, his features grew into a hard mask of hate, and he looked like the very soul of the devil. "I want only Tadd of Prydd."

Sorcha's world was black as the depths of hell. Her father was dead; she would never see him again, and tears of grief threatened her eyes.

She had heard the rumors all her life—that she was not her father's daughter—and yet Eaton had been so close to her, loving her and teaching her, letting her learn the skills of the knights, not denying her just because she was a woman. And now he was gone.

Her soul writhed in agony.

Darton had locked her in her chamber, and other than the numbing news of her father's death, she'd learned nothing. She'd had no word of Hagan, nor of Leah and Bjorn. The soldiers whom Darton had sent to find Hagan came back with neither the man nor his body, and Sorcha prayed that he was alive and safe. In her mind's eye over and over again she heard the sickening thud of arrows piercing his muscles, saw him pitch over the horse and crawl into the forest. "Please, God, protect him and keep him safe," she prayed so often that her desperate prayers became a litany.

She refused to eat, and each time Ona came in with food from the kitchen, Sorcha left the trencher on a stool, untouched. Ona returned later in the day, retrieved the uneaten portion, and clucked her tongue. "It serves no purpose, you not eatin' Ada's good brawn, m'lady," she admonished as she picked up the stale bread platter and greasy meat thereon. "You need yer strength." With a sly glance in

Sorcha's direction, she continued. " 'Tis said you will soon be Darton's bride—"

"Never!"

Ona shrugged as if she cared not what Sorcha did, then left the room. Sorcha barely noticed. The girl was a twit, and she would never, *never* marry Darton. She'd die first. Sorcha stared out the window and wondered how she could trick the girl so that she could escape. The only window, though it looked over the bailey, was far too high to jump from, and the oaken door with its thick timbers and iron bands was barred from the outside. The chimney was impossible to scale, though she'd attempted to climb its blackened tunnel and ended up coughing and covered with soot. She had no weapon to lay against Ona's pale throat whenever she appeared with food, water, or a bucket in which Sorcha was supposed to relieve herself.

Sorcha's only hope was to ask for a tub of hot water for her bath. More than one man would have to carry up the tub and take it down again. The door would be open longer than normal, and if she could cause some confusion . . . by spilling the scalding water on the two guards or . . . using her fire to ignite the rushes on the floor and create panic within the castle, she would have a chance to free herself. But she had to wait for the right moment. Patience had never been one of her qualities, but as she thought long and hard, she decided that the plan with the bath might just work. As long as she moped and said little and seemed to be wasting away, no one would expect her to try and escape. Looking grief-stricken would not pose her any trouble, for she thought of Hagan constantly and her heart was heavy.

However, she cautioned herself to watch her tongue and not be so forceful in her denials of marriage to Darton. She had to lull the guards and Ona and Darton into believing that she would actually take the holy vows of matrimony with the cur. Christ's blood, it would take all of her strength to pretend that she would do the horrid deed.

Staring out the window, hoping for some sign of Hagan's return, she chewed her lip and plotted a way to escape, but her hopes, so recently soaring, fell like dead birds to the earth when she heard the men's shouts and the portcullis, with the low grind of metal gears, opening. "Oh, no," she whispered as the soldiers—all men loyal to Darton—entered the bailey. A company of twelve men surrounded the captives, and Sorcha felt tears pool in her eyes as she recognized her sister and Bjorn.

She bit her knuckles so that she wouldn't cry out.

Both prisoners looked haggard and drawn, and thick ropes surrounded their torsos, holding their arms to their sides. Leah's mud-spattered face was white with fright, her eyes cast down to the ground, but Bjorn sat proudly upon his horse. His shoulders were stiff, his chin thrust forward at a mutinous angle, his eyes looking neither left nor right.

Near the stables, they were yanked to the ground, and Leah slipped, her feet sliding away from her. A guard pulled her roughly to her feet, and she screamed. To Sorcha's horror, the guard slapped Leah soundly.

"No!" Sorcha screamed, pounding her fists futilely against the window ledge.

The sudden silence in the bailey was deafening.

The prisoners were shepherded into the great hall, and Sorcha was frantic to see her sister. Running to the door, she cried, "Guard! Guard!" and pounded upon the rough timbers. "Open up! Guard!" Her fists thudded, and pain jarred up her arms. "Open the door!"

Clunk! The bar was lifted out of its brackets. "By the gods, woman, you're makin' enough racket to wake the bloomin' dead," the guard, a portly man with a red-veined nose, said. His breath smelled of stale mead and he belched loudly.

"I want to see my sister," Sorcha demanded.

"Yer what?"

"I just saw some soldiers return with Lady Leah, and I demand to see her." She tossed her head imperiously.

"I'll be havin' to talk to Lord Darton—"

Sorcha didn't wait. While the dullard was making his plans, she raced by, pushing him out of her way.

"Hey, wait! Bloody Christ!" The soldier gave chase, but Sorcha had already scurried along the corridor and to the stairs. Her feet were swift and sure on the steps. "Hey! One of the prisoners is escaping. Sir Brady! Elwin! For the love of Jesus! Stop, you fool woman!" Other footsteps pounded through the halls, and Sorcha was met at the bottom of the stairs by Sir Brady and Darton, the lord of Erbyn himself.

Brady grabbed at her, but Darton held up a hand. "What is it?" he asked.

"I want to see my sister." From the corner of her eye she caught sight of Tadd, his face red from too much wine as he backed Lucy into a corner and grabbed at her breasts. Lucy giggled, had the decency to blush, and ducked out of his drunken embrace.

Sorcha's stomach turned over, but she pulled her gaze back to Darton's. "I saw Lady Leah being brought in. I need to talk to her."

"In good time," Darton said with eminent patience.

"Now!" Sorcha cried. "Tadd . . ." She turned to her brother, and he growled back at her. "Leah is here!"

Tadd's eyes were glazed from too much wine, but he managed to lean against the wall, and his thin lips pulled into a smirk. "Just in time to marry her off."

"You cannot!"

He stepped closer, swaying slightly. "I can do anything I damned well please, sister. I'm the ruler of Prydd now."

"Then Prydd is dead."

He reached up, intending to strike her, but Darton's sword came fast from its sheath and settled at Tadd's throat. "Remember that the lady will be my wife."

"Then I pity you," Tadd said thickly. "She's nothing but trouble and will be your curse for as long as you live."

"I think not." The blade pinched a little closer to Tadd's Adam's apple, and Sorcha thought she would be sick.

Small dots of sweat collected on Tadd's upper lip. "My mistake," he said carefully, and Darton quickly sheathed his weapon.

"As long as we understand each other. As for your request," he said, turning to face Sorcha again, "Mayhap Lady Leah would like to bathe."

Sorcha tried to remain calm, though inside she was screaming. "Then let me talk to Bjorn."

"The stableboy who stole the horses?" Darton shook his head slowly. "He's been thrown in the dungeon and will stay there until he's hanged."

"Hanged?" Sorcha whispered, her throat catching over the horrid word. Surely he was joking. "You would not . . ."

Darton's leer was as cold as a snake's skin. "He's a traitor, m'lady, and here at Erbyn, we hang traitors."

sixteen

"Have you lost your mind?" Anne called after her brother. Darton seemed to have gone daft, and she wouldn't believe a word of his nonsense. He didn't look around at her, just kept walking through the rain to the armorer's hut. Blast the man. Frowning at the mud, she gathered her skirts in her fingers and followed him. Rain splattered the ground and peppered her shoulders, and the hood she wore was little protection as water began to soak through the heavy wool, but she was damned if she was going to let one of her bullheaded brothers destroy the other.

In the bailey, men shouted and hammers banged. Several carts, their wheels creaking and thick with mud, rolled into the yard.

"You can't just say that Hagan's dead," she insisted, catching up to Darton as she sidestepped a puddle. Her strides were as long as her brother's, but she was still hurrying to keep pace with him.

"Hagan's dead or dying. Either way, he deserted us."

Had he no conscience? The castle gossip rang in her ears. "Since you sent no one to find him or his body I think you were behind the attack so that you could steal his castle!" The mud was squishing over her boots, but she didn't care. Her heart was heavy with fear and dread. Asides, she was furious. Darton had no right, none, to attack Hagan. 'Twas against everything in which she'd placed her faith.

Anne had always known her brothers didn't get along and had long sensed Darton's vexation at being born just a few minutes after Hagan, but she never thought he would do anything so vile, so wicked, so utterly blackhearted as to try and overthrow Hagan. "Don't think I don't hear things, Darton."

He turned on her, his eyes burning bright, his scarlet mantle swirling around him like the very cape of the devil. "What have you heard?"

"That your soldiers chased down Sorcha and Hagan, that you intended to murder him."

Darton's skin tightened over his face. "Anything else?"

"Yes. You've detained his soldiers and have kept them prisoner, and you left your own twin in the forest to die like a wounded dog." She was furious now because he didn't deny anything, just stared at her with his hate-filled eyes. "He's your brother. My brother. *Our* brother. How could you—"

With a smack that rang through the bailey, he struck her hard in the face. She gasped and stumbled back a step, and the pounding of the hammers ceased. Her hood fell away from her hair, letting the rain pour down her neck. Tears stung her eyes. Slowly she lifted her hand to her face, holding her cheek where a welt was forming, and watched in horror as he reined in his wrath so he wouldn't strike her again. "So 'tis true," she said, and wondered how his brotherly rivalry had festered into a hatred so intense that he would resort to murder. As children, she and Darton had been close, sharing secrets, playing together, and excluding Hagan, who had always been groomed to be heir. Often she'd seen Darton's face tighten as he'd fought tears when their father had ignored him in favor of his firstborn son, but Anne had never believed that his torment would lead him to such murderous deeds.

"You cannot stay on this path, Darton."

His nostrils flared and his lips curled in disgust. "You don't understand, Anne. I can do as I wish. No one can stop me."

"So you would murder your own brother, and kill a stableboy for helping a woman escape?"

"Bjorn's a traitor."

"No, Darton, you're the traitor. You kidnapped a noblewoman, forced her to lie with you, and she tried to free herself by taking her life. There is no betrayal in that. But you . . . you've plotted against Hagan for years, turning his own soldiers against him, and now this . . . this murder. What's happened to you?" She took a step forward, and he stopped her with the fearless hatred that etched every one of his features. He looked evil and hard. No light of remorse lighted his eyes.

"Leave it be, Anne."

She couldn't. Her own rage was so great that she had no control of her tongue. " 'Tis rumored that you and Tadd of Prydd have some sort of agreement to marry off Leah to Sir Marshall." She shuddered at the thought. "Have you no conscience?"

"Be careful, Anne. I have spoken to a messenger from the house of Derwen. Someone is asking for your hand."

"No . . . there is no one at Derwen save Lord Spader . . ." She felt the color drain from her face.

"His last wife, poor thing, died in childbirth, and he's looking for a new mate."

Anne's lips curled in disgust. "Lord Spader—by the gods, the man's near eighty and can barely walk. Surely you are joking." But the gravity in his eyes caused her blood to congeal.

"Spader only wants a young wife for his amusement. And he needs an heir; none of his five wives gave him a son. He has spoken to me of you."

"No."

Darton smiled without a trace of warmth. Rain dripped from his nose.

"You would not," she whispered, but knew it to be true. Had he not tried to kill their brother? "All of Lord Spader's wives are dead—either by their hands or his, I suspect—and if you think I'll marry that old man, you're wrong," she said.

"You forget, sister, Hagan is no longer running the castle. If I make an arrangement for you to wed Lord Spader, you'll damn well marry him." Darton managed a sneer, and she felt her blood begin to boil. As Darton had always resented being treated as the second-born, she had resented both her brothers treating her with less respect because she was born a woman—as if her womanhood were her fault. Not that she wanted to be a man, but it galled her to think that just because she had not male parts dangling between her legs, she was considered less able to think for herself. As if the man's sex and brain were connected. She dared not voice her feelings, however, for it seemed that most noblewomen were perfectly satisfied with their lot in life. They would not want to ride off to war, or worry about the thievery or quarrels in the fiefdom, or take part in jousts or have to answer to the king, but Anne felt differently. A part of her resented the fact that she was never asked her opinion. As if her thoughts didn't matter. Neither Hagan nor Darton considered her ideas worth much, and she had spent years trying to keep the family name away from scandal, trying to fit the part of the baron's sister.

No longer. Not if Darton could strike her and make her appear a fool to the peasants and then insult her by suggesting that he'd marry her off to a man who might be buried within the week. If Darton thought she would meekly accept his edict, he had better think again.

Darton was still glaring at her, and she had the urge to kick him between the legs and let him feel how important his member really was. "You can't treat people this way," she said, her body shaking with rage.

"Of course I can." His voice was even and smooth, though hatred burned like hot embers in his eyes. "I'm the baron."

"Not unless Hagan's dead."

"Believe me, sister, our brother will never return, and unless you obey me and recognize me as the new baron, I will have to consider you a traitor." He glanced meaningfully toward a grassy knoll near the well where the carpenters were busy building a gallows.

"You cannot do this, Darton," she said wretchedly, and swallowed over a sudden knot of fear. "You cannot hang Bjorn for helping Sorcha—"

"Just watch me, Anne. And be careful that you obey me as well. For if you cross me, I will see that your life is a living hell. Lord Spader is an impatient man." He strode across the yard, and geese and hens flew out of his path.

Anne, her cheeks flaming in embarrassment, was left standing near the fishpond as work in the castle resumed. The carpenters were busy building their death trap, the tanner was scraping hides near the door of his hut, and the silversmith tooled a new platter, but even as they began working again, they cast curious glances in her direction, and she knew they had overheard some parts of her horrid conversation with her brother. Most of the men had stopped working at their tasks until Darton had slapped Anne, but now, as if embarrassed for her, they gladly resumed their labors.

Gathering the frayed strands of her dignity, she tossed her hood over her head and turned back to the great hall. She'd always been loyal to her brothers and felt that, above all else, she should show her allegiance to her castle and the man who ruled Erbyn. She'd believed in family honor and keeping personal squabbles hidden. Pride and honor and the preservation of Erbyn above all else.

But that was before Darton had become a murderer and declared himself baron.

Splashing through the puddles, she realized that all the stories she'd heard about him had been true. She had turned a blind eye and a deaf ear in his direction whenever there had been gossip. More often than not she'd chosen to ignore the rumors that had swarmed around him. There had always been gossip—about his taste in women and his sexual pleasures that had bordered on the perverse or his far-sighted ambitions—but she'd been stalwart in her belief that the treacherous stories had been grossly exaggerated, that this was her brother, for God's sake, and he would never, *never* do anything so ruthless and wicked as plot the murder of Hagan.

Her stomach wrenched painfully.

Now it appeared as if he'd ordered their own brother slain!

"Oh, Hagan," she whispered, staring at the ground as tears ran from her eyes, "forgive me." She had been a fool where Darton had been concerned, and her elder brother had probably paid for her foolishness with his life.

Biting her lip, she vowed that she would never make the same mistake twice. Now that she knew the depths to which Darton had sunk, she'd find a way to save those he planned to harm. The list was long, but it started with Sorcha of Prydd.

By the gods, he could walk! One leg didn't work very well and he was still stiff and sore, but whatever that bitter concoction was that old Isolde had forced down his throat, it seemed to have worked. He'd drunk the stuff, coughing and spitting, for two days while she'd applied an ointment to his wounds. Now Hagan was able to stand and walk with no assistance, though his back and legs still throbbed.

He'd been lucky, Isolde had told him. None of the arrows, save the one in his forearm, had pierced deep. Even his old wounds throbbed. His thigh muscle ached, and his back, near the shoulder, burned, but the pain was not great enough to keep him lying on the pallet in Wolf's tent.

Too much was at stake.

He couldn't wait another minute, for the dull ache from his wounds was nothing when compared to his tortured thoughts of Sorcha. He'd been tormented for three days with the sickening image of her standing before a priest and swearing to honor and obey Darton. Guts roiling, Hagan had tried to push himself to his feet, demanded that Wolf find a way to free her, ranted, raved, and cursed until he was hoarse and could speak no more. But it seemed Wolf had his own plans and was in no hurry.

Grinding his teeth, Hagan walked stiffly out of the tent, and with each stride his sore muscles began to respond. He found Wolf near the embers of the fire. 'Twas twilight and the forest was beginning to shadow.

Some of the men were out hunting game, others were guarding the camp, and a few others had ridden away on their own missions. Several of the ruffians and the old woman, Isolde, lingered in the camp. Hagan hadn't asked about them; he was better off not knowing which laws were being broken and by whom.

"We must go back to Erbyn," he said as Wolf began to sharpen his dagger on a whetstone. "We have little time."

"There is time."

Hagan's temper flared. "Nay—"

"Patience," Wolf snapped, sliding his thin blade over the smooth rock. His eyes shadowed over with a memory that he didn't bother to share. "I learned patience a long while ago; now 'tis your time to understand so simple a virtue."

"But Sorcha—"

"Is not married yet."

"How do you know this?"

"As I told you, I have spies at Erbyn," Wolf said with more than a hint of pride. Click, click, click, the tiny weapon gleamed in the firelight.

Hagan's fists curled in vexation. Never had he felt so helpless, and the feeling gnawed at him. "Who are these traitors?"

"None of your trustworthy men, rest assured, but a few of Darton's followers who drink too much. When their tongues are loose and their loins hot, they lie with poor wenches who, for a little silver, are willing to share their tales."

Hagan snorted. "You rely on gossip from whores."

Wolf grinned and wiped his knife upon his leggings. "This bothers you?"

"Everything bothers me, and there is no time to waste. Look, outlaw, I would reward you well if you would help me free Lady Sorcha."

Wolf considered. "How well?"

"All your crimes would be forgiven."

He sheathed his dagger and lifted a shoulder. "I care not that there be a price upon my head."

"That is not all. Half of all that is mine, I will give to you."

Wolf rubbed his hand over the back of his neck. "Land?"

"Aye, and a castle. One that is not far from Prydd."

"That is a great amount, Lord Hagan," Wolf said with a sneer. "You are generous."

Generous? Nay. Desperate. And impatient. "My offer only stands if we start today to save the lady."

"I want none of your wealth, m'lord," Wolf said with more than a trace of sarcasm. Hagan felt as if a stone had been thrust upon his soul, for without Wolf's help, he would have to return to Erbyn alone—trick the outlaws, steal his horse, and begin the journey back to the castle. He wasn't afraid of returning by himself, but he knew that there was might in numbers, and even this tattered group of robbers was better than no army at all.

Wolf's eyes slitted at the darkening heavens. "I want only Tadd of Prydd," he said with such a low voice that Hagan wondered at his intense hatred.

"He is yours. But we must hurry."

Wolf lowered his blue eyes and gazed at Hagan. "Worry not, I ride in the morning."

"To Erbyn."

"Nay, to the north. To Abergwynn."

"Abergwynn?" Hagan said, remembering the huge castle from his youth. As large as Erbyn, the castle was a fortress with wide curtain walls and tall towers. Its battlements, ramparts, and towers were said to be impenetrable. Garrick, the ruler, was fearless, a warrior whose reputation cast fear into many who rode outside the law. Yet this outlaw seemed to think the baron could be persuaded to their cause.

"How do you know the Baron of Abergwynn?" Hagan asked suspiciously.

Wolf's eyes clouded and he refused to answer. He motioned to the silent one, the big man known as Jagger. "We ride in the morning," he said. "To Abergwynn."

Hagan said, "I will go with you."

Wolf considered. "This is personal."

Hagan didn't give a damn. "If you want me to deliver Tadd of Prydd to you, then you must take me with you."

Scratching his beard, Wolf frowned, but seemed to be wavering. "You are in no position to bargain."

"This is my battle, Wolf. I will reward you greatly, but I must be a part of the battle plan. I needs speak to Garrick of Abergwynn myself."

"You are not healed."

"I will ride swiftly. Without complaint." Hagan reached for his sword and drew it deftly, placing the point at Wolf's throat. "I will not slow you," he vowed.

Wolf wasn't pleased. His blue eyes turned to ice in his anger, but he lifted a shoulder. " 'Tis your own death you seek."

"So you still defy me." Darton stormed through the door to her chamber and kicked aside Sorcha's uneaten trencher. Venison and gravy sprayed upon the walls and floor, and the hard bread sailed into the fire, where it was quickly consumed by hungry, hissing flames.

Sorcha, leaning against a post to the canopy of her bed, lifted her chin and pinned her bridegroom with a gaze of pure hatred. "I feel not like eating," she admitted, and knew she'd failed. She'd told herself that she had to appear to accept her fate, that she should eat her meals and smile at Darton, but her pride would not allow her to grovel at the boots of someone she detested.

" 'Twill do no good, this moping and starving yourself." He walked to the foot of the bed, near enough to her that she could touch him, and he said, "We will be wed tomorrow."

"Nay."

Darton curled strong fingers over her arm. Squeezing painfully, he said, "You have no choice in the matter. Tadd has agreed. The arrangements have been made."

Sorcha's heart was thundering with rage, and she wriggled free of his hurtful grasp. "I will never marry you, Darton of Erbyn. Nor can you torture me into agreeing to be your bride." Turning swiftly, she walked to the window, where the air was fresh and the wind blew softly over the curtain wall. In the orchard, apple and pear trees lifted their bare branches to the darkening heavens, and Sorcha felt foreboding as dark as the middle of the night.

She heard him approach, and stiffened. His breath was hot against the back of her neck and she tried to move, but he used his body to block her escape, and she was forced to stare out the window.

"I want you to be my bride, Sorcha," he said.

"Why?"

His finger trailed along her neck, and she shuddered. "Because I'm captivated with you."

"I detest you."

"You're very powerful, m'lady. We could use that power, you and I."

"Did you not hear me? I loathe being in the same room with you, I cannot stand to hear your voice, and I will never, *never* agree to marry you!"

He chuckled softly. Hideously. "I think I can persuade you." His voice had a deadly ring that caused her heart to stop. When she turned to face him, his eyes were dark with lust. He motioned at the window, and one of his guards scurried through the bailey. A few seconds later the guard returned, dragging Bjorn with a noose slung over his neck.

"What . . . what is this?" Sorcha whispered, her words frozen in her throat, the silent knell of doom resounding through her brain. The first stars were beginning to wink through heavy clouds, and she could barely see.

With curses and kicks, Bjorn was shoved up the steps of the scaffold and forced to stand upon a stool.

Horrified, Sorcha cried, "No, you must not! This is madness. Bjorn did nothing—oh, my God." She saw a movement from the corner of her eye and turned to watch as her sister was being led—half dragged into the yard as well. *Oh, God, no! He couldn't mean to kill them!* Leah was crying, her hands over her eyes, her screams muffled. She tried to run to the gallows, but a huge guard restrained her, and her wails rent the bailey and cut into Sorcha's heart.

"You bastard!" Sorcha spat. "What are you doing?"

"Taming you."

"I will never—" The words died in her throat.

"It seems your sister has taken a fancy to the stableboy, and her bridegroom, Sir Marshall, does not like anyone else vying for her affections."

"Sir Marshall?" Sorcha whispered, conjuring up the gaunt knight with devious eyes, bony skull, and long fingers. Cold, cruel, and heartless. *This* was the man to whom Leah was betrothed? Nay! Nay! Nay! "No!" She felt sick inside. "Leah will not marry—"

" 'Tis arranged. Tadd has agreed."

"But Leah—" Oh, Lord, what of her sister?

Leah was on her knees in the bailey, sobbing wretchedly and letting the rain pound upon her head and shoulders.

"Noooo!" Suddenly catapulting to her feet, she lunged up the stairs, screaming and scratching, begging the guards to stop as the noose settled upon Bjorn's neck.

Cursing loudly, a burly soldier hauled her back down the stairs, and she let out a keening wail that brought goose bumps to Sorcha's neck.

"Release him and let her be!" Sorcha screamed from the window, but the guard ignored her pleas. Turning to face Darton, Sorcha cried, "You must stop this madness! Bjorn deserves not to die. 'Twas *my* plan to steal the horses and escape the castle. 'Twas I who begged him to help us!"

"So you want to join him?" Darton cocked his head toward the gallows.

She angled up her chin. "I will replace him. Rather than marry you."

"Careful, my love," he said, and she wanted to spit in his face. She didn't, however, for fear he would give the signal to have Bjorn's stool kicked from beneath his feet. Gritting her teeth, her fists clenched at her sides, she said, "Please, don't do this."

Darton hesitated, then cast a bored glance out the window. He held his hand in a signal, and as Sorcha watched in silent relief the noose was tossed away from Bjorn's neck and he was led back to the dungeon. " 'Twas not planned for this day anyway," Darton said, slowing twisting a coil of Sorcha's black hair around his finger. " 'Twill be done at dusk tomorrow."

"No!"

He let the loop of hair slide from his finger. "You are willing to plead for the stableboy's life, eh?"

"Yes."

"And bargain with me?"

Her heart nearly stopped when she realized his ploy. Her stomach rolled over, and she had to swallow hard not to retch. "This show was only for me, was it not?"

"Smart girl." He lifted his brows. "Bjorn's life as well as your sister's happiness is in your hands. Marry me, and Bjorn will live. Leah will not be forced to marry a cold man who would as easily slit her throat as lie with her."

"And Hagan?" she asked, barely daring to breathe.

"Is dead."

"But his body has not been found," she said, horrified at the twist of her thoughts. She felt as cold as death when she realized that if Hagan were found alive Darton would surely kill him. Darton would not stop short of murdering his brother to remain Baron of Erbyn. She swallowed back the lump of fear in her throat, but said, "I will marry you, Darton, if you promise Bjorn's freedom and that Leah will be allowed to return to Prydd or go where she pleases. If Hagan is found alive, you will not harm him."

Though there was no wind, she felt as if a gale as sharp as a blade of ice cut out her soul. The thought of marrying Darton was vile.

"Hagan is dead."

"So you say," she whispered over the thickness in her throat. Tears threatened her eyes, and her voice was low and uneven. It was all she could do to keep from falling on the floor and sobbing for the man she loved. She clenched her fists and refused to show Darton any more of her weakness. "But there is a chance that Hagan is alive, and I want your word that you will look for him no longer, and if he is alive, you will let him live as a free man."

"Think you I would ever hand back Erbyn to him?"

"Nay. I did not ask for that, Darton," she said, forcing her gaze to meet his. His face was blurred as she stared through tears. "It matters not if he is stripped of his possessions, but you must vow to me that he will live."

"And for this you will marry me?"

The words lodged in her throat, but she forced them over her tongue. "Aye, my liege," she said, hoping to sound obedient when she wanted to spit in the cur's face. Oh, for her small dagger with the wicked little blade! "I will be your wife."

"Then we will make haste. The wedding will be tomorrow at dawn."

Bjorn stared at the moon through the small window high over his head. In the rat-infested dungeon, he glared at the night sky and vowed his vengeance. He'd been toyed with today, and he still felt the scratch of hemp at his throat. More frightened than ever in his life, he'd learned something vital when the hangman had tightened the noose around his neck. He could face death, but not without some sense of dignity, and he would not willingly be led back to the gallows until he'd tried to pay back Darton in kind for all the evil he'd brought to Erbyn . . . and to Leah.

For, in truth, Bjorn felt little loyalty to the castle or the lord, but for the first time in his life, he cared for another person; someone other than himself.

In the few days he was with Leah, he'd fallen in love with her. Though Sorcha was the forceful one, the sister with the ideas and the power and the birthmark proclaiming her the savior of Prydd, it was Leah, sweet, simple, and good, to whom he had been drawn.

Mayhap it was because she seemed so quiet. She hardly dared look a man in the eye, and yet he sensed in her an inner strength. He'd heard the rumors, knew that Darton had forced her into his bed and raped her. His teeth gnashed and hate poured through his blood.

During their one night alone together in the forest, Bjorn had heard Leah scream in her sleep, and when he'd tried to awaken her, to hold her until the demons of the darkness left her mind, she'd scratched and fought, pushing him away with more strength than he'd expected. Perhaps she was terrified of all men. Because of Darton. His lip curled and he spewed a curse at the new master of his fate.

Bjorn and Leah had become close during their few hours together, and she had seemed to come to trust him. But he'd failed her and they had been ambushed by Darton's men and brought back in humiliation to Erbyn.

By the blood of Christ, he would save her.

In the darkness of the dungeon, Bjorn swore on the grave of his mother that he would seek revenge upon the evil one who called himself baron. For himself. For Sorcha. But most of all, for Leah.

Somehow, he intended to kill Darton with his own hands before he'd let the hangman kick the stool away and snap his neck.

Anne had never considered herself a coward, and yet sweat ran down her spine as she faced the guard at Sorcha's door. For once, her usually graceful bearing seemed forced. She smiled sweetly, but wanted to kick the man into doing what she wanted.

"I didn't hear nothin' about a visit," Sir Patton, the dullard of a guard, said as he scratched his head.

Anne looked down her nose at the man. "The lady has not been eating. My brother is concerned and thought she might need company to bring back her appetite."

The guard didn't move. "Brady says no one goes in but the servant girl."

"Brady is not the lord. Now, Sir Patton, the baron has

asked not to be disturbed while he and Lord Tadd work on the details of the truce between our houses, but if you will not allow me to visit his bride and take her the meal Darton so wants her to eat, then I'll go fetch him and he can tell you himself. Maybe he'll bring Lord Tadd along as well." She smiled coldly and let her words settle into Patton's thick skull.

He swallowed and shifted from one foot to the other. He knew that Tadd and Darton were drinking together and that Darton was hoping that under the influence of wine and Lucy's considerable charms, Tadd would ask for less compensation for the trouble of the kidnapping and the murder. Darton would be furious if he was interrupted, and Sir Patton had tasted Darton's wrath once before. He still bore the scars of Darton's whip from the last time he'd stupidly disobeyed the new lord of Erbyn.

"You'll not be staying long," he said.

"But a few minutes, just to assure myself that she eats some of Ada's eel pie." Grinning coyly, she opened the linen covering, and in a warm cloud of spice, the scent of onions and fish wafted through the hallway.

Patton licked his lips and moved the bar from the door. "See that you hurry."

"I promise," she said sweetly as she swept into the room and found Sorcha huddled before the dying fire. The door clanged shut behind her, and Sorcha looked up sharply, expecting Darton and finding his white-faced sister.

"What do you want?" Sorcha asked. She'd never trusted Anne because the woman was often with Darton.

"Only your company," Anne replied, glancing over her shoulder, then letting out a long sigh. She held out the pie tin.

"I'm not hungry."

"You must eat."

"I'll not—"

"Come, Sorcha, we have little time," Anne whispered firmly as she cast another worried glance over her shoulder. "If you are to escape before Bjorn is hanged, we must work quickly."

"Escape."

"Aye. Look, I know I've not been . . . kind to you, but I cannot stand idly by and watch my brother . . . Oh, Lord, please, just trust me."

Sorcha didn't know if she should bother listening. Anne had not been overly friendly to her since her arrival at Erbyn, and she'd seemed closer to Darton than to Hagan. Could this be a trick to test her allegiance? "You want me to plan my escape? Why? So you can run back to your brother and tell him?"

In vexation, Anne blew a strand of hair from her eyes. "Nay—"

"Why should I trust you?"

"Because you have no choice."

"But—"

"Because your sister's life depends upon it."

Sorcha bit her tongue.

"Because you love Hagan and tomorrow you are to wed Darton." Anne's fingers coiled anxiously in her hair. "Please, Sorcha, listen to me. For Hagan's sake. I have an idea, a way to help you escape, but I'll need your help, for I know not the ways of the old ones," Anne said, though in truth, she shuddered as she thought of it. Again she gave the pie tin to Sorcha. "Eat . . . eat . . . in case Sir Patton returns."

"This is no trick?"

"I, too, wish for Hagan's return, though I fear . . . Oh, God, if Darton has had him killed . . ." Anne's voice caught and her brown eyes filled with tears. Sorcha realized the horrid truth: Anne was right, she had no choice but to put her faith in Hagan's sister.

She took a large bite from the pie. "What do you needs know?" she asked around a bite of the succulent eel.

Anne's shoulders relaxed a little. With one eye trained toward the door, Anne reached up beneath her skirt and withdrew not one, but two small daggers. The very knives that Isolde had given Sorcha oh, so long ago. "This one is yours," Anne said, handing her the knife with a curved blade.

"And the other?"

"Is for me." Anne shifted her gaze to the dying fire and said a quiet prayer for strength. "I think I have found a way for you to escape to your freedom, but we must work fast. Tonight. If I am to help you, I need you to swear on all that you hold holy that you will find Hagan or proof of his body."

Seventeen

"Abergwynn," Wolf said, his voice barely a whisper.

From inside, as if in answer, a wolf or dog howled, and Hagan felt a finger of ice draw down his spine. The small band of thugs pulled up their horses at the edge of the forest, but Hagan rode forward, staring at the castle.

Like towering giants the battlements of Abergwynn rose in the dusk, and Hagan admired the sturdy stone walls. If only the baron was as strong as his castle, there might be a chance that he could rescue Sorcha. For the first time in his life, Hagan felt powerless, and all of his possessions and wealth meant nothing to him. Darton could have it all.

Except for Sorcha. The thought that Darton was marrying her was a weight upon his shoulders Hagan couldn't dislodge. Why had he been such a blind fool—trusting a brother who had always begrudged him? Now, because of his stupid pride, because he wouldn't see Darton for the traitor he was, Sorcha and all of Erbyn would suffer at his brother's cruel hand.

His teeth gnashed together in his impatience. A sentry shouted and a horn blared, signaling their arrival. Hagan knew only a little of Garrick of Abergwynn, and yet he was trusting his life and the fate of those he loved to an outlaw and a baron he'd never before met. He glanced at the rogue, a man named Wolf with cold blue eyes and a savage grimace. Hagan didn't know what ties bound Wolf to Abergwynn, but he guessed that the baron owed the outlaw a favor—perhaps in payment for some murderous deed Wolf had done under the cover of darkness.

Though not a God-fearing man, Hagan sent up a prayer for Sorcha's safety and resigned himself to the fact that the meeting with Garrick was necessary, though time seemed to be running out.

Wolf felt Hagan's impatience, and in truth, he, too, was anxious, for at last, Tadd of Prydd would be his. Tadd would finally pay. A cruel smile twisted his lips as he stared at the massive curtained walls of the keep. It had been ten years since he'd been in the castle. He'd left when he was but a boy. He'd been foolish and young and thought himself a man at the time, but he'd been proved wrong.

Hot injustice, banked for years, simmered to the surface of his blood. Inside his gloves, his fingers clenched tightly around the reins. It had been so long. Memories of his youth flitted through his brain, and he found it hard to believe that he'd been gone for so many years. Would they remember? Or did they believe him dead?

He smiled coldly, for it would do his heart good to think that he might scare the living hell out of his brother. There had always been a rivalry between them, and the one time he'd tried to prove his manhood, Wolf had let Garrick down. He'd vowed never to return, but here he was, ready to beg a favor. He was anxious and sweat began to dampen his spine, but he showed no outward sign of emotion. He'd grown into a man in the past ten years, seen the hell that life could be, and he'd learned to keep his feelings deep in his soul, hidden away from anyone else's eyes. 'Twas weak to show emotion, and Wolf wanted his men, aye, and his brother, too, to believe him strong.

"Who goes there?" a guard yelled from the tower. A young man whom Wolf didn't recognize glared at the ragged company of riders. The guard's gaze narrowed in suspicion and his bow and arrow were at ready.

"I'm here to see the baron," Wolf said, ignoring the fact that the sentry's weapon was aimed at his heart. He remembered another time when he'd stood outside this very keep, a knife pressed to his throat.

"That doesn't answer me question," the sentry said. "Who are you?"

Wolf leaned forward on the saddle, and his gaze was fierce as he stared up at the man blocking his entry. There was a guard at ground level, too, a wary lad with a long sword. Wolf thought about knocking the sword from the younger man's hands and grabbing the sentry by the front of his tunic, then hauling him off his feet and scaring the devil out of him, but he couldn't. For if he made a swift move, a dozen arrows would be showered upon his men. "Tell him Wolf from the forests near Erbyn has come. I bring with me Baron Hagan, and we have a request for Lord Garrick."

The guard's gaze moved to Hagan, his eyes slitting a bit as if he didn't believe a grand lord would look so pale and weak. "Is this true?"

Hagan stiffened and his own gaze turned to stone. "Aye. I'm Hagan."

"Come in then," the guard said, waving them through the portcullis, "but just you two." He blocked the way of the rest of the outlaws, and though Cormick and Odell grumbled loudly at being mistreated, Wolf did not argue with the guard.

"Baron Hagan's wounded," Wolf said. "We seek but a few hours' rest and an audience with—" He saw her then.

Through the opening in the gate, he watched her dash across the bailey. As slender as he remembered and even more beautiful, she ran with four girls chasing after her, all with the same wild black hair and small white faces as their mother. Behind the last girl a dog—nay, a wolf—loped with an uneven gait.

She was hurrying from the new chapel, a small church that hadn't been built when Wolf had last seen Abergwynn. As if she'd heard him speak, though he hadn't uttered a word, she turned and noticed him. The temperature of the air in the bailey seemed to drop ten degrees. She gasped, her hand flying to her throat. The wolf-dog sniffed the air and growled. "Merciful God," she cried. Her eyes locked with Wolf's before she smiled widely and picked up her skirts, running forward and leaving her dazed daughters to stare after their mother. The dog followed his mistress, his tired old eyes trained in Wolf's direction.

She didn't seem to care that the guards and men could see her legs as she ran to him. Her green eyes were filled with joy. "Ware!" she yelled. "Ware! You're alive! I knew it! I've seen visions of you . . . Oh, thank God, you've come home!"

Leaping off his destrier, he swept her into his arms and twirled her off her feet. " 'Tis good to see you again, Morgana."

For a minute his men, watching from the other side of the gate, were confused. Was this, their leader, the Baron of Abergwynn? No. Wolf was not Garrick! And yet this woman who seemed the lady of the castle was greeting him warmly, tears of joy running from her beautiful eyes. She clung fiercely to him as if she were afraid he might vanish . . .

" 'Twas sinful of you to let us think you were dead," she teased, but couldn't stop smiling.

"Morgana!" a harsh voice boomed across the bailey, and the lord himself, his face set in a savage scowl, stood at the top of the stairs to the great hall.

"Look, Garrick," she said, wiping the tears from her eyes. " 'Tis—"

"Wolf, the outlaw from Erbyn," the rogue said as he let go of Garrick's wife. Head cocked arrogantly, he swaggered up to the great lord.

Garrick's jaw was firmly set. Hand on the hilt of his sword, he swiftly crossed the wet grass and glared at the leader who had the audacity to take his wife into his grubby arms. "I've heard of you," he said as he drew closer and his eyes narrowed upon the man.

Morgana giggled. "Oh, my love, do you not recognize—"

"My God!" Garrick whispered hoarsely. "Can it be? Does the ghost of my brother visit me?"

One side of Wolf's mouth twisted into a cynical smile. "I assure you, Garrick, I am no ghost."

"Ware!" Garrick said, his harsh features relaxing. "By the gods, I thought you were dead. Morgana has been prattling on and on about you, saying you were returning, but . . . well, I found it impossible to believe. It's been so long . . ." His voice caught.

"*This* is Ware?" A lad of about thirteen with red-brown hair curled his nose at the outlaw as if he smelled foul.

"I'm afraid we've told Logan many tales of you," Morgana said with a smile. "All of them very heroic."

"He's a bloody outlaw," Logan said.

"Aye. And my brother as well." Garrick clapped Wolf on the back, and Wolf, too, embraced his brother. Until this moment he didn't realize how much he'd missed Abergwynn. It had been too long he'd been hiding in the woods.

Morgana touched him on the arm. "You must tell us everything as soon as you meet your nieces."

"Nieces only? No sons?"

"Aye, there are enough women here to make a man daft," Garrick agreed as his daughters raced up to him. "Jillian, Jane, Millicent, and Margaret." He shook his great head. He swept two of the raven-haired vixens into his arms. "Logan keeps hoping for a brother."

The boy rolled his eyes to the heavens, and Garrick ruffled his hair as he ducked away.

As Garrick set his daughters back on their feet, Morgana took Ware's arm. "Come," she said, the laughter in her eyes slowly dying. "I knew you were alive, I could feel it, but there are still so many questions . . ."

Ware's smile vanished and a shadow passed behind his eyes. "You are asking of your brother, Cadell," he said sadly, and shook his head. "I know not," he said with a sigh.

She blinked rapidly and looked away.

"Come, bring your men inside and tell us all," Garrick said, waving to the guard to allow the rest of Wolf's band into the castle. "Give these men food and drink."

Hagan slid down from his mount and extended his hand to Garrick as Wolf introduced him as the rightful Baron of Erbyn. "His brother is now, through trickery, ruling the castle."

"Darton?" Garrick asked.

"Aye, he's trying to wrest the power from Hagan, and it would do me well to help restore the rightful lord to his castle," Ware said. " 'Twould fulfill my promise to myself."

Garrick's eyes locked with those of his younger brother. "You still blame yourself for losing control of Abergwynn?"

"Aye. You had faith in me and left me in command. Strahan would never have attacked had you stayed behind."

" 'Tis long over now," Garrick said. " 'Twas not your fault."

Ware frowned but didn't seem relieved. "We've come here for your help, brother."

"Help?" Morgana whispered, and her voice faded on the wind. "You are not staying?"

Wolf shook his head. "We have not the time."

Hagan was restless. The hours slipped by. Even now, Sorcha could be married to Darton. His fists clenched silently and his mind was back at Erbyn imagining the horror that his brother had brought upon the castle. He ate the Baron of Abergwynn's fine meal of salmon, venison, fruit pies, pigeon, and custard, yet he hardly tasted a bite, and it was all he could do to keep from storming out of the great hall, climbing upon his horse, and riding back to Erbyn as fast as the beast could run, though he knew as one man, he could accomplish nothing. He needed the strength of Garrick's army as well as Wolf's bravery and cunning.

The brothers and Morgana talked long and hard, and from the pieces of their stories, Hagan learned that ten years before, Garrick's son, Logan, had been kidnapped. His most trusted knight, Strahan of Hazelwood, Garrick's cousin, had suggested asking Morgana of Wenlock, whom some believed to be a witch, to locate the boy by using her powers of seeing the future.

At the time, Garrick, whose wife was dead, had felt he had no choice and he'd fallen in love with the sorceress, but had promised her to his cousin. The battles had been bloody, and Strahan, who had instigated the kidnapping of Garrick's son in the hopes of luring Garrick from his castle and overthrowing him, had been found out. Morgana had located Logan and married the baron, but Ware, Garrick's younger brother, and Cadell, the brother to Morgana, had been feared dead. Morgana had seen them tumble off the cliffs and into the sea, presumably to their deaths.

"Sometimes," she said, leaning over the table and dabbing at a spot of gravy at the corner of her smallest daughter's mouth with her napkin, "I feel as if Cadell is calling to me. When the wind is silent, I hear his voice."

Ware sighed and shook his head. "I saw him not that night. 'Twas as if the sea had swallowed him whole. I waited until morning, searching the rocks for either him or his body. But I found nothing, no hint of what had happened to him. I was half-dead myself, but a fisherman found me." His voice lowered a bit. "The fisherman, Alan, took me back to his village, where I worked for him until I was ready to leave."

Hagan sensed that there was more to the story, but Wolf fell into silence, and Morgana dropped scraps of venison to the wolf-dog that was always at her side.

"You chose not to return to Abergwynn," Garrick said, his frown becoming more pronounced.

Ware drank long from his cup, and though there was much more he could tell them, he kept his silence. Only Hagan knew of the hatred he harbored for Tadd of Prydd, though the rightful Baron of Erbyn knew not why. No one would ever know the truth, for 'twas too private—just between Tadd and the outlaw Wolf. Mayhap he should have slit the bastard's throat and slain him when he'd posed as a messenger to Prydd, but Wolf had sensed that the time was not right. He'd waited nearly ten years, he could wait a few more days.

His eyes narrowed in the candlelight. He'd been happy working with the fisherman, learning a trade and falling in love with Alan's pretty daughter, Mary. Even now, as he thought of her, his heart lifted, then he remembered how it ended. Mary was but fourteen when Tadd of Prydd had ridden through the village, seen her, and decided that he would like her to warm his bed.

Alan objected loudly, defending his daughter's virtue, and for that crime Tadd had used his sword to sever Alan's arm at the elbow. Ware, too, intervened, and Tadd's sword felled him, slicing his face, sending him nearly to his death. They hadn't been able to save Mary, and Tadd, in front of his men, in her father's bed, had raped her. When Ware had finally come to consciousness, she cowered in the corner, half-dressed and shivering on the bloody sheets. Ware had tried to comfort her, but she'd screamed at his touch and would let no man near her.

Weeks had passed into months and Mary retreated into herself, not speaking to anyone, cowering at the very voice of any man other than her father. During a storm with Mary aboard, Alan's boat had disappeared in the ocean, and Ware, who had stayed ashore upon the fisherman's orders, had vowed that he would seek vengeance on Tadd of Prydd. From that day forward he'd called himself Wolf and had become an outlaw. He shuddered at the memory and silently pledged that he would finish it with Tadd, make him suffer as Mary had, or end up dead himself.

As he stared into the flames of the white tapers of Abergwynn, he felt his brother's gaze and he pulled himself from the depths of his memory.

"You did not answer my question. Why did you not return?" Garrick asked.

"I felt that I had failed you, Garrick. Strahan had taken over the castle when you'd entrusted its welfare to me."

"You were foolish," Morgana said. "No one blamed you."

Wolf lifted his shoulder and finished his wine in one long

swallow. "Now I am back. And I need your help. Lord Hagan needs your help."

Hagan leaned forward so that he could look the lord of Abergwynn straight in his eye. " 'Tis important that we move quickly," he said with all the patience he could muster. "If you help me quiet this rebellion, Lord Garrick, I pledge that should you ever need my help, my entire army will stand with you." Looking at each person sitting at the table, Hagan shoved up his sleeves. "Gaining entrance to Erbyn will be difficult. Darton will be wary. But I have a plan . . ."

Anne had never been more frightened in her life. In truth, she wished she'd never met Sorcha, that she felt no obligation because of her brother, but she had no choice. What Darton had done to Hagan was horrid, and now, as she realized that all the rumors about her brother—the very rumors she'd denied—were true, she knew it was up to her to preserve her family's honor.

Darton's kidnapping and rape of Leah were hideous, his plan to hang Bjorn just plain cruel. He could never be allowed to rule Erbyn. So, despite her fear, she was duty-bound to go through with her part of the bargain. Sorcha had told her what to do; it was just a matter of drinking the potion that she'd made from the roots and herbs she'd begged off the apothecary.

The apothecary, John, hadn't been pleased to give away his precious herbs, but he hated Darton and was loyal to Hagan. John's son was one of Hagan's soldiers who was still missing, and John would do anything to wrest the power of Erbyn from Darton. "These medicines are dangerous," he'd warned Anne as he'd reluctantly handed her the vials. "I wish there was another way."

"There isn't, John. This will work."

His spotted forehead had wrinkled over bushy gray eyebrows. "Be careful."

"I will," she'd promised. Noting the worry in his old eyes, she'd tucked the vials into the folds of her tunic and turned toward the door.

"God be with you, Lady Anne, and with Erbyn."

"And with you, John."

She'd hurried back to the castle and waited until dark. Now the time had come. With her heart thudding in fear, she prayed God to give her strength, lifted the cup to her lips, and drank the bitter liquid. Camphor and narcissus, jasmine, and herbs she couldn't remember the names of, concocted into a horrid-tasting brew. Despite her urge to retch, she drank it all, gagged, but forced the vile concoction to stay in her stomach. Then she lay back on the bed, waiting . . . feeling her heart begin to slow and her breathing become heavy.

There was a chance her hastily conceived plan would not work, and she worried that she would never live to see the dawn, but her life was now out of her hands. "God help me," she whispered drowsily.

Now she had to rely on the savior of Prydd.

Sorcha paced the room and silently prayed that their plan would work; 'twas risky . . . too risky, and she worried that another death would be on her hands. "Please, Lord, help us," she whispered as the breeze rolled softly through her window. She stared outside to the bailey, where darkness had settled over the castle. The clouds that had poured rain all day had disappeared and the moon was full, casting silver shadows along the landscape and reflecting in the puddles that had formed during the day's showers.

She flung herself on the bed, ignoring the cupboard

where her wedding dress had been hung. If her plan did not work, she would marry Darton and the thought sat like a stone in her stomach. She tried to still the racing of her heart. She had to be patient and feign sleep. If the plan was to work, Darton must never realize that he'd been duped. Closing her eyes, she let out a slow breath and thought of Hagan. A wretched pain sliced to her soul. Was he dead? Had he been found by Darton's men and slain at his command, or had he crawled off like a wounded animal to die in the forest, without food, without water, and burning from the fever of infection? Her fingers clutched the fur coverlet in a death grip. She'd never told him she loved him, hadn't wanted to accept the truth herself, and yet she missed him horribly. Tears welled in her eyes and she sniffed as quietly as was possible.

There was a chance, though a slim one, that he was alive, and she clung to that slight hope, thinking she might see him again. Telling herself she couldn't fall victim to grief, that she had to be strong, she slapped away her horrid tears and swallowed against the sudden thickening of her throat.

She tried to sleep, but her eyes refused to close. She lay stiffly on the bed, her ears straining at every creak of the rafters, or the shuffle of footsteps in the hall, or the quiet cough from a guard or a snort as a sentry tried to stay awake.

Why hadn't she been summoned? Had something gone wrong? Could Anne, even at this very moment, be lying on the brink of death? "Please, please, be with her," she prayed, though fear made her lips tremble.

The minutes slowly passed and the moon moved in the sky. This was wrong. It was too close to morning. The morning of the day she was to marry Darton. Her stomach churned. Oh, God, if Anne, too, had died . . . another death would be at her feet. For she was at fault. She shivered. Some had called her the savior of Prydd, and yet she felt at this moment like the very death of everyone who had known her.

It must be time!

She thought she would go mad with waiting when she heard the thud of hurried tread, the groan of the bar being removed from her door. Forcing her eyes shut, she kept her breathing even as the door was yanked open to bang against the corridor wall.

With a start, she sat up and feigned surprise. Her gaze settled on Darton. "What're you doing here?" she demanded as he entered. Sir Ralston, the cruel one, was at his side, and as they approached, she cowered to a far corner of the bed.

" 'Tis Anne," Darton said in vexation.

"What of your sister?"

"She needs your help."

"My help?" Sorcha said, arching a brow as her pulse began to race. "How . . . ?"

"Don't ask questions, just get dressed and come with us." Darton's face was white with fury and impatience, and there was something else in his eyes, an evil suspicion that lingered just below the surface. "No matter what happens, we are to be married this day."

Sorcha watched as he and Ralston left her alone to dress, and her fingers fumbled as she placed the hated velvet dress over her head, then shoved her feet into her boots. With a prayer, she slid her dagger into the inside of one boot, where it pressed against her leg. "God be with us all," she whispered as she shoved open the door and found Darton pacing the hallway. Ralston leaned insolently against the wall, propped by one shoulder, as if bored by the drama unfolding.

Only a few of the sentries had been awakened, and

Sorcha suspected that Darton had not wanted the entire castle to be disturbed, but he smiled wickedly when he noticed her gown of gold velvet.

"What is wrong?" Sorcha asked, half-running to keep up with his long, angry strides.

"Anne is near death, though I know not why," he said tightly, and she was surprised to notice how much this seemed to bother him. She hadn't thought him capable of caring for anyone but himself. "Lord Spader has asked for her hand, and he won't be interested in a corpse."

So there was no love in his heart for his sister.

"You must work your magic, Sorcha. Whatever ails my sister, you must bring her back to life!"

"And if I fail?"

His lips tightened. "Don't."

They entered Anne's chamber, and Sorcha had to repress the urge to gasp. The room was dark and cold as the winter rain. Anne lay pale as death upon the bed. Oh, Lord, she'd drunk too much, Sorcha thought as she dashed to the bedside and took Anne's cool hand between her own. "Lady Anne! Wake up!" Anxiously she rubbed the insides of Anne's white wrists and noticed in the flickering candlelight the way her veins webbed beneath her thin skin. "Lady Anne!" Sorcha flung herself to her knees. " 'Tis I, Sorcha . . . Please, wake up."

Fear clawed at her heart. This had been a foolish plan, and now Anne, whose pulse beat so faintly, it could barely be felt, was dying. It was all her fault! No! No! No! She swallowed hard and, remembering that she should not know the truth as yet, turned worried eyes to Darton. "What happened?"

Ona, the sparrowlike little maid, was standing near a stool in the corner and wringing her hands. " 'Tis my blame," she whispered, tears rolling down her pale cheeks.

She coughed loudly. "The lady asked me to check on her as she'd felt ill, and . . . I fell asleep, and when I woke up, she was like this." The pitch of her voice had lowered with each of her words, and she could barely be heard.

"Stop that sniveling!" Darton ordered, then turned his eyes upon Sorcha. "Do your magic, m'lady. Save my sister."

"I need . . ." Her words failed her for a second before her eyes met Darton's. "Does not Bjorn have the necklace of knotted thread?"

Darton threw a hand up in the air in exasperation. "I know not."

"I need the necklace." When he hesitated, she added, "Without it I will not be able to save your sister . . . or her marriage . . ."

Scowling, he motioned to the guard. "Bring me the prisoner."

Sorcha didn't wait. She turned back to Anne's still form and rubbed her hands. "Lady Anne, please hear me," she pleaded, her heart hammering as sweat began to dot her brow. "Do not leave us." She touched the pulse at Anne's wrists and felt nothing, not a breath of life in her. "Anne, can you hear me?"

Darton paced from the curtained bed to the hearth and back again. His boots shifted the rushes and rang on the stone floor, and candlelight flickered on his hard features.

"Why is it so damned cold in here?" he growled, then noticed the fire, nearly dead, in the hearth. Only a few red embers glowed through a thick layer of ash. "Is this your fault?" he demanded of the maid.

"Nay, the lady asked that the fire be not lit tonight," Ona said, her voice trembling with fear. "Mayhap even then she had the fever."

"Fever?" Darton said under his breath.

"Why else?"

Darton's eyes flew to the stand near the bed where the empty cup stood. As Sorcha chanted over Anne, he crossed the room, picked up the mazer, and sniffed at the contents.

Sorcha's muscles tightened in fear. Had she told Anne the wrong potion? She'd only been half listening when Isolde had told her how she'd caused the guard to sleep on the night Sorcha had fled Prydd. What if Darton suspected?

"What's this?" he asked, and Sorcha felt as if bands had been tightened around her chest.

"Lady Anne wanted wine to help her sleep."

Damn Ona, why couldn't she keep quiet! The tension in the room began to pulse, and from the corner of her eye, she watched Darton. His eyebrows drew together to form one long black line. Slowly he rimmed the cup with a finger and lifted the dregs from the mazer to his lips. His face contorted violently and he spat onto the rushes. " 'Tis not wine she wanted but something in which to disguise some herbs." His eyes slitted with a dangerous wrath. "What know you of this, Sorcha?"

"Only that she is near death," Sorcha replied as the guard returned and pushed Bjorn into the room. The stableboy half stumbled, nearly falling against the bed. His wrists were bound and he smelled of the rot of the dungeon.

"Anne was in your chamber this night? Did she speak of trying to kill herself?"

"Nay—she said not much." Sorcha's heart pumped loudly.

"Take the damned necklace from him," Darton ordered Sir Ralston, "and then stoke the fire. 'Tis as cold as a demon's breath in here." Suspiciously, he eyed Sorcha. "And when you're finished with the fire, Ralston, fetch the priest. 'Tis time the Lady and I are married."

"But Anne—" Sorcha whispered.

" 'Twill matter not if she be alive or dead. Still we will wed. Now," he added angrily, pinning the guard with a harsh stare, "get the damned necklace."

The guard reached around Bjorn's neck, but the stable-boy stepped away quickly, agile despite being bound.

"Bloody bastard," Ralston growled, "I'll cut out yer black heart with my knife." He reached for his dagger.

Sorcha shot to her feet and placed a hand on Bjorn's chest. She lifted her gaze to him, silently begging him to trust her, and wondered if he would. He was a prisoner, his very life threatened because he'd once before placed his trust in her. "Please, Bjorn," she said softly. "We must help Lady Anne." Bjorn's strong jaw thrust forward and his lips flattened over his teeth. " 'Twill be all right," she murmured, though she doubted her own words. Mayhap Anne would die, Bjorn would be hung, and she would be forced to marry Darton. *Oh, Hagan. Where are you, my love? Please be well.*

Reluctantly Bjorn bent his head, and Sorcha removed the string from his neck. She stared deep into his eyes, trying to reassure him, then turned back to Anne.

"Take him back to the dungeon—" Darton said as Sorcha placed the magical necklace around Anne's neck, but as the guard tried to push him out of the room, an alarm sounded throughout the keep.

"What the devil?" Darton said.

Footsteps thundered through the hallways. Men shouted and pounded on thick doors, waking everyone who had been sleeping. "Lord Darton! Lord Darton! Come quickly!" A breathless sentry, sword unsheathed, rushed into the room. His scabbard clattered against the doorway. "There is an army outside the castle! An army of more than a hundred men!"

The wind rushed in through the open window, and

voices, loud and anxious, shouts and cries, echoed through the bailey.

"Hagan?" Darton asked, his voice a rasp.

Hagan! Sorcha's wretched heart soared for an instant—

"Nay! 'Tis a baron from the North."

—then fell to earth, dashed against the sharp stones of truth. She nearly cried out in pain.

"Who?" Darton demanded.

"I know not, m'lord."

Oh, Hagan, would you were alive. Sorcha closed her mind to thoughts of Hagan or worries over the army standing on the other side of the thick stone walls of Erbyn. Taking both of Anne's hands between her own, she squeezed her eyes shut tight. "Live, Lady Anne," she whispered. "By all that is holy, arise . . . walk with us . . ."

The noise of the castle seemed to mute. The air was suddenly cold and the silver ring pulsed warm against Sorcha's finger. The serpent seemed to glow in the shadowed room and clouds covered the moon.

With one hand Sorcha clutched the twigs in the necklace, and the ring turned hot. Her eyes closed and the room seemed to swim about her.

"Whose army is it? Go find out," Darton told Ralston and the sentry. As the men departed, he stayed in Anne's room, unable to move, as if he were fascinated as he watched Sorcha work her magic. With a shriek the wind raced through the castle, rattling the stone walls and echoing against the timbers, but Sorcha barely heard. She felt the warmth of her blood leave her body to heat Anne's as she prayed for Anne's life.

Slowly her eyes opened. The candles flickered and died, and still Sorcha's chants were unbroken. Carried on the wind, voices from the bailey seeped into the room. Soldiers shouted, swords clanged, horses neighed, as Darton's men made ready for battle. The acrid smell of war hung heavy on the air swirling within the dark chamber.

Sorcha's heart constricted. She gasped and swayed.

Anne's breath rushed out as if in a long sigh.

Darton's own heart nearly stopped. He couldn't tear his gaze away as his sister's eyes fluttered open and she retched. The miracle of life was restored by this small woman who would be his wife. He saw his future stretched out before him—golden, perfect, without a flaw. Yes, his bride would surely—

Crack!

Pain exploded in Darton's leg. Bones splintered and his kneecap shattered. With a scream, he felt his legs wobble and fold. His head struck the floor with a thud, and as quickly as the vision of his life had entered his head, he was swallowed in a deep, black void.

"Bloody son of a dog!" Bjorn, his face twisted in hatred, stood over the baron and shoved his boot onto Darton's throat. "You sick bastard," he snarled. "I swear I'll kill you in your own castle and spit on your body."

"There is no time for that now." Sorcha reached under the covers where Anne's knife was hidden and sawed through the thick rope binding Bjorn's wrists. Within seconds he'd yanked the frayed hemp off his arms, but never once did his boot move, and Darton's face darkened with his lack of breath.

"Do not kill him," Sorcha warned, though she knew he deserved no better.

"Why not?"

Darton squirmed and Bjorn's foot settled deeper at his throat. "Go ahead," Bjorn said to the man who would have killed him. "I would love to send you to hell."

"No. He is our prisoner. As he kidnapped Leah, so shall we kidnap him."

Bjorn smiled at this little twist of irony and he hauled Darton to his feet. Darton screamed in pain.

Anne roused, her low moan whispering through the chamber.

"Come, you must wake." Sorcha helped her to a sitting position, but she was still spinning from the effects of the potion she'd drunk, mumbled something, then sank back onto the bed as if she had no bones in her body.

"We have no time for this, Anne. Wake up! We must free Leah now."

"Free Leah?" Marshall's voice whispered through the room, and Sorcha stiffened. "I think not."

Turning, Sorcha saw the gaunt knight. He cast a look at Darton and his lip curled in disgust. "Fool," he muttered, then glared at Bjorn, Sorcha, and Anne. "You may go with your sister, but I assure you that you will not free her. You see, you're all my prisoners now, and I have an audience with Garrick of Abergwynn."

"Abergwynn?"

"Aye—Baron Garrick is here now. Seeking shelter." Marshall's grin was evil.

Ralston, who had returned, looked confused. "But what of the baron?" he asked, eyeing the groaning mass that was Darton.

Marshall smiled wickedly. "Break his other leg, then kill him."

Eighteen

Never before had the gates of Erbyn been closed to him. Now, as the wind keened across the heavens, Hagan glared up at the looming castle that had been his home all his life—a fortress impossible to scale. No battering ram could break through the gates, no catapult could throw stones large enough to pierce the thick curtain walls, and no ladder was long enough to reach the battlements. Laying siege was not an answer, for it would be months before the supplies ran out, and in that time Darton would have married Sorcha, taken her to his bed, and got her with child.

Curses filled his mind, and his fingers curled around the reins of his mount. If given the chance he would strangle his own brother—his twin—for all the evil Darton had brought to Erbyn.

Astride an unfamiliar horse, wearing the hauberk and surcoat from Abergwynn, Hagan eyed the castle and wondered if, even now, as the first gray light of dawn pierced the clouds to touch the forests of Erbyn, if Sorcha and Darton were married. Wolf had finally admitted that he had several spies within the castle, and one girl, Ona, had a loose tongue. It had been she who had told one of Wolf's men of the impending marriage.

Again he silently cursed the fates. Though his head was hidden by a skull cap and helm with a nose guard, he felt the sentry's eyes upon him. In the darkness of early morn, he appeared just another knight in the vast army of Abergwynn, though he was not far back, his own horse stood close to the flank of Garrick's steed.

His lips pressed together as he waited. If his plan failed, then all was lost. Desperation scraped at his soul until he heard the surprised shout of a guard and the unlikely clang and grind of the gears of the great portcullis as it was raised.

"The gods are with you this dawn," Wolf said as he leaned closer from his own horse. He, too, was dressed as a soldier rather than the ruffian outlaw who had terrorized the forests of Erbyn and Prydd for years.

Garrick held up his hand, and Wolf and Hagan rode forward with him at a slow trot.

"State yer business," the first guard said, his surly gaze, in the thin light, passing over Wolf and Hagan without much interest.

"I'm Garrick of Abergwynn. My army and I come seeking shelter. Some of our men were wounded by outlaws in the forest, and we cannot ride on without them."

"You are out late, m'lord."

"Aye . . . The battle was long and hard, the ride tedious. It took us all night to outwit the bastards."

The guard did not doubt him, for Garrick's face was streaked with grime from hours in the saddle and the lathered, mud-spattered horses were weary.

"Lord Darton bids you welcome," the guard said, standing aside to let them pass.

"I thought Hagan was baron here."

"Aye, he was, but he was killed recently."

"A pity," Garrick said, and Hagan felt his lips curve into an evil smile.

* * *

Sorcha turned and faced her tormentor. "I'll not be locked up," she said to Marshall. Quick as lightning, Ralston reached for his sword.

But Bjorn was fast. He struck first, springing like a cat and shoving his knife deep between the stunned soldier's ribs. Ralston let out a groan, faltered, stepped back, and swung wildly with his sword. Blood spurted, spraying the walls and the front of Sorcha's hated dress.

"Idiot!" Marshall roared, grabbing his own weapon as Ralston's sword clattered to the ground. Marshall aimed for Bjorn, but the stableboy twirled away and scooped up Ralston's weapon.

"So now we're even, Marshall."

"Hardly." Marshall grinned with an evil leer, and Sorcha felt as if death was surely upon them all. Marshall was an accomplished knight, and Bjorn, though lithe and strong, was no match for him.

Quickly Sorcha reached into her boot, her fingers searching for her knife. She heard shouts from the bailey and then the thunder of hooves, as if a hundred horses had raced through the gates, but she could not worry about whoever had intruded, not while there was an ounce of breath left in her body.

Her fingers coiled around her knife as Marshall pressed forward, pushing until Bjorn was backed to the window.

"Stop!" Sorcha commanded.

But Marshall drew back as if to cleave Bjorn in two. "Go now and meet Satan," he said as Bjorn ducked. The sword struck the windowsill, showering sparks through the room. Anne screamed as Bjorn whirled, and Sorcha threw her knife as she had so many years ago when she'd first learned how to use a dagger. The blade sliced through Marshall's tunic and delved deep into his back. With a hideous roar, the traitor spun around, his eyes round in horror, spittle collecting near the corner of his mouth to run down his beard, as he faced the woman who dared attack him.

"You . . . By the Gods . . ." He staggered.

Bjorn swung his sword without mercy. The blade sliced Marshall's shoulder before hitting bone, and the evil knight crumpled with a sickening squeal. He writhed on the ground before his soul swiftly fled this earth.

"Thank God," Anne whispered.

"Come!" Sorcha pulled Anne off the bed and, stepping over Darton and Ralston, said, "We must find Leah and make good our escape before any more who are loyal to Darton find us."

Bjorn paused to grab the weapons, which he handed to Sorcha and Anne. "Oh, God," Anne whispered, shaking her head at the sight of the blood dripping from the curved blade of the dagger. "I cannot."

"You must!" Sorcha curled the older woman's hands over the carved handle. "You may need it. We know not who is laying siege to the castle." Through the halls, she heard the sound of swords clanging and men fighting. Curses and screams and the sickening stench of death filled the castle. "Hurry! There is no time!" Together they scurried down the hallway to the room where Leah was locked. Torches nearly dead from burning throughout the night flickered faintly as they passed, casting moving shadows on the walls.

No guard was standing outside Leah's chamber, and it was little trouble to throw off the bar. The door swung open, and Leah, her face white as death, stood waiting, as if she'd heard the skirmish. "What is happening? I heard fighting—swords and men cursing and—" She gasped. *"Bjorn!"* She threw herself into his arms and began to sob. "I thought you were dead!"

Bjorn held her close and caressed her hair. "Beautiful Leah," he whispered. Sorcha thought of Hagan and how he had once touched her, how his body had felt pressed against hers. To think that he was dead, that she would never see him again . . . Tears studded her eyes, but she sniffed quickly and would not dissolve into a weeping woman, not yet. There would be time for grieving later. Clearing her throat, she said gently, "Come, we must make haste. There is not much time."

Leah, her eyes damp with tears, finally let go of the man she loved.

Sorcha started for the hall. "We have not yet escaped."

"And you won't," an authoritative voice boomed from the shadows. Sorcha's heart turned to stone. *Tadd!*

Spinning, she was sickened to find her brother filling the doorway. "What has happened here? Where's Darton?" he commanded, looking as fierce as the night. "Don't tell me, sister, that you have been plotting some kind of rebellion against the man you're to marry?"

There was confusion in the yard. Without a leader, Darton's army was nervous. A few men drew their swords. Curses were muttered and threats issued.

Garrick stood his ground. "I asked for an audience," Garrick yelled over the wind that screamed over the cliffs and brought a sudden lash of rain.

"Darton was to come out and meet you," one of the men Hagan recognized as a traitor said. Sir Brady. The bastard. He seemed as much in charge of the men as anyone.

"I'll not be kept waiting." Without another word, Garrick slid off his destrier, and Ware and Hagan did the same. "Let in the rest of my men."

"I have orders—"

"Change them," Garrick growled, and Hagan could stand the deceit no longer. He grabbed Brady around the waist and pressed his knife to the Judas's throat.

Ware jumped from his steed to challenge the guard at the gate. The sentry cried, "Wait! What think you—"

Without a word, Ware slit the sentry in the arm, and as the man howled, he cranked on the portcullis. The gate ground upward just as some of the soldiers realized they'd been caught unawares.

"What the bloody hell—" Brady whispered, then caught sight of the eyes behind the nose guard. "Lord Hagan—?"

"Aye," Hagan bit out, wishing he could kill the man right here. He tossed off his helmet and let the rain drive down against his hair. In a voice that resounded throughout the castle, he shouted, "Lay down your weapons, for I've returned. Those of you who wish to obey me, swear again your fealty and drop your weapons; those who oppose me, let it be known that I will see that you're all slain." He pressed the knife point closer to Brady's thick throat, and the traitor squealed. A drop of blood slid down his neck as the army from Abergwynn rode into the keep. Through gritted teeth, Hagan growled, "What say you soldiers?"

"We know not of a rebellion," Sorcha said, her fingers tightening around the handle of her knife, her gaze pinned to that of her brother.

"You lie, sister," he said, his lip curling with disdain as he fingered his own dagger.

"Nay—"

Outside she heard voices, and imagined Hagan was among the men in the yard. But that was a silly dream, a dream she had to give up, for Hagan was surely dead.

"You're a liar, Sorcha, but then you've always been a liar,

haven't you? Even your birth was a lie," he said, advancing into the room and leaving two men to guard the door. "And that damned birthmark was a falsehood as well. To think that you had everyone believing you were the savior of Prydd. Now 'twould seem that you need saving."

"I fear you not, Tadd."

"Never too smart, were you." He studied the blade of his knife, then said, "Now, tell me, where's Lord Darton?"

Bjorn stood, feet apart, eyes centered upon Tadd as if he would gladly kill him with his bare hands. "Darton's with Satan."

Tadd's eyes moved to the stableboy. "Pity Satan. Tell me, did you kill the Lord of Erbyn?"

"I would have tried."

"One of his own men," Sorcha said. "Sir Marshall betrayed him."

"And where is Marshall?"

"Dead as well." Bjorn's fingers clenched his sword in a death grip.

"So that leaves the castle to . . ." Tadd's eyes swung to Anne, who was still pale, but managed to square her shoulders.

"Aye. Lady Anne is in command," Sorcha said, reading the turn of Tadd's thoughts and stepping between her brother and the single heartbeat that controlled Erbyn. Anne stood at the window and gazed down at the bailey. "And . . . and . . . Lady Anne commands everyone to lay down their weapons," Sorcha added, shooting a meaningful glance in Anne's direction.

"Yes . . . yes," Anne said quickly. "To meet Garrick of Abergwynn, we will go unarmed."

"The Baron of Abergwynn is here . . . now?" Tadd asked, disbelieving. "I think not—"

"Have you not heard the commotion in the bailey?" Sorcha asked, her heart pounding as loudly as the heavy tread of more soldiers' feet in the hallway.

"Aye," Anne said, "I've seen him. He is with his army, and one of his men has Sir Brady by the throat. Now, as the lady of the castle, I ask you to lay down your weapon, Baron Tadd."

Tadd looked unsure but held his ground. He listened for a second to the noise from the bailey, and the end of his tongue nervously rimmed his lips. "What matter if Garrick of Abergwynn is here? It is of no consequence. 'Twould still be easy to turn the tables on Erbyn, would it not? As for Garrick, I've no use for the bastard." Tadd's face was taut, but he managed a smile that looked like pure evil as he reached for his sword. "I'll take Lady Anne as a hostage, and bargain with her for Erbyn."

"Nay!" Anne cried.

"Why not?" Tadd lunged then, and Sorcha shoved Anne aside, for though Lady Anne's words were strong, she could still barely stand from the potion she had drunk.

"I will not allow it," Sorcha proclaimed as Anne nearly lost her balance and leaned against the wall.

"*You* will not allow it, sister?" Tadd barked out a sinister laugh. "We are not in Prydd any longer. No one here believes you to be their savior. Here, you are just a small woman with a sharp tongue. Now, get out of my way, you stupid bitch!" He swung at Sorcha with his blade. Her dress ripped with a sickening rending of threads.

"Nay, Tadd, do not . . ." Her dagger seemed a poor weapon against the sharp blade of his sword. "There has been enough death. Run!" she screamed to everyone in the room as she kicked a stool in Tadd's direction and he fell over the upturned wooden legs. "Run!"

"Nay!" Tadd roared, holding his shin. "You will not—"

Bjorn led Anne and Leah through the doorway, pausing only to run each guard through with his sword before guiding them through the dark corridors of Erbyn. Rushlights flickered as they passed, and Sorcha hurried through the door, trying to close it. Tadd threw his body against the oaken slats, and she could do nothing but run down the stairs and into the bailey, where the very depths of hell were breaking loose.

Tadd scrambled after her and caught her at the door of the great hall. She stumbled out the door.

Tadd swung his horrid sword, and Sorcha jumped.

Bjorn rounded the corner, his knife raised.

"Halt!" Hagan's voice reverberated through the bailey.

Hagan! Sorcha could barely believe her ears. He was alive! Her spirit seemed to soar. Turning her back on Tadd, she began to run to him.

"Watch out!" Hagan shouted as Tadd twisted and, growling in fury, swung again at Sorcha. Bjorn intercepted the blow, his arm gushing blood against the walls. He stumbled and knocked Sorcha backward to teeter on the stairs.

With a roar, Hagan hurdled a cart and vaulted up the stairs. He caught Sorcha, then, seeing that she was unharmed, turned and jumped upon the man who would dare hurt her. His fist connected with Tadd's jaw, and the burly man staggered backward.

"Nay, Hagan! He's mine!" a strong, male voice insisted, and Hagan, muscles bunched and the cords in his neck straining hard, spat on the steps near Tadd's face. Though he seemed to want to tear his enemy limb from limb, Hagan stood aside.

As Sorcha watched, a tall man with a cleaved eyebrow strode up the stairs with measured gait, so slowly that she believed he was enjoying Tadd's discomfort, as if he was stretching out this scene that would surely be a battle to the end. The blade of his sword glinted in the early morning light.

Sorcha's throat turned to sand. Death lingered in the air.

"You . . . But you are only a messenger," Tadd said, his voice trembling slightly as he took up his sword.

"Aye, a messenger from Lucifer," the tall man said. "Remember me not, Tadd of Prydd? I'm Wolf, the outlaw, but before that I was Ware of Abergwynn. We've met before, you and I—"

Remembrance flashed across Tadd's face, and along with it came fear.

Ware kept closing the distance. " 'Twas you who cut my face"—he motioned quickly to the cleaved eyebrow—"you who raped Mary the fisherman's daughter, who let your men have sport with her, who ruined what was left of her poor life!"

"I know not what you're saying," Tadd said, but his voice sounded strangled, and as he eyed the tall warrior his face lost all color.

"Prepare to die, Tadd of Prydd. It's time to face God for your sins!"

" 'Tis you who will die!" Tadd declared.

"No!" Sorcha said, hoping to stop the bloodshed.

Tadd lunged, and the tall man agilely stepped aside.

"Son of Satan, you will not live another day." Tadd turned quickly and managed to keep his balance. He swung his sword wildly, a man possessed by the scent of blood. But the soldier dodged the blow and seemed to be toying with him.

"Stop this madness!" Sorcha cried, her knees weak at the sight of Hagan. "Please, Hagan—" He looked up at her, and in that moment Tadd twisted away from his attacker and, spying Sorcha, he struck, thrusting his sword toward Sorcha again.

"No!" Hagan threw himself in front of the blow just as Ware rammed his deadly sword between Tadd's ribs. Tadd's blade ripped through Hagan's flesh.

Blood poured onto the stone steps as Tadd fell, striking his head. Hagan, too, staggered, and Sorcha ran to him, cradling his head in her hands, pressing hot kisses against his crown. "You're alive!" she cried, tears streaming down her face. "Hagan, love, you live!"

His eyes blurred, and then she realized how badly he was wounded. Blood stained his tunic a horrid shade of scarlet, and his lips moved but no sound escaped.

"Oh, God, no . . ." she whispered, her throat swollen with sudden fear. "You cannot . . ." She would not watch him die again. She could not. She placed her hands over the blood, but still it ran hot and sticky through the folds of his tunic and through her fingers.

From the corner of her eye she watched Tadd try to struggle to his feet. He smiled though blood drizzled from his mouth. "You cannot save him, Sorcha. You have no power."

"Nor do you, bastard." Ware delivered yet another blow with his sword, and Tadd fell silent, his body jerking until all motion stopped.

Sorcha barely noticed, for Hagan was dying in her arms. She tore off his clothes and ripped strips of cloth from her hated dress. Though tears clogged her throat, she bound the ugly gash in his side and yelled, "Bring me water! Call Nichodemas! Oh, Hagan, no. No, no, no!" She held him close, willing him to live, praying to a God who seemed to turn deaf ears in her direction. "You cannot die!"

"Sorcha—" Leah tried to peel her away from the man she

loved, but still, while soldiers gathered around, she clung to him, silently praying as her tears fell onto his chest.

"Lady Sorcha—" Garrick tried to be gentle with her, but she would not listen. She'd endured Hagan's death once before; she couldn't bear the thought of living without him again. "He's gone—"

"Nay!" she screamed. "He is not yet dead!" She wouldn't believe that God would bring Hagan back only to steal him from her again. She stared into his eyes and knew they were unseeing, that he was leaving her as surely as the wind was rising over the hills.

"Someone help her," Garrick said. "Hagan is no longer with us."

"No. Leave her." Anne's voice was filled with quiet authority as she placed the necklace of red twine in Sorcha's bloody fingers. "Only you can save him," she said. "As you saved me."

Sorcha's heart ripped a little further as she placed the knotted red strands over Hagan's head and let the twigs settle on his chest. "You will not die, my love," she said, though her voice trembled as she touched his chin gently, her fingers brushing the coarse stubble of his beard. "I cannot live without you."

His gaze, so bleary, centered on her, and he struggled with words before he gave up a rattling breath and closed his eyes. Disbelieving, she felt the life draining out of him. As surely as sand slipped through the hourglass, Hagan was leaving this world. "Please, God, if ever you have listened to me," she whispered, "spare this man, this warrior. Dear Jesus, please . . ." She kissed his crown tenderly and fought back the sobs that racked her body and tore at her soul. "Hagan, can you hear me? You must live . . ." Her fingers wrapped around his, and she closed her eyes, chanting, praying, hoping that he would be strong enough to turn back the hand of death.

She felt the eyes of a hundred soldiers turned toward her. The air went suddenly still and cold, and somewhere in the distance the wind began to rise. "Come, love," she whispered, coiling her fingers around the tiny sticks of the necklace.

The serpent ring began to pulse, and heat encircled her finger. "I've waited for you. Don't leave me now."

Behind her eyelids she saw the flash of eerie light, and thunder rumbled through the heavens. She shuddered as rain began to pour. "Please, please," she whispered, her voice breaking with raw emotion. "Hear me, Hagan. I love you. I'll always love you. Come back to me . . ."

He didn't move, but the ring pulsed hot and Sorcha felt a shudder rip through her body.

He coughed, then was still.

"Come, Sorcha . . ." Garrick's voice was firm, and Anne began to sob.

The strength ebbed from her as she felt her arms being pried from around his neck, her heart breaking a hundred times over. What cruelty was this—that she should find him alive only to watch him die?

Inside she, too, gave up life and hardly noticed that Bjorn lifted her from her feet. Though he was wounded he carried her into the keep, to Hagan's room, where the lord was laid upon his bed. Sorcha was beside herself, and though both Anne and Leah tried to force her from his chamber, she stayed at his side, as long as even the tiniest breath of life was in his lungs.

Holding his hand in hers, she kept her vigil throughout the day and into the night, refusing food and sleep, never failing to touch him, to talk to him, to beg him to come back to her.

The gossip of the castle was spoken around her, and bits and pieces scattered through her mind. Anne, as Lady of Erbyn, gave Bjorn his freedom, and Leah planned to leave with the man she loved. There was still talk of Bjorn being of royal birth, and he was determined to discover his birthright.

Tadd was dead, struck so by Ware, who, once his mission was accomplished, disappeared. Garrick of Abergwynn was furious with his brother and planned to have him hunted down like a dog, but Anne absolved Ware of his crimes.

But Sorcha paid no attention. She cared not for what the others would do. She stayed with Hagan until Isolde crept into the shadowed room.

" 'Tis no use," Isolde said, touching Sorcha's shoulder. "He's dying."

"Where there is life, there is hope. Is that not what you once told me?"

"But, child . . ."

"I will not give up," Sorcha proclaimed, and she eyed the sticks around Hagan's neck. They seemed so small and useless. His chest barely moved, and though his wound was beginning to heal it was as if his soul had lost its way and he had no reason to live.

"Child—"

"Damn it all! Hagan, do not leave me!" she yelled, her voice raspy and desperate. "I love you." With all the strength in her hands, she grasped the damned red cord from his neck and yanked it hard, tearing the threads, the knots unraveling, the twigs falling apart. With a fury born of lost hope, she flung the useless necklace into the fire. Sparks sputtered upward, and the flames crackled in hungry anticipation.

The tears she'd fought so valiantly against welled in her

eyes, and as she leaned over him for one last time, she whispered, "I love you. I have always loved you and I vow to you that I will love you forever." Heart in her throat, she placed her lips over his and kissed him goodbye.

He was gone to her. Lost forever.

As she lifted her head, she felt Isolde's old fingers clutch her arm. "Come, child. 'Tis over."

"Aye," she whispered but could not tear herself away. Somewhere outside the castle the wind rose, sighing loudly through the trees, rushing across the battlements.

Hagan's eyelids moved.

Sorcha stood stock-still. 'Twas only her imagination, but—

One of his long fingers stretched upward, and she felt a gladness soar in her heart. "He lives," she cried, hardly daring to believe the truth.

Blinking hard, Hagan opened his golden eyes to stare up at her as if he'd been in a dream.

"Hagan!" she whispered, tears of gladness raining from her eyes as she threw her arms around him. He let out a low sound, somewhere between a cough and a laugh.

"Wha—what is this?" he asked in a voice that sounded as if it were made of gravel.

"I thought I'd lost you—"

"Never," he vowed, lifting one arm to surround her and draw her close. Though he winced with pain, he would not release her. "Did you doubt your own powers?"

"What powers?"

"You are truly a savior," he whispered, his fingers coiling in the strands of her hair. "And I love you."

The words, spoken so softly, echoed in her heart.

"Do not leave me, Hagan," she cried, sobbing against him.

"Never, my love." He pulled her head to his and kissed her with a desperation that ripped through her heart to her very soul.

Sorcha stared at the gown she was to wear. Soft white with gold threads for her wedding. Isolde's smile was tired. "I lived to see this day, m'lady," she said, "that you will marry the man you love."

Sorcha slithered into the soft silk and pulled her hair from the neck. "Without you, Hagan may not have lived. I owe you much, Isolde."

The old woman shook her head. "There are things I have not told you, m'lady," she said, "about your birth."

"I've heard the story—"

A bony hand reached out and covered hers. "Then you know that Eaton was not your father."

Sorcha blinked hard. "Nay—"

" 'Tis true. That is why the prophecy was fulfilled. You have the blood of the great Llywelyn running through your veins—"

"No!"

"Would it be so bad?" Isolde asked.

"Father—"

"Eaton loved you. As his own. He never knew. But were it not for your heritage, this"—she lifted Sorcha's thick hair and touched the back of her neck—"would have meant naught. You're a true daughter of Llywelyn, and as such, you were destined to save Prydd."

"Is that what I did?" Sorcha asked.

"Aye."

'Twas true, Leah would now be the Lady of the castle while Sorcha stayed here, at Erbyn, to marry Hagan. Leah would wait for Bjorn, hoping that he would someday find the truth to his own birth. Tadd's reign of cruelty had been short-lived.

"Come now, 'tis time," Isolde insisted as she tucked a wayward strand of Sorcha's hair behind her ear.

Sorcha gathered her gown and walked through the corridors of the castle she'd called home. Hagan was waiting for her at the bottom of the stairs. He still walked stiffly; his wounds had healed but still pained him. But as he gazed up at her, he smiled.

Her throat filled, and tears threatened her eyes as she hurried to him and he wrapped his arms around her.

The priest cleared his throat, but Hagan ignored him and pressed his anxious lips to those of his bride. The ceremony be damned, right now all he wanted to do was embrace the woman who had been his tormentor, his prisoner, his lover, and, at the very last, his savior.

"Come," Father Thomas said.

"You are sure of this?" Hagan asked.

"Oh, yeah, m'lord," she replied with a saucy smile. She brought his hand to her flat stomach. "Think you not that your child deserves a name?"

His intake of breath was swift. "My child?"

"Aye," she whispered, laughing as she tossed her wild hair off her shoulders. "Born during a tempest, with hair the color of a raven's wing . . ."

"Come, witch, we have no time for this now," he growled into her ear. "And if I remember, we still have a bargain that you've not yet paid."

"A bargain?"

"Struck long ago," he said with a wicked grin. "Now, priest, make haste. 'Tis time for this one to become the Lady of Erbyn as well as the savior of Prydd."